3/

THOSE IN PERIL

Recent Titles by Margaret Mayhew from Severn House

A FOREIGN FIELD
I'LL BE SEEING YOU
THE LITTLE SHIP
OLD SOLDIERS NEVER DIE
OUR YANKS
THE PATHFINDER
QUADRILLE
ROSEBUDS
THOSE IN PERIL

THOSE IN PERIL

Margaret Mayhew

This first hardcover edition published in Great Britain 2006 by
SEVERN HOUSE PUBLISHERS LTD of
9–15 High Street, Sutton, Surrey SM1 1DF.
This title first published in the USA 2006 by
SEVERN HOUSE PUBLISHERS INC of
595 Madison Avenue, New York, N.Y. 10022.

British Library Cataloguing in Publication Data

Mayhew, Margaret, 1936-
    Those in peril
    1. World War, 1939-1945 - Social aspects - England - Fiction
    2. Dartmouth (England) - Social life and customs - Fiction
    3. Love stories
    I. Title
    823.9'14 [F]

    ISBN-13: 978-0-7278-6444-4
    ISBN-10: 0-7278-6444-0

All Severn House titles are printed on acid-free paper.

Typeset by Palimpsest Book Production Ltd.,
Grangemouth, Stirlingshire, Scotland.
Printed and bound in Great Britain by
MPG Books Ltd., Bodmin, Cornwall.

For Sylvie and Malcolm

Acknowledgements

I thank these kind people for their generous help: Richard Parkes, Reg and Sheila Little of Kingswear; Michael Pollard who served on clandestine wartime MTB operations; Commander Michael Sizeland, Lieutenant Commander Charles Addis and Commander Mark Thistlethwaite of the Royal Navy; Sylvie and Malcolm Bates for material on Brittany and the early days of the French Resistance; Derik Quitmann and James McMaster for information on fishing boats and sailing; Linda Evans, my editor; and Philip Kaplan for everything.

One

The news was very bad. In spite of the beautiful weather, Louis Duval had spent the spring of 1940 indoors in his studio, painting the view of the Pont-Aven quayside from the window. In that way he could listen to the bulletins on the wireless while he worked – his eyes directed outside, his ears attuned inside to the babble of news being broadcast, interspersed, optimistically, with dance music. At the beginning of June he realized that the battle for France was all but over. By then, most of the communiqués being broadcast were out of date and unreliable and there was no advice from the Government to the people on what they should do next.

From the talk and rumours circulating like wildfire in the bars and cafés in the town he knew that there were still plenty who clung euphorically to hope, but he was not among them. The facts, as he saw them, were unpleasantly clear. Holland and Denmark had been taken and the Belgian king had handed over his country on a plate. Thanks to that unexpected betrayal, the Germans had since surrounded most of the British Expeditionary Force in northern France and the British had been attempting the near-impossible feat of rescuing their trapped army by sea. Those of the French forces not trapped with them were – with some honourable exceptions – in disarray and panic. The remnants of the British army still fighting elsewhere in France were being overrun by the German panzer divisions steamrollering merrily across the country. The battle for the Somme had been lost. Within weeks, perhaps even days, all remaining resistance would collapse. He had no doubt that an armistice was already being sought by certain members of the Government and that, in the end, some kind of shameful deal would be struck with Nazi Germany in the name of France.

By the second week in June he had reached a decision. He cleaned his brushes and put away his paints. At the foot of the stairs his landlady, Mademoiselle Citron, intercepted him.

'Have you heard, monsieur? The Boche are at Rouen. It is a disaster.'

The more terrible the news, the more gratified she looked. He guessed that she was probably already wondering how much she would be able to charge to billet members of the occupation forces. A German officer or two of the old-fashioned Prussian school would suit her nicely – well-behaved, clean and tidy and prompt with the rent. A far more appealing option than any of the ragtag French refugees reported to be streaming towards Brittany with their belongings piled high on carts and wheelbarrows. Louis himself rented the whole top floor of the house from her – a very large studio, bedroom, bathroom and kitchen. The daylight was excellent, the views delightful and it suited him admirably, or he might have taken the trouble to look elsewhere for a more congenial *logeuse*.

Mademoiselle was a businesswoman, before all else. It was difficult to place her age – somewhere in the mid-forties, he judged. Unattractive, with a sallow skin, a thin mouth, poor teeth and a sour disposition. It was a nice irony that birth had bestowed on her such a suitable name: Miss Lemon. When he had first rented the attic rooms from her, she had kept coming up the stairs on this and that flimsy excuse until he had finally realized, wearily, what she was hoping for. He had rebuffed her as politely as possible but knew he had not been forgiven for the slight. Nor, he suspected, for the fact that he had never shown any interest in painting her – with or without her clothes on. There was a rich fund of far more interesting subjects in and around Pont-Aven. She was eyeing him now, speculatively.

'Will you be staying, monsieur?'

He'd been right: she *was* thinking about accommodating the Germans. 'I'll let you know, mademoiselle.'

'As soon as possible,' she called after him. 'I need to know how I am placed.'

He caught the next train for Paris, travelling

via Rennes. After Rennes, the compartment was empty except for a little old nun huddled in the corner like a bundle of black rags, her veiled head bent low over a prayer book – bent so low that her nose almost touched the pages. He smoked and watched the Breton scenery passing by – woods, lakes, streams, apple orchards, stone farmhouses embedded for centuries in the landscape, cows grazing, tethered goats – and then dozed for a while. When he woke up later they were on the outskirts of Paris. The nun had put away her prayer book and was sitting with her gnarled hands folded neatly in her lap. Her face was pale as parchment and webbed with fine lines. He smiled at her. 'It seems not many of us are in a hurry to go to Paris these days, sister.'

She looked at him serenely. 'I go where God sends me, monsieur.'

At the Gare Montparnasse, he had to elbow his way through a huge crowd of people fighting to board trains to Brittany. The mood was close to panic and, he thought, ugly: insults hurled, blows struck, no quarter given. He took the metro to Monceau and walked across the park towards the rue de Monceau. The trees and grass were a fresh, new green, the sky blue, the sun shining, the air pleasantly warm. Paris was looking her best, which made her present situation all the more tragic, all the more terrible and all the harder to bear. There were no young lovers entwined on benches, or lying on the grass, only one woman out with her poodle. He admired her as he passed – not beautiful but very elegantly dressed with a charmingly provocative little hat tilted over her brow. Even the dog, trotting along beside her in a jewelled collar, had style. Otherwise the park was deserted. The rue de Monceau was also empty except for a Citroën parked at the kerbside halfway down. He opened the outer door to the apartment building and went into the sunless courtyard with its row of metal mailboxes against the wall. Before he had reached the staircase beyond, the glass door to the concierge's flat had opened.

'Monsieur Duval?'

He turned. 'As you can see, Madame Bertrand. It's me.'

'One cannot be too careful these days.'

'No, indeed. I might have been a German. Madame Duval is at home?'

'I believe so.'

She would *know* so. No-one passed her glass door, going in or coming out, without her noticing.

'How is your husband?'

'Poorly. It's his liver again. Another crisis.'

Monsieur Bertrand's liver had given trouble for years and been the subject of much discussion, but now Duval could not afford the time to stop and listen to the latest state of affairs. He went on up the stairs to the first floor, knowing that the old woman would be watching him every step of the way, her nose questing upwards inquisitively like a bird's beak. He still had his own key but, out of politeness, he rang the bell at the

13

apartment door. Simone opened it. Almost a year had passed since they had met. Time improved her looks, rather than the reverse, he thought. She was one of those rare women who grew in attraction with maturity – in spite of the thickening waistline, the little crow's feet round the eyes, the sprinkling of grey hairs. And she knew how to choose and wear clothes. He had never seen her look anything less than chic.

'I'm sorry to call without warning.' He had always been careful to avoid walking in on any of her lovers.

She smiled drily. 'There's nobody else here. Come in, Louis.'

He walked into the apartment. Nothing seemed to have changed since his last visit – or indeed, for many years. The furniture and furnishings, like the apartment lease, had belonged to Simone's mother and had been passed on intact when she had died. He had got on well with his mother-in-law – rather better, it had to be said, than with his wife.

'A drink, Louis?'

'Certainly.'

While she went into the kitchen, he lit a cigarette and stood looking out of the half-open window at the street below. A middle-aged man and woman were feverishly loading suitcases and boxes and bags into the Citroën, piling them to the roof. The woman scurried back indoors and came running out again carrying a wicker basket in her arms that emitted furious cat yowls. The doors slammed and the car went off fast down the street, skidding round the corner as though pursued by a pack of panzers. He turned away from the window and caught a glimpse of himself reflected in the big gilt-framed mirror over the mantelpiece. He looked rather worse than usual, he thought, passing a hand over his uncombed hair: a poor specimen of humanity in a creased linen suit – overweight and out of condition. Too much drink, too many cigarettes, too much food, too little sleep and, probably, too many women.

Simone came back into the room with two glasses of Pernod. 'So, Louis, what on earth are you doing here? Everyone is leaving, not arriving. There has been a big exodus – people running away like frightened rabbits. Everyone says the Germans will be in Paris within days.'

'So it would seem.'

'They've been burning papers at the Quai d'Orsay. We've seen the smoke. What do you suppose is going to happen next?'

He shrugged. 'The Government will desert Paris and run away too. Reynaud will resign and Pétain and his weaselly defeatists will deliver up France to the Nazis.'

'So, you think it's hopeless?'

'I'm afraid so.' He offered a Gauloise but she shook her head.

'Not those horrible things.'

He lit her Chesterfield for her – the brand she liked best. 'I thought it might be difficult for you to get those now.'

'There are still Americans in Paris – newspaper correspondents, broadcasters, diplomats . . . I know one or two of them.'

'Perhaps not for much longer.'

'Why should *they* get involved in this stupid war? They'd be crazy.'

'I think they will, in the end.' He pocketed his lighter. 'I came to tell you that I'm planning to get out.'

'Whatever for? You should be safe enough where you are. I doubt the Germans will bother much with Brittany.'

'They will. There are too many useful harbours.'

'So . . . where else would you go?'

'To England.'

'*England!* Whatever for? Switzerland would be a far better choice. The Boche will have England next on their list and the British army is on its knees – what little is left of it. The Germans will only need to walk in.'

'Swim in,' he corrected. 'That's not so easy. Tanks don't float very well.'

'They'll manage it. Nothing and no-one is capable of stopping them. We may as well accustom ourselves to the idea. But they'd leave you alone at your age, Louis.'

'Do you think they'll leave *you* alone?'

'They're not all savages. I'm staying put. I have my business to consider.'

'Is it worth it?'

'Of course it is. I've spent years building it up

and I've been making a good profit. I'm not just walking away.'

He thought of the smart little boutique in the Avenue Victor Hugo and of the deserted streets and shuttered shops that he had seen. 'Who is going to be buying expensive handbags and scarves, I wonder?'

'The Germans. For their wives and girlfriends. Perhaps they'll want to buy your paintings. One must be practical. If we are to be occupied by them, then somehow we must survive.'

He said slowly, 'I don't believe that things will be quite so simple. France is going to be made to suffer under the Nazis. Suffer badly. I think you should come with me.'

She stared at him. 'Come with you? To England? I hate the place! You know that very well. And it's going to be invaded too, so what's the point? I'd far sooner spend the war here in Paris, thank you. You go, if you want. *If* you can get there. They say it's almost impossible to get on a boat now.'

'I'm taking my own.'

'Your own?'

'A small motorboat I've had for a while. It's been useful for getting around the coast, finding places to paint.'

'How small?'

'Eight metres or so.'

She burst out laughing. 'Do you seriously expect me to go with you in some little tub like that?'

'It's quite a reliable little tub,' he said mildly.

'It will need to be. It's a long way across to England and you're no sailor.' She shook her head. 'You're completely mad, Louis. *Mad!* It's a stupid risk and for no point. You'd do far better to stay here and get on with your painting. It's all you care about. All you've *ever* cared about, let's face it.'

'Not entirely,' he said. Once he had cared a great deal for her. 'I'd like to do something more useful – in the circumstances.'

'What, for example?'

'I don't know – yet.'

'Well, you're too old for the military – they wouldn't take you.'

He gave a mock bow. 'Thank you for reminding me, Simone. In any case, it seems there would be little point. Our army is apparently giving up the unequal struggle. And I've no desire to end up in a labour camp either. Still, at fifty-three I don't feel like retiring completely from the front line of life.'

'If you're sensible, you'll do nothing. Just stay out of trouble.'

'Sound advice, certainly. I'll try to remember it. I can't persuade you, then?'

'To come to England with you? No, thank you. Absolutely not.'

He finished the Pernod. 'I'll make arrangements with the bank for the monthly payments to be made to you, as usual. There shouldn't be a problem.'

She tilted her head. 'You've been doing rather well, I gather, Louis. Getting quite well known at last. I stopped by Gerard's gallery the other day and he was singing your praises. He says your paintings sell well, and to some rather important people. But I doubt if they'll appreciate you the same in England. The English don't like us, any more than we like them, and they're philistines. You'd do far better to stay put.'

'Personally, I don't much like the idea of selling my work to the Nazis.'

'Well, you never were very practical. Another Pernod? Did you eat lunch? I can cook something for you, if you like? There's no great rush surely?'

She had moved deliberately closer. If he stayed, they would certainly end up passing a very agreeable afternoon. Whatever differences they might have had, they had not been of the marriage bed. For a moment he was tempted, as he had been on several other occasions when they'd met over the years. She was still his wife, after all. He stubbed out his cigarette. 'I have to get back, Simone. There's lots to do.' He bent to kiss her cheek. 'I'll try to let you know where I am. Look after yourself.'

She shrugged, moving away. 'I always do.' She saw him out. 'Good luck, Louis.'

As he passed the glass door downstairs, the concierge emerged. 'You're leaving already, monsieur?'

'Evidently, madame.'

'Shall we see you again soon?'

'I doubt it,' he said. 'My regards to Monsieur Bertrand and his liver.'

He called at several banks, trying to get francs changed into English sterling, but without success. The cashiers all regretted that there was none to be had. The crowds outside the Gare Montparnasse were even worse than before, filling the Place de Rennes. When he finally forged a way inside the station, the bad situation became chaotic as people fought like animals to get on board the trains. Alone and without luggage, he was able to squeeze himself into a carriage where there was space, at least, to stand. He closed his eyes and ears to the pandemonium and panic around him – women weeping, children howling, babies screaming.

Simone would probably be all right. He certainly hoped so. One could not be married to a woman for more than thirty years and not feel some concern for her, even if the last fifteen of them had been spent apart. In the beginning he had felt a great deal more than concern for her, but that had been long, long ago. He was hard put now to remember how it had been when they had first met in Paris – to recapture the feeling of being young and wildly in love. He had been a penniless art student of twenty-one and she had been a year older and working in the Galeries Lafayette on the glove counter. She had sat down at the next table in a café and he had asked to borrow her newspaper. Naturally, it had been an excuse. They had been married within a year and lived happily in terrible lodgings on almost no money – but not, unfortunately, happily ever after.

Reasonably enough, she had wanted him to get a proper job too and not spend his days painting pictures that never sold. To please her, he had found work in an advertising agency, which he had hated. The First World War had begun and he had volunteered to serve in the army, largely to escape the advertising agency. Instead of dying in the trenches, along with the hundreds of thousands of others, he had been invalided out with a leg wound that still gave him trouble at times. By the end of the war Simone's mother had died and they had moved into the rue de Monceau apartment. Simone had become pregnant but miscarried at five months and never conceived again. With her inheritance she had opened a small boutique and he had gone back to painting.

As time passed, he had begun to sell some of his work but, by then, he and Simone had grown apart – she occupied with her boutique, he with his painting. He had moved out of the apartment and lived for a while in Provence, painting whatever pleased him. Later he had spent some time in England in St Ives in Cornwall, doing the same thing. Then he had travelled some more – Italy, Greece, Turkey and across the Atlantic to the eastern seaboard of America – Maine and Massachusetts. Finally, he had returned to France and rented the studio in Pont-Aven on the south coast of Brittany. Simone had stayed put in the

Paris apartment and she had opened a bigger and better boutique in the Avenue Victor Hugo. Since they were both Roman Catholics there had never been any question of a divorce; not that he had set foot inside a church for many years, but Simone went to Mass regularly. Neither had interfered in the other's life and there had been no shortage of women in his or of men in hers. It was what might be called a very civilized arrangement.

In Pont-Aven he paid a visit to his bank. As a favour, the manager unearthed a few English pound notes for him.

'You are proposing to go to England, monsieur?'

'No, but one never knows what currency will come in useful these days.'

'Very true. Though American dollars would be safer.'

He went to buy some more paints and canvases. The art shop was empty of customers, its owner deeply depressed. 'Nobody has been in here for three days, monsieur. If things go on like this, I shall be ruined.'

Back at the apartment, he packed a suitcase. His paintings were stacked around the walls of the studio. He went through them, as a farewell gesture, and came across the portrait he had done years ago of Simone when he had been in love with her and which she had disliked, thinking it made her look fat. He held it up for a moment, admiring a good-looking young woman with dark brown eyes, a retroussé nose, soft hair and a rather hard mouth. But the magic that she had once held for him had gone.

He did a little more work on the painting of the quayside and then cleaned his brushes before going in search of Mademoiselle Citron in her rooms on the ground floor. She opened her door, unsmiling. The grudge of his rejection was always there.

'I'm going away in the morning,' he told her, 'but I want to keep the studio on.' He produced an envelope from his pocket. 'Here is six months' rent in advance.'

She lifted the flap of the envelope and took a lightning glance at its contents – it was all she needed to gauge the sum precisely. 'Very well, monsieur. I will reserve it for you. Where will you be going?'

'To friends, in the south.'

She nodded. 'It may be safer there. You are wise. God knows what is going to happen to us all. But supposing you do not return, monsieur, what shall I do then? I can't keep the rooms for nothing.'

'I have arranged with the bank to pay you another instalment at the end of the six months – if I am not back.' That satisfied her all right. He went on, 'I shall leave the studio locked. Everything is to be left exactly as it is. Nothing is to be moved or disturbed in my absence.'

'As you wish, monsieur.'

He knew that she had a key and would

23

certainly poke and pry into everything once he had gone, but there was nothing he could do about it. Her excuse, whenever he had raised the subject, was that the place needed cleaning – which was certainly true enough since he never bothered to do much himself. He said pleasantly, 'Perhaps you could give me a receipt for the six months' rent, mademoiselle.'

'Certainly, monsieur.'

He ate at the bistro, *Chez Alphonse*, in the rue du port, where he was a regular – a modest place with steamy windows and a smell of garlic, herbs, coffee, caporal tobacco, its walls proudly decorated with prints of paintings by once-local artists: Paul Gauguin's *Breton Girls Dancing, Christmas Night, The Young Christian Girl, Christ Jaune* with his three Marys resembling farmers' wives, Paul Sérusier's cutout-like Breton women wearing their peasant shawls, Emile Bernard's panoramic vista of the town bridge from the Bois d'Amour. The original colours were all dulled by grease, nicotine and time. As Louis was finishing an excellent onion soup, Alphonse came to his table. He was a small, thin man and his clothes – a white apron tied over black – were as much a part of him as another skin. He sat down to join him in a glass of wine, shoulders slumped, moustaches drooping – the picture of dejection. 'People are leaving. People are arriving. Nobody knows what to do or where to go. Me, I have to stay where I am. This is my living. All I have. I'm too old to start all over again somewhere else. What of you, monsieur?'

'I'm thinking of getting out.'

'Well, there is nothing to keep you here, I suppose. You can paint anywhere, isn't that so? You're lucky. Who knows what the Germans will do when they get here? We could all be put against a wall and shot. It wouldn't surprise me. They are capable of anything. Yes, I think you would be wise to leave. What about your studio?'

'I'm keeping it on, in case I want to come back.'

'Will you take your car?'

'No. The tank is only half full. And who knows if I could get more petrol.'

'What about your boat?'

The less he said to anybody, the better. 'I'll probably sell it.'

Alphonse nodded gloomily. 'If you don't, the Boche will take it.'

From the bistro he went to the boat which he kept moored at a quiet part of the quay. The *Gannet* had certainly seen better days and, in places, her blue paint had peeled down to the wood. But she was seaworthy, with an engine that usually worked and a small wheelhouse that sheltered him from the worst of the weather. He checked the preparations he had already made: the compass, the full reservoir of petrol, the spare drums, the hand-torch and batteries, the drinking water, the tin of biscuits, the smoked sausage and ham, the round of Camembert, the cigarettes,

25

the bottles of wine and one of brandy – not forgetting a corkscrew.

He unrolled the chart, smoothing it down with the flat of his hand while he studied it once again. Down the river to Port-Manech at the mouth of the estuary. Hug the coastline as far as the Pointe de Trévignon and then cut straight across to the Pointe de Penmarch, where he would alter course to go north-west across the Baie d'Audierne towards the Pointe du Raz – the most perilous part of the voyage. He would have to time it very carefully so as not to be caught there with the wind over tide when the seas would boil up into a seething white cauldron. On across the Douarnenez Bay towards the port of Brest and then, from there on, due north for England where the wind would be behind him. If he could make a steady five to six knots, he could reach Falmouth within roughly forty-eight hours. But it was a far cry from the kind of gentle pottering around up and down the coast that he usually did. He wondered if he, and the boat, were up to it.

On his way back, he checked on his Citroën, kept in a shed near the quay. He was fond of the old machine – they had done many miles together – but there she would have to stay. He removed the rotor arm and took the keys with him. The idea of the Germans making use of her was abhorrent.

Back in the apartment, he turned on the wireless, poured a glass of cognac, lit a Gauloise and stood at the window, looking out over the harbour. In the room behind him a newsreader's grave voice began the latest bulletin. The Germans had already taken Amiens and were now advancing on Le Havre. And after Le Havre, he thought, it would be Cherbourg, St Malo, Brest . . . and so on until they had secured every Atlantic port in France worth having, which would include Lorient and St Nazaire. There was no chance, as Simone had naively put it, of them not bothering much with Brittany. He finished off the cognac and went to bed.

It was a while before he slept, and he lay thinking things over. He had spoken nothing less than the truth to Simone when he had said that he wanted to do something useful. Being too old to serve in the Second World War had not bothered him much at first, but the crushing advance of the German army across the Low Countries and France and the prospect of another humiliating surrender had appalled him. He had little to offer except for the fact that he was a Frenchman who spoke reasonably good English and had a certain knowledge of France. Some use might perhaps be made of him over in England. He did not share Simone's dislike of that country – the time spent there had been very agreeable – but it was not for love of England that he was proposing this crazy journey. It was for love of France.

He was up early, before six, and let himself out of the house quietly, carrying a suitcase, his box of paints, some spare canvases and an easel. Since it was his custom to take the boat off on painting trips, he would arouse no comment, and, in any case, many shutters were still closed. High water had been an hour earlier and the fishing boats had already left harbour. The quayside where the *Gannet* was moored was deserted except for a few gulls strutting about and a small black cat with four white paws who was sitting at the edge, scratching itself. It watched him lowering himself and his baggage on board and, as he was making ready to leave, jumped down onto the deck. He picked it up and put it firmly back on the quayside. The engine started up first go and he set off downstream.

The steep and rocky riverbanks, crowned with pine trees, were golden with summer gorse. He had passed Kerdruc before he realized that the cat must have jumped back on board again. It came into the wheelhouse, wandered around and rubbed itself against his legs. Too late to take it back, he decided. And anyway the animal looked like a homeless stray – nothing but skin and bone with dull, mangy fur and a tail as thin as a rat's. When he had picked it up it had weighed almost nothing. He shrugged. It might as well take its chances in England as in France. If it didn't fall overboard en route.

As soon as he left the safe shelter of the estuary, the wind and the North Atlantic waves grabbed hold of the *Gannet*, tossing her about. He held her on a north-westerly course, ploughing along the south Brittany coastline, the boat pitching and rolling. The cat had retreated to a corner of the wheelhouse and was clinging to the deck with its claws. From time to time Duval chewed on some bread and cheese or sausage or ham, drank some of the wine, or smoked a cigarette. Seasickness had never bothered him. Nor did it seem to trouble the cat, who, crouched in its corner, devoured the scraps he threw to it.

It took him more than six hours to reach the Pointe de Penmarch and begin the long haul across the Baie d'Audierne, and another seven to gain the other side. Navigating a course round the treacherous granite fortress of the Pointe du Raz with its vicious tidal streams took all his concentration. He had timed it well and the tide was still with him, but the wind force increased and the surge and swirl of the sea and the pull of the current swept the *Gannet* perilously close to the rocks. A huge wave swamped the boat and he lost his grip on the wheel and was hurled into the corner. He lay stunned for a moment until he could scramble back and yank the boat clear of the rocks. The cat had lost its grip as well and was swirling around in seawater, scrabbling wildly with its paws. He seized it by the scruff of the neck and threw it into the locker before it could be swept overboard.

Then, once round the headland, he passed suddenly and miraculously into calmer waters. The wind had dropped and the temperature risen, the waves flattened to a mere swell. He set his course due north for the port of Brest, counting on another three hours of daylight. The cat, when he let it out of the locker, went back to its corner and started trying to groom its sodden fur. He doubted that he looked much better – soaked to the skin and with a lump on his forehead where he had hit it that felt the size of a pigeon's egg.

Around two o'clock in the morning he reckoned that Brest must be ahead on his starboard bow. The temptation to steer for its harbour was very strong but he resisted it. The Germans could well have taken the town already and the risk was too great. He pressed on, checking his course regularly and fortifying himself with more snacks and more wine and some nips of brandy, feeding more scraps to the cat who was invisible now except for the glint of its eyes in the torchlight. He followed a course that kept him well away from the reefs and islets and jagged rocks that infested the Brittany coast, and by dawn he had sighted the Ile Vierge lighthouse. There he turned his back on France and headed north towards Falmouth in England. Some dolphins came and played alongside the boat for a while and an RAF plane circled overhead a few times before it, too, left him alone. In the distance, he caught sight of a large convoy of merchant ships steaming north-east before they were lost to view.

In the early evening of the second day, the engine faltered and died. It took time to discover the cause of the trouble – a blocked carburettor –

and to deal with it and, by then, he knew that the south-westerly wind and the tide must have carried him several miles to the east. No matter. So long as he continued due north he would make landfall somewhere along the south coast of England. He kept himself awake during that night by talking to the invisible cat – keeping up an absurd, one-sided conversation through the hours of darkness until dawn finally came. *We are both completely mad, little one. We are very lucky, you know, not to find ourselves at the bottom of the sea. If we had any sense between us we would both have stayed in France – Germans or no Germans. On the other hand, perhaps you, at least, made the right choice. You will certainly be welcomed in England. They like animals there – even a French cat – whereas they are not so likely to welcome me, a Frenchman.*

Within two more hours he had sighted land ahead – a long dark smudge low on the horizon. He could see a lighthouse blinking and then, as he gradually drew nearer, a gap in the cliffs where a river flowed out to meet the sea. Not Falmouth, though. Fowey perhaps? Or even Plymouth? His tired brain declined to make any sense of the chart. What did it matter, anyway? It was somewhere in England.

As he steered the boat towards the tall cliffs and the mouth of the estuary, the sun came out and lit the scene for him. He could see two ancient-looking forts guarding the river entrance – one on each side. Most probably English defences against the marauding French in years gone by. In a moment of triumph, or maybe defiance, he rummaged for the *tricolore* kept in the locker and attached the flag to the *Gannet*'s stern. He went between the two headlands, flying his country's flag, and entered sheltered waters. The riverbanks were steep and thickly wooded, the trees growing down to the water's edge. Further on, as the estuary narrowed, the woods gave way to houses – whitewashed cottages built of stone and clinging to the hillsides in much the same way as those built on the river valley slopes of Pont-Aven. He passed some naval launches moored at buoys in midstream; further upstream, he could see larger vessels. He cut his speed and steered the *Gannet* gently towards a quay on the east side of the river, aiming for a flight of stone steps. As he reached them, a man in fisherman's clothes, smoking a pipe, leaned over.

'Morning.'

'Good morning.'

'Nice day.'

'Yes, indeed.'

'Reckon it might rain tomorrow, though.'

I have come all this way, risking my life, he thought wearily, to find myself discussing the weather. '*Vraiment?*'

The man came down some of the steps – a big man with a chest shaped like a barrel of English beer. 'Want a hand?'

'Thank you.' He threw the painter and it was

made fast to an iron ring. But when he climbed ashore, staggering on the unaccustomed dry land, he found his way up barred and he realized that the reception was not so amicable, after all. The *tricolore* had been noted.

'French, are you?'

'Yes, indeed. I have come from Brittany.'

'That so?'

'From Pont-Aven on the south coast. Perhaps you know of it?'

'Can't say I do.'

'What is the name of this port, please? I have no idea where I am.'

The man took hold of his arm without answering the question. 'You'd better come along with me.'

He went along – there being little alternative. Other people had gathered on the quayside – also fishermen, by the looks of them, and some women who stared at him with hard eyes. He was marched past them under an archway and round a corner to the entrance of a building guarded by a naval rating with a bayonet tied to the end of a broomstick. My God, he thought, is that really all they have left after Dunkirk? A shove in the shoulderblades propelled him forward for inspection.

'This foreigner's just arrived by boat. Says he's come from France.'

The sentry looked him over uncertainly. 'From France you say, sir? Do you mind showing me your passport?'

He handed it over, waiting while it was scrutinized carefully and doubtful comparison made between his photograph and himself after two days at sea.

'I'll have to keep hold of this, sir – for the time being. And I'm afraid I'll have to ask you to step inside, if you don't mind.'

He was shown into a room with a table and two chairs and a small window. Not quite a cell, but almost. Somebody brought him a cup of tea the colour of old leather and, to him, undrinkable. He could see faces outside peering through the window and fists rubbing at the grimy glass to see him better. He realized that they thought he was a spy – though what sort of a spy would make no effort whatever to conceal his arrival in broad daylight? Or perhaps they were simply suspicious of all Frenchmen, in the same way that most French were suspicious of the English. He finished the cigarette and lit another, and was halfway through a third before the door opened and a naval officer entered the room – a short, stocky man, many years younger than himself and with a crushing handshake. He had the clear, keen eyes of an intrepid explorer – typically set on a distant horizon or raised to some snowy peak.

'How do you do, Monsieur Duval. I'm Lieutenant Reeves, Royal Navy. So sorry to have kept you waiting. Just a few questions to ask you, if you don't mind. It won't take very long.' He sat down at the table and took out a silver case.

'Cigarette? Ah, you already have one on the go, I see. More tea?'

The politeness of the English gentleman was legendary, Duval knew, but it was a fatal mistake to believe that it meant he was on your side. 'No, thank you.'

The lieutenant leant forward to peer into the full cup. 'Not too keen on tea, perhaps? I'd offer you something stronger, but the bar's not open yet.'

'The bar?'

'This was a hotel before us naval chaps took it over. We let them keep the public bar going in the basement. Rather handy.' He lit a cigarette. 'Lovely weather we're having.'

'Yes, indeed.' It was unbelievable how they always brought up the subject. 'Very agreeable.'

'You've just come across from France, I gather?'

'That is correct.'

'Alone?'

'Yes, alone.'

'Is that your boat – the *Gannet*?' He pronounced the seabird in the English way, sounding the t firmly at the end.

'Yes. I am the owner.'

'Jolly small for crossing the Channel.'

'There are not many bigger boats leaving from France for England these days,' he said drily. 'And those there are are completely full. Otherwise, I might have chosen a more comfortable means of arriving here.'

'Quite. Where exactly did you leave from in France?'

'Pont-Aven on the south coast of Brittany. It's not far from Lorient. Perhaps you know it? It's very charming.'

'Not personally, I'm afraid. Pretty long haul, though.'

'Haul?'

'A long way. You must be a fairly experienced sailor.'

He shook his head. 'Not at all. In general I keep close to land. It is the first time I have undertaken such a voyage.'

'May I ask why you did?'

'Why? Perhaps you do not know how things are in France . . .'

'Actually, we have a pretty fair idea – our chaps have been over there quite a bit. But it doesn't really answer my question.'

Duval drew hard on his cigarette. 'My country is on the point of surrendering to the Germans, as you will know, Lieutenant. In the first place, I have no desire to remain in a France occupied and controlled by Nazis, and, in the second, I thought I might perhaps be of some service here, in England.'

'Oh? What kind of service exactly?'

He gestured with both hands, palms upturned. 'To tell you the truth, I have no idea. As you can see, I am too old for military service, but it had occurred to me that there may be other ways. That it may be possible to make some contribution from this side of the Channel. I simply wish to place myself at your disposal.'

'I see. That's awfully decent of you, of course.' A pause. 'Do you happen to have a French identity card on you?'

He felt in his pocket and handed it over without comment. Photograph, full names, nationality, domicile, place and date of birth, height, colour of hair and eyes, shape of face, profession, print of right thumb . . . all officially stamped twice over in a frenzy of French bureaucracy. That should satisfy them, he thought grimly.

The Englishman studied it for a moment. 'This states that you're an artist.'

'That is correct.'

'What kind of artist exactly?'

'I paint on canvas – usually in oils. In general, I paint landscapes. Or nudes. Sometimes still life. Whatever interests me.'

'And you live and work in Brittany?'

'Yes, I have a studio in Pont-Aven.'

'But you were born in Rennes?'

'Yes. I have lived also in Paris, and in Provence and in other countries, including the United States. For a short time, I lived in England.'

'Which is how you learned such good English, of course.'

'I'm afraid it's not so good these days.'

A dry smile. 'It's rather better than my French. Are you married, Monsieur Duval?'

'Yes, but I have been separated fom my wife for many years. She lives in Paris.'

'No children?'

'No, none.' He rubbed a hand over his sore eyes. Tiredness was making it difficult to remember the correct English words. 'Listen, Lieutenant, I have been at sea for many hours. My clothes are wet and I need a bath. Most of all I should like to be able to sleep. Perhaps that could be arranged and we could continue this conversation later?'

'Yes, of course.' His identity card disappeared into a pocket. 'I'll fix you up with somewhere to stay. We'll have to ask you to remain in Kingswear for the time being, if you don't mind.'

If you don't mind. Whether he minded, or not, it was an order. He wondered how many more times he was going to hear that polite but empty phrase. There was really no such equivalent in French. One used a variety of phrases to express a similar meaning. 'Kingswear? Is that where I am?' He had never heard of it. He must have been carried much further east than he realized.

'Well, it's called Kingswear on this side of the river and Dartmouth on the other. You came up the river Dart.' The lieutenant got to his feet. 'There's not a lot in the way of accommodation over here, but I'll do my best. I take it you've brought some funds with you?'

'Funds?'

'Money.'

'Oh yes, I have money – unfortunately nearly all in French francs.'

'There's a bank in Dartmouth and they may be able to change some of it for you. You can take the ferry across later. The naval college is over there – the big building up on the hill. Our school for sailors. Perhaps you've heard of it?'

'I regret not.'

'Not to worry. By the way, if you've been at sea for a couple of days I don't suppose you're aware that the Italians have just declared war on us?'

'No, I did not know.' He shrugged. 'But I think we need not worry about them so much as the Germans.'

The lieutenant smiled. 'Organ-grinders and ice-cream sellers? Well, we'll soon see.'

After another period of waiting, he was taken back to the *Gannet* by a young naval rating to collect his suitcase. He realized then that he had forgotten all about the cat, but there was no sign of it on board so, presumably, it had jumped ashore. He wished it good fortune in its new life in England; he had a feeling that his own might not be quite so simple. According to the lieutenant, he had been found a room in some kind of lodging house run by a Madame Hillyard. He sincerely hoped that she was not anything like Mademoiselle Citron.

By now the day was warm, the sun climbing in the sky. He trudged up a steep road, following the rating who was good enough to carry his case. The sailor took the incline like a mountain goat and he had a hard job keeping up with him. The road went by a church, between houses built on the hillside above and below, following the curve of the riverbank. Eventually, they reached a white-painted house with a grey slate roof and – unusually for England – shutters at the windows. It stood close to the road, behind a high stone wall, and an iron gate bore a plaque with its name, Bellevue. The rating stopped and put down his case. 'Here we are, sir. You'll be all right now.'

He felt anything but all right. His heart was pounding, he was out of breath, and he was dripping with sweat. But the rating was off down the hill at once, leaving him alone. The gate, he discovered, opened into a small courtyard with a door. He pressed a brass bell beside it and, when the door eventually opened, it was not some forbidding *logeuse* who stood before him but a child – a small girl of about eight or nine, pale, skinny and painfully plain. He bowed to her gravely.

'My name is Louis Duval. I believe that I am expected.' She stared at him open-mouthed and he realized that he must present a frightening aspect – unkempt, unshaven, red-eyed, bruised, breathing heavily – probably fumes of brandy – and with a foreign accent. He smiled as reassuringly as possible. 'Is Madame Hillyard at home?'

The child vanished without a word and he wiped his face with a handkerchief and leaned wearily against the doorpost. After several more minutes a woman appeared. No, she was not in the least like Mademoiselle Citron, he saw with relief. Considerably younger and infinitely better-looking and nothing sour about her at all. He heaved himself away from the doorpost and, again, bowed.

'I am Louis Duval, madame. I understand that you have a room for me.' He could tell that she, too, was appalled by his appearance, though she tried to conceal it.

'Yes. They telephoned me. Please come in.'

He picked up his suitcase and stepped onto stone flags in a blessedly cool hallway. There was a long-case clock ticking quietly in a corner and a vase of pink and yellow roses on a table. He could smell their sweet scent.

'Please come this way, Monsieur Duval.' He followed the Englishwoman up a staircase to the floor above and then along a corridor. At the far end she opened a door. 'I am afraid the room is a bit smaller than the others but it's the only one I have vacant.' She flattened herself against the door to let him pass inside. He knew that he must smell, as well as look, disgusting.

It was simply but charmingly furnished: a brass bed with white cotton covers, an old armoire, a chest of drawers, a table and a comfortable chair, a looking glass, a framed print or two, another vase of roses . . . He set down the suitcase and went over to the open window. The house was well-named. There was, indeed, a most beautiful view of the estuary and the open sea beyond. The wooded slopes that he had observed from the river lay below, tall pines rising above the rest to frame the scene. A flight of steps led from a terrace at the back of the house to a narrow lawn bordered by thick shrubs and lush ferns, with a very un-English palm tree and a very English bed of beautiful roses like the ones in the vases. A bench with scrolled ironwork ends and a slatted wooden seat was perfectly placed to enjoy the view.

He turned. 'Thank you, madame. Everything is delightful.'

Even in his exhausted state, he appraised her automatically. Lovely skin – like many English-women. Thick and naturally curly brown hair, nice features – especially the large grey eyes. Not such a good nose – it was too broad – but the mouth more than made up for it. The generously curved body was tragically hidden away beneath dowdy clothes, but he could see through them easily enough. He wondered if her husband appreciated his good fortune. Most Englishmen, in his experience, did not.

'The bathroom is just two doors down. I do hope you don't mind sharing with the rear admiral.'

Again the word *mind*. He was in no position to mind anything, and who was the rear admiral? 'But of course.'

She looked worried. 'You *do* mind?'

'No, no,' he said hastily. 'I meant that I do not.'

Her brow cleared. 'I charge twenty-five shillings a week – that includes all meals and laundry. Will that be all right?'

'Certainly.' He groped in his jacket pocket. 'I have some money here.'

She shook her head. 'No, no, that won't be necessary.'

'But I should like to pay in advance.' He held out two English pound notes. 'I'm sorry that I do not have the exact amount.'

She took it, but unwillingly and blushingly. Mademoiselle Citron would have shown no reluctance at all, let alone embarrassment. 'I'll give you your change later. Would you like a cup of tea?'

He repressed a shudder. 'No, thank you.' He had probably given offence. It would have been better to accept even if he had never drunk it. 'All I want is to . . .' The English word for sleep eluded him and he was forced to do a childish pantomime of resting his head on clasped hands. She understood, though.

'I'll see that you aren't disturbed.'

As soon as she had shut the door, he stripped off his outer clothes, pitched face down on the bed and fell instantly into a deep sleep.

Two

'He's not going to stay here, is he?'

'For the time being.'

'He looks horrid. Like an old tramp.'

'It's not his fault, Esme. He's been on a long journey across the sea.'

'I couldn't understand anything he was saying.'

'He's French, that's all.'

'Well, I hope he's not going to be here long.'

She hoped so herself. If the Frenchman had simply turned up on the doorstep she would have taken one look at the frightening sight and turned him away with any excuse that she could think of, but Lieutenant Reeves had specifically requested her to take him – almost insisted on it, in the politest possible way.

'We must welcome him, Esme. He's had to leave his own country because of the war.'

'Why? Why couldn't he stay there?'

'Because the Germans have invaded it. Just the same as you couldn't stay in London in case they bombed it.'

'Well, they haven't, have they? Mum just wanted to get rid of me.'

'She wanted you to be safe.'

'No, she didn't. She doesn't care about me one bit. She'll be having more fun without me – specially with Dad away. He doesn't care about me neither.'

Barbara Hillyard said firmly, 'That's quite enough, Esme. Go and finish that homework you're supposed to be doing this weekend.'

'I've done it.'

'No, you haven't. Don't argue. Off you go at once.'

The child did so with dragging feet and a mutinous expression. Originally, soon after the war had started, there had been four evacuees in the house – two sisters and a brother from one family who had been happy, easy children; and Esme. More than two hundred evacuees had arrived by train from London at Kingswear station. From there they had been taken by bus round to Dartmouth on the other side of the river, where they had been herded into the Guildhall like bewildered animals at market. Barbara had gone to take one and had come back with four. The billeting officer had wanted to keep siblings together where possible and the little trio had been clutching each other's hands tightly, the two older sisters trying to comfort their small brother who had had huge, heart-breaking tears rolling down his cheeks. She had been ready to leave with her charges when the officer had come up to her again. There was one child left who, it seemed, nobody wanted. When she had turned to see Esme standing there, so plain and unappealing, a furious scowl on her face while she kicked hard at the floor, she had not been surprised.

From the first, the girl had been difficult and disruptive and there had been many times since when she had regretted agreeing to take her. None of the expected bombs had fallen on London and the other three had eventually been collected by their mother to return home. She wished very much that Esme's mother would do the same but it seemed unlikely. In six months there had been only two letters to her daughter, and neither had mentioned wanting her back. The father who was apparently in the Navy on active service had never communicated.

She went into the dining room and started to lay the tables for lunch. Three separate tables were placed near the window so that her residents – Mrs Lamprey, Rear Admiral Foster and Miss Tindall, a newcomer since the three evacuees had left – could all enjoy the sea view. Unfortunately, there was no room there for a fourth so the Frenchman would have to sit further away, without the view. She dragged another small table into the centre of the room, found a clean cloth and began to set out cutlery.

Mrs Lamprey entered, stage left, in a little cloud of Guerlain's *L'Heure Bleue*. She never simply came into a room; it was always a theatrical entrance with a scarf trailing from one hand, the other held a little to one side with the palm upwards and always a slight pause for effect, as though allowing time for an audience's traditional applause for a star. She took in the extra table at a glance. 'A new resident, Mrs Hillyard?'

'Yes. A Frenchman, actually, Mrs Lamprey.'

'A *Frenchman*. How interesting. I never liked that Czech who was here before. And those Poles were rather strange. Scarcely a word of English between them. When did he arrive?'

'Early this morning. He came over from France by boat.'

'Fleeing the Germans, I suppose. Does he realize they'll probably come here too?'

'I don't know. He's upstairs sleeping at the moment.'

'Is he in their navy?'

'No, he's a civilian. He came on his own.'

'Really? That was very brave. What does he look like?'

How to describe him – the swarthy, unshaven, unwashed stranger who had appeared on her doorstep with long matted hair, bruised forehead and bloodshot eyes? 'Rather like a pirate.'

'I can't *wait* to meet him. A French pirate! How romantic! Will he be at luncheon?'

'I doubt it. I should think he'll sleep for a long time. He seemed utterly exhausted.'

'Poor man. Does he speak English?'

'Rather well.'

'I must brush up my French. I was quite good

47

at it once. Such an elegant language. And the French are so cultured. I wonder if he knows the London theatre at all.'

When Mrs Lamprey had exited, Barbara shifted the fourth table a little further away from Mrs Lamprey's, out of consideration for Monsieur Duval. She could, and would if given the chance, talk at great length about her days in the theatre. Her stage name had been Vera Vane and she had, apparently, worked with the very best. Henry Irving was often mentioned, Gerald du Maurier, Herbert Beerbohm Tree, Ellen Terry, Sarah Bernhardt, Mrs Patrick Campbell . . . she had known them all. The actual roles she had taken were not all that clear, but she could quote lines at random from a number of plays. She had, apparently, been on the very point of making her name when she had met Mr Lamprey and sacrificed a glittering career by finally accepting his (fifth) proposal of marriage. He had been dead for more than twenty years now and Mrs Lamprey was probably the wrong side of seventy, but her sacrifice obviously still rankled. The rear admiral's marriage, by contrast, must have been a contented one because there was a very beautiful silver-framed photograph of his late wife close beside his bed, whereas Mr Lamprey's image was conspicuous by its absence.

Barbara finished laying the tables and went back into the kitchen to begin preparing lunch. Macaroni cheese, followed by baked apples and custard. If she did an extra apple, it might just

48

stretch to feed Monsieur Duval though it would be a big help if he went on sleeping until dinner-time. The prospect of cooking for the Frenchman worried her. He might look like some fearsome pirate but he had not behaved or spoken like one. She had a feeling that he would be accustomed to much better fare than she could produce. The French were said to be the world's best cooks – adept at making wonderful dishes out of even the most unpromising ingredients. Her own repertoire was strictly limited by the wartime rationing: scrag-end stews, rissoles, fish cakes, toad-in-the-hole, mock this and pretend that, followed by rather dull puddings. Mrs Lamprey, who had a large appetite, rarely complained, neither did Miss Tindall who pecked as sparingly as a bird, nor Rear Admiral Foster who simply ate whatever was put before him. Monsieur Duval might not be quite so easy to please.

As she was putting the macaroni cheese into the oven, she heard the rear admiral return from his morning walk, wipe his feet briskly on the front door mat and go into the sitting room where he would immerse himself in *The Times*, holding it up in front of him like a shield to discourage Mrs Lamprey from conversation should she happen to go into the room. His partial deafness provided another buffer. Miss Tindall, a retired schoolteacher, had no such defence and therefore spent a good deal of time upstairs in her room, reading and writing letters to other retired teachers and former pupils. The former pupils, she said, kept her in touch with the modern world, and she took pride in hearing of their achievements.

At one o'clock Barbara rang the brass handbell in the hall. Mrs Lamprey came down the stairs, trailing her scarf, *L'Heure Bleue* and a little whiff of Stone's Original Green Ginger Wine which she occasionally took, as she explained, for a tonic and which the grocer obligingly delivered for her at regular intervals. Rear Admiral Foster – a spare and courtly figure – emerged from the sitting room and Miss Tindall, in her uniform of blouse, skirt, cardigan and single row of pearls, came down the stairs. They sat at their separate tables facing the view – Mrs Lamprey calling across every so often to one or the other, or both. The rear admiral would respond politely, Miss Tindall guardedly.

Barbara served up the macaroni cheese which, with so little cheese, looked dull and unappetizing. To her great relief there was no sign of the Frenchman.

When he finally awoke it was dark. Pitch black, in fact. He lay still, wondering where on earth he was. The room was unfamiliar to him, he could tell that much, and there was no sound he could identify – nothing to give him some clue. Just silence. Then, after a moment, as his sleep-fogged brain cleared, he remembered. He was in England *chez* Madame Hillyard and he must have slept for hours. There was a very urgent need to find the bathroom which could not be ignored, and he groped for the lamp that had been on the bedside table and knocked it over onto the floor. After more groping, he discovered a switch but when he pressed it nothing happened. Almost certainly he had broken the bulb and very probably the lamp too. He swore softly to himself. His torch was still on board *Gannet* so he must find some other light switch in the room – beside the door, surely, if he could remember where the door was.

He got out of bed and began feeling his way along the wall, bumping into a large piece of furniture – the armoire, by the size of it – before he had the luck to find the door and, on the wall beside it, a light switch. He surveyed the room. The curtains were still open at the window, his suitcase on the floor where he had dumped it, his clothes thrown onto a chair. The table lamp, mercifully, was undamaged – only the bulb had been broken. His watch showed that it was two o'clock in the morning. He opened the suitcase and rummaged for his old dressing gown. He had no desire to alarm Madame Hillyard more than he had already done, by encountering her in his underclothes. What exactly had she told him about the bathroom? Somewhere down the corridor? Fortunately there was a light burning and he found it easily enough because there was a notice on the door, and returned to his room. One discomfort had been dealt with but he could do nothing about his hunger. Like the torch, the remains of his food rations were all still on the boat. Also the wine and brandy – if they had not been stolen.

He lit a cigarette and smoked it standing at the open window, looking towards the sea and his country. No moon. No stars. Silence. He wondered if he had done the right thing? If he might not have been more use if he had stayed in France? The naval lieutenant had been polite but clearly unimpressed and who could blame him? A middle-aged French civilian, arriving out of the blue with vague offers of help. And they were not only unimpressed, they were suspicious. Who could blame them for that either? If France fell – no, he corrected himself, *when* France fell the English would be on their own without allies. They were wise to trust nobody. He finished the cigarette and went back to bed. Before he fell asleep again, he remembered that, as well as his identity card, they still had his passport.

When he awoke again, it was day. His watch had stopped because in his stupor he had forgotten to wind it up; from the sun's position and the light he judged it to be around six o'clock. Too early to expect breakfast but he found himself too hungry and restless to lie in bed any longer. Perhaps if he took a walk he might find some café or bar open, or even retrace his steps to the *Gannet* and his stores there. He went in search of the bathroom once again. In the mirror over the handbasin he looked an alarming sight with the three-day-old beard and a black pigeon's egg on his forehead. He shaved, took a bath in tepid water and dressed in clean clothes. He was padding quietly towards the head of the stairs when a door on the landing opened and Madame Hillyard came out. She was wearing a dark blue dressing gown of some thick material – the kind more usually worn by a man. Perhaps it belonged to her husband who was still asleep in bed? Her thick hair, tousled from the pillow, looked most alluring.

He bowed. 'My sincere apologies, madame, if I disturbed you. I could not sleep any longer. I thought I would take a walk.'

She was clutching tightly at the collar of the robe, highly embarrassed. 'A walk? But you must be hungry.'

'A little,' he admitted. 'But it's nothing.'

'If you would like to wait in the dining room, I'll be down in a few moments to cook you some breakfast.'

'Please do not trouble yourself.'

'It's no trouble. What would you like? We do have some eggs and bacon.'

Normally, he would have eaten hunks torn off a baguette, still warm from the *boulangerie*, with good Breton salted butter and some local ham or cheese or sausage, maybe a little pâté, or perhaps, on occasion, jam. And a bowl of very strong coffee – with a small cognac to finish, if he felt the need. But just now he would have eaten anything. 'That would be very nice, thank you.'

'Would you like tea to drink?'

He hesitated. Politeness had its limits, after all. 'Do you have coffee?'

It was her turn to hesitate. 'Not exactly. It's not real coffee, I'm afraid – that's getting rather scarce. Just an essence, but it doesn't taste too bad.'

He smiled at her. 'Thank you, madame.' He started down the stairs in obedience to her request and then stopped. 'Excuse me, but where is the dining room?'

'Oh, I'm so sorry – I should have said. It's the door facing you at the bottom.'

He wound up his watch and set it by the old long-case clock in the hall – twenty minutes to seven – before he went into the dining room. He saw, with amusement, the four separate tables set out at a discreet distance from each other, each laid for one person, a little vase of fresh flowers beside the salt and pepper and bottles of what appeared to be different sorts of terrible sauces. The English respect for privacy; the desire, at all costs, not to intrude upon another. The problem was, which table was his? As the new boy, he guessed that it would be the one away from the window and set at a further distance from the others. He went over to admire the view once again – the delightfully secluded and lush garden with the beautiful roses and the exotic palm tree, the woods on the hillside below and the green-blue sea beyond.

'Here is your change, Monsieur Duval.' She had come into the room without him hearing –

dressed now in another disastrous cotton frock printed busily all over with blue and white flowers. The alluringly disordered hair had been combed firmly into place and she had put on some lipstick – but the wrong colour. He admired many things about the English, but not the dress sense or style of their women. 'My change?'

'From the two pound notes you gave me. I owe you fifteen shillings.' She placed the money carefully into his hand – a paper note, and, on top of it, a little pile of coins, all different sizes. He had forgotten how complicated their money was. 'I'm sorry but I didn't have two half-crowns.'

He put them all in his pocket. 'Thank you, madame.'

'Would you like something to start with? There's wheat flakes or shredded wheat.'

He had never eaten either of those things. When he had lived in England before he had always catered for himself, buying whatever he could find that was eatable. 'Whichever is convenient. Where would you like me to sit?'

She indicated the table he had predicted. 'If you don't mind.'

He sat down, not minding at all, and presently she came back carrying a laden tray. He rose to his feet. 'Permit me to help you, madame.'

'No, no, it's quite all right, thank you. I'm used to it.'

He sat down again reluctantly while she set the tray on the sideboard and brought things over to his table: a china bowl containing something that looked rather like a straw pincushion, a jug of milk, a smaller bowl containing a little white sugar, and, finally, a cup and saucer containing what he supposed must be the coffee essence. 'Thank you, madame.' She went away again and he tested the drink cautiously. In France, he took his coffee black – very black. This was made with milk and had a curious taste and smell that had nothing whatever, so far as he could tell, to do with real coffee. However, it was infinitely better than the cell tea. The pincushion almost defeated him. He tried it first without milk and then with milk, which was slightly better, and chomped away doggedly. It not only looked like straw, it tasted like it. He was just forcing down the last mouthful when she came back with the tray to remove the bowl and set before him a fried egg, a single piece of bacon, and a triangle of something that he recognized as a piece of bread that had been fried too. She was looking embarrassed again.

'I don't suppose it's quite what you're used to, Monsieur Duval. I'm afraid the rationing is getting to be a bit of a problem here. We have to make do with what we can get. Perhaps it's easier in France?'

It certainly seemed so to him – in Brittany, at least. In spite of the *cartes d'alimentation* and all the restrictions, if one knew where to go it had not been too difficult to eat perfectly well. Almost as normal. One could still, for instance, get plenty of local oysters, langoustines and crabs. Though doubtless that would all change soon. He said gallantly, 'This looks delicious, madame. But I must be taking your rations.'

'Oh, it's quite all right. Lieutenant Reeves is providing an emergency ration book for you, so we'll be able to manage.'

After the eggs and bacon she brought more little bread triangles, toasted this time and slotted stiffly into a silver rack. There was a small pat of butter and a pot of some dark conserve that tasted very good. 'It's blackberry,' she told him, in answer to his question when she came back into the room. It was not an English word that he knew, so he was none the wiser. 'You made it yourself, perhaps, madame?'

'Yes. We can get extra sugar for that, you see.'

He declined another cup of the coffee essence. 'I regret to have disturbed you so early. Your other guests will certainly not descend until much later.'

'Not until eight o'clock,' she said. 'That's usually when I serve breakfast.'

'I shall remember tomorrow. I hope I did not also disturb your husband.'

She said awkwardly, 'There isn't a husband. I'm a widow.'

'I'm so sorry. I hope I have not given you any distress.'

'No, not at all.'

'It was the war? He was a soldier, perhaps?'

She shook her head. 'He died several years ago – long before the war.'

'How sad for you. You were living here?'

'No, we lived in Eastbourne then – on the south coast.'

'I do not know Eastbourne.'

'It's very nice.' She looked at his now empty plate. 'Can I get you some more toast?'

'No, thank you, madame.' He stood up. 'I think that I will walk down to find my boat again. There are still some things on board that I must fetch.' He bowed to her once more. 'Thank you for the breakfast.'

In the hallway he met the child who had first answered the door to him. In spite of his improved appearance and placatory smile, she scuttled past as though he were an ogre.

'That French man's still here.'

She turned from washing up at the sink. 'I told you, Esme, he's going to stay for a while.' Shaved and dressed in clean clothes, with his hair combed, Monsieur Duval had looked rather different. Not nearly such a frightening prospect as yesterday.

'How long?'

'I really couldn't say. Do you want some breakfast now?'

'I suppose so.'

Barbara reached for the shredded wheat packet.

'I hate that stuff. It's horrible.'

'Well, how about some wheat flakes instead?'

'I hate those too.'

58

She put both packets back in the cupboard. Mealtimes with Esme were one long battle. 'Then you'll have to go without cereal because there's nothing else. You can have a boiled egg and toast.'

'I don't want it.'

'That's a pity because it's what you're going to be given. And you're to eat it all up. Eggs are too precious to be wasted.'

The Frenchman had probably hated his breakfast, too. In her anxiety to do it well, she had undercooked the egg, overcooked the bacon and burnt one side of the fried bread. Maybe he had only finished it because he was so hungry.

She stood over Esme while the child ate the egg, pulling silly faces at every mouthful. The rear admiral's bedroom was immediately above the kitchen and presently she heard him moving about quietly. He would come downstairs soon and take his early morning pre-breakfast walk along the coast path and back. It was unlikely that he would encounter Monsieur Duval who would have gone the other way, down to the harbour.

Gannet was where he had left her, close to the steps and barely afloat on a falling tide. He went into the wheelhouse and found the provisions all still safely stowed in the locker. The bread was no longer eatable but he sliced off some cheese and poured a stiff shot of brandy to erase the memory of the coffee essence. He was lighting a cigarette when he felt something touch his ankle and looked down to see the black cat rubbing itself against him – thinner and mangier than ever. He gave it some sausage and watched it eat ravenously, gulping down the pieces. 'Poor little one. What are we to do with you? We should certainly both have stayed in France. We are not welcome here.' He poured some water into a tin lid and put it down for the animal.

'Good morning, Monsieur Duval.' Lieutenant Reeves was standing on the quay above, very spruce in his uniform.

'Will you join me in a glass of cognac, Lieutenant?'

'Bit early for me. Another time, though. I say, is that your cat?'

'No. It came on board in France without my permission.' He searched in vain for the English word he needed. 'A clandestine passenger.'

'A stowaway.'

'Yes. And now it wants to stay.'

'Has it got a passport?'

He smiled politely at the joke. 'I'm afraid not. Must it be sent back?'

'Strictly speaking, yes – according to our quarantine laws. But you can tell it that we'll grant it asylum – so long as it behaves itself. Have you settled in all right with Mrs Hillyard?'

'Thank you – yes. A charming lady.'

'She is, isn't she? Perhaps she'd take a French cat in too.'

'I should not like to ask such a thing.'

'Worth a try. It looks like it's in need of a good home. By the way, one of our Royal Navy chaps is going to have a word with you sometime soon.'

'A word?'

'Just an informal chat. Nothing to worry about.'

'You still have my passport and identity card, Lieutenant. I am worried about that.'

'So we do. We'll hang onto them for the time being, if you don't mind.'

'Supposing that I do mind?'

The lieutenant smiled. 'There's not actually an awful lot you can do about it, is there? You'll get them both back in the end. Have you heard the latest news this morning?'

'What news?'

'The Germans are in Paris.'

'Ah . . .' It felt like a physical blow to his heart; the breath seemed to have been knocked from his body. He stood, head bowed, in choked silence, unable to speak.

'Yes, I'm sorry. It's a jolly bad show.' The lieutenant touched his cap, moving away. 'We'll be in touch, Monsieur Duval. The ferry operates from the slipway just along there if you want to go across to Dartmouth and find a bank.'

He finished off his cognac and then poured more. Clear images passed through his mind of Nazi troops marching down the Champs-Elysées and all the civilization and history and culture and beauty of his beloved country being crushed beneath the brutal stamp of jackboots. He sat for a long while in the boat, drinking and smoking and thinking, the cat beside him.

With an effort, he roused himself. It was still too early for a bank to be open in the town but he might as well go over and take a look around. He left the cat chewing at a last piece of sausage and walked to the head of the ferry slipway. The few people he passed seemed untroubled, even cheerful, without a care in the world. Most of them, he supposed, would have no idea of how grave the situation was, how terrible the might of Hitler's forces. A few miles of sea had lulled them into thinking themselves safely out of reach. They had not yet, of course, been truly tested. That was still to come.

He could see the river ferry on the opposite bank and leaned against the wall in the sunshine, smoking a Gauloise while he waited for it to come back, and watching the seagulls scavenging at the water's edge. His thoughts returned to Paris. To Germans strutting round the streets, gorging themselves in the restaurants, drinking at the bars, strolling in the parks, leering at the women, swarming like vermin over the city while Parisians stood meekly by. He was very glad that he was not there to witness the humiliation. And what of Simone? How would she fare? *Who is going to be buying handbags and scarves? The Germans. For their wives and girlfriends. One must be practical.*

The ferry came back and he walked up the

gangway, proffering one of Madame Hillyard's coins for the fare and receiving several more different ones in return. The journey across took only five minutes or so and he stood in the bows, looking upstream towards the green hills and fields and woods of Devon where the river curved gently away out of sight. The shops in the town were still closed, also the two cafés he passed, and the several pubs, and the bank, too. In France, he thought regretfully, the cafés, at least, would have been open. Alphonse would have been setting out chairs and wiping tables and there would have been strong coffee and freshly baked bread.

One shop *was* open – selling newspapers and cigarettes and violently coloured English sweets. He bought a *Daily Express* with one of the coins he had acquired from the ferryboat man and took it to read on a bench by the harbour. The Germans' entry into Paris was not yet reported but there was other equally depressing news. Their army was racing across France and meeting little or no resistance. There were unedifying accounts of French soldiers throwing away their arms and fleeing south. The Government had decamped first to Tours and now to Bordeaux. Prime Minister Reynaud was expected to resign shortly and the armistice-seeking Marshal Pétain and his supporters were in the ascendant. None of it surprised him in the least; all of it dismayed him. There was an article by an English journalist warning that the French Navy should not be allowed to fall into German hands – he read it with particularly close attention.

When the bank had finally opened, he went to queue at the counter and, as his turn came, smiled winningly at the middle-aged woman behind the grille. She smiled back, patting her coil of greying hair into place, but his request to change French francs into English money caused consternation. Apparently she would have to talk to someone about it, and she hurried away to do so. Presently an elderly man wearing an old-fashioned suit and a starched wing collar emerged and introduced himself as the manager. Duval gave his name and found himself being ushered into his office and offered a seat in front of an immense mahogany desk. The manager cleared his throat.

'I'm afraid there may be a slight problem about changing your French francs into sterling. I shall have to refer the matter to our Plymouth office. With the present situation so delicate, it may well be out of the question – much as we should like to help you. You do understand?'

The poor fellow was looking quite upset. He said reassuringly, 'Oh, yes, I understand perfectly. France is falling, and, with her, the franc.'

'Exactly how much currency had you in mind?'

He gave the substantial figure and the manager shook his head. 'I very much doubt they would be prepared to consider anything like that amount. But I'll do my best for you.'

'Thank you.'

'Have you just come across from France?'

64

'Indeed I have.'

'How are things over there – if you don't mind my asking?'

He smiled inwardly at the *mind*. 'Not at all. Things are very bad. Which is why I have chosen to come here. I'm afraid that my country will soon surrender completely to the Germans. Perhaps within a week.'

'We're rather afraid of that too.'

'Then you English will be on your own.'

'Yes, we will.' The manager didn't seem at all alarmed by the idea – in fact, he looked rather pleased about it. 'Do you have some sterling to keep you going?'

'A little.'

'Well, I'll do the best I can. If you could tell me where you are staying, I'll be in touch as soon as possible.'

I'm getting to be quite popular, he thought drily. The Royal Navy and now the bank manager are going to be in touch with me. He was shown to the door courteously and the manager shook his hand.

'Good luck, Monsieur Duval.'

He smiled. 'I think it's you English who are going to need the luck now.'

He walked back to the ferry, passing two girls in some kind of female naval uniform – rather chic, in fact. He particularly liked the black stockings.

Back on the other side of the river, he found that the falling tide had left his boat high and dry.

The cat had jumped down onto the mud and was chewing away at a dead fish. He lit a cigarette and reviewed his situation. Four English pound notes in his wallet and a pocketful of coins; the remainder all in French francs that might prove worthless to him. No passport, so it was necessary to stay put until it was returned to him. No identity card either. There was no going back, in any case. The whole of France, not just Paris, was on the point of surrender – within a week, he had said to the bank manager, who had thought so too. Well, he might as well get out his paints and do some work. He might even be able to sell it.

Three

Lieutenant Commander Alan Powell left his desk at the Admiralty and walked the short distance to Pall Mall. He walked briskly, as he usually did, striding along at a good pace so that he arrived at the entrance to the club rather sooner than he had intended – ten minutes earlier than the time arranged, in fact. The porter took his service cap and respirator.

'Commander Chilcot is already here, sir. I'll tell him that you've arrived.'

He waited in the hall and presently his host came down the staircase, hand outstretched. Rather more grey hairs now – like himself – but otherwise little changed. 'Good to see you, Alan. Too long since we last met, don't you agree? Let's go and get a drink before we have lunch.'

The club room upstairs had deep, well-worn leather armchairs and sofas, oak panelling hung with impressive oil paintings and fine Georgian windows, somewhat marred by criss-crossed strips of anti-bomb blast paper. A waiter shuffled over, stooped with age.

'Pink gin, Alan? Or do you drink something else these days?'

'No, the same, thanks.'

He still stuck to the old wardroom drink, out of habit. Gin, angostura, no ice. They raised glasses to each other. How long was the too long, he wondered? Five or six years at least and probably more. During the peace between the two wars, they'd met occasionally at the odd function and they'd had lunches, like this one, a few times, but Harry had a wife and four children and had been posted for some considerable time to the Far East. The bond of friendship, though, had somehow held since their time at Osborne and later Dartmouth. *The men that were boys when I was a boy.* That shared experience made it virtually unbreakable.

They'd been eleven when they'd first met at the Royal Naval College at Osborne. Same entry, same age, same passion for the sea – a lot in common in those days. At thirteen they'd gone on to Dartmouth together – four years of rigorous discipline intended to bring about their eventual metamorphosis into naval officers: intensive instruction, exams, strenuous exercise, sailing up and down the Dart – the two of them cox and crew in the same dinghy, both revelling in their seamanship. They'd done their stint in the college training ship *Vindictive* together and passed out together, rising from midshipman to sub lieutenant as they continued their training at Greenwich and Portsmouth and Chatham and at sea, and then, finally, to full-blown lieutenant with their two stripes so arduously won and so proudly worn.

After that their paths had diverged. They had served on different ships in the Great War and in different theatres. He had been so confident then of the future – of rising, in time, to the top of the Service – until his own life had changed course suddenly and radically when his ship had engaged in action with a German cruiser. He'd been in one of the gun turrets when an enemy shell had scored a hit, wounding him badly in the arm and chest. The exploding shell had also started a major fire close by and he'd managed to stop it spreading and get the damn thing put out before he'd collapsed. Unfortunately, the effect on himself had been longer-lasting. The ship's surgeon had saved his arm but the damage done had put him in hospital for a long time. Infection, complications, setbacks, more operations on his arm, another on a lung . . . months of convalescence.

They'd let him stay on in the Navy – courtesy of strings pulled by his father – even given him a medal for doing what he had only considered to be his duty in action, but, meanwhile, others had passed him by and the high-flying career that might have been – that he had always strived for and counted on – was virtually finished. He'd instructed at shore training establishments for a while, been given another promotion, and then, eventually, sidelined, like a shunted engine, into a

desk job at the Admiralty. He had schooled himself to accept the fact, to make the best of things,
and, for the most part, he had succeeded. The
outbreak of another war, though, had brought
him face to face with the painful truth that he
had no real active part to play in it. At forty-six,
he could still have served his country in some
useful capacity – something rather better, he
knew, than moving papers from an in-tray to an
out-tray.

'How've things been with you, Alan?'

'Fine, thanks.'

'Admiralty keeping you busy?'

'Pretty much.'

'They've put me in dry dock too, you know.
Not what I wanted, as you can imagine, but
there's not much one can do about it. I'd've given
my eye teeth for another command in this war
but it doesn't look like there's any chance of it.
Still, one can make oneself useful. As a matter of
fact, that's what I wanted to have a chat with you
about, but it can wait till after we've had some
lunch. The menu's not what it was these days, I'm
afraid, but I suppose we mustn't grumble.'

It was not unlike the sort of food they used to
eat at Osborne and Dartmouth: cottage pie and
steamed chocolate pudding with custard. They
talked of those far-off days – as they usually
did. He was never quite sure whether he saw
them through rose-coloured spectacles, but he
certainly remembered them as happy days when
the future had seemed so full of promise and

bound eternally to the sea. *And all I ask is a tall ship and a star to steer her by.* He still sailed, of course. Not a tall ship but a small one that he kept at Maldon in Essex. At the time of Dunkirk he'd moved heaven and earth to take her across himself and help bring back the troops from the beaches, but he'd been refused leave to do so. A bitter pill to swallow.

'Haven't gone and got yourself spliced since we last met, Alan, have you?'

'I'm afraid not.'

'I recommend it – if you ever meet the right woman.'

'Yes, I'm sure.' It was advice he had been given many times by many people and regularly by his older sister, but he'd never met anything like the right woman. During their time at Greenwich, Harry had owned a Morris 8 tourer and whenever possible had roared off to parties in London. Sometimes he'd gone along too, but Harry had always been more at ease in female company than himself. And then the blow to his expected career had also dealt a resulting blow to his self-esteem, and he'd pretty much given up on the whole idea.

'Still . . . there's something to be said for being footloose and fancy free. A lot of married chaps probably envy you. Are you still in Dolphin Square?'

'Yes, still there.' The small flat suited him. There was a very pleasant view over the river, porters, a restaurant, tennis courts, a swimming pool. If the weather was fine, he sometimes

71

walked to work for the exercise. It helped to keep him fit. And a private, inherited income ensured that there would never be any great money worries.

They returned to the leather chairs for coffee and a smoke, Harry leading him to a quiet corner of the room, away from other members. He wondered what precisely he wanted to have a chat about.

'What are your views on France, Alan?'

He said, surprised, 'France? Well, the same as most people's, I suppose. They're in a tight corner and they seem to be giving up.'

'The word is that they'll only hold out for four or five more days.'

'More than likely. Thank God we didn't let them have any more of our fighter squadrons over there. We're going to need every one of them ourselves.'

'I'm afraid so. Once they've taken France, the Germans will be giving us their full and undivided attention.'

'I almost look forward to it.'

'Me, too. Still, it's going to be pretty tough. They have most of the advantages at the moment. Superior forces, armament, experience . . . they're on a winning streak. Apparently unstoppable.'

'They'll find the Channel and the Navy will slow them up a bit. And they'd have to do something about the RAF.'

'Very true. We do hold the odd card. Fortunately. The thing is, Alan, that one thing we don't have is good first-hand intelligence about the situation now in France. If the Germans are planning to invade us from there we need warning – where, when, how. At least seventy-two hours' warning, to be precise. That's what I've been told. The Prime Minister has given an order. We're to send agents over there and find out exactly what the Germans are up to, and get the information back as quickly as possible. It's vital. And there's another aspect. We know that France is going to fall and that the Germans will then have the use of all those excellent North Atlantic ports. We, and the RAF, are going to need to know as much as possible about German naval movements – especially about the U-boats.'

'Surely the Secret Intelligence Service already has contacts over there?'

'Unfortunately not. Nothing to speak of. Apparently things were allowed to run down badly after the end of the last war. There have been all kinds of problems – underfunding, betrayals, no new recruiting, bad security, not taking enough notice of what the Nazis were cooking up in the Thirties. The SIS gave no warning of German preparations to invade Poland, you know. Incredible! And they had some ludicrous gentlemen's agreement with the *Service de Renseignements* not to conduct espionage in France. It means starting pretty much from scratch. Recruiting, training, briefing agents, finding ways to get them in and out of German occupied territory.'

He frowned. 'It sounds quite a tall order.'

'It is. That's rather where you come in, Alan. At least, I hope so.'

'*Me?* I don't quite see . . .'

'No, I didn't suppose you would.' Harry tapped the ash off his cigarette. 'The point is, I've been roped in to help set things up as far as the seaborne landing attempts are concerned – to co-ordinate various departments and do a spot of recruiting myself to find chaps who I think could do a good job. I thought of you. I know that you can be trusted one hundred per cent. No question of that. You're a first-class sailor. You speak good French, if I remember correctly. And you know Brittany rather well, don't you?'

'Reasonably.'

'Your family always used to take summer holidays over there – right?'

'Well, yes . . .' His parents had rented a Breton farmhouse for years and they'd cycled all over the peninsula, exploring. He'd made friends with two French brothers in the village, close to his own age who spoke no English and, in later years, he had gone back several times on his own to visit the family. 'But, Christ, I haven't been there for a long time, Harry, and my French must be pretty rusty. I don't think I'm your man.'

Harry grinned. 'I wasn't suggesting landing *you* in France, Alan. You'd stick out like a sore thumb. I want you to help me set up an organization down in Dartmouth and get things going. At the moment, we haven't got any naval high-speed

74

craft with the range and speed to penetrate further south than Brest, which leaves submarines as a possibility. They'd be ideal for sneaking in and out but, as you can imagine, most of them are otherwise occupied at the moment. As luck would have it, though, events have been playing into our hands. Quite a number of Breton fishing vessels have been doing a bunk across the Channel – they've been turning up at Falmouth and their crews want to stay. It seems they don't think too much of the prospect of fishing for the Germans.'

'I don't blame them.'

'Nor I. And you see how handy they could be? We could use them. A genuine Breton trawler complete with a crew of genuine Breton fishermen, plus a hand-picked addition of ours, coming and going without suspicion.'

He said doubtfully, 'The Germans aren't fools.'

'Of course they aren't, but then neither are we. It needs very careful planning, of course. Attention to every detail, tight security, brave men. We have to try, Alan, or we'll be playing blind man's bluff, not knowing where the hell the Germans are going to strike or what they're playing at. We have to get agents on the ground. The RAF think they could make a parachute drop by night, or even land a plane, but they need time to experiment and practise – and time's something we don't have. The Admiralty resources are stretched to the limit and they can't spare us much help. It's got to be done on a shoestring at the moment. That's one reason why the Breton fishing boats are the answer to our prayers. So, what do you say? Will you join us?'

He could scarcely believe that he had been given this chance. 'I'd be glad to, Harry. But are you sure I'm the right man? I've no Intelligence experience.'

'Damn sure, or I shouldn't have asked you. Actually, asked is the wrong word. You've already been seconded. It's all fixed. You'll find a first-class rail ticket on your desk when you get back. The night train leaves at seven this evening so you'll just have time to pack some gear. We've requisitioned a house down there and there'll be some staff already in place. I'll fill you in on all the details.'

'You knew I'd want to do it, in any case?'

'Of course I did. By the way, there's another little piece of luck that's come our way. Some Frenchman has just turned up there in a small motor boat. He came over by himself, all the way from a place called Pont-Aven on the south coast of Brittany.'

'It's an artists' colony – very picturesque.'

'Well, this chap's an artist. Quite well known, apparently. I'm afraid I'm clueless about the modern ones. Don't care much for their stuff. We've checked him out, as far as we're able, and there's no reason to doubt he's who he says he is.'

'Did he say why he left France?'

'Same reason as the Breton fishermen – didn't fancy life under the Germans. Also, rather interestingly from our point of view, he offered his services. Said he wanted to do something to help. He didn't know what, though, and he's rather left that to us. It occurred to me that we might as well take up the offer. He's on the old side – fifty-three – but I don't think that's necessarily a disadvantage. Rather the contrary. Nobody over there in France is going to wonder why he wasn't called up. And, by all accounts, he's an educated, intelligent chap. See what you think of him.'

'What's his name?'

'Louis Duval. You'll find a file on him when you get there. And files on everything else we could think of.'

He nodded. 'I'll get down to work straight away.'

'Good show. As I said, Alan, there's no time to lose.'

The washing line was positioned out of sight on a piece of rough land below the garden. Barbara hung out towels and tablecloths and table napkins, the next peg gripped at the ready in her teeth. She left the sheets until last – folding them lengthways and pegging the open edges together in long loops to the line so that they caught the breeze and filled out like ships' sails. When the war had started she had dug up the rest of the patch for a vegetable plot, except for the far end which she had left for a chicken run. The hens were a motley band, bought as chicks from local farms, but they laid well. One of the very few things that Esme seemed to enjoy doing – perhaps the *only* thing – was collecting the eggs. There was never an argument or a sulk about that. The child would go off with the basket and come back with the warm eggs carefully stowed in it and, for once, without a scowl on her face.

When Barbara had finished hanging out the washing, she did some work in the vegetable patch. Unlike the hens who had been an un-qualified success, the vegetables were hit and miss. Last year the potatoes and runner beans had been a hit. This year the early potato crop had got some sort of blight and half the bean plants had been eaten by slugs, but, on the other hand, the cabbages and the onions were looking healthy. She had sown three rows of spinach and it remained to be seen to which category they were going to belong.

On her way back up the steps to the house, she noticed that the Frenchman had moved his easel and paints out into the garden. He was working at the end of the lawn with his back turned to her and she was able to slip past without disturbing him. For his sake, she hoped that Mrs Lamprey would not decide to take a stroll in the garden, or, worse, sit out there on the bench and practise her French. At mealtimes she had taken to trotting out phrases, in an accent not unlike Mr Churchill's. '*Il fait beau aujourd'hui, n'est-ce pas? Avez-vous dormé bien, monsieur? Est-ce que vous aimez la cuisine Anglaise?*' He always replied very politely, in slow, clear French. Yes, it was a beautiful day. Yes, thank you, he had slept very well. And, yes, he liked English cooking very much. This last Barbara seriously doubted.

She went into the house. Rear Admiral Foster was reading his *Times* in the sitting room but there was no sign of Mrs Lamprey who was probably up in her room, perhaps sampling a glass or two of green ginger wine before lunch. Monsieur Duval was safe for the moment. But what must he think about his country surrendering to the Germans? About all the terrible news of the past few days? He had listened impassively to Mr Churchill's speech on the wireless in the sitting room . . . *the Nazi regime, with almost all Europe writhing and starving under its cruel heel . . . We do not yet know what will happen in France . . . the Battle of France is over . . .* He had given no hint of his feelings. And if he had left any family there, he had never spoken of them – not even when grilled archly by Mrs Lamprey. '*Êtes-vous marié, monsieur?*' '*Oui et non, madame,*' he had replied enigmatically. Yes and no. And he had turned the conversation adroitly to other things. If the Navy had taken an interest in him on his arrival, it must have waned, as the lieutenant had not telephoned since. There had been a call for him from the bank in Dartmouth, but that was all.

She was crossing the hall with a vase of fresh flowers to put in the sitting room when the doorbell rang.

79

'Mrs Hillyard?' He was a tall, rather severe-looking Royal Navy officer. 'I believe you have a Monsieur Duval staying with you. I wonder if I might have a word with him?'

Had they come to arrest him? To make trouble for him of some kind? She stalled, instinctively. 'I'm afraid he's busy at the moment.'

'It's quite important. I'm sure he won't mind being interrupted.'

There would be no prevarication with him, she could tell. She led him reluctantly out into the garden. 'This gentleman would like to speak with you, Monsieur Duval.'

The Frenchman turned from his easel, wiping a paintbrush on a piece of rag, and she saw his face light up. '*Enfin*,' she heard him say. 'At last.'

At first sight, Alan Powell thought that the Frenchman would be a liability rather than an asset. He was too noticeable a figure. True, he was only of average height – not more than about five foot ten – middle-aged and rather overweight, but the features were strong, the face memorable, the voice deep and resonant, and the black hair, streaked with grey, was worn unusually long. And his clothes were anything but conventional – loose-fitting linen shirt and trousers, no tie, casual loafers. What was required, surely, was a man who could pass virtually unnoticed and unremarked. A pale negative of a man, not one nearly so positive. However, he let none of these misgivings show as he shook Duval's hand and introduced himself. He addressed him in careful French, apologizing for any mistakes he might make.

Louis Duval smiled. 'You speak it well and it's a great relief to me to be able to converse in my own language for a change. It's tiring for me to find the right words in English. Lieutenant Commander, you said? Then you are from the Royal Navy. They promised that they would be in touch. I had almost given up hope.'

'I'm sorry to interrupt your work.' He glanced at the easel and the painting in progress – not of the sea view, as he might have expected, but of the house and part of the garden. Bold slabs and blocks and daubs of colour with no fine detail at all. Not to his personal taste.

'I have plenty of time.'

He indicated the bench facing the view to the sea. 'Could we sit down, perhaps?' It was a lovely garden, he thought, looking round at the shrubs and ferns and the bed of roses. And a palm tree lent a sub-tropical feel to the place. A garden was something he had missed out on in London and in life. He offered a Players but the Frenchman produced his packet of Gauloises. When their cigarettes were lit, he said, casually, 'I believe you have already talked with Lieutenant Reeves on your arrival.'

'He still has my passport and my identity card.'

'Actually, *I* do now. He passed them on to me. I wonder if we could just go over what you have already told the lieutenant – just to make sure we've got it right.' The slightly acrid smell of the Gauloise brought back his golden memories of France, and the language was returning more easily now; the odd mistake wouldn't matter, so long as he made himself clear. 'I've seen your boat *Gannet*. It must have been quite a trip all the way from Pont-Aven to here, on your own.'

'Not quite on my own.'

'Oh? I understood . . .'

'I had a companion – a small black and white cat. A stray. It stowed away in France. Did you notice it hanging about the boat?'

'Now I come to think of it there *was* one sitting out on the deck. Extraordinary. Amazing what cats will do.'

'Perhaps it thought England was a safer place to be.'

'I'm sure it did. Tell me, Monsieur Duval, are you an experienced sailor?'

'Lieutenant Reeves asked me the same question. On the contrary, I have used the boat to potter round finding things to paint, that's all. I stuck to the coastline.'

'Then you are familiar with that part of the coast – around Pont-Aven, Lorient, Quimper? You know it well?'

'Yes, you could say so.'

'And how long have you lived in Pont-Aven?'

'Nearly six years.'

'So you are also familiar with the town and the countryside around?'

'Yes. I have done a good many paintings in the region.'

'And you're acquainted with a number of people there?'

'You could say that, yes . . . but I'm not a very sociable person.'

'But you know important people in the town?'

'Important to me. The manager of the bank, the owner of a very good bistro, the man who cuts my hair, the one who sells me paints, the woman who runs the *boulangerie* which bakes wonderful bread . . . people like that. Oh, and I do know the mayor. He bought one of my paintings once. He's what you might call a fan of mine.'

'And where do you live? Do you own property?'

'No, I rent the top floor of a house. It makes an excellent studio.'

'Who is the owner?'

'A Mademoiselle Citron. Citron by name and sour as a lemon by nature. She lets out the other rooms below as well.' Duval smiled. 'She is not at all like Madame Hillyard.'

'What did you tell your landlady before you left?'

'That I was going south – so were many others, to get away from the Germans. I asked her to keep the studio until my return. I paid her six months' rent in advance. I also left paintings there, and other things.'

'So she has no idea that you planned to come to England?'

'None at all.'

'You told no-one?'

'Except my wife.'

'Ah . . . your wife. She lives in Paris, I believe.'

'Yes, in the rue de Monceau. But, as I told Lieutenant Reeves, we have been separated for many years. We live different lives. I pay her money every month through a bank and I visit sometimes, that is all.'

'But nonetheless you told her you were coming to England. Why?'

'I thought she should come too. The Germans were almost in Paris. I thought she should get out before they arrived. She refused. She has a business there – a boutique selling bags and scarves, that sort of thing. It does quite well and she's not afraid of the Germans. She thinks they'll be good customers. She's probably right. Also, she doesn't care for England.'

'And you do?'

'I spent a year here once. I like many things about it.'

'But you prefer France?'

A very Gallic shrug. 'Of course. It's my country. France is in bad trouble and I want to do what I can to help her. That's why I came here. As I told Lieutenant Reeves.'

One couldn't fault him for that, Alan thought. His own love for his country was deep, immutable, unalterable. He'd die for England without a second's hesitation, if it was required – had very nearly done so once. 'But you didn't say exactly how you want to help.'

'Because I don't know. I'm too old to fight as a soldier. I rather hoped you might be able to think of something else.'

He gave himself a few moments to consider the next step, watching a bird with a speckled breast pecking about by some shrubs. A song thrush. He could remember seeing them in the gardens of the Royal Navy convalescent home, smashing open snail shells on stones. Leaving the debris scattered. Messy eaters. 'Does your wife know that you're in England – for certain? Have you written to her? Communicated with her?'

'No. Not at all.'

'So, for all she knows, you're still in France? You changed your mind, after all?'

'Yes. It's possible.'

'Would she believe that of you?'

'That I changed my mind – decided to stay? Yes, I think so. She would think it sensible. Practical. I'm seldom so, but it's possible.'

'And Mademoiselle Citron, and everyone else that you are acquainted with in Pont-Aven – as far as they know, you have never left France? You went south to see if things were better there, that's all?'

'That's so. The manager of my bank changed a few francs into sterling but he, too, believed I was going south for the time being.'

'Do you have other family? Parents alive, sisters or brothers?'

'I have a sister who lives in Tours but I haven't seen her for years. She is married to a town hall official and he doesn't approve of my way of life.'

'What exactly *is* your way of life, Monsieur Duval?'

Another shrug. 'I'm an artist. I drink too much and smoke too much. I get up late. I go to bed late. I paint. What else is there to say?'

Powell coughed. 'Do you have a mistress?'

He was given a dry look. 'Like all self-respecting Frenchmen are believed to have by the English? No. Not in the terms you mean. Naturally, from time to time I sleep with women – one who has sat for me, perhaps, or one I have come across by chance who pleases me.'

'But there is no-one who would expect to know your whereabouts . . . and everything that concerns you? *Demand* to know it?'

'No-one. I much prefer it that way.'

Powell thought for a moment. Harry had already pointed out the advantage of Duval's age and background, and he saw now that there was another advantage too. He lived as he liked, did what he wanted, went where he pleased, answered to none. There was nobody – not even his wife – who had any claim on him, other than the maintenance paid monthly by a bank. Add to that the fact that he knew the area so well and that he went everywhere with his easel and paints, and it began to make sense. 'You say, Monsieur Duval, that you want to help your country. Now that she has surrendered and signed an armistice with the Germans, that presents a bit of a problem for you. Her fate is sealed – for the time being. You have my deepest sympathy, of course.'

'Thank you.'

There had been a definite trace of irony in the response. 'I assure you, though, that we, in this country, have no intention of giving up the fight. We shall go on to the end, whatever happens.'

'So your Prime Minister declares.'

'He means it. And you can help your country by helping us to fight on until we can liberate France and the rest of Europe from the Nazis.'

'You will need the Americans' support to do that, I think.'

'Very possibly. But the Americans will need *us* also. We have to hold out.'

'So . . . what can I do?'

'I can't give details at the moment, I'm afraid. All I *can* say is that it would involve you returning to France for a time – a few days, perhaps – and finding out certain things that we need to know. Would you be willing to do that?'

'Return to France? My God, that's asking a great deal! I went to a lot of effort to come here.'

'I know.'

'And now you want me to turn round and go back again?'

'Not immediately. But as soon as we can arrange it.' Powell hesitated. 'You would be putting yourself at considerable risk, of course. I can't deny that.'

The Frenchman seemed amused. 'Yes, that

does occur to me. But I'm curious to know how you propose that I should return. Not, I hope, in the *Gannet*? I should not want to repeat the experience.'

'No. In a French fishing boat, as a matter of fact. Quite a number of your fellow countrymen have just turned up on this coast. Fishermen from Brittany. They're not the only ones. Did you know that your General de Gaulle is in London?'

'No, I had not heard but I am not surprised. He would never serve under Marshal Pétain. It's good news that he has escaped.'

'Even better for him than you think. Apparently, he has been tried and condemned to death in his absence by your government.'

'Not *my* government, Lieutenant Commander. Not mine. They are not my choice.'

'Quite. It's rather an affair of honour, when it comes down to it, isn't it? The honour of France.'

'Of dishonour, rather. My country has been dishonoured, I am ashamed to say.'

Silently, he agreed. 'So, would you be prepared to go?'

Louis Duval drew on his cigarette, apparently considering his answer. He shrugged his shoulders. 'Yes, I will go. After all, I offered to do something, so it might as well be that.'

'Thank you, Monsieur Duval. There is a good deal of preparation still to be done, so in the meantime, we'd like you to stay on here, if you don't mind. Carry on with your painting. I don't, of course, have to ask you not to speak of this to anybody.'

'No, it is not necessary to tell me that. What will be necessary for me, though, is to have English money in order to pay Madame Hillyard. The bank in the town can only change a few pounds' worth of my francs.'

'You brought French francs with you?'

'Quite a sum.'

'Don't worry, I'll get them all changed for you. French francs will come in very handy for us. And, of course, you'll be recompensed for your services. Not riches exactly, I'm afraid, but we'll see you're not out of pocket.' Powell stood up. 'We'll have to move your boat, if you don't mind. She's rather in the way.'

'Where to?'

'I'll find another mooring further upstream.'

'I should like to empty the locker before she's moved.'

'By all means.' They shook hands. 'Goodbye for the moment, then.'

'There is one other thing, monsieur . . .'

He turned. 'Yes?'

'I should like my passport and identity card back,' Louis Duval said. He smiled and added in English, 'If you don't mind.'

Alan Powell encountered Mrs Hillyard by the side door. She was carrying secateurs and a flower basket, on her way into the garden. He said, 'I'm just leaving, Mrs Hillyard. I'm sorry to have disturbed you.'

89

'I hope there isn't any problem for Monsieur Duval?'

'No. None at all. Everything's fine.' He guessed that she took him for some busybody official, causing trouble. 'I didn't introduce myself. My name is Powell. Lieutenant Commander Powell. I just wanted to clear up a few points with Monsieur Duval, that's all. We have to check on these things, you know – can't be too careful these days. All part of national security.' She looked relieved – though whether for the Frenchman's sake or her own, it was impossible to say. He thought of Duval's smiling remark about his landlady, *not at all like Madame Hillyard.* There was certainly nothing sour about her. The word womanly came into his mind, and the word warm. Warm and womanly. She had beautiful thick, wavy hair and large grey eyes. He realized that he was staring, pulled himself together and went on hurriedly, 'I hope it will be all right with you if Monsieur Duval stays on here, for the time being?'

'Yes, of course.'

'He's going to make himself useful to us doing some translating and interpreting. Very handy having him around for that sort of thing. We'll need to call on him from time to time.' He had made it up on the spur of the moment and she seemed satisfied as well as relieved.

Later on, he phoned Harry at his number in London. 'I've just been to see Louis Duval.'

'What did you make of him? Any good?'

He said cautiously, 'Yes, I think he should be fine.'

Barbara clipped away with her secateurs, dead-heading the roses and keeping at a distance from the Frenchman who was at work again on his painting, back turned. She clipped as quietly as she could but he must have heard her because after a while he turned round and called to her, smiling.

'Madame Hillyard . . .'

She walked over to him, carrying her basket of dead rose heads. 'I'm sorry if I disturbed you once again.'

'You did not. But I need to rest for a moment. To smoke a cigarette. Will you have one? I only have the French kind, I'm sorry to say.'

She hesitated. 'I've never tried those.'

'Then you should. A new experience – that's always good.' She put down the basket and the secateurs and took one of the French cigarettes. He lit it for her and one for himself. The foreign tobacco scented the air. It smelled of France, she thought; or how she imagined France might smell. He was watching her closely as he put away the matches. Artists must see everything, notice everything. It was an unnerving thought.

'Well, do you like it?'

'It's quite nice.'

'Only *quite*? In English that is a polite way of saying that it's not nice at all. I have learned this. Don't finish it, if you don't want to.'

'No, really . . . it's all right.'

'All right is much the same as quite. If an English person says they are all right, very probably they are not all right at all – but they would sooner die than say so and become a nuisance.'

She smiled. 'Are French people so different?'

'Oh yes. Very different, in so many ways. If you were French you would have said to me, this cigarette is *dégoutante* – disgusting – and thrown it away. And I should not be in the least offended.'

'Well, it *is* a bit strong . . .'

'So, you can throw it away.'

She ground it out carefully under her shoe and put it in the flower basket with the dead roses. 'I'm sorry to have wasted it.'

'I have plenty more. I brought some packets from France. Also bottles of wine. Still on my boat. Do you like to drink wine?'

'I'm not sure. I've only drunk it once or twice.'

'*Mon dieu!* How is that possible? Life without wine. What a tragedy!' He drew on the French cigarette, exhaling the smoke. She liked the smell of it much better than the taste. 'In France wine is like a mother's milk. And just as good for you. Have you never been to France?'

'I'm afraid not.'

'Do you speak any French?'

'A little. We were taught at school. I'm afraid I've forgotten most of it.'

'But you still remember some, perhaps? A few words.'

'Yes, a few words.'

'And your charming house is called by a French name. Bellevue – which means beautiful view.'

'Yes, of course.'

He pointed to the bench. 'Shall we sit down for a moment to enjoy it?'

'I ought to get on.'

'Get on?'

'Start getting lunch ready.'

'Ah . . . for a woman, there is always something that must be done in the house and especially in the kitchen. But a few moments will make no difference – while I finish my cigarette.'

She sat down at the very end of the bench, the flower basket balanced on her knees, practising what she had preached to Esme: that they must make the Frenchman feel welcome. But his presence, so close, disturbed her. Everything about him was foreign – the way he looked and dressed and spoke and behaved. The way he seemed to study her all the time. He had taken some sunglasses from his pocket and dangled them loosely from his fingers. 'It is you who has done all this garden, madame?'

'Oh, no. It was here already. I just planted some new things – the roses for instance.'

'The English love to garden, isn't that so?'

'Don't the French?'

'Not in the same way. French gardens are not at all like yours.' He gestured round with the cigarette. 'This is very natural. Very English – except, of course, for the palm tree.'

'They can survive in Devon. We hardly ever get frost.' His forearms and the backs of his hands, she noticed, were covered with thick black hairs, like a monkey's. It should have been repulsive, but wasn't. And she noticed his hands – not sensitively thin and tapering as she would have supposed an artist's hands to be, but broad and strong with thick, short fingers, like a workman's. She found herself fascinated, her eyes drawn to them.

'Tell me, how long have you lived here?'

'Eight years.'

'It is that long since your husband died?'

'More or less.'

'You decided then, to leave the nice place on the south coast that I remember you spoke of and to move all this way?'

'I had been here for holidays and I liked it very much.'

He nodded. 'It is very pleasant. Pont-Aven where I live in France is not so different. On a river by the sea.'

'How sad for you to leave it.'

'Indeed, it was a great sadness.'

She sought for something encouraging to say. 'The lieutenant commander told me you are going to help them with translating and interpreting.'

He nodded. 'Yes, I have put myself at their disposal.'

'So, you'll be staying on here for a while?'

'If you have no objections, madame?'

'Of course not.' Far from it, she was glad. His cigarette was almost finished. She half-rose. 'Well, I'd better get on.'

'There is something that I wished to ask you . . . if you have just one more little moment.'

She sat down again warily. 'Yes?'

'It concerns a cat.'

She said, surprised, 'A cat? I don't have one.'

'No, I know. This is a French cat. A stowaway, you call it. He or she – I am not certain which it is – came with me in the boat, all the way from France to England. And now it will not leave. It stays with the boat and the boat is to be moved somewhere else – Lieutenant Commander Powell tells me that it cannot remain where it is. So, I'm not sure what will happen to the cat. And I think to myself that, perhaps, it might be able to come here – for the time being.' As she made no comment, he spread his hands apologetically. 'No, it is too much to ask of you. I regret that I spoke.'

She found her voice. 'Not at all. It can come here. Of course it can.'

'I must be honest – it's not a very beautiful cat. Rather ugly. In fact, very ugly.'

'It doesn't matter. If it needs a home.'

'You are very kind, madame. I will pay for the food.'

'We always have some scraps . . . I'm sure we'll manage.' She looked at her watch. 'And now I really must go and get on.'

Mrs Lamprey was making her entrance into the garden, pausing for effect against a backdrop of pink hydrangeas before she advanced across the grass. As Barbara went into the house, she could hear her voice, pitched as if to the upper gallery. *'Bonjour, Monsieur Duval . . . il fait chaud, n'est-ce pas?'*

The requisitioned house that Harry had spoken of was on the Kingswear side of the river. It was an early Victorian building with large, airy rooms, built on the hillside above a small creek and surrounded by overgrown gardens and trees that almost completely concealed it in summer. The owners, Alan Powell discovered, had not been in residence since long before the outbreak of the war and the place had obviously been neglected for years. All private furniture and furnishings had been removed to storage and in their place he found assembled a collection of desks, lamps, typewriters, filing cabinets, tables, chairs, carpets, beds, crockery, pots and pans . . . As Harry had promised, some naval personnel were already installed – a small band of people gathered together in haste, like the equipment, and without any clear idea of why they were there.

'Nobody's told us much, sir,' the young naval lieutenant seconded to assist him said. 'But I gather it's pretty hush-hush.'

Lieutenant Smythson, Harry had informed him, had been picked out for some good reasons. 'His mother is French and he's completely fluent in the language. Also he's a damn good yachtsman and knows the Brittany coast well. He'll be a useful man to have around.' Fresh-faced and very keen, he reminded Powell of how he had once been himself, long ago.

He took him with him to Falmouth to look at the French fishing boats that had taken refuge there and to interview their crews. The lieutenant's superior French proved a valuable asset, since he himself found the Breton accents of the fishermen almost impossible to understand. The five-strong crew of a crabber from the Ile de Sein impressed him as good, reliable men. They volunteered at once to return for the purpose he outlined but, on closer questioning, he discovered that all of them had left wives and a large number of children in France. The risk on such a perilous venture was too great for men with families, he decided. Two other possible crews had become disenchanted with Falmouth and already decided to take their boats back to Brittany.

In the end, the choice fell on a sardine trawler from Douarnenez, the *Espérance*. Rather a suitable name, he thought: Hope. She was sixteen metres long and fitted with an excellent engine. Her only fault seemed to be a small leak that could easily be repaired. The crew of three Bretons who had brought her over were all single men and declared themselves eager to help. It only remained to take on board the petrol needed and to victual the ship. He began arranging for

97

British naval rations to be loaded, but the Bretons' faces at the prospect were comical in their disgust, and so he took the lieutenant off on a foraging expedition round the harbour and found an abandoned French vessel with a barrel of Algerian red wine and tins of French beef and biscuits on board. He left Smythson to organize their transfer to the *Espérance* and to sail her with her crew round to Dartmouth while he drove back alone. The next step, he decided, was to talk again with Louis Duval.

Duval unloaded the remaining bottles of wine and the quarter-full brandy bottle from *Gannet* and put them in the empty suitcase. The ham was finished and the last of the Camembert and the sausage were both past keeping, so he threw them to the seagulls who swooped on them in a shrieking frenzy. The cat sat on the deck and watched him, scratching from time to time. 'Well now, little one,' he said to it. 'It seems you are in luck. Lodging has been offered – at least for the time being. But will you permit me to take you there, I wonder?'

He picked up the animal and held it under his free arm, carrying the suitcase in the other. Its four legs dangled limply and without protest. He set off from the quayside, up the steep road leading to Madame Hillyard's house, pausing from time to time to rest. The cat weighed next to nothing but the suitcase and the bottles were heavy and grew heavier as he went on. He let himself into the house, put down the suitcase and knocked on the door that led to the kitchen. She opened the door, wearing an apron over her dress and with a long white streak of flour down one cheek.

'I have brought the cat, madame – as you were kind enough to permit.'

She stared at it hanging under his arm. 'Poor thing – it looks awfully thin. Shall I give it some milk, do you think?'

'I am sure it would be very grateful.'

He followed her into the kitchen – a most agreeable room, he noted, not having seen it before. Glass-fronted cupboards, an old-fashioned dresser, a white enamel-topped table in the centre with a mixing bowl and rolling pin on it – some pastry rolled out. The domain of a home-making woman. She took a bottle of milk from the larder, poured a little of it into a saucer and set it down on the floor. They both watched as the cat sniffed gingerly at the saucer and then began to lap up the milk. He regretted that the animal was so unappealing – so dull-coated and scrawny and with the patch of mange on its neck.

'It seems to like it,' she said. 'Does it have a name?'

'I regret not. The truth is that I know nothing whatsoever about this animal, madame. Perhaps you could think of a name for it? Or your daughter?'

'My daughter?'

'The little girl.'

'Oh, Esme, you mean. She's not my daughter. She's an evacuee.'

'What is that?'

'They sent a lot of children out of London at the beginning of the war – so they'd be safe. In case the Germans bombed the city. I had three others as well but they went home.'

'Ah . . . I understand.'

'I'm afraid she's not very happy here. She wants her mother to come and take her home.'

'But the mother is not coming?'

'She doesn't seem very interested in Esme.'

'Poor little one.'

'I know. It's awfully sad.'

'Perhaps she will like the cat.'

'Yes, it might help.'

'I must warn you, though,' he said solemnly. 'There is a difficulty. This cat does not understand any English. Not a word.'

She laughed and he thought, watching her, that in the same way that Mademoiselle Citron did not comprehend her unattractiveness, this woman did not remotely realize her appeal. Perhaps no man, not even her late husband, had ever complimented her or made her feel desirable. It was perfectly possible, especially in England. He said, 'I also brought some wine from the boat, madame. And a little brandy. Perhaps you would like to share it with me?'

She shook her head. 'No, thank you. But I think Mrs Lamprey might, and the rear admiral, too. I'm not sure about Miss Tindall.'

'I shall ask them. At dinner.' He gestured at the table and the pastry. 'You are cooking for this evening?'

'Just a vegetable pie.' She seemed embarrassed again. 'The meat ration doesn't go far. I'm afraid you must find our food very dull.'

'Not at all,' he said politely, though he did. In general, very dull and with so little flavour. Except the fish and chips. Eaten very hot, out of newspaper, it was magnificent. 'Excuse me, madame, but you have something on your face . . . *de la farine.* I don't know the word in English. No, on the other cheek.' He removed the streak with the tips of his fingers, brushing it away gently. '*Voilà* . . . it has gone.' The cheek was red now instead of white, and she was looking shaken as though he had taken a great liberty. 'I'm sorry, I should not have done that. My apologies.'

'It's quite all right,' she said, avoiding his eye. 'And the word's flour.'

At dinner that evening he produced one of the bottles of wine. As predicted, Madame Lamprey was delighted to join him, raising her glass and shouting at him across the safe divide between their tables, '*À votre santé, Monsieur Duval.*' He responded gallantly in French. Miss Tindall declined but the rear admiral accepted with a dry smile. Before very long it was necessary to refill Madame Lamprey's glass.

*   *   *

Esme climbed into her bed. 'I don't like that cat. It's got a disgusting bare patch. Does it have to stay here?'

'It's got nowhere else to go. It came with Monsieur Duval on his boat from France and I said we'd look after it.'

'It's a horrible French cat, then.'

'Don't be silly. You haven't given it a chance yet. I thought perhaps you'd like to think of a name for it.'

'I don't care what it's called.'

Barbara gritted her teeth. 'Very well. *I'll* think of a name. I know, we'll call it Fifi.'

'That's a stupid name,'

'It isn't at all stupid. It's very appropriate for a French cat.' She kissed Esme goodnight – though the child seemed to hate her doing so – and went downstairs to the kitchen. They were taking longer than usual in the dining room. She could hear Mrs Lamprey's voice raised even above her normal level in a bizarre mixture of English and French, and Monsieur Duval's deep voice answering. The cat had jumped up onto one of the kitchen chairs and was sitting with its front paws tucked neatly under its chin. Poor thing, it really was nothing but skin and bone. She stretched out a hand and stroked the top of its head gently. It blinked yellow eyes at her in a sort of smile and, presently, it started to purr.

Four

Lieutenant Smythson who came to collect Louis Duval by car spoke French like a native. His mother was French-born, he told him; she had married an Englishman whom she had met as a student in London and he was the result. Although he had been born and brought up in England, she had talked to him in French from the very beginning and he had spent holidays with his grandparents in Lille.

'I'm hoping my grandparents will be all right, sir. It's a bit of a worry.'

'I hardly think the Boche will be troubling elderly people.' But he did not believe his own words. The Germans would trouble anybody if it suited them. Young or old. Rich or poor. Dangerous or harmless. Anybody who got in their way or was a handy example for encouraging the others to behave. One did not subdue a country and its people by being nice. He had no illusions, either, about the perils that might lie ahead for himself. But then, nor did he much care. His own life seemed to him to be of little importance. No wife, except in name. No child, no family. Only his work and such as he had already produced would still remain, whatever happened.

'Did you hear that de Gaulle has arrived safely in London, sir?'

'Yes, I have heard.'

'And about two thousand other French servicemen managed to get out as well. They're all rallying round him.'

'That's very good news.'

'I thought so too, sir. One wouldn't want people to think the Marshal speaks for all the French.'

'No, indeed.'

It amused Duval to converse with him – looking so English in his Royal Navy uniform and yet speaking like a Frenchman.

The lieutenant turned the car into a narrow lane that wound steeply upwards above a creek. 'We've moved your boat down there, sir. It's a nice quiet spot, though it's a bit muddy at low tide.'

'I shall be permitted to take it out, then?'

'Well, of course, there's the problem of the petrol.'

'Problem? There were still two full drums on board.'

'Oh, we had to take those away, I'm afraid, and siphon out the rest. You see, we can't leave anything lying around that the Germans might be able to use – just in case they turn up.'

He smiled to himself. The lieutenant might speak French like a Frenchman but he was perfidiously

English to the core. The lane reached an open gateway and, from there on, a potholed drive led to the house – a whitewashed, slate-roofed mansion that looked sadly run-down. He followed the lieutenant into a bare hall that smelled of damp and mustiness. No carpet on the floor, no pictures on the walls. Makeshift blackout curtains tacked across the windows – the only daylight coming from an open door, together with a machine-gun clatter of typewriter keys. He followed Lieutenant Smythson to another door at the far end of the hallway. The room beyond contained a desk, a long trestle table, several chairs and Lieutenant Commander Powell who rose from behind the desk.

'Thank you for coming at such short notice, Monsieur Duval.'

As he sat down on the chair indicated – the upright, hard sort that belonged to a school or institution – he wondered wryly if he had had much choice in the matter. For once, nobody had asked if he minded. A cigarette was offered across the desk, which he declined in favour of his Gauloise.

The lieutenant commander said, 'We've been making some progress since we last met.'

'Indeed?'

'We have a suitable boat – a French sardine trawler from Douarnenez called *Espérance*. She has a crew of three who seem to fulfil most of our requirements.'

'Which are?'

'They are patriotic Frenchmen who wish to do what they can to help your country against the Germans. As far as we can ascertain, they are experienced sailors who know the coast of Brittany very well. In addition, they are all single men. Like yourself, they have no families to – er – to complicate matters.' He had hesitated a little over the last bit. Unlike Lieutenant Smythson, his accent was unmistakably English, though nowhere near as excruciating as Madame Lamprey's. 'I take it, Monsieur Duval, that you are still willing to take part in this exercise – in spite of the great risks?'

'Certainly.'

'You have given it careful thought? You are quite sure?'

'Yes.'

'Very well.' There was a pause, a clearing of the throat. 'This is how things stand. We understand that the German occupying forces have divided France into two zones – the northern one will be occupied and controlled by them, the southern – roughly south of Tours – is to be an unoccupied area administered by Marshal Pétain's government from Vichy.'

'I don't know which part I feel the more sorry for.'

'Quite. I have to warn you, though, that we have very little information at our disposal as to the present situation in Brittany. It's logical to suppose that the Germans will be keeping a close watch on the northern coast since it's the nearest to England, but we hope that the southern coast of the peninsula may be less patrolled – as yet. We know from the French fishing crews that have just arrived here that the Germans are imposing a ban on them sailing beyond four miles from the coast, deep-sea trawlers excepted, that all fishing boats must fly a white flag over their national colours and that they must return to port before sunset, or anchor outside. But that's *all* we know. It seems almost certain that there will be a curfew but we have no idea from when to when, or how strictly it's enforced. We know virtually nothing about what other identity papers are required for French civilians, what rules and regulations the Germans are busy making, the price of things, new rationing – in short, what any agent landed there would need to be completely familiar with in order not to attract suspicion. And that's what we want *you* to find out for us – as quickly as possible. I'm asking you to return to Pont-Aven in the *Espérance* to gather as much detail as you can and bring it back for us. Find out as much as you can. Bring back samples of permits, documents, proof of demobilization or military exemption, ID cards, ration cards, newspapers . . . anything you come across that you consider will be vital to know, or be useful.'

He nodded. 'I understand.'

'In addition, anything you can learn yourself about German troop movements, about their methods of controlling the population, and about the morale and mood of the French people in that area would be very valuable to us.'

Again, he nodded. They were asking for the moon, but so what? All he could do was his best.

'We know something about their secret police, the Gestapo, and their SS. Not people you'd want to get to know.'

'I hadn't planned to introduce myself.'

The lieutenant commander gave a brief smile. 'Lieutenant Smythson will accompany you and be in charge of the crew. For the crossing, while on board the *Espérance*, you will wear Breton fishermen's clothing and assume a Breton name which will be entered on the crew list. Before disembarking, you change into your normal clothes – just as you're wearing now. From that point on, you are to be yourself – Louis Duval, the artist, who has just returned from the south.'

'Why have I returned? And from where?'

'You returned because you wanted to check on your studio apartment – you were afraid that it might be taken over by either the Germans or refugees, and that the paintings left there would be stolen or destroyed. Paintings of considerable value on the market. Once you have been reassured that all is well – and we have to hope that it is – then you can depart again to resume work you have left unfinished in the south. Or elsewhere, if you prefer. So long as your story is believable and accords with how you would normally behave. As to exactly where you have been staying, that's for you to choose. Somewhere that you know well and can be convincing about.'

He thought for a moment. 'I have been in Toulouse.'

'Where have you been staying?'

'In a rented apartment – in the rue St Georges. I did so once. The landlady there would certainly lie for me, if I ask her.'

'Are you sure? The Germans are very thorough. They check facts.'

'She can be trusted,' he said blandly. 'I knew her well.'

The lieutenant commander cleared his throat again. 'Very good. Let's take a look at the chart.'

They stood looking down at the chart spread out on the table – at the intricate Brittany coastline with its endless promontories and bays and islands and coves and inlets. The Englishman said, 'What I am proposing is this. We've run some trials and established that the *Espérance* has a cruising speed of six knots. Her departure will be timed to make maximum use of the hours of darkness. The hold will carry fish in case you are challenged and boarded. I estimate that you should be approaching Le-Guilvinec the following evening, where you will anchor in the bay for the night. At daybreak you leave. Your time of arrival off Pont-Aven must be before sundown so that you can enter harbour in company with the other fishing boats returning. You, Monsieur Duval, go ashore before any curfew is in force. Exactly how long you stay will be for you to decide – one day, perhaps two, or even more. The *Espérance* will wait as long as Lieutenant Smythson considers it's safe to do so. If suspicions are aroused, she may have to leave without you. Do you have any questions?'

'If the boat *does* leave without me, what do you suggest I do next?'

'That's rather up to you, as well. The *Espérance* will try to return at some later time, but it might be out of the question. In either case, there's unlikely to be an opportunity for Lieutenant Smythson to get any message to you. You wait to see if the boat does return reasonably soon.'

'And if it doesn't?'

'You make your way south and cross the Pyrenees into Spain. You then approach the British Embassy in Madrid and give them the information you have gathered.'

'And I would then be returned to England?'

'If possible you would be flown back from Gibraltar.' The lieutenant commander coughed. 'Of course, if you have been compromised in any way – if, say, you are under suspicion or surveillance, then you would be of no further use to us.'

He smiled at the baldness of it. The cool, matter-of-fact observation. He said, 'Lieutenant Smythson's French is completely fluent, of course, but his appearance and mannerisms are English. I wonder how well he'll pass for a Breton fisherman?'

'Don't worry. He'll look and act the part.'

'I've been taking lessons,' the lieutenant informed him cheerily. 'First hand.'

'So . . .' he stubbed out his cigarette. 'When do we leave?'

'The day after tomorrow. There's no moon – an important requisite. We don't want you spotted outside the four-mile limit after sunset. Lieutenant Smythson will collect you first thing in the morning for a final briefing here.' The Englishman paused. 'You *are* quite sure you want to do this? The thing is, you see, if they arrest you you won't be able to claim any kind of prisoner-of-war status. The Germans could pretty much do what they liked with you. You understand that?'

'Of course.' He was rather proud of himself for sounding so insouciant. So British. Perhaps it was catching. 'And what shall I tell Madame Hillyard? How to explain my absence satisfactorily?'

'You've been asked to go to London . . . to do some interpreting and translation for the Free French there. General de Gaulle's organization. Liaison work. You're uncertain when you'll return.'

'Yes,' he observed drily. 'I can see that.'

The lieutenant commander opened a drawer of his desk. 'By the way, this is from your boat. I thought you might like to have it, to keep safe.'

He took the *tricolore* and held it in his hands – the blue, white and red banded flag so dear to his heart. He found it impossible to speak.

*   *   *

When he knocked on the kitchen door she answered it – this time without the flour on her cheek but with a knife in her hand. She had been peeling potatoes instead of making pastry.

'Excuse me, madame, but I wish to inform you that I shall be absent for a while in London. I am to do some liaison work there. I regret that I am unable to say for how long this will be. Perhaps only a few days, perhaps longer. Naturally, I will pay for the time that I am away.' He took some notes from his pocket. 'I should like to give you a payment in advance.'

She shook her head. 'Please don't. That won't be necessary at all, Monsieur Duval. I'll keep the room for you.'

How unlike Mademoiselle Citron – in every way. 'You are very kind.' He looked round the kitchen. 'How is the cat?'

She pointed to a shopping basket on the floor in a corner. 'Fast asleep in there.'

'I can see it has made itself at home. I hope it is not a nuisance to you?'

'Not at all. It's very well behaved. I took it to the vet yesterday. He gave me something for the mange and to get rid of the fleas.'

'Fleas?'

'Little insects in the fur.'

'Ah . . . *des puces*. It had many?'

'I'm afraid so. A lot. It's a she, by the way. About a year old, the vet thinks. I thought I'd call her Fifi, as she came from France.'

He chuckled. 'That's a very good name. I knew

a Fifi once – many years ago. I hope the cat is better-behaved.'

'Well, she's learning English very quickly.' She smiled at him – a warm, natural smile that was altogether charming to him.

'How clever of her. But I am sorry about all the fleas.'

'It doesn't matter in the least.'

It would have mattered a great deal to Mademoiselle Citron, but then she would never have taken in a mangy stray in the first place. Nor would Simone. Or any other woman of his acquaintance, he realized. Not one of them. He stared at Madame Hillyard. 'You are so good, madame. So *very* kind.' Her smile faded and her cheeks reddened as they had done before when he had touched her to wipe the flour away. She turned back to the sink and began peeling potatoes again.

'When will you be leaving, Monsieur Duval?' Her voice was distant now and formal.

'Tomorrow morning. Would it be possible to have an early breakfast?'

'Of course. What time would suit you?'

'Seven o'clock. If it's not too early.'

'No, that's quite all right.'

The child, Esme, came into the kitchen from the outside entrance, wearing her sullen expression and dragging her sandalled feet. She glowered at him as he left.

*   *   *

The *Espérance* left harbour in the early afternoon, her hold full of fresh fish, gutted and packed in ice in wooden boxes, her lockers stocked with tins of French beef, biscuits and a barrel of Algerian red wine. A square of white material had been stitched over her French flag to comply with the known German regulations. It was the unknown ones that were going to be the worry, Duval thought. Germans were sticklers for rules and regulations. They loved notices and permits and rubber stamps that permitted this and forbade that and, by now, they would have had time to think up a nice long list. Failure to comply could land them instantly in trouble. His fears about Lieutenant Smythson's appearance giving them away, however, had been groundless. With his hair dyed dark brown and wearing Breton fisherman's clothes, including the heavy sabots, he was almost unrecognizable. As for himself, he should pass any casual German inspection easily enough. The people who could never be fooled by either of them would be the real Breton fishermen, and how far other Frenchmen in France could be trusted remained to be seen. Occupation by the Nazis would bring out the best in some and the worst in others. Terror was a powerful weapon and the Germans would be fools not to use it.

As well as being much larger than the *Gannet* the trawler was a good deal faster, making a steady six knots, and on this trip he could take a back seat. Lieutenant Smythson and the three

Breton fishermen did nearly all the work; his turn would come later.

At first light on the following day they were several miles west of the island of Ushant and by eight o'clock they were approaching the Raz de Sein in a relatively calm sea, but well outside the four-mile fishing limit. It was then that an aircraft appeared out of nowhere and flew over them almost at masthead height. A German Dornier. They looked busy on the aft deck, pretending to be handling nets, and, out of the corners of their eyes, watched the Dornier turn to come back and make another low pass. Duval fully expected a hail of bullets to spatter the deck but instead the pilot fired a red, yellow and green rocket, presumably in warning. The *Espérance* reduced speed and headed obediently towards the nearest land. They watched the German plane fly off, apparently satisfied.

It had begun to rain and they continued south at a top speed of eight knots, vanishing into a lucky curtain of grey drizzle. As night fell, they anchored off Le-Guilvinec, opened more tins and unstoppered the barrel. The Algerian wine was rough but he had drunk a lot worse in his time. He stayed up talking to the lieutenant when the other three had taken unsteadily to their bunks, and they went over their plan of action again.

Later, lying in his bunk with the sour taste of the wine in his mouth, smoking a cigarette and contemplating what might lie ahead, he began to have second thoughts; to wonder if he had been totally mad to commit himself so readily to such a venture. He could have lived out the war in France, minding his own business and keeping out of trouble, as Simone had shrewdly recommended. The Boche would probably have left him alone. The English would have left him alone, too, if he hadn't volunteered his services. Tolerance towards refugees was one of their noblest traditions. They might not understand foreigners, or like them, but they gave them shelter. Heroics would neither have been expected of him, nor required – especially as a Frenchman. He understood well enough the cynical view that most English held of the French. There had been no need to offer himself up like some sacrificial lamb. And there was, after all, still some point to life. Work still to be done. Things to be enjoyed. Yes, he must have been totally mad.

Five

'I'm sorry to disturb you again, Mrs Hillyard.' Uncertain that she remembered him, he added, 'I'm Lieutenant Commander Powell.'

'Yes, of course. You came to see Monsieur Duval. He's not here, I'm afraid.'

'I realize that. He's in London, giving the Free French chaps a hand. Actually, he's asked me to call by to collect some papers from his room that he needs.'

She stared at him. 'I'm sorry but I don't think I could let you in there without his permission.' She was the antithesis of most people's perception of a dragon-like landlady, and seemed absurdly young for the job, but she was standing her ground.

'No, I quite understand. But it *is* rather urgent. And very important. A question of national security, in fact.'

She ran her fingers through her hair, frowning. He could see her weighing up his Royal Navy credentials – his rank, the uniform, the reassuring gold braid, the medal – against her quite proper protection of her lodger's privacy. In the end, the Royal Navy won – just.

'Well . . . in that case, I suppose it would be all right.'

'Thank you.'

He stepped into the hall. There was a savoury smell of something frying – a homely, comforting sort of smell that he hadn't experienced since his childhood when he used to sneak into the kitchen at home to chatter to Cook, who'd let him dip fingers into pudding and cake mixes and scrape out bowls. His life, since those far-off and almost forgotten days, had been spent in places where the cooking was done elsewhere, out of sight: in school and college kitchens, in galleys on ships, hidden behind swing doors in clubs and restaurants.

She was moving away from him towards another door. 'Would you excuse me a moment? I think the onions are burning. You turn left at the top of the stairs and the room's at the end of the corridor on the right.'

He made his way upstairs. The onions were a piece of luck or else she might have shown him to the room herself and waited while he pretended to look for some imaginary papers. As a matter of fact, he had no idea what he was looking for. Anything, he supposed, that might cast doubt on Louis Duval. Anything that gave the faintest suspicion that he could not be trusted – that whatever information he brought back from France might not be accurate, might, on the contrary, be deliberately misleading. His boat, the *Gannet*, had been thoroughly searched already. These were days when nothing could be taken for granted, not with so much at stake.

The file on Louis Charles Duval was thin: no more than a couple of sheets of paper. Born in Rennes in 1887. Studied art in Paris. Married to Simone Eloise Petit in 1909. No children of the marriage. Served as an officer in the French army from 1914 to 1916 when he had been wounded and invalided out. There was a brief summary of the nomadic years afterwards spent painting in other countries, including England. His address in Pont-Aven was given, his wife's in Paris. No known Nazi sympathies or communist associations. One of General de Gaulle's Free French coterie in London had known him reasonably well in Paris and vouched for him in both those respects. Duval was not thought to have any interest in politics or axes to grind. He was a painter *tout court*. He drank a good deal, he womanized somewhat, he lived a bohemian style of life . . . but there was nothing surprising or reprehensible in that. A man was entitled to live as he pleased, especially a man on his own. To be honest, Powell rather envied him. Service life, he was well aware, had its constraints and limitations.

The room had been left remarkably neat and tidy. Artists, he had always imagined, would be most unlikely to be anything of the kind. The easel with its part-worked canvas stood near the window and there was an aroma of oil paints and French tobacco. The ashtray, he noted, was clean, the furniture dusted, the carpet swept – Mrs Hillyard, it seemed, looked after her lodgers well. He shut the door behind him and began a thorough search through the chest of drawers, the wardrobe, the suitcase, the bed and in any possible hiding place, careful to replace everything exactly as before. He found nothing that gave any real clues to the man – no photographs, no letters, no diary, no papers, no personal mementoes of any kind. If Louis Duval possessed such things then he had left them all behind in France.

Before he left the room, Alan paused by the canvas on the easel, studying it for a moment. It was the same painting that he had seen Duval working on in the garden. Now that he looked at it again, and more closely, the apparently slapdash brushstrokes and daubed colours began to make more sense. The style might not be to his taste, but he realized that the execution was masterful.

Downstairs, he knocked at the kitchen door and opened it. Mrs Hillyard was busy at the stove.

'Did you find what you needed, Lieutenant Commander?'

'No luck, I'm afraid. The papers must have got mislaid. Easy enough to happen in the circumstances. I'm sorry about the onions. I hope they weren't beyond saving.'

'No, I got there just in time. I shouldn't have left them.'

'Whatever you're making smells awfully good.'

'It's only cottage pie.'

It might be only that, he thought, but he'd be willing to bet that it was superior to most of the cottage pies he'd eaten over the past years.

She had taken a saucepan off the back of the stove and moved across to the sink to drain it through a colander. Over her shoulder she said, 'Would you mind very much just giving the mince a bit of a stir while I mash these potatoes?'

He picked up the spoon lying beside the stove and prodded gingerly at the contents – mince and onions, simmering away in gravy. He stirred on more boldly, rather enjoying the novelty, and was sorry when she finished with the potatoes and took over. 'Well, I mustn't keep you any longer.'

'Thank you for the help.'

'It was a pleasure,' he said truthfully. It had been a perfectly sound and sensible idea to search Duval's room while he was away and, of course, he had wanted to do the job himself to be quite sure that nothing of significance was missed. But, even so, he knew that he had also, subconsciously, wanted to see her again. And, now that he had done so, he found himself even more attracted by her. It was an absurdly romantic notion but he felt that he had been looking for this woman all his life.

A small black cat with four white paws

had appeared from nowhere and was rubbing itself against her ankles. 'It's a French cat,' she said, bending down to stroke it. 'It came with Monsieur Duval on his boat. I'm looking after it for him.'

He remembered about the stowaway. 'That's very kind of you.'

'Oh, it's no trouble. She's sweet.'

'And intelligent. She knew when to get out.'

'Like Monsieur Duval.'

'Yes, indeed.'

'I wonder if they were right to come here, though. It could be us next, couldn't it? Being invaded and occupied by the Germans. There's not much to stop them, is there?'

He said firmly, 'They'll find us rather different to deal with.'

She accompanied him to the front door. He paused, delaying his departure, looking at her a moment longer. 'Well, thank you again, Mrs Hillyard. We appreciate your co-operation.'

She said, 'When do you think Monsieur Duval will be back?'

'Difficult to say . . . perhaps only a few days, perhaps longer. Is there a problem about keeping his room?'

'Goodness, no. None at all.'

'Well, I'll let you know if I get any definite information about his return.'

Back at his desk, he pulled himself together. He was a middle-aged, confirmed bachelor. Any fanciful thoughts he might entertain about Mrs

122

Hillyard, a married woman, were ridiculous, not to say dishonourable.

The phone rang. Harry's voice sounded in his ear. 'Any news, Alan?'

'They should be there now, with luck.'

'Let me know as soon as you have anything.'

A Wren brought in a cup of tea and left it on his desk. He drank some and then lit a cigarette and went over to the chart on the trestle table. The Channel looked alarmingly narrow in places. *There's not much to stop them, is there?* She had a point. The Germans could take their pick and launch an invasion force from anywhere along the whole northern coast of France. With defensive military resources still meagre from the shambles of Dunkirk, it would be impossible to cover every potential landing beach on the English side. Reliable and up-to-date intelligence was more than important; it was crucial. He traced a finger thoughtfully from the port of Cherbourg all the way round the peninsula of Brittany down to Pont-Aven. The *Espérance* should be there now. Within a few days – perhaps no more than three or four at the most, if all went according to plan – she could be back. There was nothing to be done but wait. And pray.

At sundown they approached the mouth of the Aven estuary, joining the fishing boats returning with the day's catch – some of them with sails hoisted. Duval stayed below out of sight, enduring the heat, the petrol fumes and the stink of dead fish. Lieutenant Smythson and the three Bretons were strangers to the port, but he had mixed with too many Pont-Aven men – sketching and painting them, chatting to them in bistros, passing them in the street – to risk being seen and recognized on board the *Espérance*. He delayed changing into his own clothes since they had no idea what kind of reception might await them. It was very possible that the Germans might be making inspections and come on board. The letters and numbers on the port bow of the *Espérance* identified her as from Douarnenez, which matched with their story, but what other permits and papers would be required and expected of them?

He could hear the three Bretons up on deck calling out to crews on other boats as they converged on the harbour. The lieutenant was sensibly keeping his mouth shut. Smythson came below. 'Well, we've learned something. The Germans are rationing petrol to fishing boats – some of this lot have used theirs up, that's why they're under sail. We've spread the word that we've got engine trouble and are putting in for the night to do some repairs.'

'What about them searching the boats?'

'Apparently, they pick on them at random as they come back to port. It's landlubber Wehrmacht soldiers – not Kriegsmarine – so they probably don't know one end of a boat from the other, but if they take it into their heads to search us, we're going to have a hell of a job explaining our forty-gallon barrels of extra fuel. So, the plan is this. We're going to hang back and wait till they've boarded one of the other boats, then go in fast and tie up as far away from them as possible. Us four will nip ashore and go and sit in one of the bistros on the quayside and see what happens. That'll be your chance to get ashore too, sir. Curfew starts at nine o'clock, by the way.'

Duval changed into his own clothes – the loose-fitting jacket, shirt and trousers and, thank God, comfortable shoes instead of wooden sabots. The engine speed had slackened and the *Espérance* was trundling along, the seawater slapping gently against her sides. If it came to it, he reasoned, he could explain his presence on board by spinning some story about painting a seascape, but there was no story that he could think of to account satisfactorily for the presence of all the extra fuel. The boat surged forward in a spurt of speed and then slowed down again until she came alongside the quay. He could hear the slither and thud of ropes on deck and, after a while, Lieutenant Smythson called down to him quietly. 'Well, that all went OK. The Germans have boarded a boat right up the other end of the quay. We're going ashore now, sir. There are a couple of other soldiers standing around a bit further along but they aren't taking much notice. They're not asking for papers, or anything.'

'Good luck, Lieutenant.'

'Good luck to you too, sir.'

He waited another minute or so and then slipped ashore and strolled along the quayside. The two Wehrmacht soldiers in their grey-green uniforms lay directly in his path but they were more interested in a young girl walking by and barely glanced at him. He let himself quietly into the apartment building. As he started up the stairs, he heard Mademoiselle Citron's door open behind him.

'Monsieur Duval! You're back! I did not expect . . .'

He turned and saw the consternation in her face. 'Is something the matter, mademoiselle?'

'I had no idea that you would be returning – so soon.'

'Nor I. But I grew rather tired of Toulouse and so here I am. In fact, I am rather tired altogether – the journey was not a good one. I bid you goodnight, mademoiselle, if you will excuse me.'

He continued up the stairs. She called something after him but he ignored her. He unlocked the door to his apartment and opened it. The lights were on and someone was sitting in his easy chair, making himself very much at home, drink in one hand, cigarette in the other, his highly polished, booted feet propped up on a stool while he listened to one of Duval's favourite records. An officer of the German Wehrmacht.

For a moment they stared at each other, then the German swung his feet off the stool and stood up. An older man, an Iron Cross adorning his uniform, his manner courteous – one of the old school and just the type to appeal to Mademoiselle Citron. He said in halting, German-accented French, 'May I be of assistance, monsieur?'

'I hope so. This happens to be my apartment.' There was no need to feign anger; he felt it.

The German looked taken aback. 'I'm sorry – there has been some mistake. A confusion . . . Mademoiselle Citron has let it to us. It was understood that the former tenant had departed in a hurry and was not expected to return.'

'She misled you. I paid her six months' rent in advance to keep the rooms for me.'

The officer frowned. 'Then she is being paid double.'

'Evidently. She's a very shrewd business-woman.' He glanced round the studio. So far as he could see it was exactly as he had left it. 'I hope there has been no damage.'

'Nothing has been harmed, I assure you. It has only been myself here and I have been most careful. Permit me to introduce myself. My name is Major Winter. You must be Louis Duval, of course. I have seen your signature on your paintings here. I have studied them with great interest and I should like to say how much I admire your work. It's excellent. Most remarkable.'

He shrugged. 'Is that my cognac you're drinking?'

'Not at all. It's my own.' The major held up the bottle of Courvoisier. 'Will you join me?'

'No, I don't think so.'

'Just a small one. Please. Before I leave. It's not every day that one is fortunate enough to meet an artist of your great talent. I used to paint myself once, but unhappily I was never good enough to be more than an amateur. A big regret to me. And, of course, Pont-Aven has been an inspiration for French painters for many years, isn't that so? Gauguin, Moret, Bernard, Chamaillard, Sérusier, Seguin . . . I have learned of all these. I have made some study of their work. Art is a passion of mine. I am fortunate enough to possess a small landscape by Ernst Ludwig Kirchner that I acquired before the war. I was reminded of his style when I saw your work – rather the same use of bold and simple form and strong colour. And I am reminded of Kandinsky whom I also admire greatly.'

Things were going better than he could possibly have imagined and he knew that he must make the most of it. He grudgingly accepted the glass of brandy pressed eagerly into his hand. He accepted a cigarette, too, and a light offered with a flourish from a silver lighter, and sat down with the air of one according a big favour. His record of the Mendelssohn violin concerto was still playing quietly on the gramophone turntable. The music of a Jewish composer played by a Jewish violinist and conducted by a Jew. An ironic choice for a Nazi. 'I have just come from Toulouse. Your people are making life impossible. I was kept hanging around for six hours because, apparently, I didn't have the right papers to cross into what you call the Occupied Zone. In the end, I had to bribe a guard to let me through.'

'Regrettably, some sort of control is necessary. You must appreciate that.'

'I have an identity card. It has my photograph, my name, my date of birth, my profession, my physical appearance . . . everything about me. What more can possibly be needed?'

'To be properly in order you must carry other papers – an *Ausweis* is required to cross the demarcation line between the two zones. Will you wish to return to the Unoccupied Zone?'

'Certainly. My work takes me everywhere. It knows no borders or boundaries.'

'Naturally. I understand this. You could obtain this pass at the *Kommandantur* here, but it may take you some time. There are always long queues. If you wish, I could get one for you almost immediately. I have some influence.'

He nodded curtly. 'I should be obliged.'

'You are not of military age, I think, or you would also need proof of exemption from conscription so that you are not taken for an escaped prisoner of war or a deserter. Or papers to show that you have been officially demobilized. But I would strongly advise that you obtain a document to declare that you are excused from any forced labour scheme.' The major paused and added, 'I am afraid that painting is unlikely to be considered a reserved occupation.'

'How do I come by such a thing?'

'I could obtain this also for you, if you wish. I

shall need your identity card for the information required. May I see it, please?'

He handed over his card. For all the major's helpfulness, Duval noticed that he looked at it closely and carefully before he put it away in his pocket. 'Did you perhaps fight in the last war, monsieur?'

'Yes.'

'Like myself. But on the opposite side, of course. Were you wounded?'

'As a matter of fact, I was. They invalided me out.'

'There we have it, then.' Major Winter smiled. 'Such an injury exempts you from obligatory labour. Very simple. More cognac?'

He accepted graciously. 'I suppose you've been imposing all kinds of regulations since I was last here. I shall have to watch my step.'

'As I said, unhappily some rules are necessary. There is a curfew, as no doubt you are aware. Rationing was here before we came, of course, and your French system of tickets works well, but we have been obliged to make it more stringent, I'm afraid.' The major raised his glass. 'The good things of life, like this excellent cognac, are in sadly short supply but otherwise, I hope, you will find things tolerable in the Occupied Zone. How was it in Toulouse? At least, there things are being run by your own government which must make it somewhat preferable. I'm a little surprised that you returned here.'

He said with a contempt that he saw no reason

whatever to conceal, 'I have no regard for Marshal Pétain and his cronies.'

'Nor I, to tell the truth. It is hard to have respect for them. I found myself shocked by the easy surrender of France – I hope you will forgive me saying so. There has been dishonour . . . even shame.'

'Believe me, I feel it myself.'

The major drained his glass. 'I will obtain an *Ausweis* for you and your military exemption document. As soon as I have them, I will deliver them to you – perhaps even tomorrow, or the day after. Tell me, do you possess a car?'

'An old Citroën.'

'You will need a permit that authorizes you to drive a motor vehicle. I can arrange that for you and I might be able to get you a few gasoline coupons, though that may prove more difficult – I'll see what I can do. After all, even in a war, artists should be given every assistance. The culture of France must be allowed to survive and thrive. It must not wither. That is of great importance. And now, I will collect my possessions and leave you to your apartment.' He went into the bedroom and reappeared after a few minutes carrying a suitcase and his high-peaked cap with its impressive Nazi insignia. 'Please keep the cognac, with my compliments and my apologies. On my way out, I shall give myself the pleasure of a word with Mademoiselle Citron.'

Major Winter was not the only Wehrmacht officer billeted in the building. On his way down the stairs the next morning, Duval encountered three more of them. Mademoiselle Citron was clearly making hay while the sun shone. He knocked on her door and was not surprised to find that, unlike the major, she was not in the least apologetic.

'I was afraid to refuse, monsieur. The Germans act as they please, take what they want. What can one do?'

'Not what you did, mademoiselle. We had a legal agreement, in case you have forgotten. The Germans are great respecters of the law, as no doubt you will have learned from Major Winter. You will oblige me by keeping strictly to it in future and not subletting my apartment to any more of them.'

'So you will be remaining here now, monsieur?'

'My plans are my business, mademoiselle. You have been paid and will continue to receive payment. There is no need for you to concern yourself with my affairs.'

He saw the naked animosity in her eyes, as well as the old-maid bitterness.

He breakfasted *Chez Alphonse* – weak coffee, coarse, grey bread, a smear of butter, a miserable little spoonful of jam. A mere sprinkling of local customers where, once upon a time, almost every table would have been taken. Alphonse was desolated – his face as long as a fiddle. 'Things get worse and worse. The Boche have been bleeding us dry. They cram their suitcases and trunks with everything they can lay hands on to take back to Germany. Everything is scarce now – even fish because they will not give enough petrol to the boats. And there are almost no shellfish to be had, except those that the Germans confiscate for themselves. It's a tragedy.'

'Do they come in here to eat?'

'Oh yes.' Alphonse spread his hands. 'I have to keep my best rations aside for them. They demand it. I hate the bastards but I can't refuse to serve them or they would close me down. Or worse. There have been arrests, you know. One cannot be too careful.'

'People are afraid?'

'Naturally. You should have stayed in the south, monsieur. It must be better down there.'

He lit a cigarette. 'Tell me, Alphonse. You hear and see what's going on. You listen to what people say, watch how they behave, who is collaborating willingly with the Germans, for example.'

'Ah, those I know . . .' Alphonse reeled off names of those he considered suspect – among them, Mademoiselle Citron.

'And our esteemed mayor?'

'That's different. You know how clever he is. He works with the Boche because he must, but he plays his own game, while seeming to obey all their little rules.'

He paid and strolled along the waterfront in the hot morning sunshine, smoking his cigarette. Most of the fishing boats were already out, but the *Espérance* was still moored at the far end of the quay. As he drew nearer, he could hear the sound of tools clanging loudly on metal. Jean-Luc, one of the Douarnenez crew, was up on deck, apparently mending a net. When he caught sight of him, he vanished below and presently Lieutenant Smythson appeared in his fisherman's blouse, canvas trousers and sabots, his dyed hair uncombed for days, his chin unshaven, his hands filthy with grease. Really, Duval thought, amused, one would never ever take him for an officer in His Majesty's Royal Navy. Smythson came close to where Duval was standing on the quayside, and filed away intently at a tube of metal while he spoke.

'The fishing brethren seem to have swallowed the story about the engine OK but I'm not sure how long we can spin it out. It's not so much the Germans we need to worry about but the French – the maritime gendarmes and the port authorities. Some of them have taken to the new order with gusto, apparently. And we haven't got the papers and permits for the boat that we're supposed to have. How long do you think you'll need?'

'At least until tomorrow. Perhaps longer.' Duval briefly related his conversation with the German major. 'I must wait until he brings those documents. This morning I'll go and see the mayor. He's a friend of mine. He could be a mine of information. Also, he may be able to get papers for the boat.'

Smythson nodded. 'We'll do our best to hang

on.' He blew on the tube. 'We got rid of the fish before it went off completely. Flogged it cheap.'

Maurice Masseron was about his own age. A big man with a head of thick, grizzled hair, a loud laugh, many friends and relatively few enemies. He worked hard at being a popular mayor and all things to as many people as possible, but he was nobody's fool and nobody's tool. In his office, in pride of place on the wall behind the desk, there was the painting Duval had done some years ago of the ancient standing stones outside the town. 'I'm glad I bought it from you then. I couldn't afford you now.' He clapped Duval's shoulder. 'Sit down, Louis, my old friend. Have a cigarette while they're still to be had. And a glass of cognac.' A bottle and glasses surfaced from the bottom desk drawer, good measures were poured, the glasses raised and clinked loudly, one against the other. 'It's good to see you again. I'd heard that you'd gone south to the Unoccupied Zone. I was surprised. Frankly, I never took you for a Pétainist.'

'I'm not.'

'Thank heavens for that! The old fool has just given us the gift of himself – did you hear his broadcast? *Je fais à la France le don de ma personne*. He has remained on French soil, he tells us, only so that he can preserve the government and the honour of France and save us from military rule. Our flag, he says, remains unstained. What a load of crap! He means that he can do deals with the Germans to shame us even more. But the Germans will use him and his cronies to do all their dirty work for them, wait and see – just like they'll use the rest of us. They'll take their revenge for Versailles, with interest. My God, we must pay them for the privilege of being occupied! Not all the soap in the world will ever wash the stain from the *tricolore*. Sit down, my dear friend, and tell me what I can do for you.'

He said without hesitation, the decision to confide in Masseron already made, 'I didn't go to the southern zone, Maurice. I went to England.'

The bushy eyebrows shot up. 'To England? How did you manage that?'

'In my boat, the *Gannet*.'

'My God – in that little pisspot! You're not kidding me?'

'No. Not a pleasant voyage, I admit, but I arrived – in the end. And I've been there since France fell.'

'But why come back? You must be mad, my friend.'

'The English asked me if I could find out information for them and, like a cretin, I agreed. I came over on a Breton fishing boat that had fled to England. There are a lot of them over there.'

'So I heard. Nobody can blame them.' Masseron sipped his brandy and puffed at his cigarette, watching him closely. 'Who did you come with?'

'Three Bretons and a lieutenant of the Royal Navy.'

'Not in his fine uniform, I trust?'

'No. If you saw him, you'd take him for a Breton fisherman.'

'That's lucky for him. The English Navy stinks like rotting fish here at the moment. Have you heard the latest news?'

'We were at sea for two days. What news?'

'They've just destroyed most of our fleet at Mers-el-Kebir in Algeria. Sent their Royal Navy to do the deed while our ships were tied up in harbour. I imagine that Monsieur Churchill didn't trust the Germans' solemn, cross-their-heart promise not to make use of them.'

'I shouldn't have trusted them either.'

'Nor I. Naturally, the Boche would have used our ships to attack England. They're not stupid. But you can see why it wasn't too popular here . . . a lot of French sailors died. Perfidious Albion up to her tricks again. So, you'd better warn your lieutenant. What information do the English want exactly?'

'They need to know everything possible about the German Occupation regulations. They want samples of permits, exemptions, ration cards, papers of any kind that must be carried in order to comply.'

'For what purpose?'

'So they can forge them and send their agents to France without them being picked up the minute they set foot in the country. They want to find out everything they can about the German plans for an invasion of England, about the

Wehrmacht troop movements, about Kriegs-marine and Luftwaffe activity, about the morale of the French population, about who might help against the Boche and who will not. And they need to know it fast.'

Masseron whistled. 'Not much! And you have come to me. I'm very flattered.'

'You can be trusted, Maurice. I know that.'

'Fortunately for you, you are right, or I might be telephoning the Gestapo at this very moment. But this is a very dangerous game for us two old men to play – you realize that?'

'Yes, I realize it.'

'The Boche are not plodding morons. I have already found that out in dealing with them. To their face I treat them with great respect. It's only when they turn their backs that I spit on them.'

'But you'll help?'

'Naturally. Some shreds of honour must be salvaged.' Masseron unlocked a drawer in his desk, took out an old newspaper photo and waved it. 'This is the man I pin my hopes to: General Charles de Gaulle. But I pin them in private. It's safer that way.' He replaced the photo and relocked the drawer.

Duval said, 'I've had one piece of good luck. A German major who has been occupying my apartment – without my consent, I might add – has promised to supply me with an *Ausweis* and also military exemption papers.'

The eyebrows went up again. 'How did you manage that trick?'

'He is an admirer of my work. He felt guilty at using my apartment. And, naturally, he believes them to be for my use alone.'

'What is his name?'

'Major Winter.'

'I have come across him. A decent enough fellow. I think you may rely on him to produce the goods. So, what other things can I get for you?'

'Anything you can. Copies of work permits. Travel authorizations. Ration cards. Lists of regulations.'

'You have no idea of the tidal wave of decrees and dictates coming from the *Militärbefehlshaber* and the *Kommandantur* but I will do my best.'

'I have to work fast. How much time will it take?'

The mayor shrugged. 'Impossible to say. I'll move as speedily as I can, but I shall have to be careful. Come here again at the same time tomorrow and you'll see what I've come up with.'

'There is another thing. The sardine boat I came on, the *Espérance*, is tied up in port here at the moment, pretending to have engine trouble while she waits to take me back to England. She came originally from Douarnenez but she has no up-to-date papers, no authorized crew list, no fishing permit, no customs clearance . . . nothing that can be shown if she is inspected.'

'You may safely leave that to me. One would think this place was Brest by the way our port Administrator likes to throw his weight around

139

but Georges Tarreau owes me a favour or two. Give me the names of the crew – true or false, whichever you are using – and I'll do the rest. There must be an official list and they will each need a document to show that they are an *inscrit maritime* – I told you, it's endless. You say the English want information on German troop movements, but that's more difficult. Their security is generally tight. All I can say is that there are only three hundred or so Wehrmacht soldiers garrisoned in Pont-Aven and the surrounding district. Obviously, their main interest lies elsewhere in far more important ports – Brest, Lorient, St Nazaire, La Rochelle . . . There are rumours of big submarine pens being built at all those places and much naval activity – but they are only rumours. As to plans to invade England, I have also heard stories of converted barges assembled all along the coast of Normandy, and of the cafés being full of German soldiers bragging about how easy it will be to cross *La Manche*. But they are just stories – somebody had heard it from someone who had heard it from someone else . . . You know the sort of thing. There is no proof.'

Duval nodded. 'But it's all of interest. It gives a picture. Major Winter told me that civilian rations have been cut.'

'Inevitably. The Germans have to feed themselves here in France and the war must still be fought against England. Also, they are fond of looting. What victor is not?'

'What about morale, Maurice? Have they lost all courage, all pride, all hope?'

'Hard to say. Some have. Some have not. Those who follow the old Marshal will doubtless delude themselves from here until eternity that the honour of France has been saved and that our defeat was all the fault of the socialists. The rest of us must come to terms with the situation, each in our own way.' Masseron shrugged. 'Here in Pont-Aven, the few men who remain are mostly too aged or feeble to do anything other than they are told by the Boche, or else they are very young and reckless – like my son – which bodes ill for them. As for the women, they range from the whores who are making good extra money to the *demoiselles* who will not raise their eyes to a German's face. In between, I think there are still a few who could perhaps help you.'

Duval passed a list of names across the desk. 'Alphonse spoke of these. The first column is those who he thinks can be trusted. The second, those he believes can't.'

Masseron ran his eye quickly down the sheet of paper. 'Very few in the first category, I see. And he has missed several in the second. But, yes, I agree with him in general. Of course, what you have to remember though, my dear Louis, is that where there are families involved, the Germans will take full advantage. That makes a difference. Who would be willing to risk sacrificing his family in order to help the English, if it came to such a choice? For myself, I'm thankful that my wife and I can barely stand the sight of each other.'

Duval smiled. It was a slight exaggeration, of course, but it was common knowledge that the Masserons had had a combatant relationship for years. Insults and recriminations were the stuff of their existence. He said, 'How is Anne-Marie?'

'The same as usual. She drives me crazy. And my son drives me even more so. Luc is one of the reckless young fools that I spoke of. He amuses himself taunting the Germans – writing rude things over their posters, tearing down flags, that sort of thing. I have warned him against it many times but at sixteen one believes one can get away with anything.' The mayor studied the list, fingering his chin. 'Robert Comby, Paul Leblond, Jacques Thomine . . . if they were approached, I think they could make themselves useful. There is another name I would add: Jean-Claude Vauclin. Have you come across him ever?'

'No.'

'He was a commercial traveller in lace before he got some lung disease. Now he mends and sells bicycles for a living. But he will still have contacts all across Brittany and he went every-where. Shops, homes, offices, farms . . . Also he thinks General de Gaulle is our saviour and that Hitler is Satan. He has a wife, Marthe, but no children. I would put him at the top of the list. I have not seen him for some time, myself, but he is the kind whose beliefs never change.' Masseron got out his pen. 'This is where to find him.'

'Thank you, my friend.'

'So, what will you do next?'

'Go to see Vauclin and the others, if I can. After that I will return to my apartment and wait patiently for the major to turn up.'

Masseron handed back the list. 'Beware of Mademoiselle Citron. She belongs well and truly in the second category. Just the type of woman to settle old scores by shopping people to the Gestapo with any trumped-up story.'

'I hope you're not suggesting that I sleep with her, just to be on the safe side?'

'I don't know of any man in Pont-Aven who has yet had the stomach to do that. Seriously, though, Louis, take care. These are early days. The Germans are not yet completely organized and there is some disorder in their control, but it won't be so for much longer. Then nothing and nobody will be safe.'

He found Jean-Claude Vauclin at home in his small cottage high up on the hillside – a younger man than he had expected, perhaps not more than thirty-eight. Young to have a disease that clearly threatened his life. He was sitting outside his front door in the sunshine, working away at an old bike upturned onto its saddle and flanked by a veritable scrap heap of old spare parts: wheels, chains, handlebars, mudguards, brakes . . . all piled high in a rusting heap. As Duval approached, Vauclin glanced up. His thin face had the yellow-grey look of chronic ill health, and every breath that he took sounded a painful effort. 'I have no more bikes for sale, monsieur, if that's what you've come for. It's impossible to find them these days.'

'I'm not after a bike. Maurice Masseron sent me.'

'What for? Unless you are looking for a bike or have one that needs mending, I can do nothing for you.'

Duval indicated another chair close by. 'May I sit down for a moment, nonetheless?'

'If you wish. Forgive me if I carry on working. I'm very busy. Also, it's tiring for me to speak much.'

'I'm sorry. Let me do the talking, then. My name is Louis Duval. I am an artist and I have lived in Pont-Aven for several years.'

Vauclin looked up again. 'I know. The mayor has one of your paintings in his office. The one of the standing stones.'

'That's so.' Duval shaded his eyes to study the view of the river better as it raced and tumbled down towards the town. He had painted it many times, but not from this precise vantage point. 'He tells me that you admire General de Gaulle.'

'Certainly. He will be the saviour of France. The Free French forces will return one day to liberate us, you may depend on that.'

'The English may have to lend a hand, perhaps.'

'Of course. They stand alone now against the

Nazis. We will need their help. And their island as a vantage point.'

'Still, they have sunk our fleet . . . Not so good, eh?'

'It was necessary. The General himself will agree, I'm sure. If not, our warships would have been commandeered and used by the Germans. They could not be trusted to keep their word.'

'Does your wife feel the same?'

'Certainly. Marthe thinks like I do. In every way.'

'So we must help the English – if only to help us. Would you be willing to do that?'

'I wish I could, but I'm a sick man, as you see. Quite useless.'

Duval turned his head away from the view. He looked at Vauclin. 'On the contrary, my friend, I think you could be very useful indeed. You were a commercial traveller, isn't that so? You know people all over Brittany. People that you could ask to keep their eyes and ears open and report what they learn about the activities of the Germans.'

Vauclin said, 'Some of them might be willing – some not. It would be very risky.'

'You could perhaps find out?'

He shook his head. 'You don't understand, monsieur. It would be impossible for me to travel any more – my health is too bad. I can barely walk up the stairs. My spirit is willing, but my flesh is too weak.'

Duval nodded. 'I understand, my friend. And I

am sorry to have troubled you.' He stood up. 'Well, I shan't keep you from your work any longer.'

'A moment, monsieur.' Vauclin looked up at him. 'As I said, I myself could not go, but my wife, Marthe, could. I still have a great many lace samples, all kept safe in boxes. It would be easy for her to pass herself off as a traveller. She could call on the people I used to visit, find out every-thing she can and see who would be brave enough to help.'

'She would do that?'

'Of course. I told you. She and I think the same. We are as one.'

'And you would be willing for her to go – to take the risk?'

'That will be her decision. She has gone to the market but when she learns that you were here she will want to know why and when I tell her – as I must because we never hide anything from each other – I don't believe that anything will stop her. She could take the horse and cart and follow my old route.' Vauclin smiled. 'Perhaps you have come to the right place, after all.'

The Wren put her head round the door. 'Lieuten-ant Reeves is here to see you, sir.'

Powell said, 'Thank you. Send him in.'

The lieutenant came straight to the point. 'I thought you'd like to know, sir, that the Admiralty orders we received have been followed to the letter. We've impounded every French vessel that has taken refuge in the port and their crews have been put ashore.'

'We can't be very popular with them at the moment.'

'Not exactly,' Reeves agreed. 'But it's left us with some rather handy boats. Several very useful tugs and, even better, a couple of brand new MTBs. They were actually built over here at Hythe for the French Navy. The Free French naval chaps have their covetous eyes on them, unfortunately, and so have our Coastal Forces. I just wondered if you might like to declare an interest, as it were.'

'I appreciate the thought, Lieutenant. Thank you.'

Lieutenant Reeves's brief from London, Powell knew, had been to make himself as helpful as possible to the organization – to smooth paths, provide ways and means, to solve problems. They were to operate independently from de Gaulle's *Deuxième Bureau*, while maintaining a cordial relationship so that their French personnel could be pinched, if necessary. The prospect of getting his hands on two high-speed surface vessels that could cross the Channel overnight was certainly appealing, even if it upset the cordiality somewhat. Sardine fishing boats, and the like, had their advantages but there were also big snags, the main one being that they were desperately slow. Another drawback, to his way of thinking, was the use of Breton fishing crews. Their courage was not in question, but their discipline was. They could do as they pleased with impunity – get drunk, fall asleep, go off when they felt like it – and since they didn't officially come under naval control, there wasn't much that could be done about it.

The lieutenant said, 'How's Duval shaping up, sir?'

'Early days. We'll have to wait and see.'

'I was rather impressed by him actually, sir. The old boy at Mrs Hillyard's place has been keeping a close watch on him, by the way.'

'What old boy?'

'I must have forgotten to mention him. Rear Admiral Foster. He's out to grass officially but he worked with Naval Intelligence in his day. We've sent one or two odds and sods to stay at the Bellevue who just turned up out of the blue – same sort as Duval. People we're not too sure of and want to keep an eye on while we find out more about them. Poles, Czechs, Belgians . . . all the ragtag and bobtail.'

He frowned. 'Doesn't Mrs Hillyard mind your sending those sort of people to her?'

'They're just lodgers to her. We don't tell her anything else and we do ask her very nicely. Our tame rear admiral gives them the once-over, watches them, listens to them, takes a peek in their rooms, that sort of thing. He's a very quiet, retiring sort of chap but he doesn't miss a trick, I can tell you. Warned us off one of the Poles – quite rightly.'

Powell thought of his pointless search of the

room which, presumably, would already have been thoroughly gone over. 'I see. And what does he make of Louis Duval?'

'He thinks he's all right.'

He said grimly, 'That's a comfort.'

The lieutenant grinned. 'Actually, we have a file on Mrs Hillyard, too. Did a spot of checking up just to make sure that *she* was in the clear. Can't be too careful these days. Would you like to see it, sir?'

'Will you give Fifi her supper, Esme? There's some fish in that saucepan ready for her.'

Big sigh. 'I've *just* gone and got the eggs.'

'Well, now you can do this for me, please. I'm rather busy at the moment and she's waiting very patiently to be fed.'

Another big sigh. 'Oh, all *right.*'

Barbara watched the child out of the corner of her eye as she plonked the cooked fish into the tin dish and banged it down for the cat. 'You could give her a brush when she's finished, if you like. It would do her coat good.'

'I don't want to. She's still got that horrid place on her neck.'

'It's getting much better. It'll be gone soon.'

'I still don't want to.' Esme hauled herself up on a kitchen stool and sat slouched over and kicking her heels against the legs. Kick, kick. Kick, kick. 'When's Mum going to come and get me?'

The same question was asked repeatedly and

149

Barbara always gave the same answer. 'As soon as she's sure it's safe.'

'The others went back when their mum came for them.'

'Well, it really would have been better if they'd stayed. The Germans have started to drop bombs over here. They could easily bomb London.'

Kick, kick. 'I wouldn't care if they did.'

'Don't be so silly, of course you would. Your mother doesn't want you to be in danger, and nor would your father.'

'Dad doesn't know anything about it – he's away at sea all the time.'

'That doesn't mean he wouldn't want you to be somewhere safe. Why don't you write him a letter? Tell him all your news?'

'I haven't got any. And there's not much point writing if he's at sea, is there?'

'Yes, there is. My brother is in the Navy and I write to him all the time. The letters always reach them eventually.'

'Dad's probably forgotten all about me.'

'He'd never do that, Esme.'

'Well, Mum has, hasn't she?'

'No, of course she hasn't.'

At supper Mrs Lamprey lamented the absence of Monsieur Duval.

'Such an interesting man. Will he be back soon, do you think, Mrs Hillyard?'

It was a day for being asked questions she couldn't answer. 'I'm afraid I don't know.'

'He's in London, you say?'

'Yes, that's what he told me. Some liaison work – for the Free French forces there.'

'It must have been dreadful for them to have to abandon their country. The French did their best, don't you think, Rear Admiral?'

As always, the rear admiral agreed with her politely. If he ever held different views – and Barbara suspected that he quite often did – they were never expressed. Miss Tindall, as a relative newcomer, knew her place and rarely offered opinions.

Later on, Barbara went upstairs to Monsieur Duval's room to check once again that everything was in order – clean towels ready for him, clean sheets on the bed, the furniture dust-free. She had aired the room daily but there was still a smell of oil paints and, very faintly too, the smell of the cigarettes he smoked. Not that she minded either of those things. There was an open packet of Gauloises, lying crumpled on the bedside table, and she picked it up and breathed in the foreignness of the tobacco. Then, for a while, she stood at the window, looking at the sea and at the sun going down, thinking of the Frenchman.

After visiting Vauclin, Duval had gone in search of the other three men named by Maurice Masseron. Paul Leblond, a shoemender, and Jacques Thomine, a greengrocer, proved very willing to help. The third, Robert Comby, had also been willing but he had wanted to know how much he would be paid. 'Nothing whatever, my friend,' Duval had told him, striking him from the list. Those who demanded payment were, in his view, those who could never be trusted. In the morning, he returned to the *mairie*, as arranged, and Masseron gave him copies of all the permits and papers that he had been able to lay his hands on.

He went straight from the *mairie* to his studio to wait for Major Winter. To occupy himself he did a pencil sketch, from memory, of the garden at Bellevue – the shrubs and the ferns and the roses, the palm tree and the wrought-iron bench. He added the figure of Madame Hillyard, putting her at one end of the seat with a flower basket on her lap. He spent some time trying to recapture her just as she had appeared to him that day – seated on the edge, head half-turned away, as though poised for flight. He was putting the finishing touches to the sketch when, at last, the major knocked at the door.

'I am pleased to say that I have been able to obtain an *Ausweis* for you, monsieur, as well as the military exemption papers and the driving permit. All is in order now and there should be no difficulty for you travelling in France in future. So far, I have had no success with the gasoline coupons but I will continue to try.'

'I am obliged.'

'And here is your identity card as well, safely returned.'

When it came to returning things, the Wehrmacht were a definite improvement on the

Royal Navy. Duval said pleasantly, far more pleasantly than at their last meeting, 'A glass of your cognac, Major?'

The offer was accepted, the glasses raised politely to good health. The major noticed the sketch on the table and picked it up. 'Where is this?'

He shrugged. It had been careless to leave it there. 'Nowhere particular. I imagined it.'

'Strange . . . if it were not for the palm tree, it might almost be England.'

'You think so?'

'Oh yes. I know England rather well. My maternal grandmother was English and I spent several summer holidays in Kent as a child.'

Duval said drily, 'Perhaps you plan to spend more time there soon?'

The major smiled. 'Who knows? It would certainly be very pleasant to see the countryside again. My grandmother had a beautiful garden – and with a seat exactly the same. That is why it reminded me of England. Have you also been there?'

'I did some painting in Cornwall years ago – it's very similar to Brittany.'

'So I understand. I have never been in that part of the country myself – always the south-east.' The major was still studying the sketch. 'And the charming lady – does she also exist only in your imagination?'

'No, she is real.'

'She also looks English – the clothes, the hair,

the flat basket made for carrying flowers. My grandmother had such a basket to gather roses.'

He saw no point in denying it. 'Yes, she's English. Someone I met once. For some reason, I was remembering her.'

'I have always admired the English – not just because of my grandmother. It is a great pity that we must now fight them. In that respect it is fortunate that my grandmother is dead. It would have grieved her very much.'

'And does your admiration also extend to the French?'

'Of course, I admire a great deal about your country – your culture, your ancient history, your beautiful language, your cuisine . . .'

'But not our politicians. Or our soldiers.'

'Some of them, it has to be said, are a disappointment. It's difficult to have respect.'

'You're not the only one to feel so, Major.' Duval removed the sketch from the table. 'I am grateful to you for your help. If there is any one of my paintings that you would like to have, please take it.' What he would never have sold, he was prepared to give. The major must be cultivated as much as possible.

'That's extremely generous of you. I should be delighted to possess such a treasure.'

He indicated the canvases stacked against the walls. 'Choose whichever you prefer.' While the German went through them, he smoked a cigarette and drank the cognac, taking a surreptitious glance at his watch. There was less than half an hour before the curfew. All the fishing boats would have returned to port at sunset. The *Espérance*, if she were still there, could not sail until the morning, but he should be on board before and ready to go with her at first light. At last, the major reached a decision.

'This I should like very much – if I may be permitted?'

It was one of his own favourites – a small landscape of the Aven river with two thatched-roof cottages in the background. He would be very sorry to part with it. Especially to the enemy.

'But of course.'

'I thank you. I shall have it framed and on my next leave I shall take it to my home in Dresden to hang on the wall in a place of honour.' The major finished his cognac. 'Well, I hope to have the pleasure of meeting with you again. Will you be remaining in Pont-Aven for a while now?'

'I'm not sure. I am always in search of interesting subjects to paint and the hunt can take me anywhere at any time. I act on impulse.'

'I understand. And now that your papers are in order, there should be no problem for you. Please let me know if there is anything else that I can do for you.'

'There is just one thing, Major. If I am away, I should be obliged if you would see to it that Mademoiselle Citron does not billet any of your people in my apartment.'

'Have no fear. I assure you that she will not.'

When the major had left, he looked at the

sketch once again before he tore it into small pieces.

He waited another ten minutes before leaving. The documents were stowed away in his pockets, a newspaper that he had bought earlier tucked under his arm. The fishing boats were in, the light fading fast and the quayside deserted except for a Wehrmacht soldier who addressed him in clumsy French. 'A pleasant evening, sir.' He nodded curtly and walked on. The *Espérance* was still there, tied up at the far end. He lit a cigarette and stood around for a while smoking until the German had moved off in the other direction. Then he went aboard. Lieutenant Smythson was triumphant. The port Administrator had been more than helpful. He had provided them with a quantity of blank crew and customs clearance forms, already stamped and signed, which they could fill in and retain for future use. 'How did you get on, sir?'

'Not so bad.' He felt very tired. The lieutenant had the boundless energy and enthusiasm of youth – something that he had lost long ago.

'It's a good thing you came back now, sir. I couldn't have waited any longer. Our three chaps were drinking themselves silly in the bistros and talking their heads off, and everyone was wondering why the engine wasn't fixed yet and wanting to help. Then some bossy little port gendarme turned up here earlier, asking to see our papers – damn lucky we had them by then. Nasty piece of work. I told him that we were leaving first thing in the morning. By the way, one of our crew's decided to stay here. Daniel says he wants to go off and see his girlfriend.' Smythson raised his eyebrows comically. 'He says he misses her too much.'

He changed into his Breton fisherman's clothes and lay down on a bunk. They'd drunk all the Algerian wine – waiting around for him, they explained apologetically – and there was nothing to eat but the tinned meat and biscuits. Not that he cared. He smoked another cigarette, thinking about what he'd achieved. Not such a lot, perhaps, but it was a start. And he thought he could see the way forward.

At dawn the *Espérance* sailed for England.

'Lieutenant Reeves left this for you, sir.' The Wren laid the file on the edge of his desk. 'He said you'd requested it.'

'Thank you.' Powell waited until she had left the room before drawing the buff-coloured folder towards him and opening it. There was only one sheet of paper inside – the information it contained very basic, but all of interest to him. Barbara Ann Sutcliffe had been born in Croydon on 12 April 1906. Her parents were British – her father an accountant by profession. Both parents were now deceased. She had attended Croydon High School and left at sixteen to take a domestic science course at a college in Eastbourne. Afterwards she had worked as a receptionist at the Grand Hotel, Eastbourne. In 1928 she had married Noel Hillyard, a dentist with a practice in Eastbourne. He had died of an aneurysm in 1931. In 1932 she had sold their home there and bought the property, Bellevue, in Kingswear which she ran as a lodging house. Her brother, Frederick John Sutcliffe, had been born in 1915. He had joined the Royal Navy four years before the outbreak of war and was now serving as a lieutenant on a destroyer. There was nothing whatever in Barbara Hillyard's past to indicate any connection or sympathy with the Nazi party in Germany – he would have been astonished if there had been. And she was a widow.

Six

Louis Duval and Lieutenant Smythson came straight to the headquarters in Kingswear, still in their Breton clothes and smelling strongly of fish. After seven days of Smythson playing his part, Powell reckoned that his own mother wouldn't have recognized him – the young Wren who showed them into his office, wrinkling her nose, clearly hadn't. Duval produced the documents that he had brought back with him: passes and papers and permits demanded by the German overlords of France – some unwittingly furnished by a Wehrmacht officer himself – together with a sheaf of notices giving new regulations, lists of conditions, instructions, warnings, threats. Smythson handed over the signed and stamped crew and customs clearance forms. The town mayor had, apparently, been more than helpful. Altogether, it was an impressive haul that had opened the way for future missions and he congratulated them. 'What else can you tell us?'

Duval said, 'Well, it seems there are only a few

hundred German troops in Pont-Aven and the surrounding area, but there is talk of large numbers of them assembling along the coast of Normandy and of the canals and rivers there being full of barges. The Germans apparently brag in the local cafés about how easy it will be to invade England. How accurate or true all this is, I can't say for sure. Also, there are rumours of submarine pens being built at Brest and Lorient. Lieutenant Smythson heard much the same in the bars when he went ashore.'

It all fitted with the latest aerial reconnaissance results, Powell thought. The photos had shown a lot of activity between Courseulles and Ouistreham. The invasion threat was real enough, the U-boat threat to shipping and convoys carrying vital supplies even more so, and he found that much the more alarming. The Germans would find invading England a great deal harder than they imagined, but U-boats roaming the North Atlantic like packs of savage wolves would be deadly. 'What else?'

'The four-mile fishing limit is strictly enforced,' Smythson told him. 'We were buzzed by a Dornier when we were outside the limit on our approach, and lucky not to be spotted in daylight on our return. Also the rule of all fishing vessels returning to port at sundown definitely applies – except for tunny boats fishing much further off-shore who can stay at sea for two or three nights. As far as we could tell, the Germans inspect boats randomly as they enter harbour. Fortunately, they didn't bother us. There is a curfew at the moment from nine o'clock in the evening until daybreak.'

'Anything else?'

'Yes, sir. Unfortunately, the Germans are rationing petrol for the fishing boats. A number of them are already having to operate under sail. Any vessels crossing in future ought to be rigged so that they can make the final part of the journey under sail. Also, we'll need another man for our crew. Daniel decided to stay so he could go and see his girlfriend. I couldn't exactly order him to leave with us.'

Duval laid a French newspaper on his desk. 'This might be of interest as well. Articles, local news, and so forth The newspapers are effectively under German control, of course.'

He glanced at it. There was a large photograph on the front page of smiling Wehrmacht troops chatting to a group of French children. 'Are they really so friendly?'

'They're trying to be – in Pont-Aven, at least. They've put up posters everywhere: *Put your trust in the German soldier*, with a picture similar to that one. The commanders seem to be keeping their men well in line. Their behaviour is generally very correct.'

'And the French themselves?'

Duval considered his answer, frowning. 'Lost at the moment, I would say. Bewildered at what has happened. They feel betrayed but they're not sure by whom. There is a slogan that one sees chalked on walls: *Vendu pas vaincu.*'

Betrayed not beaten. 'Betrayed? By whom?'

Duval shrugged. 'Whoever they care to point the finger at. The British, of course, who deserted them, the Belgians who threw in the towel so unforgivably, German agents, communists . . . even their own people. The French betrayed the French. Soldiers can blame their commanders, right-wing politicians can blame those on the left, the communists blame the fascists, the fascists, naturally, blame the Jews.'

Smythson nodded in agreement. 'I heard that sort of talk all the time. And I'm afraid the British certainly aren't too popular just at the moment – after what happened to the French Navy.'

'That's understandable,' Powell said. 'We have to hope they'll get over it.'

Duval said, 'It will pass. There will still be those in France who have kept their heads.' He leaned forward. 'I have been thinking about the best way to gather the intelligence you need as quickly as possible. I already have the names of three men in Pont-Aven who can be relied upon and who are willing to help – to amass all the useful information they can about the Germans. One of them has contacts across Brittany and will make good use of them if need be. We only need to give the word – to let them know exactly what you need to know. In my opinion, it's the ordinary men, and women, that you should use in France – people who belong to a region, who have lived there all their lives and know every stick and stone of it. The baker, the farmer's wife, the bank clerk, the tiler, the shunter who works in the railway marshalling yard, the schoolmaster, the doctor, the lawyer . . . hundreds of eyes watching. Perhaps thousands. Agents who look normal because they *are* normal. They can watch the Germans while they go about their daily work and gather information to pass on. These men and women would be completely unknown to each other, and the man who is in charge of them would receive his directions from another source. A secret network of anonymous people extending across the whole of France. Do you see, Lieutenant Commander?'

Powell said dubiously, 'It's a very tall order. It would take a long time to set up – even if such a thing were possible.'

'But consider this, also. Suppose the Germans abandon their plan to invade and conquer England? We know that it would not be so easy. They must then think instead in *defensive* terms. If they fail to take this country they will have to guard against being attacked and invaded themselves. That's a different game altogether. And the war could go on for years. There would be plenty of time to set up big networks of people such as I have described.'

It made some sense – in the long term, at least. Meanwhile, they had to carry on as planned. He had been told that Free French agents from General de Gaulle's *Deuxième Bureau* had just been landed by boat in Normandy in an attempt to get more information on the German invasion plans, and he had received instructions to arrange for a second trip to be undertaken to Brittany as soon as possible. In addition to all the enemy activity in Normandy, reconnaissance photos had shown the Germans to be very busy on the coast between Quimper and Douarnenez. Two of General de Gaulle's Free French had been lent to him for the purpose of investigating that area. They would cross in another Breton fishing boat, equipped, this time – thanks to Duval and Smythson's successful mission – with all the necessary papers. He cleared his throat. 'Could we discuss the possibility of your returning to Brittany, Monsieur Duval? You are not, of course, under any military orders and so there is no obligation for you to do so, but would you be prepared to make a return trip – soon?'

'Yes.' A simple answer to his simple question.

'There was no suspicion at your returning to Pont-Aven?'

'No. Artists seldom conform to normal patterns of life. I can go more or less where I please. It's expected. And now, I have the papers that permit and authorize me to do so – the personal support of a respected officer of the Wehrmacht. I can travel to Paris to see my wife without attracting comment or suspicion. I sell my work through a gallery there and I have friends there, just as I have friends in Brittany and in other parts of France. I could begin the work of recruiting trustworthy agents such as I spoke of to you just now.'

Powell hesitated. There was no doubt that Duval would be useful in a limited way, but he had to disabuse him of any wild notion of freelancing. To involve a whole lot of French civilians could be a security nightmare. And the man himself was scarcely unnoticeable.

'It's not for me to approve such an idea, or otherwise. But I'll pass it on to the people whose job that is and let you know what they say.' He paused. 'Would you like a cup of tea?'

Duval smiled. The offer had evidently amused him. 'No, thank you. But I should like to be able to change my clothes and clean up before Madame Hillyard sees me and wonders why I have returned from London filthy dirty and stinking of fish.'

He knocked gently on the kitchen door and opened it. She was busy at the sink, an apron tied round her waist and scrubbing away at a saucepan with some kind of scouring pad. The tap was running and so she had not heard the knock.

'Madame Hillyard.'

She swung round. 'Monsieur Duval! I wasn't expecting you back yet.'

Mademoiselle Citron had been equally startled by his reappearance but there the parallel ended. Madame Hillyard, he could swear by the rush of colour to her cheeks, was pleased to see him. Or so he hoped. 'I'm sorry to disturb you when you are busy, but I thought I should let you know that I had returned.'

She fumbled hurriedly with the tap – turning it quite the wrong way at first so that a sudden burst of water splashed everything before she could stop it. 'I was just cleaning this pan.'

It was a great pity, he thought, that she had to slave away like a domestic. 'Do you not have someone to help you with such things?'

'I did – before the war. A girl from the village used to come but she joined the ATS.'

'The ATS?'

'The women's army.' She was mopping round the sink, her back still turned to him. 'Did you have a good trip to London?'

'Yes, indeed. It went quite well.'

'I hope the train wasn't too crowded. It's sometimes hard to get a seat.'

He lied smoothly. 'There were many passengers, but I was lucky.'

'Was it the first time you've been to London?'

Here, at least, he could speak the truth. 'No, I have been there several years ago – before the war. It's a beautiful city.'

She turned round again, surprised, and he saw, with appreciation, that the tap water had soaked the front of her blouse, making it cling to her. 'You really think so? But Paris must be much more beautiful.'

'No. It's beautiful in a different way, that's all. And it will certainly not look so beautiful now that it is full of German troops.' He took his eyes tactfully, but reluctantly, away from the wet blouse. 'You were born in London?'

'Not exactly. In Croydon. It's just south of London. In Surrey.'

'And then you went to Eastbourne. And when your husband died, you came here?'

'Yes.' She turned back to the sink and did some more mopping. 'It was a bad time after my husband died. I didn't know what to do, or where to go at first. But then I thought of Kingswear. I'd been here as a child, you see. My parents used to rent a holiday cottage in the summer and I'd always remembered it.'

He nodded, understanding. 'We always remember the places where we have been happy as children.' His own childhood was hazy now, but the smell of ripe apples took him instantly to the orchard next to an aunt's house in the country outside Rennes. One sniff and he was a boy again, climbing trees and running wild with his cousins. Torn clothes, scratched limbs, endless energy and not a care in the world. Golden days, gone, alas, for ever.

'You must be tired after your journey, Monsieur Duval. Can I get you a cup of coffee?'

He didn't want one in the least – or not the terrible substitute kind – but he wanted to stay. 'That would be very kind, madame – if it's not a difficulty.'

'It won't take a moment. Do sit down.'

She filled the kettle and put it on the stove to heat. He was amused to see that she had noticed the way the blouse was clinging and kept tugging at it surreptitiously. He watched her take a cup and saucer from one of the cupboards and a bottle from another, which she set down on the counter. From where he was sitting, he could make out the curious label on the front showing some Scotsman in Highland regalia outside a tent, and read the words: Camp Coffee. She picked up the bottle again to measure a spoonful of brown liquid into a cup.

'Would it be possible to have it without milk, madame?'

'Yes, of course.' She looked at him apologetically. 'It's awful stuff, isn't it? Nothing like the real thing.'

'Not at all. But for me it is better without milk.' He felt something touch his ankle and looked down to see the black cat rubbing herself against him. The improvement in her appearance was remarkable. There was flesh on her bones and the mangy patch had almost gone. He bent down to stroke her. 'You have not forgotten me, then, Fifi? But I think you are enjoying your new home. And you know how lucky you are. You might still have been alone and starving in France, and with the Germans.'

The kettle began to hiss and then, finally, to whistle a high, piercing note. Madame Hillyard went to fill the cup and brought it to him at the table. 'Will you have some sugar?'

'No, thank you.'

He drank it valiantly while she began to slice up a loaf of bread. 'You are always working, madame.'

'It's a pudding – for tonight.'

'What kind of pudding?' He had experienced a number of English puddings and few of them with any pleasure.

'Bread and butter pudding. It's made with milk, egg, currants and some sugar.' She smiled a little. 'Nothing too terrible.'

'I'm sure that I shall enjoy it.'

'It's the rear admiral's favourite.'

'He has lived here a long time?'

'Several years. Longer than Mrs Lamprey. Or Miss Tindall – she's quite new. Incidentally, Mrs Lamprey has been asking after you almost every day. She'll be very glad you're back so that she can go on practising her French.'

'Ah . . . alas, it's very probable that I must leave again.' He caught her eye and she laughed.

'Oh dear, is it that bad?'

He shook his head, smiling. 'No. Not at all. But, unfortunately, I am serious. I *will* have to go away again. Not because of Madame Lamprey.'

She stopped laughing. 'Oh? Soon?'

'Yes,' he said, pleased that she seemed sorry about it. 'Probably quite soon.'

He finished the dreadful Camp coffee. Far from perking him up it seemed to have made him feel worse. His eyes were gritty from lack of sleep, his body stiff and sore after the rough sea crossing and his bad leg was aching. He dragged himself to his feet. 'If you will excuse me, madame, I think I will rest a little now. Thank you for the coffee.' Crossing the hall, he had the misfortune to encounter Madame Lamprey.

'*Monsieur Duval. Quel grand plaisir! Nous vous avons manqué.*'

He mentally unscrambled the last bit to make sense. 'Thank you, madame. I have also missed you.' Her heavy perfume assailed his nostrils. Like the smell of apples bringing back his boyhood, perfumes evoked women from his past – in this particular case a beautiful but rapacious countess of a certain age who had used the same scent.

'We shall see you at dinner this evening?'

'Yes, indeed, madame.'

She wagged a finger at him. 'We shall want to hear *all* about your trip to London. *Toutes vos nouvelles.*'

He hoped he was up to the invention of them. 'Yes, of course, madame.' He bowed and went on up the stairs. His room was pristine. Everything swept and dusted and tidied, the window opened for fresh air in the manic English fashion. His painting stood on the easel and he considered it critically for a moment. It was almost finished but some things were still not quite right. Tomorrow he would do more work on it to occupy himself while he waited to return to France.

Mrs Lamprey put her head round the kitchen door. 'Monsieur Duval is back, Mrs Hillyard. I just met him in the hall.'

'Yes, I know he is, Mrs Lamprey.'

'He looks rather tired, poor man. I expect he had a busy time in London. I've told him he must tell us all about it – unless it's Top Secret, of course.' She poked her head round a little further. 'Do you know, he reminds me a little of dear John Barrymore – not in looks, of course, but in manners.' The rest of her followed her head into the kitchen. 'He was such a fine actor and a perfect gentleman. The two, I may say, do *not* always go hand in hand. I well remember when John was playing Hamlet and how charming he was to the rest of us in the company, even on matinée days when he would be quite *exhausted*. It's such a demanding role, you see. No chance to rest at all except during Ophelia's mad scene. You know the bit, I'm sure. *There's rosemary, that's for remembrance; pray, love, remember: and there is pansies, that's for thoughts . . . There's fennel for you, and columbines; there's rue for you; and here's some for me . . .'*

Mrs Lamprey was wandering about the kitchen, head flung back and running her fingers abstractedly through her hair. Barbara only half-listened. She beat the eggs and milk together and poured them over the bread and butter slices, currants and sugar. He was back. But he would be going away again soon.

Alan Powell took a train from Kingswear station on the day following the return of the *Espérance*. It was a long, irksome journey to London, involving several changes, and he passed it reading his report and making further notes. Sometimes, though, he found himself simply staring out of the window and it was Barbara Hillyard's face that he saw, not the scenery. He couldn't get her out of his mind. What hope was there, though, that she would be in the slightest bit interested in him? Too old, too set in his ways, too reserved, and a not very impressive naval career. Nothing that would recommend him.

The train was almost an hour late arriving at Paddington. To save time he took a taxi to the address that Harry had given him, north of Wigmore Street. A woman in civilian clothes, her face devoid of expression, answered his ring at the door of the Georgian house and he was shown into a waiting room that looked remarkably like the one at his dentist's, whose surgery happened to be just round the corner. There was the same sort of ugly modern gas fire installed in the fine marble fireplace, the same sort of impersonal furniture, the same kind of landscapes of nowhere in particular on the walls. After ten minutes or so, the woman came back and he was shown up into a large and elegantly proportioned room on the first floor which must once have been the drawing room of the house. Harry was seated behind a government-issue desk and surrounded by grey metal filing cabinets. Powell apologized for his late arrival and handed over his report on the *Espérance* mission, together with the documents and information that Duval and Smythson had brought back. Harry examined them all carefully.

'Well done, Alan. We'll get to work on these straight away. You did a damned good job.'

'Not me.'

'Well, you got the show on the road. Fixed it all up.'

'And they carried it out.'

'Good for them. Give them a pat on the back from me, will you? Now we can get down to the serious business of sending in trained agents, properly prepared. And let's hope we have more luck than the *Deuxième Bureau* so far. Their last expedition ended in bloody disaster.'

'What happened?'

'The navigator made a complete cock-up and got them to entirely the wrong place, miles away from the Ouistreham area where they were supposed to land, and the French chap who'd been sent refused point-blank to go ashore. Then the boat's engine broke down and they only just made it back. By the way, those impounded French Navy MTBs you told me about have been nabbed by Coastal Forces. I did my best to get them for you, but it was no go. The *Deuxième Bureau* are livid about that, of course. They were after them for themselves.'

'We'll just have to do our best with the fishing boats.'

'They're too damn slow – it takes too much time. They can't make it all under cover of darkness like the fast motor boats, can they? That's what we need. Unfortunately, the Admiralty are hanging onto all theirs like a dog with juicy bones, but I'll keep on trying. Submarines are far the best way of landing agents, to my mind, but try borrowing one of those from their lordships . . . You've got two Free French chaps on loan for the next trip to Brittany, haven't you? Do you think they're up to scratch?'

'I hope so. Apparently, they both know the Quimper to Douarnenez stretch very well. One of them has relatives living near Audierne – an aunt and uncle. They'll go across in a tunny boat with a Breton crew and row ashore in a dinghy at night at a beach not far from the house. We're giving them five days to find out everything they can before we pick them up again. And they're taking carrier pigeons to send back messages. What we desperately need, of course, is some radio transmitters.'

'I know, Alan. I know. It's the same old problem, though: none available right now. However, if I've got anything to do with it, you'll have 'em within the next month or two. The Prime Minister's very keen on our clandestine operations. We've got his full backing. He wants the answers we ought to be able to give him, and he wants them today.'

'I'm well aware of that.' Powell waited a moment, choosing his next words. 'As I understand it, Harry, there's the short-term view – get these agents over and back with as much general information as they can gather up, as fast as we and they can accomplish it. And there's a longer-term view – setting up agents who'll stay

there on the ground for a period of time –
perhaps for the duration – and send back coded
messages via radio. The longer term applies, of
course, if the war goes on for some years.'

'Which it almost certainly will.'

'Quite.' He went on slowly. 'Louis Duval has
something in mind that I thought I ought to
discuss with you.'

'Oh? What exactly?'

'His suggestion is that he should start to recruit
ordinary French civilians on the spot in France
– as opposed to agents trained over here. The
sort of people who've lived and worked in one
place all their lives and who could secretly gather
information about the Germans, unnoticed as
they go about their daily business. The idea
would be gradually to build up a network across
the country of men and women who don't know
each other's identity and receive their instructions
from another source . . . in watertight com-
partments, as it were. For security.'

'Hmm. Sounds a bit far-fetched. The French
can't keep a secret, you know. Simply not in their
nature. And there's not much evidence that there
are many people in France who are in favour of
General de Gaulle rather than Marshal Pétain.
We couldn't trust them.'

'Duval swears there are.'

'How could he really know? Anyway, spying's
not a game for amateurs, Alan. The Germans
would soon root them out.'

'I agree, in principle, but I think it's an

interesting idea, all the same. Duval has already spoken to people in Pont-Aven who would be willing to risk it, and one of them has established commercial contacts all across Brittany. It's quite a hot spot in France just at the moment, as we know. Lots of German military and naval activity all along the coast and so on . . . it's worth giving it some consideration. As Duval points out, he himself can come and go pretty much as he pleases now. He's even on excellent terms with a Wehrmacht major in Pont-Aven. A big fan of his painting, apparently. The man arranged all his personal papers for him.'

'Did he, by Jove? That's handy.' Harry nodded. 'OK. I'll give it an airing at a higher level. I suppose we've nothing to lose by investigating all possible avenues. I'll let you know.'

'Thank you.' Powell stubbed out his cigarette. 'It's the rumours about the U-boat bunkers being built on the French Atlantic coast that worry me the most. If it's true, our merchant ships are going to be easy meat for them.'

'The whole damn business worries me, Alan, to tell the truth. Every bloody thing. We're in a very tight spot.'

An hour later he left the house and walked down towards Wigmore Street. It was a beautiful July afternoon – warm and sunny and with a cloudless blue sky above the London rooftops and chimney pots. Civilians were dressed in lightweight summer clothes and looked in holiday mood. It was almost possible to forget that there was a war on, let alone a threat of imminent invasion. He had yet to see, or hear, any signs of fear or panic among either civilians or service people. On the contrary, it seemed that since France had fallen, they were, if anything, more cheerful and more determined than ever. United we stand, he thought. *Hitler knows that he will have to break us in this island or lose the war.* Churchill's memorable words had summed it up.

He called into the Times Bookshop on Wigmore Street – a favourite stopping-off place whenever he was in that area – and browsed for a while before catching another taxi to Dolphin Square. The flat awaited him – silent, orderly, everything in its proper place, and rather stuffy. He opened the windows onto the Embankment and let in the breeze from the river. There was some post to sort through and one of the letters was from his sister. *Where on earth have you got to, Alan? I've been ringing you for days and there's never any answer. Do let me know if you're all right.*

He phoned her reluctantly. 'Henrietta? Sorry I haven't been in touch lately. I've been a bit busy.'

'I was beginning to get *really* worried. We wondered what had happened to you.'

Once the older sister, he thought, always the older sister. It would probably be just the same when they reached their nineties. His first memories were of Henrietta – five years his senior – fussing over him. Picking him up, dusting him down, scolding him, hugging him. He had put up with it all then and, to a certain extent, he still put up with it today, though at a safe distance.

'I've been away, actually.'

'Oh? Where did you go?'

'They sent me off to Devon. I'll be based down there for a while. I'm only in London for tonight, then I go back tomorrow morning.'

'Then you must come and have dinner with us this evening.'

'I was rather thinking of getting an early night.'

'Oh, nonsense, Alan! Get yourself over here around seven thirty and we'll have time for a drink beforehand. William will be awfully pleased to see you, and so will I.'

He got his car out of its garage and miraculously found a florist on the way to his sister's home in Highgate. She gave him a hug and a smacking kiss on the cheek, much as she had done when he was three years old, except that now she had to stand on tiptoe to do it, rather than bending down.

'Yellow roses! My favourite. How clever of you to find them, Alan, and how extravagant! William's going to be late at the hospital so he'll be a while. And Julian's still away at school – they don't break up until next week. So we can have a nice cosy chat – just the two of us.' He followed her into the cluttered drawing room – ornaments, photos, knick-knacks, books, magazines, all fighting for space. 'Help yourself to a drink, while I go and put these flowers in water.'

He poured a gin and added a dash of angostura,

then lit a cigarette. Henrietta's cosy chats usually took the form of not-very-subtle inquisitions, but were preferable to her other tactic which was to produce a single, unattached female to be dangled under his nose. It was some time since she had tried this approach but he knew perfectly well that she had never given up hope of him taking the bait. After a few moments she returned, carrying the roses haphazardly arranged in a crystal vase. He wondered where she was going to find room to put them, but she solved the problem by shifting a pile of magazines further up one end of a table.

'Be a dear and do me a large gin and tonic. There's some ice in the bucket. Of course, you never take it, do you? That horrible Navy pink gin of yours . . . we only keep that bitter stuff for you.'

She was becoming an almost exaggerated version of her earlier self with the passing years, he thought affectionately. A kind-hearted, no-nonsense Englishwoman who pursued her way blithely on a well-worn path. Sensible girlhood, contented marriage, motherhood, doing good works. He poured her drink and lit her cigarette before he sat down, prepared for the cosy chat. She put her head on one side. 'So . . . you've been sent off to darkest Devon. Where in Devon?'

'Dartmouth, as a matter of fact.'

'Your old stamping ground. How nice for you. I suppose I can't ask what you're doing there?'

'I'm afraid not.'

'I didn't think so. Well, at least it gets you out

of London before the Germans start dropping bombs on us. William wants me to go and moulder away in the country somewhere but I absolutely refuse to leave. There's far too much to do here. We're rushed off our feet in the WVS just now.'

'It would be safer if you did.'

She pulled a face. 'But very boring. I like being busy. Besides, William really needs me around. I wouldn't want to leave him to cope alone.'

'How is he?'

'Overworked, as usual, but he loves it.'

'And Julian?' The beloved only child, born after eight barren years.

She sighed. 'As lazy as ever. Your nephew, unlike his father, never does a stroke of work as far as we can tell. He'll probably get the most frightful end-of-term report. Still, he seems to get by on charm. You know what he's like – it's hard to be cross with him. Do you realize, Alan, that he'll be seventeen this year? If this wretched war goes on much longer he'll be called up. He keeps talking about going into the RAF and learning to fly. Mad on the idea. You can imagine what I feel about that . . . I worry about him all the time. And I worry about *you*, Alan.' She studied him closely and anxiously for a moment. 'Actually, you're looking better than you've looked for ages. Quite different. Have you met someone at last, by any chance?'

'Someone?'

'You know what I mean. A girl. A woman.

180

You know how I hate the idea of your being on your own. It's not so bad now, but when you're older it'll be terribly lonely for you. And you'll need someone to take care of you.'

He smiled. 'It's nice of you to worry on my account, Hattie, but there's no need. I'm perfectly happy as I am. Much happier than I'd be married to the wrong woman.'

'Well, I wish you'd hurry up and find the right one. It can't be that difficult, surely? What about all those Wrens you mix with? There must be some nice ones. You're quite a catch, Alan. A good-looking lieutenant commander with a private income . . .' She went on looking at him in her earnest, troubled way. 'You've always been pretty special.'

He knew that she would never understand. So far as he was concerned, the man she was talking about had died when the enemy shell had blown apart his career. He had lived on with a ghost at his elbow – the ghost of what he might have been – and he didn't think much of what he had become. But because he knew that his sister's concern was deep and genuine and because of his own fondness for her, he said consolingly – and rashly, 'As a matter of fact, I did come across someone recently.'

She brightened up at once. 'You did? Who? Where?'

'Oh, in Dartmouth. Just someone.'

'Is she a Wren?'

He was already regretting he'd said anything.

The interrogation was only just beginning. 'No.'

'What does she do?'

'She runs a lodging house – I suppose you'd call it that.'

'A *landlady*! Heavens, Alan . . .'

He smiled. 'It's not like you might imagine. She doesn't wear carpet slippers and curlers and it's a lovely place.'

'How did you meet her?'

'I just happened to.'

'How old is she?'

He knew exactly, to the very day. 'In her thirties. She's a widow.'

'Children?'

'No.'

'She sounds perfect, Alan. Not some giddy thing – you wouldn't want that – but still young enough to have *your* children. Are you in love with her?'

He protested, half-laughing. 'For heaven's sake, Hattie, I hardly know her. I've only met her a couple of times.'

'Once is enough. One look, even. I knew I wanted to marry William the second I laid eyes on him. Have you taken her out?'

'There aren't exactly many places to take people to in Dartmouth in wartime. Besides, I told you, I've only just met her.'

His sister groaned. 'Oh, Alan, you're hopeless. Get on with it before someone else does. If she's lovely, and I'm sure she is or you'd never have noticed her, then you won't be the only admirer.'

He was saved by his surgeon brother-in-law coming into the room. He was glad to see him, not only because he liked him, but because he had mercifully cut short the cosy chat.

He travelled back to Dartmouth early the next morning, driving the Riley down rather than taking the train this time. In the early afternoon there was a meeting with the two Free French lent by General de Gaulle, who were due to make the next trip to Brittany. They were both level-headed and intelligent young men, but they were inexperienced. Neither had ever done any espionage work before and their training, he soon realized, had been rudimentary, to say the least. British Intelligence was still lagging behind in a John Buchan world of teaching special agents to look after carrier pigeons and make invisible ink.

He spent the rest of the day going over every detail of the proposed operation with them, and taking them step by step through the questionnaire that had been compiled for them to work from, briefing them exactly on what to look for and how to recognize it. Each man was to cover approximately twenty square miles in the five days allotted before the tunny boat returned for them. The boat itself was ready, so was its crew, the two men were now as ready as he could contrive, their papers would be ready soon. The rest was in the lap of the gods.

On Sunday he went to Matins – from long habit as much as from anything else. The Kingswear church was packed with civilians and service men and women, instinctively gathered together in the face of danger. The preacher rose to the occasion with a strong sermon on the need to be of good courage, to hold fast to what was right, to fight the fight against evil and tyranny to the bitter end, and to trust in God. Afterwards they stood to sing the sailors' hymn and he had no need to look at the book: the words were engraved on his heart.

> *Eternal Father, strong to save,*
> *Whose arm doth bind the restless wave,*
> *Who bidd'st the mighty ocean deep*
> *Its own appointed limits keep:*
> *O hear us when we cry to thee*
> *For those in peril on the sea.*

We're all of us in peril, he thought. Not just our sailors on rough seas, but every man, woman and child in this country.

As the service ended and the congregation streamed out of the church he caught sight of Barbara Hillyard a little further ahead in the crowd, with a small girl beside her. He managed to squeeze past enough people to catch up with her by the lychgate.

'Mrs Hillyard . . . good morning to you.'

She smiled up at him. 'Good morning, Lieutenant Commander. It was a lovely service, wasn't it?'

'Yes, indeed.' She was wearing a white leghorn straw hat with a blue and white spotted ribbon round the brim. He thought it suited her beautifully. 'A very good sermon. Just what was needed.'

'I don't think you've met Esme.'

The child glowered up at him from under her boater. He smiled at her, nonetheless, wondering who on earth she was. A daughter? There had been no mention of any children in the file. 'Hallo, Esme.' She kicked at the ground with the toe of her shoe.

'Esme is from London. She's staying with me until it's safe to go back to her home.'

Light dawned. An evacuee. He said encouragingly, 'I'm sure it soon will be.'

They were in the way where they were standing – people bumping into them, trying to get past. He searched for something else to say, to detain her. *Oh, Alan, you're hopeless. Get on with it before someone else does.* But before he could think of anything, a middle-aged woman dressed in WVS uniform came bearing down on them. She was built like a Matilda tank and equally impervious to any obstacles in her path.

'Mrs Hillyard! The very person I wanted to see. Are you coming to that meeting I told you about? I do hope you are. I'm going to need twenty helpers to run the new canteen . . . meals for the troops, tea and refreshments. We're going to have our hands full.'

Barbara Hillyard sent him an apologetic look but there was nothing to be done but retreat, defeated. He touched his cap and walked away.

Seven

In the first week in August, another letter arrived at last for Esme. The postman, Stan Fairweather, came to find Barbara in the garden where she was weeding the rosebed. When she saw him plodding solemnly across the grass towards her, her first terrified thought was that he had come to deliver a telegram with bad news about Freddie. But it wasn't a telegram, it was a letter for Esme. He must have known by her expression what she feared because he held it out plainly so that she could see it.

'This'll please the little girl, Mrs Hillyard. Give her something to smile about.'

She thanked him and took the letter straight indoors. Esme was lying on her bed, reading a comic.

'The postman brought a letter for you.'

Esme kept her eyes fixed on the comic.

'It's from your father. Don't you want to see it?'

'Not specially.'

'Would you like me to open it and read it to you?'

'No, thanks.'

She put it down on the bedside table. 'Well, I'll leave it here for you to open when you feel like it.'

Esme went on looking at the comic.

As Barbara went downstairs, Mrs Lamprey came out of the sitting room. 'I saw the postman through the window, Mrs Hillyard. Was there anything for me?'

'I'm afraid not, Mrs Lamprey.'

There seldom was. Mrs Lamprey had a nephew in London who wrote very occasionally but to no effect. 'Not an artistic bone in his body, you know. *Nothing* like me at all. He only writes because he hopes I'm going to leave him some money in my will. Well, he's in for a *big* disappointment.' The highlight was always the arrival of the latest copy of *The Stage* which she devoured from cover to cover, with comments to whoever was unlucky enough to be in earshot. The most recent one had been delivered the previous day and Mrs Lamprey had not yet wrung it dry. 'I see that John Gielgud has been touring in *The Importance of Being Earnest* with Edith Evans as Lady Bracknell. Of course, the role would suit her perfectly. I remember them so well together in *Romeo and Juliet* in 1935. He was Mercutio and she was the nurse. *The bawdy hand of the dial is now upon the prick of noon* . . . Laurence Olivier was Romeo, you know, but I've never thought him a patch on dear Johnnie.'

Barbara tried to return to the weeding but Mrs

187

Lamprey hadn't quite finished. 'I wonder where Monsieur Duval has got to? I haven't seen him all day.'

'He said he wouldn't be in for lunch.'

'Well, I do hope he'll be here for dinner. There's something I most particularly wanted to ask him.'

Monsieur Duval, she had noticed, had become quite adept at avoiding Mrs Lamprey. She went back to the garden and worked until it was time to cook and serve lunch. Miss Tindall had gone to visit a friend for the day and Rear Admiral Foster had to cope alone with Mrs Lamprey.

'Do tell me, Rear Admiral, what was the biggest ship you have ever served on?'

'*In*, Mrs Lamprey. One serves *in* a ship, not on it.' It was the first time Barbara had ever heard him correct her, though he did it in the mildest tone. Perhaps even *his* patience was finally wearing thin.

Esme came down late for her lunch in the kitchen.

'Did you read your letter, Esme?'

'Yes.'

'Did your father have any news – about coming back on leave?'

'No.' Esme frowned at her plate. 'I knew he wouldn't.'

'Well, when he does he's bound to come and visit you.'

'No, he won't. It's too far.'

Barbara tried again. 'Shall we go for a walk

this afternoon? Would you like that? It's a lovely day and it would do you good to get some fresh air. It's a shame to spend the holidays cooped up in your room.'

Esme poked at a piece of liver. 'I'd sooner read.'

She gave up. There was no point in forcing the child to go for a walk – she'd only sulk all the way there and all the way back. 'Well, I think I'll go – just for a while.'

A flight of steep steps led from the lawn down the hillside to a gate and a path that followed the curve of the estuary towards the town. A rocky inlet below had been a favourite spot of hers and Freddie's, and she stopped to look at the little beach where they had paddled and swum. There were no children playing there now. The beach was deserted and barricaded with coils of barbed wire.

Round the next corner, she came, unexpectedly, upon Monsieur Duval. He was sitting on the low stone wall that bordered the river side of the path, a sketch pad propped against his knee, a cigarette drooping from the corner of his mouth. He lifted his head, saw her and waved. 'I am making some sketches, madame.'

She hoped he hadn't thought she was spying on him, following him about the place. 'I was taking a walk.'

'The English are better at walking than the French. We are very lazy. Please come and sit down – just for a moment. It's very pleasant here in the sun and there is a wonderful view of the estuary, don't you agree?'

She perched on the wall, but at a distance from him. 'Yes, it's lovely. When I was a child, my brother and I always used to play on a beach just near here.'

He had flipped over a page and begun sketching again. 'And where is your brother now?'

'At sea. With the Royal Navy. I don't know exactly where.'

'Do you worry about him?'

'I try not to.' But not very successfully. She worried about Freddie night and day – especially at night when it was harder to stop her imagination painting graphic pictures of U-boats stalking convoys, torpedoes striking, ships sinking in flames, men leaping into icy black water. And during the day, every time the doorbell rang her heart would begin to pound away, convinced it was the postman with a yellow telegram for her. *Deeply regret to inform you* . . . 'Freddie's my only living relative.'

'Your parents?'

'Both dead.'

He clicked his tongue. 'How sad for you, when you are so young. No wonder that your brother means so much to you.' His pencil moved swiftly across the paper. 'I have one sister, but I'm not sure that she would worry very much about me.'

She realized that she knew almost nothing about him. Nothing of his private life or of what he had left behind in France. 'Do you have children, Monsieur Duval?'

'Alas, no. I have a wife, but no children. And my wife and I have not lived together for a long time.'

'I'm sorry.'

He smiled at her. 'There is no need for you to be, I assure you. We don't miss each other. Not at all. Do you miss your late husband?'

She hesitated. 'Not really. Not any longer. I suppose that sounds rather awful.'

'No, it sounds truthful. Most people would lie.'

'But we were very happy.'

'I am sure that you were.'

'We were married for such a short time and it's almost ten years since he died.'

'One cannot grieve for ever. Was he a good man?'

'Yes, very.' Good, kind, dependable. Safe. And, she thought guiltily, actually a bit dull.

'What work did he do?'

'He was a dentist.'

'I am always a little bit sorry for dentists. Nobody is ever pleased to see them.'

She smiled. 'Noel used to say that. In fact, it made him quite depressed sometimes.'

'And how did you meet him?'

'He was the brother of a girl who was at a domestic science college with me in Eastbourne. I was invited to lunch at her home one Sunday.'

'The English roast beef with the Yorkshire pudding?'

She laughed, shaking her head. 'No. I think it was Welsh lamb, if I remember rightly. With mint sauce.'

'*Mint sauce*? What is this?'

'Mint chopped up with vinegar and sugar. It goes very well with lamb – at least we think so in England. But I'm sure you'd hate it, Monsieur Duval.'

'I'm afraid that I might. I have never heard of eating such a thing with lamb. And so, you went to this home for this Welsh lamb with English mint sauce and there he was?'

'Yes, there he was.' She'd walked into the sitting room and Noel had been standing over by the fireplace. Nothing special to look at, but she'd liked him instantly. He'd been easy to talk to. Uncomplicated. So nice. She had felt at ease with him despite the twelve-year gap in their ages.

'But you have never married again, madame. That's strange. There must have been men who have asked you.'

It had started quite soon after Noel had died. Widows, she had soon discovered, were considered to be lonely and in need of consolation – particularly those with some money in the bank. Noel's life insurance policy had meant that she had had no need to worry financially, and his partner had bought his share of the practice. The house in Eastbourne was hers, too. 'Yes,' she said. 'But I didn't want to marry any of them.'

She had found the unwanted suitors a great nuisance and it was one of the chief reasons why she had decided to leave and go somewhere where she was not known. The college had taught her about cooking and all things domestic. It had seemed a logical step to open, first, a lodging house, and then later, if it went well, a small hotel. There was no need for her to work, but there was every need to do something with her life.

She slid off the wall. She'd stayed too long, talked too much and too frankly to him. Probably bored him. 'I'm sorry if I disturbed you.'

'But you did not. You inspired me.' He turned the sketch pad towards her. 'See.'

He had drawn her sitting on the stone wall with her hands resting on each side. Her head was tilted back, her face in profile, her figure all too clearly defined. She flushed. 'It's very flattering.'

'I never flatter in my work. This is how I see you. How you are. A beautiful woman.'

Paying compliments, of course, was second nature to him. Even Miss Tindall had received them, much to her maidenly confusion. *How charming you look today, mademoiselle.* And Mrs Lamprey lapped them up as nothing less than her due. It was meaningless and harmless and she smiled at him to show that she understood that. 'I don't think I am, but thank you.'

At dinner, Mrs Lamprey launched straight into the attack, wagging her finger in Monsieur Duval's direction. '*Vous êtes très méchant, monsieur.*'

'*Mais pourquoi, madame?* Why am I so naughty?'

'You never finished telling us about your visit to London. *Avez-vous rencontré votre Général de Gaulle?*'

'*Malheureusement pas.* I have never met the general.'

'But I thought you were working with the Free French – *avec les Français Libres?*'

'*Oui, madame. Mais le général est très occupé.* A very busy man.'

'What a pity. He sounds so interesting – *très intéressant, n'est-ce pas?* Perhaps next time? *La prochaine fois?*'

'Perhaps.'

'Will you be going there again? *Vous retournez à Londres?*'

'Without doubt, madame.'

Barbara finished serving the first course and went out to the kitchen. Esme had left her supper half-eaten and gone up to bed. Lectures on not wasting food in wartime had invariably fallen on deaf ears. She washed up the pots and pans while she waited to take in the pudding – a pie made with plums picked from the tree in the garden. When she went back into the dining room, Mrs Lamprey was still in full flood.

'*Aimez-vous aller au théâtre, Monsieur Duval?*'

'*Mais oui, madame.* I enjoy the theatre very much.'

'Did you go often in France – *souvent?*'

'Unfortunately, not so much as I would have wished. And I regret that I have never had the pleasure of seeing you on the stage, madame. It would have been an unforgettable experience.'

Mrs Lamprey looked delighted, and Barbara smiled to herself.

After they had finished dinner, she cleared the tables, washed up, dried up and put everything away before she laid the four tables for breakfast. When, finally, it was all done and the kitchen tidy, she went out into the garden. It was a warm evening, still not quite dark with the tall pines black against an opal sky, bats flitting about. She could smell the scent of the roses and then a whiff of another smell – French tobacco. Before she could retreat, Monsieur Duval spoke from the shadows.

'You have finished your work at last, madame?' He had been sitting on the bench and strolled towards her across the grass, cigarette in hand. The smoke drifted on the evening air. 'I am sorry if I offended you this afternoon – drawing the sketch of you without your permission.'

'I wasn't offended.'

'But you seemed very unsure.'

She said lightly, 'Well, I don't think I look quite like that.'

'I told you, I do not flatter.'

'Oh, I think you do sometimes.'

He smiled. 'With words, perhaps. Occasionally, it is required to lie for politeness. For instance, to Madame Lamprey.'

She smiled, too. 'Perhaps you should draw *her*?'

'I think not. If I did, it would not please her at all. My wife hated the portrait that I painted of her and yet it was exactly as she was.'

'Is she still in France?'

He drew on the cigarette. 'Unfortunately, yes. In Paris. I tried to persuade her to leave but she refused. She believes that everything will be all right under the Germans.'

'How could it be?'

'Indeed . . . how could it ever be all right to have one's country occupied and ruled by Nazis.'

There was a rustling in the shrubbery close by and a dark shape bounded out onto the lawn. Fifi on her night-time hunt. 'Fifi knew that very well,' Monsieur Duval observed drily. 'That's why she stowed away and came to England.'

The evacuee opened the door. Powell smiled at her and received a stony stare in return.

'Is Mrs Hillyard at home?' A don't-know shrug in answer. He said firmly, 'Well, perhaps you could go and see.' The child disappeared and, after a few moments, Barbara Hillyard came to the door. She looked surprised to see him. 'I'm sorry to trouble you again, Mrs Hillyard, but I wonder if I could give a message to Monsieur Duval?'

It was a pretty lame excuse, of course. He could easily have telephoned, or sent Lieutenant Smythson, not taken the time and trouble to call himself.

'I'm so sorry. I'm afraid he's out.'

'Will he be back soon, do you think?'

'I'm not quite sure. He said he was going across to Dartmouth. Would you like to come in and wait?'

He debated what to do. Duval might be hours and he couldn't afford to wait long; on the other hand, it was a golden chance to talk to her. 'If you don't mind.'

She showed him into the sitting room. It was as pleasant as the kitchen: sunny, comfortable, welcoming. He admired the big vase of flowers on the table, the books, magazines, newspapers, cushions, pictures, ornaments. A similar feel to his sister's home, but a lot tidier. 'Can I get you a cup of tea, Lieutenant Commander?'

'That's very kind of you, but no thank you.' He could see that she was about to abandon him and searched quickly for something else to say. This time, he found it. 'How's the French cat getting on?'

'Fifi? Oh, you'd hardly recognize her. She's put on weight and grown.'

'She's very lucky to have such a good home.' He gestured round the room. 'You've made this house charming, Mrs Hillyard. Do you enjoy living here?'

'Very much. I've always liked this part of the country. I used to come here on summer holidays.'

'Really? I've known Dartmouth since I was a boy – rather more years ago than yourself. I was a cadet at the College.'

'Rear Admiral Foster was there, too. I've heard all about the cold baths.'

He smiled. 'They weren't so bad – once you got used to them. Did you go sailing here when you were on your holidays?'

She shook her head. 'We didn't have a boat, or any idea how to sail one. My brother and I spent most of our time on the beach.'

'I'd be very glad to take you out sailing. It's rather a nice trip up the river to Dittisham.' He saw her face change and a wary look come into her eyes.

'The trouble is I don't get much spare time, I'm afraid. And there's Esme to look after.'

'Yes, I'm sure you must be very busy.'

She added, quite unexpectedly, 'But I'd like to do that – one day.'

Before he could say anything else, somebody appeared in the doorway – an elderly woman with hair dyed the colour of brass, dressed in an old-fashioned ankle-length gown. 'I can see that I am interrupting you, Mrs Hillyard.' She surveyed them, head inclined to one side like an inquisitive parrot.

'Not at all, Mrs Lamprey. This is Lieutenant Commander Powell. He's come to see Monsieur Duval.'

'Oh.' She looked at him with mock severity. 'I do hope you're not going to take our dear Frenchman away from us again. We're very fond of Monsieur Duval, aren't we, Mrs Hillyard? Such a lovely man.' She stepped into the room.

Closer up, he could see the heavy make-up she wore, with vivid crescents of mauve eyeshadow on her eyelids and jet black mascara on lashes that were surely false. He inhaled some overpowering perfume. She was studying him with evident approval. 'I always think the Royal Navy uniform looks so dashing. Did you win that medal in the Great War, Lieutenant Commander?'

'Yes.' To his dismay he could see Barbara Hillyard edging towards the door, leaving the room. It seemed his fate, to be interrupted by overbearing women.

'What did you do to earn it? Do tell me.'

He said shortly, 'Nothing very much. It was a long time ago. I'm afraid I'm deskbound these days.'

'Oh, I know just how it feels when one's days in the limelight are over. I was on the stage, you see. You may have heard of me. Vera Vane.'

With a great effort he said politely, 'I'm sure I have. I must have seen you a number of times.'

'Yes, indeed. I worked with all the great names, you know – Barrymore, Bernhardt, du Maurier, Beerbohm Tree . . . those were the days.'

She went on talking and talking until, to his great relief, Louis Duval returned. 'If you'll excuse us, Mrs Lamprey.'

'Oh, don't mind me, Lieutenant Commander. I'll just sit here quietly.'

'We shouldn't wish to disturb you. We can go outside.'

When they had reached the safe haven of the garden, Duval said, 'That was your first encounter with Madame Lamprey?'

'Yes.'

'You are very fortunate that you do not encounter her every day – especially at breakfast.'

'You have my sympathy.'

He lit Duval's Gauloise for him, and his own Players. They strolled up and down the lawn. The garden was already taking on a mellow look, leaves beginning to turn, early summer plants over their best, later ones in flower, a Virginia creeper changing from green to red, wasps burrowing into the overripe plums that had fallen from the tree into the grass. The year was beginning to slip away. He would not be sorry to see it gone.

He said to the Frenchman, 'I've got a piece of good news for you. There's been agreement at Cabinet level for your proposal. It's been decided that you should go back to France and try to recruit civilians as informants, as you suggested. There's a proviso, though. You have a time limit of one month. After that you must return to report any progress.'

'*One month!* That's not nearly long enough.'

'I appreciate that, but the order comes direct from the Prime Minister.'

'I might make very little progress in so short a time.'

'You'll have to do the best you can, I'm afraid. One month only.'

Duval shrugged. 'All right. How soon can I leave?'

'Probably within a week. Arrangements still have to be finalized.'

'And do I take the same route – fishing boat to Pont-Aven?'

'Not to Pont-Aven. You'll be taken to a beach a few kilometres to the west of there and rowed ashore by dinghy at night.'

'Which beach?'

'A private one – the foreshore to a château. Apparently the Parisian owner is seldom there.'

'I think I know exactly the one. But your information is not quite correct. It's a villa, not a château, and the owner is not from Paris but a businessman from Rennes.' Duval gestured with his cigarette. 'To a Breton anyone from outside his own village is a Parisian.'

'Do you know this man personally?'

'I have only met him once. I did a painting of the villa. It appealed to me as a subject. You're right, though, that he is seldom there. A good place to land. How did you find out about it?'

'Your *Deuxième Bureau* can be pretty helpful, if we ask them very politely. They've even got hold of a French bicycle for you. I hope you can ride one.'

'Naturally. One never forgets.'

'By the way, this puts you officially on our payroll and means that we'll take care of all your living expenses. There's provision in our department for that sort of thing. I'll have a word with

Mrs Hillyard about your room. She seems quite willing to keep it for you.'

'And what lie do you propose that I tell her this time?'

'The same one. You're needed in London for liaison work.' He paused. 'You do understand the risk you'll be taking?'

'We talked about that before, Lieutenant Commander. I understand very well.'

Powell glanced at his watch. 'I have to leave now but I'll be in touch again shortly. We'll need to go into more detail. To plan everything as thoroughly as we can. I don't need, of course, to remind you of the need for complete secrecy.'

'No, you do not.'

On his way out he ran into the woman, Mrs Lamprey. She fluttered her chiffon scarf at him coyly. 'Have you finished your little talk?'

'Yes, indeed.'

'And will Monsieur Duval be going away again?'

'It's possible.'

'For long?'

'I'm afraid I don't know.'

'You're being very secretive, Lieutenant Commander. I'm beginning to think there's something clandestine afoot.'

He said pleasantly, 'Nothing as exciting as that, unfortunately, Mrs Lamprey. All very dull, routine stuff.'

Eight

They crossed in the same sardine boat – the
Espérance – but this time the lieutenant
commander had been tightening things up. There
was no barrel of Algerian wine – or, indeed, wine
or alcohol of any kind – and the replacement
for the lovesick Daniel was a dour Royal Navy
rating. Duval's old friend, Lieutenant Smythson,
had greeted him brightly.

'Here we go again, sir.'

'So we do, Lieutenant.' He had nodded
towards the new crew member. 'Does he speak
French?'

'Not a word.'

'Isn't that a little dangerous?'

'Not really. He's a Geordie – from Newcastle.
If he opens his mouth *nobody* will be able to
understand a word – including us. We can pass
him off as Icelandic, or something.'

They had left Dartmouth, as before, in the late
afternoon. Lieutenant Commander Powell had
come down to see them off, shaken their hands,
and wished them good luck. As the fishing boat

had pulled away and headed down the estuary the Englishman had stayed on the quayside – an erect and solitary figure. Duval had waved in farewell and the lieutenant commander had raised an arm in response.

The crossing was unpleasantly choppy but he was getting used to that. When was it not? At dawn they were off Ushant and the sea was worse. They decided not to attempt the Chenal-du-Four passage inside the island with fang-like rocks and lethal currents, and kept well to seaward. No enemy aircraft materialized to harass them but nonetheless they took a course that kept the *Espérance* within the four-mile limit, and they stopped the engine and hoisted the sails. By the evening the wind had dropped and the sea was calm enough to make the night landing relatively simple. They hove to at about three hundred metres off the beach. Under cover of darkness, Lieutenant Smythson and Duval set off in the rubber dinghy with the bicycle lashed on board. The lieutenant nosed the boat gently onto the shore and they unloaded the bike. The beach appeared to be completely deserted – no sentries, no lights from torches, no sound but the rhythmical surge and drag of the waves on shingle.

Smythson said breezily, as though it were a question of a little holiday, 'See you in a month, sir. We'll be back to pick you up. As arranged.'

At such times, Duval thought, the English half of the lieutenant came well to the fore:

the admirable Anglo-Saxon sang froid, the casual nonchalance. No French histrionics. No foreign melodrama. There was something to be said for it, after all. He waited for a moment on the beach while Smythson rowed away in the darkness back towards the *Espérance* and then set off, wheeling the bicycle as quietly as possible. He could make out the dark mass of the villa ahead, set back a hundred metres or so from the beach. It was an old place, built in the last century and agreeably weathered by sun and wind and time. Passing by on one of his trips in the *Gannet*, he had liked the look of it enough to seek permission to paint it ashore. It had taken some time to track down the owner in Rennes, but the man had agreed readily enough; in fact, he had ended up buying the painting.

The bike made no sound as he pushed it over the lawn. No sign of life that he could see, but then he had not expected any. The information was that the owner had been arrested by the Germans in Rennes for black market dealing and was languishing in prison. The villa would be locked up, of course, but he remembered some outhouses at the side – an old dairy and some stabling. A useful place to hide and rest and wait for dawn and the end of the curfew, before taking to the road. He had almost reached the terrace outside the windows when he heard someone cough and froze instantly. A mere few yards ahead, a cigarette glowed and then faded. Another cough – the lung-deep cough of a heavy smoker, and then the sound of boots walking a little way along the terrace and the scrape of metal on stone as they turned to come back again. He waited, gripping the handlebars and not daring to move a muscle. Again, the cigarette glowed and faded. Again, the man coughed harshly. Whoever he was, he was a fool to carry on smoking; he'd end up like Jean-Claude Vauclin.

There was the sound of a door opening and more footsteps coming onto the terrace. And then voices speaking in German; the rasp of a match being struck. By the flame's light he saw their faces and their Wehrmacht caps. More talk and some laughter. No wonder they were laughing, he thought, with most of Europe cowering at their feet. Clearly, the villa had been requisitioned – something that the lieutenant commander's Free French informants had not known or bargained for. Nor he, come to that.

As he stood motionless in the dark, wondering what to do next, the two Germans strolled away down the terrace, chatting together, their backs turned to him. He wheeled the bicycle silently across the grass to the side of the house and lifted it across the gravel driveway, past the outhouses and out through the entrance gates onto the road. It was too dark to ride and so he walked as fast as he could in the direction of Pont-Aven until he was well away from the villa. A German army lorry came along, but slowly enough to give him plenty of time to conceal both himself and the bike in the deep roadside ditch while it passed by. When two more lorries approached soon after, he decided to stay where he was and rest up for a while. Mercifully, the ditch was dry and the long grasses, still warm from the heat of the day, made a rather comfortable couch, as well as good camouflage.

He dozed for a while, waiting for dawn. It was an odd feeling to be skulking in a ditch like a common criminal; to know that he dared not trust his own countrymen enough to knock on some cottage door and ask for refuge. Odd and very sad. His country was divided against itself. There were those who believed Marshal Pétain to be the saviour of their honour and would blindly follow his lead, and those who despised him for kowtowing to the Germans. And there would be those who sat on the fence, wanting to stay out of trouble at all costs. Somewhere, though, among them, there would be the people he was looking for – ordinary little people ready and willing to risk their lives for France.

In England they would be sleeping – the sleep of the just, the sleep of the free. Not for them the terrors and shame and disgrace of enemy occupation. Not yet and, most probably, not ever. Saved by a moat, as Shakespeare had so poetically described the narrow strip of water that the English, typically, insisted on calling *their* Channel . . . *this fortress built by Nature for herself against infection and the hand of war* . . . Mrs Lamprey had entertained them one evening

with that very speech – an impromptu performance in the sitting room after one of Mr
Churchill's stirring wireless broadcasts. He smiled
at the memory. Even when delivered fortissimo
by Mrs Lamprey, it had to be said that the
English language had a wonderful richness and
majesty, though most Frenchmen would sooner
cut their throats than admit it. He risked a
cigarette. If he had had any good sense he would
be safely and comfortably in bed in England as
well. Which brought him, as a natural progres-
sion, to think of Madame Hillyard. He smiled to
himself again in the darkness.

He dozed some more until the sky grew noticeably paler in the east and he could begin to see
the countryside around him – trees, fields, hedges,
materializing gradually from the night, assuming
form and dimension. A cock started crowing at
a nearby farm. Another half an hour and he
emerged from the ditch with the bicycle – a
battered old machine with near-useless brakes
and perverse steering – and set off unsteadily
on the empty road towards Pont-Aven. All he
needed was a black beret on his head and strings
of onions hanging from the handlebars to pass
throughout Brittany without comment.

The town was beginning to stir, shutters
clacking back loudly against whitewashed walls.
Alphonse had already opened up. 'Monsieur
Duval! What a surprise to see you up and about
so early.'

'I'm turning over a new leaf. Reforming.'

'Ah . . . that is a pity. Life is already difficult enough for us all without more sacrifices. You have been away?'

'Just for a while.'

He sat down at his usual table, legs aching from the unaccustomed exercise – the bad one with the old war wound stiffening up. The coffee was worse than before, the bread greyer and coarser and the butter and jam needed a magnifying glass to be seen. There was, apparently, no ham, sausage or pâté to be had for love or money. Alphonse, naturally, was desolated, his arms waving apologies.

'The Boche are responsible . . . what can one do?'

'How have things been here lately?'

'Terrible. There have been arrests – everyone is afraid of what may happen next. We are all in their dirty hands.'

'Indeed, we are.'

'And for how long, I ask myself, monsieur? How many years shall we have to endure them?'

'Who knows?'

'Next it will be England's turn. I hear them speak of it when they come in here. They talk of what they will do when they are in London. Not as much fun as Paris, they say, but interesting, and it will be a pleasure to teach the English a lesson in humility.'

'Now, that *would* be interesting.'

Alphonse took the napkin from his arm to flick a fly off the table. 'A little cognac to follow, monsieur? To give courage for the day?'

'You still have some?'

'For old customers, like yourself. I can do nothing about the miserable food rations, but I have a good store of bottles hidden safely away where the Boche will never find them.'

'You're a resourceful man, Alphonse.'

'Practical, more likely, monsieur. How could one face life as it is now without such little comforts?'

'Very true.'

The cognac – large rather than little – did much to restore him, and he lit a cigarette to go with it. Some more customers came in, regulars like himself, and he nodded to them and exchanged a few words. They all seemed resigned to their fate: to have accepted the Occupation since they could neither fight it nor ignore it. They would see themselves, he thought, not as defeatists, but realists. He was finishing the cognac when some German soldiers entered, talking loudly among themselves, and sat down. The guttural harshness of their language grated on his ears. He watched Alphonse hurry over to attend to them and the way that he bowed and scraped. But who could blame him? His livelihood was, as he had put it, in their dirty hands. As Duval paid his bill and left, Alphonse winked at him.

The hallway was empty. No Mademoiselle Citron dismayed to see him. Perhaps this time he would find his apartment unoccupied? He padlocked the bicycle, left it propped against the wall and went upstairs, limping a little. As he opened the door, he half-expected to see another German sitting in his chair, but there was nobody there and no sign that anyone had taken up residence. He shaved, took a bath, put on clean clothes and went down the staircase again. Mademoiselle Citron awaited him at its foot.

'So, you are back again, monsieur.'

If she could find an excuse, he thought, she'd sell him to the Germans at the drop of a hat. 'I am.'

'For long?'

He said equably, 'I never know. There is no need to concern yourself.'

'That is your bicycle?'

'It is.'

'I should prefer it kept outside.'

'If I do that, mademoiselle, it will certainly be stolen. How much should I pay you extra in order to keep it indoors?'

He saw by her face that she was quickly calculating a nice sum. Then she caught his cynical expression and shrugged. 'That will not be necessary, monsieur. But please put it further down the hall out of the way.'

The road up to Jean-Claude Vauclin's cottage was too steep for him to ride the bike, but he took it because it provided a good excuse to go there. On the route, he passed old men sitting on benches, staring vacantly into space, a boy kicking stones aimlessly along a dusty gutter, a woman walking with her head bowed, her eyes fixed on the ground. He could sense the hopelessness and resignation.

As before, Vauclin was outside his front door, working in the sun, his breathing painfully laboured. 'Some business for me, monsieur?'

Duval wiped the sweat from his forehead after the long climb. 'Since you ask, these damn brakes are useless. Can you fix them before I break my neck?'

'I'll try.'

He waited while Vauclin checked the bike over, smoked a cigarette and enjoyed the view of the river again. One day, when the war was over, he would like to paint it from this particular spot.

'I can fix the brakes for you, also the bad steering, but it will take time.'

'I'll wait.'

'Then perhaps you would like to talk to Marthe? About that matter we discussed. She has been wondering when you would come back.'

'She still agrees?'

'Agrees? She *insists*, monsieur. She is only waiting for you to tell her exactly what you want her to do. You'll find her indoors.'

Vauclin's wife was in the kitchen, attending to a cooking pot on the stove. It reminded him of another woman in another kitchen in another country – except that this was a small, dark, grubby hole, smelling strongly of garlic, and the woman was also small and dark and far from beautiful. She had brown skin, weathered by the sun, and eyes like sloes, set deep in her face. He smiled at her – as he smiled at all women, except the likes of Mademoiselle Citron.

'Madame Vauclin, I am Louis Duval.'

'Yes, I know. Jean-Claude has spoken to me of you.'

'And you know why I am here? What I ask of you?'

'You want me to take the lace samples and to visit all Jean-Claude's old customers. You want me to find out who would be willing to spy on the Germans. Who would keep their eyes and ears open and report what they learn.'

He nodded. 'Exactly so. It's dangerous work, you understand? If they are Pétainists they might report you.'

The sloe eyes gleamed. 'I know. But I can very easily tell a Pétainist from one who is not.'

'How?'

'For one thing, they look like wet chickens.'

He laughed. Vauclin had known what he was about. 'But you must not use your own name. You are not Madame Vauclin. Make up another one, and come from another place. And the people that you recruit must then be known by other names that you also make up. You must never speak of them by their real names and they must never know the names of any of the others. Then nobody can give the rest away. You understand?'

'Perfectly.'

He produced the typewritten list that the lieutenant commander had given him. 'These are the things that the English particularly need to know. Read it, memorize it and then burn it.

Everything must be committed to memory: this list, all the names, everything. Nothing must ever be written down for the Germans to find.'

'I understand.' She glanced at the list. 'Some of these things are strange . . . why this one, for example?'

'You do not need to know reasons, madame. You must not know them. Nor must any of the other people you recruit. They supply the information that is requested, that's all.'

'Very well.'

'How soon can you leave?'

'Whenever you wish. The horse and cart are ready. So are the samples. So am I.'

He smiled. 'You're a brave woman, Madame Vauclin. I salute you.'

'I shall take no stupid risks, monsieur, and I shall do exactly as you say. You may depend upon it.'

'How long will you be gone?'

'Perhaps two weeks. Perhaps more.'

'I have to return to England within a month. It's been arranged.'

'Then I shall be back before then.'

He watched her give the pot another stir. The cooking smell was delicious – something simmering slowly and succulently. 'What are you preparing, madame?'

'Pig's cheek, some vegetables . . . the pig was reared in our orchard. Will you stay to share it with us?'

He would have liked to – to remind himself

what good French country cooking was like. 'Un-happily, I have to leave, madame. But, thank you.'

He went out into the sunlight again; it was blinding after the dimness of the kitchen. Vauclin had fixed the bike. He spun the wheel with a greasy hand. 'See, it runs straight now, monsieur. And the brakes both work. Left and right. Be careful, though, they may be a little fierce at first. Apply them gently.'

He coasted down the steep hillside, dabbing cautiously at the brakes. They worked almost too well. Next he called on Paul Leblond, the shoe-mender he had visited before. As with Madame Vauclin, his return had been eagerly awaited and, again, he showed the list. The shoemender knew others, he said, who would be well placed to help: a cousin who was a telephone engineer in Quimper, an old friend who was a clerk in a shipping office in Brest, a brother-in-law who worked in the port at Lorient. Duval repeated the same stipulation: all must use cover names, none must know the identity of the others, nothing must be written down.

From the shoemender, he stopped for some lunch at a bistro before he went on to Jacques Thomine. While Madame Thomine served the customers in the shop, the greengrocer frequently journeyed to outlying farms, buying produce direct.

'One must search far and wide for good stuff these days, monsieur, and I can observe the activities of the German troops as I pass. And, since you were here last, I have found four more men who want to help.'

Duval bicycled back to his apartment. There was still something left in Major Winter's bottle of cognac and he poured himself a stiff measure, lit a cigarette and got out his old and well-worn map of Brittany. He unfolded it and spread it out on the table. So far, so good. But now he must decide what to do next. Who else to approach? Where to go? First of all to Rennes, he thought. The place where he had been born and which happened to be close to the north coast where the Germans were so busy. He had relatives there – an aged aunt, sister of his late father, and a cousin or two – and there might be others still living there whom he had known in his youth. It was a good place to go. Then Paris. Other friends from other years – people he knew well and trusted. Gerard Klein who owned the gallery that sold his paintings, first and foremost. He would see Simone, of course, but he knew her too well to imagine that he could trust her.

He would take the train to Rennes and then go on to Paris. No problem there, or none that he could see – not with the papers so kindly provided by Major Winter. But perhaps before he did all that, he should take a quick little painting tour south – down the coast to Lorient where U-boat pens were rumoured to be being constructed – and see what he could see. For that he would have to go by bike. It would be very slow and he wondered, from the way it felt already, whether his bad leg was up to it.

He folded up the map, poured another cognac – to the last drop – and sat down in his chair. One month was not enough to do all that needed to be done. Two would not have been sufficient. Nor three. As Lieutenant Commander Powell had pointed out, it was going to take a long time to build up a safe and solid network of agents, even in this small corner of France. It could not easily be hurried.

There was a knock on the door. Mademoiselle Citron, he thought, irritated. She wants me to move the bike again. Or perhaps to tell me that she has raised the rent. He went to the door and opened it, prepared to argue. But it was not Mademoiselle Citron; it was a young German Wehrmacht officer – blond-haired, blue-eyed, very smart in his well-pressed uniform, with shiny buttons and belt and boots. A perfect specimen of Hitler's ideal youth, saluting him with a snapping click of his heels.

'You are Monsieur Duval?'

'Yes. What do you want?'

'I am Oberleutnant Peltz. Major Winter asked me to present this to you when you returned, sir.' A brown envelope was proffered. 'With his compliments.' The French was as stiffly correct as the speaker.

'Thank you.' Duval took it. 'Where is the major?'

'He has gone on leave, home to Germany. He entrusted the envelope to me.'

His painting of the river and the two thatched-roof cottages would be hanging on the wall of an apartment in Dresden. He regretted the loss of it, and even more the absence of its new owner.

'When will he return?'

'Within two weeks. While he is away, he has instructed me to offer you any assistance you may require. Those were his orders.'

He might as well make use of them. 'Do you know where I can get some cognac – Courvoisier, if possible? And some good wine? I've run out of both.'

'I will find some for you, sir.'

'Cigarettes, too.'

'Which brand do you prefer?'

'Gauloise.'

'It should not be a problem.'

He said curiously, 'As a matter of interest, how did you know I had come back?'

'I am billeted here, sir. I asked Mademoiselle Citron to advise me as soon as you had returned.' The oberleutnant smiled silkily. 'She tells us everything.'

He closed the door and opened the envelope. Inside was a ration book of gasoline *tickets* in his name.

Lieutenant Commander Powell telephoned one evening.

'I've managed to get an afternoon off the day

after tomorrow, Mrs Hillyard, and I've borrowed a dinghy. I wondered if you'd like to come out on that sailing trip we talked about?'

'I'd need to be back for when Esme finishes school.'

'I'll make certain that you are. We wouldn't go very far. Just up the river and back.'

'In that case . . . yes, I'd like to. Thank you.'

He arrived by car the next day, dressed in civilian clothes – well-worn trousers and an open-necked shirt that made him look younger and less daunting than his naval uniform. The car was a private car and something rather special, judging by the look of it.

'We're still lucky with the weather,' he said. 'And there's enough wind. I was afraid it might go and rain.'

'Will these shoes be all right?'

He looked down at the old tennis shoes with a hole in one toe that she had found at the back of a cupboard. 'Perfectly.'

The sailing dinghy was moored down at the Kingswear quayside. He jumped on board first and offered his hand to help her step across. She sat where he showed her, in the centre of the boat, and watched while he dealt expertly with ropes and the sail. They headed upstream, threading a neat path between the naval warships at anchor out on the river. She realized that he must know the river inside out from his days as a cadet at the College.

They tacked up to Dittisham and a little further

beyond, through the glorious and peaceful Devon countryside. On the way back, she took a turn at the tiller.

'Am I doing all right?' she asked him.

'Very well indeed. Absolutely first class.'

They were back at the quayside in plenty of time, as he had promised. Driving up the hill, he said, 'Thank you for coming out today. I hope you enjoyed it.'

'Very much. It was kind of you to spare the time, Lieutenant Commander.'

'My name's Alan, by the way.'

'Mine is Barbara.'

He smiled at her. 'Actually, I already knew that.'

He changed back into his uniform before putting in some more time at his desk. A Wren brought him the usual cup of stewed tea and a plain biscuit, but he left both untouched. Instead he smoked a cigarette. On the whole, he thought the trip had been a success. She had genuinely seemed to enjoy it and he had done his level best to ensure that the sailing was as smooth and pleasant as possible – not that she had seemed at all nervous. And when he had casually raised the possibility of another outing some time, she had made no objection. Of course, she had no idea how he felt about her.

His phone rang and he picked up the receiver.

'Harry here, Alan. They're bombing London.'

'*What!*'

'Came over a few minutes ago – a whole lot of Heinkels. More than two hundred of the damned things. They went for the docks, naturally. Huge fires – a complete bloody shambles.'

'Christ . . .'

'We weren't prepared, of course. Should have seen it coming. You know what this means, Alan. The buggers are going to invade. This is just the beginning.'

The Wren came in with some letters for him to sign; he waved her away. 'Where does this leave us, Harry? What next?'

'We press on regardless. It's even more vital to get as much information as we can. We want another agent landed on the Normandy coast as fast as you can arrange it. We've got a Free French chappie who knows it like the back of his hand. I'm sending him down first thing tomorrow.'

He pulled a pad of paper towards him. 'Give me the details, Harry, and I'll get onto it straight away.'

His old Citroën was still in the shed, covered in a rich layer of dust and birds' droppings. He wiped it all away as best he could, put back the rotor arm and tried starting her up. Like a tricky woman, she refused point-blank the first three or four goes and then, finally, succumbed fretfully. He coaxed her along until she began to run smoothly and then drove to the nearest garage for gasoline. The owner, who knew him, raised his eyebrows at the *tickets* but said nothing. Black market or collaboration with the Germans, it was probably all the same to the man, so long as his business kept going. Outside Pont-Aven, Duval took the winding coastal road for Lorient. The town was only thirty kilometres or so away and he drove unhurriedly, stopping to get out where the road passed closer to the sea to make some quick sketches while he kept a watch for any German naval vessels. It was while he was doing this that a German military lorry came by. He heard the brakes squeal, footsteps thud onto the tarmac, but went on with his sketching without turning his head. Presently he felt the muzzle of a gun prod his back and heard the guttural German-French.

'Turn yourself slowly, please.'

He did so. A Wehrmacht officer was holding the gun in question, pointed directly at his chest, and, behind him, a semicircle of helmeted soldiers, all armed with sub-machine guns, also aimed at him.

'What are you doing here?'

He showed his book. 'I am sketching, as you can see.'

'Sketching?'

'Drawing. With pencil,' he held it up. 'I am an artist.'

'This is a joke?'

'No. Not a joke. First I sketch a scene, and later perhaps I paint it. That is the way I work.'

'Your identity card, please.'

He groped in his jacket pocket and handed it over and then felt again in another pocket for his cigarettes and lighter. The movement caused the soldiers to lunge forward, brandishing their guns. He produced the packet of Gauloises, shook one out from the open end and lit it.

'Why are you not at work?'

He said mildly, 'I've told you, I am an artist – as it states on my card. I *am* at work. I also have papers that exempt me from any compulsory manual labour.' He groped once again in his pocket. 'You will see that I was wounded in the Great War and invalided out.'

The exemption papers were closely examined. Thank God, he thought, for the good major.

'Why are you not in Pont-Aven where you live?'

He lifted his hands. 'I am always looking for new scenes to paint and I thought I would drive along the coast as far as Lorient where I have some friends. It's a pleasant drive with interesting views.' He added casually, 'Major Winter who is stationed at Pont-Aven is also a good friend of mine. Perhaps you know him?'

The officer stared at him. 'It is strictly forbidden to use this road.'

'I was not aware of that. There is no notice.'

'How is it that you have a car? And gasoline for such things?'

'The car is mine. I have owned it for many years. As for the gasoline, Major Winter was kind enough to let me have a few coupons. In the interest of art, you understand. He is something of a connoisseur. Without wishing to boast, I am quite a well-known artist in France.' It was the truth, if not the whole truth. He waited, smoking the Gauloise, while they searched the car, wrenching open the small valise he had left on the seat, poking and prodding with the guns. His trusty old camera was brought forth as though it had been a ticking bomb.

'Why have you this?'

'I use it for my work. Sometimes, instead of making a sketch, I take a photograph – to remember the details of the scene.' Once again this was perfectly true, though, in this case, he had been planning and hoping to photograph more than just scenery.

'Cameras are forbidden.'

'I didn't know that.'

'I must keep it.' The papers were returned to him brusquely. 'You must go back.'

'My friends at Lorient are expecting me.'

'If you wish to travel to Lorient you must take the inland road. Not this one.'

'But the scenery is not so good for me.'

'I repeat. This road is forbidden. You must go back immediately.'

He shrugged and got into the car. They let him go, watching him as he turned and drove back along the way he had come. As he glanced in the rear-view mirror, they were still standing there and still watching, the officer cradling his treasured camera.

He took the inland road instead, arriving in Lorient in the early evening. His story had spoken freely of friends there. More accurately, there was a friend. It was many months since he had visited and he rather wondered what he would find at the apartment in the Rue Lazare Carnot, or if indeed anyone at all would be there. But Violette answered the door to him – a little thinner, but otherwise unchanged. Still with the long dark hair wound into a knot on the top of her head, the milk-white skin, the Mona Lisa smile.

'How good it is to see you, Louis. And in these dreadful days . . .'

He embraced her fondly. In the past, before she had married, she had sat for him many times and was still his favourite model. She had always understood entirely what was required – how to pose with a natural grace and fluidity and how to sustain it. Some of his best nudes had been of her. He was drawn into the living room, cheaply furnished but with style: flea-market shawls camouflaging the shortcomings of the couch and chairs, lengths of antique velvet draping the windows, a cloth of soft chenille the faded pink of an old rose, covering an ugly table.

'A glass of wine? It's not good, but it's not so bad either.'

'Thank you.'

She fetched the wine and curled up on the couch, legs tucked under, feet bare. Her feet were perfect, like the feet of angels. 'And you will stay to eat, I hope. Nothing special, but I have some eggs to make an omelette. I have been saving them.'

'For me?'

She laughed. 'If I had known you were coming, then yes. Otherwise for Daniel.'

'You have some news of your husband?'

She shook her head. 'No. Nothing. He's still held as a prisoner of war – that's all I know. But I hope every day that he will be released. After all, the war is over for France. Some are already being sent home. Surely the Germans will release them all soon.'

He thought it most unlikely but he said comfortingly, 'I'm sure he will be home before long.'

She accepted a cigarette and he lit it for her. She looked up at him with her secretive smile. 'What brings you to see me, Louis? You know that I can't work for you any more. Daniel will not allow it.'

'I realize that, my dear Violette, and it's a great loss for me. But, of course, I respect your husband's wishes.' Indeed, he did. The dour Daniel with the large fists and quick temper was not the sort of husband one risked offending.

'So, why are you here?'

'I wondered how you were in these dreadful days, as you so rightly call them. And I was a little curious.'

'Curious? About what?'

'About what the Boche are up to in Lorient. When I tried to drive along the coast road from Pont-Aven they stopped me. It's now strictly forbidden to go that way. I asked myself what they were so anxious to hide.'

'I know what that is.'

'Really?'

'Oh yes. Daniel's brother, Ernest, told me. He's a technician and working for the Germans. He was conscripted and had no choice in the matter. He was very upset about it.'

'And what did he say?'

'That they are building shelters for German U-boats at Keroman – you know, the fishing village about two kilometres south of here. He has to help them.'

'Is that so? I should be interested to hear more.'

'That's all he would tell me.'

'Even so, I am curious. One should learn as much as possible about the enemy.'

Violette tilted her head with its charming top-knot of hair. 'It's not like you, Louis, to care at all about such things.'

'But still I should like to talk to your brother-in-law. Does he live in Lorient?'

'Yes. I can give you the address, if you like. But I doubt if he'll want to tell you anything more. In Lorient, we all hate the Germans but we are afraid of them, too.'

She cooked the omelettes just how he liked them, with the centres runny and filled with chopped herbs. A little salad, a hunk of bread, some more of the wine and it was almost possible to forget about the war. Afterwards, naturally, they went to bed. The marriage to Daniel had put a stop to their working relationship, but not to the rest of it – whenever the opportunity occurred. He lay beside her while she slept, smoking a Gauloise and planning his next step.

It was not possible to see Violette's brother-in-law until the next evening, after his work. Duval spent the day wandering around the town. The Germans were everywhere, erecting barriers, demanding papers, giving orders. Twice he was stopped and his papers scrutinized. Even the knowledge that they were perfectly in order didn't make the experience any less unpleasant. To be challenged by a foreigner over his right to walk freely about his own country was the worst thing of all.

Ernest Boitard had not yet returned from work when he presented himself at the address given by Violette. Madame Boitard, regarding him fiercely from the doorway, proved as inquisitorial as any German.

'What is your business?'

'A private matter, madame.'

'Private? How so? You say that you have never met my husband. Certainly, he has never spoken of you.'

But for the scowl, she would have been quite good-looking. 'We have a mutual interest – his brother.'

'Daniel? He's a prisoner of war in Germany.'

'I am aware of that.' He tried smiling at her, but, for once, without any noticeable effect.

'Perhaps it would be possible for me to wait for your husband's return?'

In the end, she gave way and allowed him in. More than half an hour passed before Ernest Boitard came back – a slightly built man with no physical resemblance to his large and pugnacious brother, and seeming a good deal more intelligent. He was apologetic on behalf of his wife.

'She is suspicious of everybody. Always on the defensive.'

'Because you have to work for the Germans?'

He looked uneasy. 'You know about that?'

'Your brother's wife, Violette, told me.'

'She had no right to tell you. I was conscripted. Forced to. I am by no means the only one – some French have even volunteered. But, even so, it is a matter of deep shame for us. We have a son whom we try to shield from any kind of trouble. You can imagine . . .'

Duval nodded. 'I can understand how it must be. I'm afraid, then, that you won't wish to hear what I have come to propose.'

'What's that?'

'First, I must ask, does your loyalty lie with Marshal Pétain? Do you believe that following him is the only way to save France?'

'My God, no! He is *selling* France, not saving her. Look how things are going. The Germans do with us exactly as they please; they make every possible use of us, even against each other. The busybody official who rings the doorbell or stamps our papers wears a French uniform, not

German. Who can we trust? What honour is there left? What hope for the future? None.'

'You are resigned to the situation?'

'Resigned? No, but what can I do? What can anybody do?'

'*You* could do something.'

'Such as?'

'You're being obliged to work for the Germans – to help them with safe shelters for their U-boats at Keroman. Violette told me. Instead of having to go north hundreds of miles all the way round Scotland, the U-boats will now have an open door into the North Atlantic to go out and sink British supply ships. Then they will return to their base, rearm, refuel, resupply and go out again to sink more. And again. And again. Isn't that so?'

Boitard shook his head. 'I can't speak of this. I should never have said a word to Violette. I must have been mad.'

Duval went on relentlessly. 'If the English are defeated then there's no hope left for any of us. If, for example, the U-boats can sink all the ships that keep them supplied, then they're finished. They need to know about the submarine shelters at Keroman. How many, how they are constructed, everything of importance. Can you help?'

'You're suggesting that I spy on the Germans? That's crazy. I couldn't risk it – I have a wife and son.'

'I understand. But I wonder what sort of life your son will have, growing up under the Nazis?

Forced, like his father, to do whatever they command. A slave. Is that what you want for him?'

'Of course not. But why should I do anything to help the English? We all know they can't be trusted either. They deserted us. Destroyed our navy.'

'They are our only hope left.'

A shrug. 'They may survive for a while longer perhaps, but, in the end, they will be defeated, just as we were. The Americans won't save them again, like the last time.'

Duval drew on his cigarette. 'There is a saying – perhaps you know it. For evil to survive, it is only necessary for good men to do nothing.'

Boitard turned away and there was a long silence. He hunched his shoulders. 'I'm an electrician, monsieur. That's all.'

'So much the better. Your skills will be needed everywhere at Keroman. There will be every chance to observe and note. I am only asking that you go about your business, just as you are ordered to do, but that while you do so, you use your eyes. You notice certain things: the thickness of the shelters, for example. What exactly they are made of. The precise placing of the U-boat pens, the layout of the dry docks, fuel stores, workshops, the position of any anti-aircraft guns. You write nothing down on paper, of course. All you do is take an exact note in your head.'

'And then what?'

'You pass on the information. To me. Or to

someone appointed by me. Not here in this house. In another place. A park, a church, a café – wherever is safe. A casual encounter of two strangers happening to sit next to each other on a bench, or in a pew, or at the same table.'

'Who is it precisely that you are acting for, monsieur? I should like to know that. For the British themselves?'

'For France, my friend,' Duval said. 'For France.'

He returned to Pont-Aven the next day and left immediately by train for Rennes. It was more than eight years since he had visited the town. After both his parents had died there had been no particular reason to return. His birthplace, historic though it was, had no special claim on him. As soon as he had grown up, he had left it for Paris. Now, it drew him back for the good reason that it was not only the capital of Brittany, but a major road and rail link to St Malo and Brest, to Normandy and Paris and Nantes.

Rennes station was crowded with demobilized French army conscripts, waiting for trains to take them onward to their homes. They were celebrating with large quantities of red wine. He approached one who seemed less drunk than the rest, and learned that they had been demobbed either because they were older men or because they had large numbers of children. The man, a happy and foolish grin on his face, was very certain that the whole war would be over soon in any case. He neither knew, nor cared, what sort of a peace would follow.

Duval's widowed aunt lived in the Rue St Michel in the old northern quarter, where half-timbered buildings had survived the great fire of two centuries ago. She had survived, like the buildings, so far as he knew. He walked there from the railway station, observing the German soldiers on the streets in their *feldgrau* uniforms – their presence as strong, if not stronger, as in Lorient. I'm getting used to seeing them around, he thought wryly. If this goes on, soon I won't even notice they are there.

Aunt Pauline, he discovered, was very much alive. Always of an acerbic disposition, she had grown increasingly so with advanced age. He was shown into her shaded salon by her faithful servant, Jeanne, almost as ancient and withered as his aunt. It was exactly as he had always remembered: window shutters closed against the offending daylight, wooden floors gleaming with linseed polish, the steady, sonorous ticking of the huge ormolu clock on the mantelpiece. The furniture and furnishings frozen in time, like his aunt, at the turn of the century.

'So it's you, Louis. You've put on weight since I last saw you.'

He bent to kiss her cheek. She smelled, as she had always done, of the camphor that Jeanne employed so liberally to protect her old-fashioned garments from moths. He wondered if it had also somehow kept death at bay – mothballing not only her clothing but her carcass. She must, he

233

reckoned, be very close to ninety. Perhaps even beyond it.

'What are you after?'

'Nothing whatever, dear aunt, except the pleasure of seeing you.'

'You don't expect me to believe that, do you?'

'It's partly true.' They had always got on well. If it was not exactly love, it was mutual respect. She had admired his painting and encouraged him to study in Paris against his parents' wishes. But she had not cared for Simone.

'What is the other part? And no, you may *not* smoke, Louis. Not in here, you know that very well. I deplore the modern habit of men smoking wherever they please.'

He put away the cigarette and played the same card that he had played with Violette. 'I'm curious to see how the Germans are treating my home town. How the family is surviving.'

She said caustically, 'A very sudden interest and concern on your part, Louis. You haven't cared a jot about the family in years. The Germans are here again – what more can one say? It's quite like old times and one must get accustomed to it once more. As for your family, as you can see, I'm perfectly well. Your cousins are well, too, so far as I am aware. André visits occasionally and he gives me news of the rest. None of them live in Rennes now – he is the only one remaining here.'

'What does he do?'

'He's a teacher, at your old school. Nothing special, but at least it spared him conscription.

He has become quite the Bolshevik, you know. Full of talk about how Stalin will crush Hitler in the end. Fortunately, he's not actually a Party member or he would certainly have been arrested by now.'

'What is his view of Marshal Pétain?'

'Naturally, he has nothing good to say of him. And nor have I. Marshal Pétain has betrayed France. Betrayed us all. But why this unaccustomed interest, Louis? Why do you care what André thinks, or doesn't think? What are you about?'

'It's safer that you don't know.'

She snorted. 'The Germans aren't going to bother me, if that's what you mean. I never leave these rooms. Jeanne runs all the errands.'

'Safer for others, too.'

She drew herself up in her chair, black bombazine inflating indignantly. 'You are not, I hope, suggesting that I would betray a confidence, Louis? I have yet to do so in my extremely long life. And I shall not do so now.'

He knew that he could trust her and he had always respected her opinion. He gave her the bare bones of it; she listened without comment until he had finished.

'Ask your consin André, by all means. He knows many people here in Rennes – how they think and feel. But he won't care at all about the English. You will have to persuade him that anything that helps defeat Hitler will also help Stalin.'

'I had also thought of Dr Duchez.'

'Then don't any longer. He's retired long since. The new one is a Pétainist. Whenever he visits, we argue. He tells me that the war will end with a victorious invasion of England before the summer is out. That the Germans will instil the order and discipline needed here in France. Last time he came, I told Jeanne to show him the door.'

'So, who else do you think I should approach?'

The black bombazine reinflated itself. 'Myself, of course. I'm greatly offended that you didn't ask me in the first place.'

He looked at the old woman with affection and amusement. 'My dear aunt, you said yourself that you never leave these rooms.'

She regarded him coldly. 'Don't mock, Louis. *I* may not, but Jeanne does.'

Mrs Lamprey's supply of *L'Heure Bleue* had finally dried up. She had tried writing to Harrods, Fortnum & Mason, Liberty's and Debenham & Freebody – all to no avail.

'Monsieur Duval will know where I can find some. I shall ask him as soon as he comes back from London, Mrs Hillyard. He's a Frenchman. He'll know where to find it. It's in their blood. Perfume, wine, good food, *savoir-vivre*. All French people know instinctively about such things.'

'I'm sure they do.'

'What is for dinner tonight, Mrs Hillyard?'

'It's cold, I'm afraid.'

'*Cold?*'

'I'm going to be out this evening. I'll leave it all on the sideboard so you can help yourselves, if you don't mind.'

It was clear that Mrs Lamprey did mind but she accepted it with good grace. 'It must be something important, Mrs Hillyard. You never usually go out in the evenings.'

She couldn't, in fact, remember the last time. And Esme was just as put out as Mrs Lamprey.

'What about my supper?'

'I'll give it to you before I go. And you can read until later in bed, if you like. Miss Tindall has said she'll make sure you're all right. If there's anything the matter, then you can knock on her door.' Esme made a face. 'I shan't be late, anyway, and I'll come and see you as soon as I'm back.'

'Where are you going?'

'Out to dinner.'

'What for? You could have it here.'

'I've been invited.'

'Who by?'

'Lieutenant Commander Powell.'

'Who's he?'

'You remember . . . he's been here to see Monsieur Duval. The tall man in naval uniform.'

'Oh, *him*. But he's *old*.'

When he'd telephoned she could have declined politely, and he was not at all the sort of man to go on insisting. But the thought of going out had seemed appealing. Dressing up a little – putting on a frock that she hadn't worn for years. Not having, for once, to cook the food she ate. Escape for one evening from her role as cook, waitress, kitchen maid.

Alan Powell arrived early when she was still changing. By the time she went downstairs, Mrs Lamprey had him in her clutches in the sitting room and was entertaining him with her version of a scene from *Pygmalion*. He caught sight of her in the doorway and as Mrs Lamprey paused to draw breath, he interrupted quickly, 'I wish I'd seen the performance myself. It must have been excellent.'

'Oh it was, Lieutenant Commander. You have no idea. Of course Mrs Patrick Campbell made a perfect Eliza. One of our greatest actresses. Why, Mrs Hillyard, there you are at last! I have discovered your little secret, as you see. No wonder you are deserting us this evening.'

In the car, she apologized. 'I'm sorry you had to be a captive audience.'

'I deserved it for being early,' he said. 'It's one of my bad habits. I can never seem to arrive at the correct time.'

She had imagined that he would take her to somewhere over in Dartmouth but instead he drove up the hill out of Kingswear.

'I've been told there's a fairly good place to eat in Torquay. I hope you don't mind a bit of a drive.'

She sat in silence, wondering whether she had been wise to accept his invitation, and then told herself that she had nothing to fear from someone like him. Unlike the other men who had wanted to take her out after Noel's death, he would never become a pest. She was surprised that he wasn't married. Or perhaps he had been? A widower, then, in the same state as herself? Divorced, perhaps? An unhappy marriage that had ended in disaster?

The place that he had been recommended was the restaurant of a hotel. Its other patrons were elderly ladies who watched them with avid interest. The waiter was equally elderly but paid them nothing like the same attention. The soup was tinned and tepid, the beef almost too tough to chew. The apple pudding, when it finally arrived after a long delay, was so sour it set her teeth on edge.

'I'm terribly sorry,' he said. 'I had no idea it would be like this.'

'Perhaps the chef was called up.'

'Perhaps he was. Would you like some cheese? They can't go too far wrong with that.'

But they could and they had. A small dry piece that would have disgraced a mousetrap, and some stale biscuits. He apologized again and, in spite of her disappointment, she started to laugh. 'There's a war on,' she said. 'Didn't you know?'

He smiled ruefully. 'So there is. I'd almost forgotten. Shall we risk coffee in the lounge?'

The lounge had dusty palms in pots, well-worn sofas and armchairs, a small dais with a grand piano – its lid firmly closed – and a large dance floor. Once upon a time, before the war, the hotel must have been rather a fine place. Elegantly dressed guests, good food and wine, faultless service, a three-piece orchestra playing for *thé dansants* and after dinner in the evenings. It was a smaller version of the Grand Hotel in Eastbourne where she had worked.

The old ladies were reassembling around them, each settling into her accustomed chair, getting out their knitting, adjusting their deaf aids, waiting for the entertainment to resume. Normal conversation was awkward since she knew they would be hanging on every word. She found that she was talking about the weather – what a good summer it had been, how warm for the time of year, though of course the garden really needed the rain.

'My sister would agree with you,' he said. 'She's a keen gardener like yourself.'

She had a vision of immaculately tended lawns, glorious herbaceous borders, topiary, marble statues. 'Her garden must be beautiful.'

He shook his head. 'Actually, it's chaotic – just like her house. But she enjoys pottering about.'

She said, grasping at suitable topics for their audience, 'Did you always have an ambition to go into the Navy?'

'Well, it's been rather a family tradition. My father was in the Navy and my grandfather, too. I was brought up to follow them. I suppose I might have resented it, but the fact is I love the sea.'

She could sense the inclining of ears towards

them, like corn ears bending on their stalks with the wind; the knitting needles had clicked to a halt.

He went on, 'I loved Dartmouth. Thoroughly enjoyed it – cold baths and all.'

'So did Rear Admiral Foster. He says they were the happiest days of his life.'

'Mine, too, I think. Or, at least, so far.'

She wondered again what else lay in his past, but with the old biddies listening, it was impossible to broach the subject. What to talk about? Whatever he did now in the Navy was forbidden ground. *Careless Talk Costs Lives*. But what exactly *did* he do? Whatever it was, Monsieur Duval was involved in some way.

She said, 'Mrs Lamprey wants to know when Monsieur Duval will be back. She's run out of her favourite French perfume and she's convinced he'll know where to get some more.'

'I'm afraid Mrs Lamprey might have to resign herself to doing without. I doubt if he'll be able to help.'

Against all the odds, the coffee, when it finally arrived, was good. They talked of inconsequential, everyday things – the weather, the shortages, the delays, a new film. Stilted, barren conversation. The disappointment of their audience was palpable. And then he spoke of her brother – just a comment, in passing, about him serving in the Navy, but she was curious.

'How did you know about Freddie?'

He frowned. 'Didn't you mention him?'

'I don't think so. Only to Monsieur Duval. Perhaps he said something to you?'

'Actually, no.'

She was still puzzled. 'I can't remember talking about him.' She wanted to ask him where Freddie's ship might be now. When he might get some leave. What his chances of survival were. But, of course, even if he knew the answers to all those things, he couldn't tell her.

They left the old ladies to their knitting and he drove her back. With double summertime, there was still no need for headlights. As they came down the steep hill into Kingswear, he said, 'I'm so sorry about this evening. I'm afraid it wasn't very enjoyable.'

She could tell that he was quite upset about it. 'It was nice of you to take me out.'

'I don't suppose you'd care to risk repeating the experience sometime? I promise to find somewhere better.'

Instead of answering him, she said, 'Alan, how *did* you know about my brother?'

The Parc Monceau was dry and dusty – leaves curling, grass bleached to the colour of straw. Nobody in sight except for two German *feldwebels*, one of them photographing the other who was grinning happily into the camera, as though on holiday. That, Duval thought bitterly, was how easy it had been for them: a joyride through France, a stroll into her capital city, redecorating her according to their taste. Huge red, white and black swastika banners flying from every flagpole, signposts in Gothic-lettered German, German banners and posters nailed to buildings. Paris had been taken and branded all over with Nazi insignia like a meek cow.

He turned into the rue de Monceau, carrying his valise, and entered the apartment building. The inner courtyard was deserted but no sooner had he set foot on the stairway than Madame Bertrand was out of her lair.

'Oh, it's you, Monsieur Duval.'

'Indeed it is, Madame Bertrand. Good evening.'

'We understood that you had gone away.'

'I have returned, as you see. How is your husband? The liver?'

'No better. How could it be with all that has happened? It's enough to make anyone ill to have these German pigs in Paris.'

'As you say. Madame Duval is well, though, I hope?'

'Oh yes, she always looks after herself.' A knowing nod.

'Somebody is visiting?'

'Not at present, monsieur.'

He went on up the stairs. Simone opened the door to him and he could tell that she was quite shocked to see him – not precisely in the manner of Mademoiselle Citron, but somewhere in that region. His unexpected reappearance was perhaps not so welcome.

'Louis! But I thought you had gone to England.'

He said smoothly, 'I changed my mind, Simone. I decided to follow your advice. It seemed a pity to let the Boche drive me out of my own country.'

'I told you it would be a big mistake. Look what's happening in England now.'

'What do you mean?'

'Haven't you heard? The Germans have been bombing London. The English are expected to sue for peace any day.'

'I rather doubt that will happen.'

'They may not have much alternative.' She noticed the valise. 'You're staying in Paris?'

'For a few days. Don't worry, not here. Gerard will give me a bed. I have some business with him.'

She had collected herself now and smiled at him. She was as chic as ever: hair, clothes, make-up all in place. It had amused him to see other Parisian women also still so defiantly elegant and well groomed. 'Since you are here, Louis, you had better come in.'

'You don't have company?'

'Company? No.'

He stepped inside the apartment. 'No Germans hiding under the bed?'

She stopped smiling. 'Don't be absurd, Louis.'

'I was only joking. I've been walking about the streets and from the look of the Germans that I have seen in Paris, they seem to be having a very happy time.'

She shrugged. 'Naturally. They think Paris is wonderful. They are delighted to be sent here.

Some of them are behaving like tourists. They are taken round in busloads and stand and gawp at the sights and take each other's photos.'

'So I've noticed.'

'In general, they are very correct in their behaviour. Very polite. Not all, of course, but most.'

In the metro he had watched a Wehrmacht officer politely giving up his seat to a woman. 'No doubt they have been told to be. I have also noticed all their flags.'

'They put them everywhere – like children at a party – even a gigantic one on the top of the Eiffel Tower. They had to climb the stairs all the way up because the lifts had been sabotaged, then the wind tore the flag to pieces so they had to climb up again with a smaller one. It's quite amusing, really.'

'Madame Bertrand doesn't seem to find it at all funny.'

'Well, you know her . . . she's a sour old bitch. Something to drink, Louis?'

'Certainly. Whatever you have.'

'There's no Pernod left but I have some Dubonnet, or some wine.'

'Wine, if you can spare it.'

She still had a store of American cigarettes, dwindling fast. 'The Americans are not quite so generous these days. Things are very hard to get, even for them.'

He had noticed a box of chocolates on a side table – an expensive French kind. 'Do you have enough to eat?'

'I manage. Friends help where they can. As you know, the rations are pathetic. I'm sure you do better in Brittany.'

'Perhaps,' he said. 'But not much, I think. And the boutique? How is that going?'

'The Germans are good customers. I told you that they would be. They have money to burn and they come in to buy nice presents for their wives and lovers. If I could only find more stock, I could make a fortune.'

'My bank pays you regularly, as usual?'

'So far, yes. Of course, one has no idea how things will go on.'

'Write to me at Pont-Aven if there's a problem.'

'You're returning there when you've seen Gerard? No more ridiculous ideas of going off to England?'

'Rather too late for that now.'

'It was wise to stay, Louis. The English are just as much in the shit as we are.'

He walked from the rue de Monceau in the direction of Montmartre. There was almost no traffic except for the odd German staff car, the French pedalling their bicycles, and an old-fashioned horse-drawn cab bowling along the Boulevard Haussman. The curfew, according to Simone, did not begin until eleven o'clock and there was time to eat, if somewhere could be found. Several of his favourite haunts had closed down but *Le Petit Coin*, hidden away in a back street behind the Sacré Coeur, had once served respectable food and was, he discovered, still open for business. He was welcomed by the patron, as the old friend that he was. The place seemed exactly the same and, better still, there were no Germans.

'They don't come here,' Michel told him with satisfaction. 'They don't like going down dark alleys. But you'll find them in all the tourist places – sitting round with French tarts on their knees.'

He dined on an excellent mutton ragout, accompanied by some passable red wine and followed by a glass or two of cognac. Much heartened, he walked on to the street where Gerard Klein lived. He had telephoned ahead and so, this time, his arrival on the doorstep was no surprise. Gerard's wife and children were already in bed.

'We can talk in peace, Louis. It's too long since we met. And too much has happened. Where to start?' They sat down to cognac and cigarettes.

'How has it been here in Paris?'

'We live by German rules. Everything is *verboten*. We must not show hostility to the occupying soldiers, we must not hide weapons, we must not listen to foreign radio stations, open windows during the curfew, take photos out of doors, gather in crowds, parade in the streets, fly our flags . . . And, naturally, the shortages are getting worse and worse and the prices are rising daily. Your paintings have been selling like hot cakes, by the way. I have only three left.'

'Who's been buying them?'

'The Germans, of course. They're the ones with the money now. Everyone else has left – *le tout Paris* has decamped: the rich Americans, the Aga Khan, the Windsors . . . all the international darlings have fled.'

'I'd sooner you didn't sell my work to the Boche.'

'Come now, Louis, I have a living to make in these hard times, and so do you. They're not all blockheads and bull-necks. Some of them – those that come into the gallery, at least – are almost human. When can you let me have some more?'

'Not at the moment.' He was surprised at how much he minded. After all, art should have no frontiers, no restrictions. But he did mind. Gerard was lighting yet another cigarette, the ash from the previous one sprinkling his shirtfront. As always, his clothes were rumpled, his hair a wild white mane. The mane had been black when Duval had first met him. At twenty-two years old he had brought a painting to the gallery, fully expecting it to be pounced upon with cries of excited admiration and discovery; instead, Gerard had turned it down flat. But he had been kind. Made suggestions. Imparted words of encouragement. The talent was there, he had said, but was not yet ready to be inflicted on a buying public. Seven years had passed before Duval had returned to the gallery, and, this time, Gerard had agreed to hang his work. Their association had begun and continued, unbroken, ever since.

Gerard was puffing at his cigarette, watching

him. 'I've phoned you several times at the studio, Louis. You were never there. So I phoned Simone. She gave me a lunatic story about your having gone to England. Naturally, I didn't believe a word of it. I thought perhaps you'd gone off down to Provence so you could paint in peace without some German looking over your shoulder.'

He had trusted Aunt Pauline and Maurice Masseron, and he knew he could trust Gerard. To succeed there had to be trust at some point. He said, 'She was right. I went to England.'

'To England? What for? The weather is terrible and now they have German bombs dropping on them. Provence would be much better for you. Several artists have gone there. But you came back, after all? Was the weather so bad?'

'No, rather good, in fact.'

'Then why?'

He told him why.

Gerard heard him out in silence. At the end he said, 'You are an artist, Louis. Forget this crazy idea. Leave it to others who are better fitted to deal with such things. It's not for you. Besides, England is close to defeat. The Germans are bombing London to bits. It's a lost cause. A waste of time.'

'Not so, my dear friend, I can assure you. They are far from defeated. And I went there, not to run away and paint, but looking for something to do for France. I was given this chance.'

'I can see that you're very serious. And you

want my help? I'm a coward, Louis, not a hero. Besides which, I am a Jew. It's prudent to keep one's head well below the parapet just now – to be as invisible as possible. Also, there is the small matter of Celeste and our five children. I could do nothing that might endanger them.'

'Names, Gerard. That's all I ask of you. Names. Nothing else. You know many people in Paris – all the gossip. You know what sort they are, where their sympathies lie, whether they could be trusted. I need the names of those who would and could help. I know of a few myself, but they're not enough.'

There was another silence for a long moment and then a deep sigh. Gerard leaned forward to grasp the neck of the decanter. 'Let's have some more cognac. I'm going to need it.'

Nine

The man was wearing a naval petty officer's badge – crossed anchors below the crown on his upper left sleeve. He looked tired and pale and was in need of a shave. 'Mrs Hillyard?'

'Yes?' Not another of Lieutenant Reeves's homeless? 'Can I help you?'

'I'm Esme's father. I've come to see her. She's still here, isn't she?'

She stared at him; it seemed miraculous. 'Yes, she's still here, but she's at school at the moment.' Barbara opened the door further. 'Would you like to come inside?'

'Thank you.' He took off his cap and stepped into the hall. 'Very nice place. Esme's lucky.'

'Would you like a cup of tea?'

'That'd be very welcome. Excuse the way I look.' He rubbed at the stubble on his chin. 'I've been travelling all night.'

She sat him down at the kitchen table and put the kettle on to boil. 'She got your last letter. She'll be so pleased that you've come to see her.'

'How is she?'

Barbara hesitated. 'She's well, but she misses her home. I'm afraid she's not very happy here. She'd like her mother to come and fetch her but, so far, that hasn't happened.'

'And it won't,' he said flatly. 'Not ever. I got a letter from Connie. She's gone off with some man – a Canadian soldier. Wants a divorce. As soon as I got back on leave, I went to the house. She's cleared out and taken most of the stuff with her. No idea where she's gone, nor had the neighbours. I've been trying to find out. Get things sorted. She won't care about Esme or what happens to her. She never liked her. Always thought she was an ugly little thing and told her so.'

'Oh dear.'

'Yes, poor kid.' He shook his head. 'It's not been much fun for her. And, of course, I haven't been there – being in the Navy and with the war on.'

She made the tea and poured him a cup. 'Will you tell her about her mother?'

His brow furrowed. 'I don't know, to tell the truth. Not too sure what's for the best. What do you think?'

'I don't think I'd say anything – not just yet. There's always hope your wife might come back.'

'Not much chance of that, I'd say. I know Connie. Maybe I could tell Esme that her mum's gone off on holiday for a while. A white lie. Just for the moment. No sense in upsetting her right now.' He drank some of the tea and shook his head again. 'Poor kid.'

She sat down at the table with him and put a hand on his sleeve. 'She still has you.'

'Not much use to her at the moment, am I? As soon as the war's over – if I'm still in the land of the living – I'll come and fetch her. We'll manage together.' He looked at her hopefully. 'I've got a sister she could go to, but she lives in London too and with the Jerries bombing the place now Esme'd be a lot safer down here. Could you keep her for the time being?'

'Of course I will.'

He gave her a weary smile. 'Thanks very much, Mrs Hillyard. She's not an easy child, I know, but it's not her fault.'

What must it have been like for him to come back from the war at sea – and whatever sort of hell that had been – to an empty house? 'Would you like to stay here tonight? We could make up the sofa in the sitting room for you.' Blow Mrs Lamprey, she thought. She'll have to sit somewhere else.

'No, thanks all the same. As soon as I've seen Esme, I ought to start back. It's only a short leave and I've got to get all the way back up to Liverpool.'

'When you've finished your tea, I'll take you down to the school, if you like. I'm sure they'll let Esme out, so you can spend some time with her.'

She walked down the hill with him. The children were out in the playground, running around and shouting; Esme, as usual, was by herself in a corner, back turned, head bent, scuffing the toe of her sandal this way and that against the asphalt. Barbara waited and watched as the petty officer went nearer and called through the wire fence. She saw the teacher in charge go over to him and Esme turn her head. The gate was opened and he went inside. The other children had stopped playing and were watching too, waiting curiously to see what happened next. Esme stood where she was, rooted to the spot, her face blank. Then her father held out his arms wide and the child ran full tilt across the playground and into them.

'How is that nice Lieutenant Commander Powell, Mrs Hillyard?'

'He's very well, so far as I know, Mrs Lamprey.'

'I haven't seen him here lately.'

'No, that's right.'

'Of course he must be very busy. I expect he's engaged on important things. Hush-hush, do you think? I somehow get that impression.'

'I've really no idea.'

'Is there any news from Monsieur Duval?'

'Not yet, Mrs Lamprey.'

'Oh, well. It can't be long now before he's back.'

Barbara took refuge in the kitchen. Alan Powell had phoned once since the Torquay evening to say that he still had no news about Monsieur Duval's return. She had been polite but distant. What he'd told her in the car still rankled – unreasonably, perhaps, but she couldn't help it.

'We have a file on you,' he'd said. 'That's how I knew.'

'A file? On *me*? What sort of file?'

'Just basic information.'

'What information?'

'Where you were born, went to school, and so on.'

'And about my family? My parents and my brother?'

'Yes. About them, too.'

She'd said coldly, 'What else?'

'Very little, really. Your marriage. When your husband died. When you came here. That's all.'

'That's *all*! It seems quite a lot to me. What right have they got to do that?'

He'd stopped the car then, drawn into the side and turned to face her. 'I'm sorry, Barbara. You're angry and upset. Please don't be.'

'Well, I don't see why the Navy need to know about me. I'm nothing whatever to do with them.'

'You are, in a way. They've been billeting people on you and they like to be quite sure of everyone they deal with, especially now.'

'You mean I might have been some sort of spy? A traitor? A fifth columnist?'

'Of course not.'

'Then why the investigation?'

'It's just routine security.'

She had hated the thought that they'd been ferreting around in her private life. Snooping on her behind her back. Putting it all into a file for anybody to take out and go through. Including him. 'So, you read this file on me, and decided that it was safe to take me out to dinner?'

'It wasn't like that at all,' he'd told her quietly. 'If you want the truth, I read your file because I wanted to know more about you. I didn't know a thing then – not even your Christian name.'

'You could have asked me what it was. Wouldn't that have been much simpler?'

'I'm sorry, Barbara. I can understand how you feel.'

'Can you?' She'd turned her head away, still furious. 'I'm not sure that you can.'

The Free French agent had returned from Normandy. Powell saw him as soon as he had landed in order to write up an immediate report for London. The man had had a tough time and was almost too exhausted to speak, but he pressed him hard for detailed answers. The Germans, it transpired, had made it very difficult to move around in that area without risking arrest. There were troops everywhere, road-blocks, searches, constant demands for papers . . . it was almost impossible to pass unnoticed anywhere near the canals or harbours. However, he had done his best to cover most of the region from Arromanches to Le Havre, passing himself off as a peasant. He had seen convoys of converted apple barges assembled at ports and had managed to take some photographs, in spite of the risk. There was little doubt that an invasion fleet of sorts was being assembled. He had then journeyed west as far as St Malo where there had been more barges but not a large quantity – perhaps fifty or so – and some old river steamers.

The agent paused for a moment, collecting his thoughts. 'I formed the impression that the Germans are not at all well prepared to invade. Yes, they are still boasting about it and yes, there are the troops and craft to take them, but it seems that they are waiting. Not ready and on the brink of an all-out attack. Though surely it must come soon.'

At least by the end of the month, Powell thought. Before the weather deteriorates. Now, or never.

He settled down to write up a report and had almost finished when Lieutenant Smythson arrived.

'We're ready to leave in the *Espérance* tomorrow, sir. All fixed to be there at the appointed hour.'

Duval's month was nearly up. It would be interesting to see how much he had managed to achieve in the short time allotted – assuming that he'd survived.

When he had finished the report and despatched it to London, he sat down at his desk again. His hand strayed towards the phone and then retreated. There seemed little point in ringing her. What more could he say? The damage had been done and he had lost whatever slim chance he might have had.

Duval returned by train from Paris to Pont-Aven. Mademoiselle Citron, who was becoming almost as vigilant as Madame Bertrand, called up the stairs after his back.

'Oberleutnant Peltz wanted to leave some things for you, monsieur. I opened the door so that he could put them safely inside your apartment.'

'Thank you, mademoiselle.'

'You will be staying here for a while?'

'Perhaps, perhaps not.'

He continued to the top floor and unlocked his door. On the table there was a case of wine, two bottles of Courvoisier and three hundred Gauloises. When he had allowed himself a brief moment of pleasure admiring the haul, he examined the black cotton threads that he had left carefully and invisibly in place round the room – on the drawers, the door to the armoire, a suitcase he kept under the bed, boxes of paints, tins holding this and that, the canvases stacked against the wall. As he had expected, they had all been disturbed. Someone had made a very thorough search of the room but whether it was nosy-parker Mademoiselle Citron or Oberleutnant Peltz checking up on him, or some other person altogether, he had no way of knowing. The only thing of which he could be certain was that there had been nothing suspicious for them to find.

An hour later, he went out again, taking the

bike, and called on the shoemender, Paul Leblond, who had much of interest to tell. The telephone-engineer cousin from Quimper had been conscripted by the Germans and sent to work at a large villa on the shores of Kernével, close to Lorient. From there, as he set up new telephone lines, he had been able to observe the construction of vast concrete shelters in progress directly across the bay on the foreshore at Keroman. It was rumoured that these were for U-boats and that the villa itself had been requisitioned as headquarters for the German Admiral Doenitz. The brother-in-law who worked in the port at Lorient had confirmed that this was so. The old friend who was a clerk in a shipping office at Brest reported that there was no sign of any invasion fleet assembling in the port.

He went on to Jacques Thomine, the greengrocer with his horse and cart, who had gathered up useful snippets of information on his travels about the movements of German troops.

He avoided calling again on Maurice Masseron. The less he and the mayor were seen in company together, the better and safer. He toiled up the hill, instead, to Jean-Claude's cottage, where he found that Marthe had returned the day before. She was in the dark little kitchen, her strong hands plunged into an earthenware bowl of dough, kneading away with her knuckles, and he saw at once by the way her sloe eyes gleamed at him that it had gone well. Fifteen people had been recruited, she told him, spread across the peninsula, north to south and as far east as Rostrenen. She had chosen them carefully; been very sure of them before she went further. She'd given them all cover names, as instructed, and done the same for herself. What kind of people? All kinds. Men, women, young and old, rich and poor. Locals who had lived all their lives in their region, knew everyone, were known by everyone. They understood what to look for and they understood how to keep their mouths shut. And they had just one thing in common: they all hated the Boche and wanted France rid of them. That was why they would help. What more needed to be said? She pummelled away at the dough as though it were the face of the Führer himself.

Later, he went out to where Jean-Claude was sitting at work. 'You have a marvel for a wife,' he told him. 'She's an exceptional woman.'

'I know that, monsieur.'

'May I ask another favour of you?'

'Certainly.'

'I leave tonight for England. If I keep my bicycle at my apartment house it may be stolen. Also, it advertises my presence or my absence – if it's elsewhere it will do neither. Will you keep it for me until I return?'

'With pleasure, monsieur. I will even do more work on it – some is needed, I think.'

He walked back to the apartment. It would also be necessary to walk all the way to the rendezvous by the villa, but there was no alternative. What was also needed, he thought wearily, was to be twenty years younger. He packed a canvas holdall with six of the bottles of wine, one of the cognac and two hundred of the cigarettes so thoughtfully provided by Oberleutnant Peltz. The balance could stay behind for his next visit. It would be heavy to carry but it would be worth it. For good measure, he wrapped the goods in the French newspapers that he had bought, which the lieutenant commander would doubtless find of interest.

An hour before curfew, he set off. No fond farewells to Mademoiselle Citron and, as luck had it, she missed his silent departure. The holdall was heavier than he had anticipated and grew steadily more so. From time to time a German army vehicle swept by at high speed. One of them – a small truck – stopped, and the driver, an older man on his own, made friendly signs at him offering a lift. With considerable regret, he shook his head. He could hardly request to be set down at the villa, and the clinking contents of the holdall might require some explanation. As he plodded on, he amused himself by inventing the conversation that might have ensued.

'If you would be so good as to drop me close by the villa, but not too close, so that I can rendezvous unobserved with the fishing boat that is coming from England tonight to collect me from the beach.'

'With pleasure, monsieur. That holdall looks very heavy.'

'Yes, indeed. It's full of excellent wine, cognac and cigarettes which I am taking with me to England where they also have severe shortages.'

'How wise of you. Will you be returning soon?'

'I hope so. I have unfinished business in France.'

'Then I trust I may be passing by to give you another lift.'

'That would, indeed, be fortunate.'

'Will this be a convenient place to drop you? The villa is fifty metres or so further on. If you take care, you will be able to reach the beach without being seen.'

'Yes, this will suit me very well. Thank you.'

'You're very welcome. Bon voyage, monsieur.'

It was growing dark as he neared the villa, but not yet dark enough, nor close enough to the appointed time. He took refuge in a dilapidated farm building that smelled strongly of pigs but was, fortunately, empty of them. He leaned against the wall since there was nowhere to sit and lit a cigarette to counter the stench. If the farmer wondered why his pigs had been smoking Gauloises, then so be it. From time to time, he used his lighter to consult his watch, smoked another cigarette and then another. At thirty minutes before the time, he left the building and made his way towards the villa, slipping in through the open gates and round the perimeter of the grounds in the direction of the beach. There was no guard on duty, nobody wandering out onto the terrace for a smoke, nobody to be seen or heard at all, though at some of the windows he could see thin slivers of light behind the closed shutters. The shingle crunched noisily beneath his feet and he took off his shoes, wincing at the sharpness of the stones. Finding a large rock, he sat beside it and waited, listening to the gentle shushing of the waves.

The sea was calm, the half-moon casting a rippling silver pathway on the water, and he half-expected the boat to come sailing magically down it towards him. In the event, it came from nowhere, stealing out of the darkness. He heard it before he saw it – the muted sound of the engine throttled back as it approached the shore, and then, later, the soft splash of oars. He stood up and walked down to the water's edge. There was a grating sound as the dinghy nosed onto the beach, the crunch of other feet, the voice of Lieutenant Smythson: 'Are you there, sir?'

He moved forward. 'Yes, I'm here.'

'Can you hop in all right?'

He clambered, rather than hopped, into the bow of the dinghy – clumsily because he was tired and unable to see properly in the dark, and because his bad leg was very stiff. The lieutenant said something else in English but he failed to understand. 'I'm sorry, what did you say?'

'I said, any more for the *Skylark*?'

'What?'

'It's just a joke, sir. Seaside trips round the bay, that sort of thing.'

He shook his head, bemused. Here he was

being snatched from enemy-occupied France in the middle of the night and Smythson was making English jokes. 'You were right on time.'

'Of course, sir. We aim to do our best. How did everything go?'

'Very well.' The holdall clinked and clanked as he settled it securely on the boards.

'That sounds promising, sir.'

He smiled in the darkness. 'Yes, certainly it does.'

The lieutenant pushed off from the beach and pulled away from the shore. Presently, Duval could make out the familiar shape of the *Espérance*, hove-to at a safe distance, engine ticking over, ready to go. Within minutes he was on board, a few more and he was lying on a bunk below, a few more still and he was fast asleep.

When he woke up it was daylight and they were in rough seas off the Pointe du Raz. The lieutenant kept a discreet course well clear of Brest but, even so, Duval had the unpleasant feeling that at any moment a U-boat might surface and challenge them. The feeling persisted until they had left the coast of France far behind. Soon after dawn on the following day, as they were nearing England, he went up on deck.

It was only by chance that he saw it – just a speck on the surface, a mustard-yellow blob on the grey sea, rising and falling with the swell. At first he thought it was some kind of seabird, or even a piece of flotsam, and then as he strained his eyes for a better view, he realized that it was neither of those things. The *Espérance* altered course towards the blob which turned into a pilot, kept afloat by his Mae West, leather-helmeted head lolling on his chest. He looked already dead, but as they drew alongside the head lifted and a hand was raised to give a feeble wave. The dinghy was lowered and they manoeuvred him first into it and then, with some difficulty, on board the fishing boat. He lay in a sodden heap at their feet on the deck. His face and hands had been badly burned. The flesh was blistered and raw on his face, peeling in shreds from his fingers, and his eyes were swollen into slits. Teeth chattering violently, he tried to smile. German or English?

'Thanks awfully.' The words were faint but unmistakable.

It might have been '*Vielen Dank*,' Duval thought. Lieutenant Smythson fetched a clasp knife and he helped him to cut the helmet carefully away from the head and then the Mae West from the body, revealing the RAF wings beneath. The pilot whimpered and moaned as they worked. They peeled off the rest as gently as possible and wrapped him in blankets. He had fair hair – the unruly hair of a mere boy, with a childish crest. Perhaps nineteen years old? Duval took out his bottle of cognac and poured some into a mug. He raised the pilot's head and held it to his mouth for him to drink.

'Thanks.'

'Cigarette?'

He lit one and put it between his lips. Smythson had got the boat under way again and he stayed beside the pilot. The smell of burned flesh was sickening. He sought for words of comfort and cheer and while he did so, the boy spoke, croaking through the charred lips, as though he felt a need for polite English conversation.

'Been a lovely summer, hasn't it?'

Ten

'Fifi's getting really fat.'

'Do you think so, Esme? I hope we're not overfeeding her.'

'I'll give her a bit less, shall I?'

Barbara watched the child putting the fish scraps into Fifi's dish and setting it down for the cat. This was a new Esme. She still had the sulks and sullens but, in between, the improvement was remarkable. There were smiles now as well as the frowns, especially when talking about her father.

'Dad said Mum's gone away on a holiday and not to worry if I don't hear from her. She hasn't been very well, he said, and she needed a rest. Besides, she ought to be away from the bombs. Dad promised he'll come and see me again on his next leave. Dad said he'd take me home as soon as the war's over. Dad said he's going to write to me whenever he can. Dad said I must write to him and tell him everything I'm doing. Dad said the war'll be over soon.' And so on.

Fifi was gulping down the fish, crouched low

in the way that cats eat. She *did* look rather fat. The sides of her stomach were sticking out quite noticeably.

The phone rang and Barbara went to answer it. Alan Powell said, 'Monsieur Duval should be back from London sometime later today. I thought I should let you know.'

'Thank you.' She hesitated. 'I'm afraid I made rather a ridiculous fuss over the file.'

'No, you didn't. You were perfectly entitled to be upset.'

'I talked to Rear Admiral Foster about it. He told me the Navy even has files on the ships' cats.'

'I don't know about that.' There was a smile in his voice.

'Yes. He says it's all to do with being ship-shape.'

'Well, he's probably quite right.'

'Anyway, thank you for letting me know about Monsieur Duval.'

She went upstairs to check on the room. It was clean and aired, ready for his return. Clean sheets, clean towels – everything as welcoming as she could make it.

He came back in the early evening when she was in the kitchen cooking. She heard a car stop outside, the front door open, footsteps across the hall, a soft knock on the kitchen door . . . and turned to see him standing in the doorway, carrying some kind of old canvas bag.

'Good evening, madame.'

She managed to speak normally and formally, as a landlady should. 'Good evening, Monsieur Duval. How nice to see you again.'

Mrs Lamprey said much the same thing to him at dinner, her body inclined coquettishly in his direction. '*Bonsoir, monsieur. Quel plaisir de vous revoir!*'

'*Merci, madame.*'

She waved her chiffon scarf. '*C'était très triste sans vous.*'

He bowed in acknowledgement of her great sadness without him. As Barbara set a dish of vegetables on his table, he exchanged glances with her.

'*J'espère que les bombes allemandes à Londres ne vous ont pas derangé.*'

'No. Fortunately the German bombs did not disturb me, madame.'

Before long Mrs Lamprey was leaning the Frenchman's way again.

'Monsieur Duval . . .'

'*Oui, madame?*'

'*Connaissez-vous où je peux trouver le parfum français qui s'appelle L'Heure Bleue? Ma bouteille est vide.*'

Barbara saw that he was having some trouble keeping a straight face. Before he could answer, though, Miss Tindall said unexpectedly, 'It should be *savez-vous*, Mrs Lamprey. The verb *connaître* means to be acquainted with, not to know *about* something.' She had gone pink in the face. 'Isn't that so, Monsieur Duval? You have two different verbs in French.'

'Indeed, that is so, Mademoiselle Tindall. It can be very confusing.'

Mrs Lamprey was looking much put out. 'I'm sure Monsieur Duval understood perfectly well what I meant, Miss Tindall.'

'Yes, indeed, madame. And I am sorry to hear that your bottle is empty. But I regret that I do not know where you could buy that particular perfume. Perhaps in London . . .'

'Harrods have run out. So has Liberty's. It's the war, of course. What a pity I didn't ask you to have a search for me while you were there. I'm sure you could have found some.'

'I should certainly have done my best.'

'Perhaps the next time? *La prochaine fois?*'

'Perhaps, madame.'

After dinner, he knocked again on the kitchen door, carrying his linen jacket over his arm. 'Excuse me, madame, but would it be possible to borrow the thing for clothes . . .' he made an ironing movement with his arm. 'This coat is very bad – even for me.'

'I'll do it for you, if you like. It's easier really.'

'You are sure?'

'Yes, of course.' She took the jacket, which looked as though he'd slept in it. 'I'll bring it up when I've finished.'

He thanked her and went away. When she had finished the clearing up she took out the ironing board and switched on the iron, using a piece of damp cloth to press out the creases in the linen. Something crackled in one of the pockets and she felt inside to remove it. It was nothing important – just a bill from a restaurant. A French restaurant called *Le Petit Coin* which he must have gone to in London. Except that the address printed below the name wasn't in London. It was in Paris. In Montmartre. And the bill was dated in September while he had been away. She studied it for a moment. *Ragoût de mouton* . . . *vin ordinaire* . . . *cognac* . . . She found herself thinking, absurdly, how much better good old mutton stew sounded in French and, very likely, tasted. While he was supposed to have been in London, liaising with the Free French, Monsieur Duval had been in Paris. But how could he have been? France was in German hands. You couldn't get in, or out. Not by normal means. How, then, had he gone there? By boat, landing secretly, at night, on some lonely beach? And what for? Did Alan Powell know that he had been there, or had he, too, believed him to be in London? Was Louis Duval working, not for the Free French at all, but for the Germans? France, after all, was no longer an ally; she had become, in real and practical terms, an enemy.

She finished the pressing, replaced the bill in the pocket and took the jacket up to Monsieur Duval's room. When she knocked on the door he opened it at once.

'Thank you so much, madame.'

She could see that he had been lying on the bed

– there was a deep dent on the pillow where his head had rested. Of course he was tired. He had been in France. Of course his clothes were so badly creased – from some long and furtive boat journey.

'It was no trouble.' She couldn't look at him. 'Goodnight.'

As she went away down the corridor, she heard him call after her, but she pretended that she hadn't heard.

'Lieutenant Commander Powell? Lieutenant Reeves here. I'm calling with a message from Mrs Hillyard for you.'

'Yes?' Was he imagining it, or was there an undercurrent of amusement coming down the wire?

'She rang me to ask for your number, but naturally I couldn't give it to her, so I said I'd pass on a message.'

No, he hadn't imagined it. He said curtly, 'Which was?'

'Would you ring her as soon as possible. Something rather urgent, she said.'

The evacuee child answered the phone at Bellevue, sounding surprisingly polite, and he waited while she went away to fetch Barbara. Then he heard her heels tapping on the tiled floor of the hall and her voice.

He said, 'This is Alan here, Barbara. I got your message from Lieutenant Reeves.'

'I'm sorry to trouble you, Alan, but I wondered

if we might meet sometime soon. There's something I'd like to discuss with you.'

She sounded strained. Upset, but in a different way from before. 'Yes, of course.' He cursed the busy day ahead of him. 'I'm afraid I can't get away until this evening. Could we make it sometime after seven?'

'Eight would be better, if that's all right with you. I'll have been able to serve dinner by then, and Esme will be safely in bed.'

'I'll come and pick you up in the car.'

'Don't ring at the door. I'll wait for you outside – just down the road.'

He put the receiver down, wondering what on earth had happened.

A good deal of the day was taken up with going over Duval's report of his month in France. Duval came to the HQ, looking in considerably better shape than when he had arrived back at dawn on the previous day. They went through it all again – the names and cover names, the places and the dates. The information given, the implications, the likely accuracy. During his time in France, Duval had succeeded in establishing a small but significant network of French men and women across Brittany. A base to build on. And much of the information, when duly sifted, would be extremely useful. The Frenchman had also set up some contacts in Paris that promised well. The lack of any sign of an imminent invasion of England was encouraging, to say the least, though the intense U-boat activity was anything but so.

Powell perceived the threat of the U-boats as far more frightening and deadly than any of Hitler's wild invasion threats. With their new and easy access to the North Atlantic, they would make it a killing ground. British merchant shipping would be forced to avoid the English south coast and take much longer routes to north-western ports.

'If I am to continue this work, then I should return soon,' Duval said. 'When can it be arranged?'

'I'll let you know.' Whether Duval went back, or not, was up to London. The various Intelligence groups worked in mysterious ways – some jealously independent, some co-operating willingly with each other, while General de Gaulle's *Deuxième Bureau* lay somewhere uneasily in the middle. And a new agency had recently come into being with an entirely different brief, from Churchill himself – not the secret collection of secret intelligence, but sabotage and acts of terrorism designed to weaken the enemy from within. All very well, in Powell's view, but the repercussions and reprisals could be devastating on other British agents being sent to operate in France, let alone the ordinary French civilians.

Duval continued. 'If we had radio transmitters, then there would be no need for me to go to and fro like this.'

'Unfortunately, there are none available. There are always the carrier pigeons, of course.'

'My God, those pigeons! They're a liability. A

positive danger, in my opinion. Difficult to conceal, hard to handle, and the Germans can shoot them out of the skies and find the messages they carry.'

'They're all we've got at the moment.'

Duval shrugged. 'I'd sooner do without.' He lit another of his cigarettes. 'Tell me, do you have any news of that young RAF pilot we picked up?'

'He's been taken to hospital in Plymouth, that's all I know. They'll probably move him on to a special unit.'

'He was very badly burned.'

'Yes, I'm afraid so.' He had overseen the ambulance transport of the pilot and been shocked by his condition. 'He was very lucky you happened to pass near enough and saw him. A chance in a million.'

Duval said thoughtfully, 'You know, Lieutenant Commander, until we picked up that boy I had been thinking only of my own country – only of France. I admit this frankly to you. But now, I find that I am also thinking of what this country – your country – is doing. The sacrifices it is making and will have to continue to make. The young pilot made me aware of that.'

At ten minutes to eight, Powell drove up the hill towards Bellevue and parked the car a short way down the road, as she had asked. He was early, as usual, and it was five past eight before she appeared, walking quickly towards him. He got out of the car.

'Have you been waiting?' she asked. 'I'm sorry. Mrs Lamprey kept me talking.'

He opened the passenger door of the car for her and then got in himself, thumbing the ignition. 'Would you like to go for a drink? One of the pubs?'

She shook her head. 'No, could you just drive – somewhere where we can talk.'

He drove out of Kingswear, towards Brixham and Berry Head. There was a narrow lane, he knew, that led up onto the cliff tops overlooking the Channel where the old fortifications still stood from an earlier invasion threat – from Napoleon. He parked and turned off the engine. 'Now,' he said. 'Tell me what's happened.'

'It's about Monsieur Duval.' She stared ahead through the windscreen. 'I know that when he was supposed to be in London, he was actually in Paris.'

'I see. Did he tell you that?'

'No, I found out.'

'How?'

'I pressed a jacket for him – the one that he'd been wearing when he was away. There was a bill in the pocket – from a restaurant in Paris, with the date on.'

Very careless of Duval. But then he'd never been properly trained. He was an amateur in the unforgiving and lethal world of espionage. Powell said, 'You're sure about that?'

'Quite sure. I looked at it closely. All the details.'

'What did you do then?'

'I put it back in the same pocket, before I returned the jacket.'

'Did you say anything to him?'

'No.'

'Or to anybody else? Mrs Lamprey, for example?'

'*Her?* Heavens, no.' Her face turned towards him. 'What I want to know, Alan, is did *you* know he was there? Or did you believe him to be in London, working for the Free French – like he told *me?*'

He debated what to say to her. 'I'm afraid I can't answer that, Barbara. I can't tell you anything. All I can say is that there's nothing for you to worry about.'

'Nothing to worry about! He's been over in occupied France. What was he doing there? Spying? For *whom?*'

'There's nothing for you to worry about,' he repeated.

'Yes, there is. I can't trust him now. He's living in my house, and I don't know what sort of a man he is or who he's working for. He might be spying for the Germans, for all I know – a double agent, or whatever they call them. A traitor. I have to *know*, Alan. Don't you see?'

He saw very well. She's in love with him, he thought bitterly. That's why she's so upset, and why she wants to know. It matters very much to her. He sat in silence for a moment. It would be easy to make her mistrust Duval; to think ill of him. So easy.

'Alan? Please tell me.'

He said quietly, 'He's not a double agent, Barbara, or a traitor. You have my word on that. He's working for us. He's a man you can trust absolutely. And a brave man.'

She gave a deep sigh of relief. 'I suppose that's all you'll tell me?'

'Yes, it's all I can say.' He took his eyes away from her face. 'Shall I take you back now? Or would you like to stop somewhere for a drink?'

'Thank you. That would be nice.'

He drove down to a pub in Brixham – a cheerful sort of place and a definite improvement on the grim hotel in Torquay. They sat in a corner of the crowded lounge bar and he bought her a gin and orange and a pink gin for himself.

'I wanted to ask you before, Alan,' she said, as he set her drink down on the table, 'but there were all those old ladies eavesdropping on us. Do you have any other life – outside the Navy, I mean? Are you married?'

'No,' he said. 'I'm not married. I never have been. And I'm afraid I don't have a very interesting life, apart from the Navy. I have a sister, a brother-in-law and a nephew, some cousins, various old friends. I have a flat in London and I keep a small sailing boat in Essex – but that's about it. I went to Osborne at eleven, then on to Dartmouth . . . it's always been the Navy.'

'How did you get your medal?'

He glanced down at the DSO ribbon. 'In the First World War.'

'*How*, not when?'

'Putting out a fire after we'd been hit by a shell from a German cruiser.'

'Were you wounded?'

'Yes.'

She persisted. 'Badly?'

'Pretty badly. I nearly lost my left arm and I was in hospital for a very long time – all kinds of problems and complications, and so on. By the time I was fit again, life and the Navy had moved on. I rather lost my place in the queue. I ended up in command of a desk. Not quite what I'd originally hoped for.' He prayed to God that he didn't sound pathetic or bitter.

She was silent, then she said, 'I can see how very much the Navy has meant to you. It's been your whole life, hasn't it?'

'Yes, I suppose it has.'

'I don't know exactly what work you're doing now, Alan, but if it's important, and I'm sure it is, it might help to make up for what happened to you.'

He summoned a smile, more hopelessly in love with her than ever. 'We'll see.'

The house was dark and silent. She stopped for a moment outside to check the blackout at the front windows before she let herself in. The hall light had been left on and, as she went towards the stairs, she heard a sound from the direction of the sitting room and expected Mrs Lamprey to emerge, demanding to know where she had been.

'I've been waiting for your return, madame,' Monsieur Duval's voice said behind her. 'Please tell me what is the matter? Why you don't speak to me, or look at me. Not since last night.'

She turned to face him. 'Nothing's the matter.'

'I have not imagined it. Tell me, please.'

She hesitated, then said, 'There was a bill in the pocket of your jacket – I found it when I was ironing. It was from a restaurant in Paris, with the date on it, so I knew you must have been in France – when you were supposed to be in London.'

'And so? What did you think?'

'I thought you might be a traitor, spying for the Germans.'

He looked shocked. Angry, even. 'You could believe such a terrible thing of me? That I would betray my country? And yours, too?'

'I know now that it's not true.'

'How do you know?' he said harshly. 'How can you be so sure?'

'I've been told.'

'By whom?'

'Lieutenant Commander Powell.'

'I see. And did he tell you anything else?'

'Only that I could trust you completely. And that you were a brave man.' He was still angry and upset, she could tell. 'I'm sorry to have doubted you.'

After a moment, he said more calmly, 'I am sorry, too – that I have not been able to tell you all the truth. I regret very much that I have been obliged to deceive you.'

'I understand. It's the war, isn't it?'

'Yes,' he said. 'It's the war. The excuse for everything.'

When she started to go up the stairs he called after her. 'You are going to bed, madame?'

'I'm rather tired.'

'Shall I turn out this light downstairs?'

'Please. If you would.'

He followed her up to the landing. 'And this one here?'

'I usually leave it on.'

'Of course. So you do.'

He stood there while she fumbled agitatedly for the bedroom door handle at her back.

'Permit me, madame.' He reached past her and opened it.

'Thank you. Goodnight, then, Monsieur Duval.'

He didn't answer. Instead he took hold of her arm, drew her inside the room and closed the door behind them.

At breakfast Mrs Lamprey was at her worst.

'*Avez-vous dormé bien, Monsieur Duval?*'

'*Oui, merci, madame.* I slept very well, thank you.'

It seemed to Barbara that the question had been put even more coyly than usual and that, as she put Mrs Lamprey's bowl of cereal on her table, the old woman gave her a sly upward glance. Perhaps it was only imagination, but her bedroom was next door to her own. Had she heard her cry out? Listened eagerly with her ear pressed to the wall?

'Is anything the matter, Mrs Hillyard? You look quite flushed this morning.'

'I'm perfectly all right, thank you, Mrs Lamprey.'

'Oh dear, you've forgotten the milk.'

'I'll get it for you at once.'

He looked up briefly as she passed his table. She made herself pause, as she usually did, knowing that Mrs Lamprey was watching. 'Can I get you anything, Monsieur Duval?'

He met her eyes. 'No, thank you, madame.'

In the kitchen, Esme was feeding her cornflakes to Fifi. 'She likes them.'

'Well, don't give her too many. Save some for yourself.'

She took Mrs Lamprey's milk back into the dining room.

'*Il fait mauvais temps aujourd'hui, n'est-ce pas, Monsieur Duval? Je pense qu'il va pleurer.*'

'It should be *pleuvoir*, Mrs Lamprey. *Pleurer* is to cry.'

'*Thank* you, Miss Tindall. It was just a slip of the tongue. Oh, Mrs Hillyard. I wonder if I might trouble you for a spoon? I don't seem to have one.'

She had forgotten to put out the rear admiral's sugar ration as well, and Miss Tindall's butter. And Mrs Lamprey, at the toast stage, found she was missing something else.

'I can't see my special pot of marmalade, Mrs Hillyard . . .'

'I'm sorry. I'll fetch it straight away.'

She cocked her brassy head at her. 'You're quite sure you're all right? You don't seem at *all* your usual self.'

After breakfast, when she was at the sink, washing up, he came into the kitchen. Esme said to him at once, 'Did you know that Fifi's going to have kittens? The vet says so.'

He clicked his tongue. '*Oh, la, la.*'

'They're going to be born in about five weeks. We don't know how many yet.'

He looked at Barbara. 'I hope it won't be a great nuisance for you.'

'No, of course not. It'll be fun.'

She sent Esme to collect her things for school. When the child had left the room he said, 'What has happened to make little Esme so different?'

'Her father came to see her.'

'And the mother?'

'Apparently, she's run off with someone else. I've promised Esme's father that I'll keep her here until the war's over and he can take her home.'

'You take in every lost soul, Barbara. Esme, Fifi, myself . . . I hope that you don't have any regrets?'

She knew what he was asking. 'No.'

'None at all?'

'None.'

He kissed her hand, still soapy and wet from the washing-up. 'I'm very glad.'

The kitchen door opened and Mrs Lamprey poked her head round its edge.

283

'Oh, there you are, Mrs Hillyard. *Et vous, Monsieur Duval. J'espère que je ne vous dérange pas?*'

He said smoothly, 'You do not disturb us at all, madame. I only wished to tell Madame Hillyard that I shall not be in for lunch.'

'*Quel grand dommage!*'

'It is also a great pity for me.' As he passed Mrs Lamprey at the door he lifted her hand to his lips. 'Until this evening, madame.'

Mrs Lamprey followed him with her eyes and heaved a sigh. 'Frenchmen know exactly how to treat us women. Don't you agree, Mrs Hillyard?'

Alan Powell took the early train from Kingswear to London. From Paddington he went by taxi to the Georgian house north of Wigmore Street, passing recent bomb damage: piles of broken glass, rubble, boarded-up windows. The same impassive-faced woman showed him first into the waiting room and then up to Harry's office. The report on Louis Duval's mission, sent up by despatch rider the day before, lay on Harry's desk.

'Sit down, Alan.' Harry flicked at the report. 'I've just been going through this again. Duval's done a good job – there's no denying it. Laid the groundwork, you might say, and collected some useful stuff for us in the process.'

'He wants to know when he can go back. Recruit more people.'

'Keen as mustard, isn't he? Well, I can't answer

that at the moment. He'll have to be patient for a while. In general, I'm in favour of this idea of his and so are others, but it's still the view that the priority is to get our own properly trained agents in the field, as soon as we can. We're working on that. Within a few months we should be getting serious answers, not what some French farmer thought he saw on the way home from the local bistro.'

'Actually, I think most of the information that Duval brought back was pretty reliable. It made sense. Especially about the U-boat pens. I don't think there's much doubt about those being built as fast as the Germans can do it – certainly at Lorient and Brest, and probably other Atlantic ports too.'

'We need more than that, though, Alan. We need definite facts and figures. Engineering data on their construction – all that sort of thing, if we're going to be able to do anything about them.' Harry turned over pages. 'This fellow, for example – the electrician in Lorient – he won't be able to get that for us. All he'll manage is a quick peek.'

'I think he might do rather better than that. He'll be helping to install miles of wire. Covered bunkers will need a hell of a lot of artificial light. And power.'

'Well, it's certainly worth carrying on. Let's try anything. I take my hat off to these people. God help them if the Germans nab them.'

'Duval has set it up as securely as possible. In theory, if one's caught the others are safe.'

'Yes, I see that. In practice, of course, who knows? Who knows *anything* where the French are concerned?'

'He's put someone in charge of each cell; the rest report only to that person. It ought to work.'

'Except that the French can't stand being organized. Hopeless at discipline. We know that only too well.'

The blank-faced woman brought in coffee and biscuits. Powell waited until she had gone out before he went on. 'The weather's going to start deteriorating soon and it's going to make the fishing-boat trips across and the landings far more difficult. Is there any news on MTBs becoming available to us? They'd be far the safest bet in winter and they could do the whole trip there and back overnight, under cover of darkness.'

'I'll do my best. This latest expedition of Duval's will certainly help oil the wheels. Want some sugar in your coffee?'

'No, thanks.'

Harry dumped a spoonful in his cup and stirred it vigorously. 'One good thing, it's pretty certain that the Führer's abandoning any idea of springing an invasion on us this year. Time's almost up so far as the weather's concerned. If you ask me, he's missed the boat completely.'

After the meeting, Powell went over to Dolphin Square. Several of the building's windows had beeen blown out by bomb blast but those in his flat were undamaged. The usual pile of mail awaited him and he sifted through it without interest. The flat had never seemed so depressing, the prospect of an evening alone more daunting. As he stood staring out at the river, the phone rang. It was his sister.

'I've been hoping to get you, Alan . . . didn't think there was much of a chance, though.'

'I just got here.'

'How are you?'

'Fine. And you all?'

'We're fine, too. Listen, are you free for dinner tonight? I've got one or two people coming round and I need another man.'

Another man meant a spare woman. He said guardedly, 'I'm not quite sure.'

'Oh, please, Alan. It would be wonderful to see you.'

'I have to get a train back first thing.'

'Then stay the night here. William will drop you at Paddington on his way to the hospital or you can always get a taxi. There's bound to be an air raid tonight and it'll be much safer than being right by the river. They always go for it.'

How clearly and obligingly the Thames must show up for the German bombers, every twist and bend and curve mapping London precisely for them. 'It's nice of you to ask me, Hattie. What sort of time?'

'Six thirty for seven. We eat early these days before the raids start. See you then.'

He arrived well beforehand to find his sister in a state of chaos in the kitchen – used pots, pans and utensils dumped everywhere. 'Cook left to do factory work last week,' she told him. 'So I'm coping. It's a stew thing. One of the recipes they give on the wireless. I hope it's all right.'

'Can I help?'

'You could be a dear and lay the table. There'll be eight of us.'

He went off to unearth mats and knives and forks and spoons and put them round the dining-room table. Then he went back to the kitchen to find Henrietta sadly surveying some kind of collapsed pudding.

'Another wireless recipe?'

She shook her head. 'I found it in one of Cook's old books. She used to make it all the time and it always turned out perfectly. I don't know where I went wrong. Anyway, it'll just have to do.'

'Who's coming this evening?'

'William's best man and his wife – you remember them? David and Susannah?'

'Vaguely.'

'He's home on leave from the Far East, so it's in his honour, really. And we asked one of the young doctors at the hospital with his wife. The wife's sister was staying with them, so I invited her along too.'

'Which is why I was needed?'

'You don't mind, do you, Alan? And you never know.'

'I never know what?'

'Don't tease – you know very well what I

mean. How's that other girl you met in Dartmouth, by the way? I hoped there might be some good news on that front by now.'

'There's no news,' he said.

'You should get a move on, Alan. She sounded ideal.'

The other guests arrived and William came home soon after, looking exhausted. Powell did his duty and made polite conversation to the young doctor's sister-in-law. She was somewhere in her early twenties, he guessed, and finding the war rather exciting, she told him. He felt like her uncle and was certainly old enough to be it.

'What do you do?' he asked.

'Sort of nursing. I'm a VAD. You know, Voluntary Aid Detachment.'

'Yes,' he said. 'I know.' He could remember the VADs in the naval hospital in the first war. Well-meaning, bright young things with little more than basic first-aid training. Henrietta had been one for a while and there was an impressive silver-framed studio portrait of her in her Red Cross uniform. 'Do you enjoy it?'

She made a face. 'Not really. We get given all the awful jobs by the proper nurses. Luckily, I'm only part-time. I don't think I could stand it otherwise. What I'd *really* like to do is drive an ambulance. I think that would be super.'

'Can you drive?'

'No, but it wouldn't take very long to learn, would it?'

She was very pretty and well made-up, with carefully arranged hair. He wondered when the reality of war would strike home. She smiled at him kindly, taking in his uniform.

'You're in the Royal Navy, aren't you?'

He almost answered, 'No, the Royal Air Force,' but suppressed the temptation. 'Yes, that's right.' She would undoubtedly have preferred someone like Lieutenant Smythson and must have been sorely disappointed by his grey hairs.

'I expect you do something frightfully interesting.'

'No,' he said. 'Nothing very interesting at all.'

He was glad that the evening finished early – in deference to the Luftwaffe. His brother-in-law was called back urgently to the hospital and he helped Henrietta to clear away and stack the dirty dishes in the kitchen.

'The daily will do them in the morning. Thank heavens I've still got her. She's a real treasure. Let's go and sit down with a large brandy, Alan, and have a nice chat.'

He poured brandies for them both and lit their cigarettes.

'Thank you for the evening, Hattie.'

'Sorry about the food. It was a dismal failure.'

'No, it wasn't. Not at all.' Teeth would have to be drawn before he admitted any such thing to her.

'Anyway, I'll do better next time. What did you think of Joanna?'

'Joanna?'

'Honestly, Alan . . . You sat next to her all evening.'

'Sorry. Very pretty and very young.'

'Too young for you?'

'The opposite way round. I'm too old for her. Much too old.'

'Well, what about the other one – the one down in Dartmouth?'

'I'm afraid that's not going to come to anything.'

'Why ever not? You seemed so happy when you were last here. Quite different.'

'I found out that she's in love with somebody else.'

'Are you sure?'

'Pretty sure.'

'Oh, Alan, what a shame.' She looked at him sadly. 'Who's the other man? Someone else in the Navy?'

'No, a Frenchman.'

'Oh dear. They can be terribly attractive. So different.'

He said, with some asperity, 'From what?'

'Well . . . from Englishmen. I remember when I was at that awful finishing school in Paris, I fell madly in love with one. Took me ages to get over him. Actually, I still think of him sometimes – never told William that, of course. You won't give up on her, though, will you, Alan?'

'You mean, faint heart never won fair maid?'

'Something like that.'

The air-raid siren started its unearthly wailing a moment later. 'Do you have a shelter here?'

'Not really. William piled sandbags all round the downstairs cloakroom, but we never bother to go in it. He's usually at the hospital anyway most nights.'

'What do you do?'

'Go to bed. I'm blowed if I'll let the Germans ruin my night's sleep.'

'You mean you sleep right through the raids?'

'Usually, yes. I put my ear plugs in and take an aspirin and that seems to do the trick.'

He shook his head, smiling. 'You really should get a proper shelter, Hattie. Get an Anderson put in the garden.'

'Half the lawn's already dug up for growing vegetables and I'm not going to disturb the roses. Besides, the Germans'll give up when they find out that bombing us makes no difference. We'll never surrender to them.'

'I'm afraid they'll go on dropping them for quite some time, that's the trouble. If you won't think of yourself, you ought to think of Julian. He wouldn't want anything to happen to you while he's away and when he's home from school, he ought to have somewhere safe during the raids.'

'That's true.' She smiled fondly at him. 'You're so sensible in so many ways, Alan. And so hopeless in others.'

After she'd gone to bed, he stayed up for a while, smoking, drinking brandy and listening to

the drone of the German bombers circling somewhere over east London, the crump of their
bombs falling and the furious reply of the ground
ack-ack guns. When the All Clear had gone
he went upstairs. Before he went to sleep, he
switched out the bedside lamp and pulled aside
the blackout curtain. In the distance, to the east,
he could see the huge, crimson glow of fires
lighting up the sky.

Eleven

October was almost over before Louis Duval
returned to France. The long wait had frustrated
and, at times, angered him. He saw no sense in
delaying things and every sense in pursuing what
he had begun, before people's courage and resolu-
tion could falter and crumble beneath the sheer
weight of German oppression. When, finally,
Lieutenant Commander Powell had summoned
him, he had said all this and more. The naval
officer had heard him out patiently and Duval,
talking at machine-gun speed and gesticulating all
the while, had realized that his protest was being
put down to French excitability. When he had
finished, the lieutenant commander had answered
him with infuriating English calm.

'As it happens, I agree with you, but unfortunately I take my orders from higher up. And they
have only just come through.'

He had said bitterly, 'And how long am I to be
permitted to stay this time?'

'Another month.'

'It's not enough. Not nearly.'

'We need you to return here before any intelligence is stale.'

He had taken a grip on himself. 'I apologize. Of course you are right about that. But when are they going to get radio transmitters so that we are not obliged to go backwards and forwards in this crazy way?'

'As soon as it can be done.'

He had lifted his shoulders silently and eloquently.

The weather was bad this time. The sea much rougher, the crossing longer, by consequence, and even more uncomfortable. The *Espérance* was undergoing an engine overhaul and Lieutenant Smythson was away on leave. The replacement boat, *Marie-Éloise* – an elderly crabber – wallowed her way along and, except for one Breton, her crew were all men seconded from the Royal Navy and complete strangers to him. As before, the plan was to arrive offshore during darkness but, on this occasion, to land on a beach at Rospico between Raguènes and Port-Manech, just south of Pont-Aven – a spot he knew reasonably well. Duval stayed on deck for the first part of the trip, smoking and watching the coast of England recede.

He thought about Barbara. He had not lied to her this time, about going to London. He'd said nothing and she'd asked no questions. All she'd said was, 'Please be careful.' There had been a long succession of women in his life, but not one

295

of them had touched his heart as she had done. Not even Simone. In the beginning he had loved Simone with the blind passion of youth, but the rest who had followed had meant little to him. They had been mostly Frenchwomen and some other nationalities, too: Spanish, Italian, German, Dutch – and English. Some had been models who had sat for him, others brief encounters, or longer, more intense affairs. Some had moved in aristocratic circles or in café society; others had been shop girls, flower girls, dancers . . . They had all been much the same – beautiful, or not so beautiful; warm or cold; amusing or boring. He never exactly forgot them, but as their successor came along they faded into the shadows of the past, where he sometimes had difficulty in recalling their names or faces – though seldom their bodies. Whether he had drawn them, painted them, or simply made love to them, he remembered the bodies rather better than their owners.

Later, he went below and fell asleep on the bunk, to be awakened after a few hours by an ominous silence. The *Marie-Éloise* had stopped her wallowing and come to a halt, her engine broken down. The petrol pipes had to be dismantled and cleaned before she could be persuaded to budge again and more than an hour was lost. There were strong seas running off the Brittany coast and getting ashore proved a treacherous operation. The naval rating rowing the dinghy had a hard job making it to the beach, and Duval landed wet through from breaking waves and spray.

He spent the remainder of the night concealed in an equally wet ditch and soon after dawn walked to Pont-Aven, trying to think of a credible reason for looking as though he had taken a swim fully clothed in late October. His guardian angel, he decided, must have risen early in order to protect him. There was scarcely anybody about and no curious or suspicious German soldier stopped him and demanded an explanation, as well as the inevitable papers. Better still, it had started to rain – rain which soon became a huge downpour and accounted quite satisfactorily for his appearance.

The angel accompanied him as he splashed through the puddles into the apartment building, ensuring also that Mademoiselle Citron continued with her much-needed beauty sleep, and seeing him safely up to his door. Inside, he took off his wet clothing and found dry things. Then he poured himself a large brandy. In normal circumstances he would have expected it to do the trick, but he had spent the past two days at sea in a draughty old fishing boat in freezing weather and most of the night in a waterlogged ditch. He felt ill. Very ill. When he lay down on the bed, it seemed to be moving up and down like the bunk on board the *Marie-Éloise*. He closed his eyes, nauseated, and, presently, he slept.

The knocking dragged him back to consciousness. He struggled to his feet and made his way unsteadily to the door. Mademoiselle Citron stood before him, staring.

'Madame Duval has been telephoning me while you have been absent, monsieur. She says she has been trying to reach you and wanted to know where you were. Since I am never informed of your plans, I was unable to assist her.'

He clung dizzily to the door jamb. 'I've only just returned.'

'Yes. There were wet footprints across the hall floor and up the stairs – I thought it must be you.'

His guardian angel had slipped up there. Her German guests, no doubt, never failed to wipe their boots. 'Did my wife leave any message for me?'

'She asked if you would telephone her as soon as possible.' She stared harder. 'Are you ill, monsieur? You don't look at all well.'

'A slight chill, that's all.'

'Do you wish me to send for the doctor?'

'No, thank you. It will not be necessary.'

He telephoned Simone in Paris. 'It's Louis. You were trying to reach me.'

'For weeks. Where on earth have you been? I thought perhaps you'd really gone off to England this time.' She sounded angry, accusing.

'What's the trouble?'

'That bank of yours has missed two payments. Unless you stopped them.'

'No,' he said. 'I didn't stop them. I'll phone them and sort it out.'

'Where have you been all this time?'

'Around, looking for inspiration. New things to paint.'

'You should try painting portraits of the Germans. They'd pay through the nose, especially if you make them look good.' She was only half-joking, he knew.

'How's the business going?'

'Not so well. I can't get the stock.'

'That's unlucky for you.' He was sweating now, instead of being cold. He wiped his forehead. 'I'll telephone the bank now.'

The manager was apologetic. The Occupation had caused chaos . . . nothing was as it should be . . . staff had gone . . . there were new regulations in force . . . it was all most regrettable . . . he would look into the matter at once and the payments into Madame Duval's account would be made immediately.

Duval lay down on the bed again. He felt worse than ever and knew that to try and get up and go out would be hopeless. In his present state he would achieve nothing. There was no option but to stay where he was and hope that whatever had struck him down would pass quickly. In fact, it took three days. Three days during which he alternately burned or froze. He ate nothing, drank brandy – when he could stomach it – and slept for hours at a time, semi-delirious. On the third day, Major Winter knocked at the door.

'Mademoiselle Citron told me of your return,

monsieur. I understand you've not been well. I trust you're better now?'

Fortunately, he was.

'A fever perhaps? The influenza?'

'Something of the kind.'

'I was away on leave on the last occasion that you were here. I hope that in my absence Oberleutnant Peltz was helpful?'

'Exceedingly. He found me some cognac and wine. And thank you for the gasoline coupons.'

'Not many, I am afraid. It was the best that I could do.' The major paused. 'I should warn you perhaps that Mademoiselle Citron is no friend of yours.'

'I'm aware of that.'

'She would like to cause mischief for you.'

'I'm sure she would. I declined to sleep with her and she has never forgiven me.'

The major nodded. 'People use us to try to settle all kinds of old scores. They even write anonymous letters. It's very distasteful.'

He wondered exactly what sort of mischief the sourpuss had been stirring up. What hints and insinuations? And since she could not know the truth, what lies?

At last he felt well enough to shave and bath and dress, and hungry enough to sally forth *Chez Alphonse* for some lunch. To his relief there were no German customers to contend with – only a few locals – and Alphonse himself, bravely continuing to bear the trials of Occupation.

'A little vegetable soup, perhaps, monsieur?

And some bread and cheese? It pains me but that is the best I can offer.'

In fact, it suited him very well. Anything more would have been beyond him. He was content to sit quietly at his table in the corner and re-habituate his stomach to the idea of receiving food. A carafe of wine on hand, and he began to feel quite normal. Alphonse found time to join him in a glass, dunking a piece of grey Occupation bread into the wine and chewing at it morosely – the only way, in his opinion, to get it down.

Duval said, 'I'm told that Mademoiselle Citron has been trying to make trouble for me with the Germans. Do you know anything about that?'

'No, I've heard nothing. But it doesn't surprise me. She's just the sort. People are denouncing old enemies to the Nazis for anything: papers not quite in order, a little black market dealing to keep body and soul together, a few indiscreet words . . . you can imagine for yourself. One is ashamed sometimes to be French. A little something now to aid the digestion, monsieur? I still have a bottle or two of good cognac hidden away.'

Afterwards he walked up to the Vauclin cottage. With the colder weather Jean-Claude was working under cover in the stables. His bike had not only been looked after but had been made to look almost like new. Jean-Claude wheeled it out with pride from a dark corner, demonstrating brakes, turning handlebars, spinning pedals. The machine stood before him, oiled, polished and gleaming. And, much as he tried, no payment would be accepted. Marthe, he was told, was away with the horse and cart and her lace samples, gathering more information and people. She was expected back within a few days.

He rode away on the rejuvenated bike, wishing that he himself could undergo a similar process.

The shoemender, Leblond, had no more news from his cousin in Quimper, but his brother-in-law had counted twelve U-boat pens being constructed at Lorient. And the shipping-office friend at Brest was now in no doubt that others were being built there. He also reported rumours of similar constructions beginning in other ports further south – St Nazaire, for example, and La Rochelle. Furthermore, the shoemender had another useful cousin who happened to be a house painter and had been doing some work for the Germans at their headquarters. He would be more than happy to keep his eyes and ears open as he wielded his brush.

The greengrocer was out with his horse and cart, but Madame Thomine left her daughter in charge of the shop while she took Duval into a back room. Her brother, who was blind, but with very sharp hearing, spent his time sitting in cafés listening to the German soldiers talking – boasting when they'd had too much to drink. The talk was no longer of invading England but of the Germans starving the English out of existence by sinking all their merchant ships, and without the trouble of getting their feet wet.

Duval returned to his studio. He left the bike in the hallway – no doubt Mademoiselle Citron would drive herself crazy wondering where it had been and how it had undergone such a transformation. He poured himself more of the cognac, lit a Gauloise and sat down to listen to one of his favourite records – the Mendelssohn violin concerto that Major Winter had also appreciated. Tomorrow he would go by train to Brest. From Brest to Rennes. From there he would go on to Paris.

It was Esme who found Fifi's litter of kittens. She came running into the kitchen, her eyes shining with excitement.

'They're in the airing cupboard upstairs. Under the shelves, right at the back.'

'How many?'

'Five, I think.'

In fact, there was a sixth, but it was already dead. Barbara removed it and arranged a suitably solemn funeral in the garden, with Esme carrying a shoebox coffin adorned with a chrysanthemum. They buried the kitten near the apple tree and marked the grave with a cross made out of two sticks tied together. The survivors were mixed colouring – two black with white paws exactly like Fifi's, two grey tabby and one ginger. Esme wanted to keep them all.

'Not all of them,' Barbara said firmly. 'Just one.

Wait and see which you like best. We'll find homes for the rest when they're big enough.'

'Could I take it with me when Dad fetches me?'

'Of course you can. It will be your very own.'

'Can I choose its name?'

'Certainly.'

She fetched some milk for Fifi and put the dish close beside her. The cat was lying contentedly on her side, her Anglo-French kittens feeding in a row.

Esme crouched down to watch them. 'Wait till Mr Duval sees them when he comes back. He'll be ever so surprised.'

Later, Barbara went upstairs to his room. She looked out of the window towards the sea, in the direction of France. What sort of boat had he gone in? How did he get ashore without being seen? Where did he go? What did he do? What risks did he take? What did Germans do to spies if they caught them?

'Lieutenant Reeves speaking, sir.'

Powell held the receiver to his ear but went on looking through the papers on his desk. 'Yes, what is it?'

'That file on Mrs Hillyard that you returned . . .'

He stopped looking at the papers. 'What about it?'

'Well, I happened to remember that she had a brother serving on one of our destroyers.'

'Yes?'

'His ship's just been sunk, sir. A signal came

through. I got the file out again, to make sure it was the same one he's serving on and it was. She was torpedoed in the North Atlantic on escort duty, about thirty miles out of Halifax. The convoy lost twelve ships at a go. I suppose the U-boats were waiting for them.'

'You're quite certain of this?'

'Yes, sir.'

'Any survivors?'

'None reported, I'm afraid. The other ships couldn't stop to pick anyone up, of course. Not in that situation. They did an air search of the area afterwards, but no luck. Of course, in that latitude and at this time of year, nobody's going to survive for very long.' Reeves cleared his throat. 'Mrs Hillyard will be getting the official telegram, of course, but I wondered if the news might be better coming from you first, sir?'

'I'll go and see her. Thank you, Lieutenant.'

'I'm sorry about it, sir.'

'So am I.'

He put the phone down and then picked it up again to put a call through to the Admiralty. The news was confirmed for him. Lieutenant Frederick Sutcliffe's ship had been sunk off Nova Scotia and there were no survivors.

The evacuee child answered the door to him and he realized that he had completely forgotten her name. An unusual one, that was all he could remember.

'Is Mrs Hillyard at home?'

Last time she had scowled at him, this time she smiled and nodded. 'Would you like to see the kittens?'

He followed her obediently through the hall and up the stairs to a cupboard on the landing. Inside there was a lagged hot-water tank, slatted shelves with neat piles of clean and ironed clothes, linen and towels. In its way, he thought, it was as comforting a place as the kitchen.

The child pointed under the lowest shelf. 'She's at the very back. You'll have to get right down to see them.' He got down on his hands and knees and crawled a little way underneath. In the far corner he saw the dark shape of the cat, the white of her paws, the shine of her eyes and a huddled heap of small furry bodies. 'They're different sorts,' the child said. 'Two like her, and two grey tabbies and a ginger. I like the ginger one best. It's a boy. Did you know that most ginger cats are boys?'

'No, I'm afraid I didn't.'

'The vet says so. It's going to be mine when it grows up. I'm calling it Tom.'

As he backed out from under the shelf, knocking his head in the process, Barbara said from the doorway, 'I didn't know you were here, Alan.'

He got to his feet, brushing the dust off his knees. 'I only just arrived. I was being shown the nursery.'

'Esme takes everyone to see them. Luckily Fifi doesn't seem to mind. In fact, I think she rather enjoys all the attention and being told how clever she is. We should leave her alone now, though, Esme.'

The child went off somewhere and he followed Barbara downstairs, dreading his task. They reached the hallway. 'Would you like a cup of tea, Alan?'

'Please don't bother. I wonder if we could talk somewhere in private for a moment?'

She saw his grave expression and her face changed. 'Yes, of course. The kitchen's probably best.' Inside the cosy room which he had liked so much, she faced him. 'Has something happened to Louis Duval?'

Naturally, it would have been her first thought; he should have guessed that. He shook his head. 'No, it's nothing to do with him.'

She looked instantly and happily relieved. 'What is it, then?'

He could hardly bring himself to tell her, but surely this way was better and kinder than a telegram. He said quietly, 'I'm afraid I've got some rather bad news for you.'

She stared at him. 'What bad news?'

He could tell that she still had no inkling. 'It's about your brother.'

The colour drained from her face. 'Freddie? What's happened to him?'

She had to know, sooner or later. 'I'm so sorry, Barbara, but he's been reported missing at sea. His ship was sunk.'

'Sunk?' She seemed stunned. 'Where? What happened?'

'I'm not actually allowed to give any details.'

'He's not dead, though, is he? There would have been lifeboats, wouldn't there? He would have been picked up?'

Her brother, he knew, was her last living relative and he would have given anything to let her have hope when it seemed there was almost none. 'There are no reports of any survivors, unfortunately. But that doesn't mean that there's no chance at all. It's perfectly possible that he did manage to get to a lifeboat or raft.'

'And he could drift for days, couldn't he? Some other ship could have picked him up?'

He thought of the icy seas off Nova Scotia, of the November weather in the North Atlantic, of the rest of the convoy steaming on relentlessly because to slow or divert or to stop would almost certainly mean going to the bottom too. 'Yes, of course that may have happened.'

She stared at him, the hope dying. 'But you don't really think so, do you, Alan?'

He said heavily, 'To be honest, it doesn't sound much like it. The area was thoroughly searched afterwards and no survivors were reported. None. It would be wrong of me to give you false hope, Barbara, but there *is* always a chance. Always. So, please don't give up yet.' He could see, with deep pity, how hard she was struggling for self-control. 'You'll be sent an official communication from the Admiralty, of course, but I thought it might help if someone came in person.'

'Thank you, Alan. It was very thoughtful of

you. Very kind. You know, I always felt it would happen. I just *knew* it. Oh, Freddie . . . my poor, poor Freddie.' Tears were running down her cheeks now and she started to sob.

He moved forward to put his arms gently around her and she buried her face against his chest.

Twelve

To save the precious gasoline as well as to be less conspicuous, Louis Duval took the train down to Lorient. It would have been pleasant to stay *chez* Violette but he resisted the temptation, not out of deference to the absent Daniel languishing in his POW camp, but out of regard for Violette. It was safer, for her sake, to avoid going near her apartment, just as it was safer for Ernest Boitard's family if he kept away from their home. He booked into a cheap hotel near the port, run-down and flea-ridden enough to discourage any Germans.

He had contacted Boitard by telephone from Pont-Aven the previous evening, using their pre-arranged message, and made his way to the café where they were to meet at six o'clock. It was a café like a thousand others in France – which was why Duval had chosen it. The gilt lettering on the glass windows read: *Joseph. Vins. Tabacs.* The *c* in the last word had worn away. Inside, there were the usual marble-topped tables, red leather benches with brass rails, mirrored walls, zinc bar, coffee machine bubbling away, and the smell of rough wine mingling with a thick haze of even rougher tobacco. The obese *patron*, Joseph, presided at the bar, dispensing *apéritifs* to the town's tradesmen with his bear-like hands.

There was no cognac and having no faith in the drinkability of the *ordinaire*, Duval ordered a Cinzano, sat down at one of the tables in the corner and lit a cigarette. One or two glances came his way, but for the most part he seemed to be ignored. At the next table two elderly men, smoking blackened pipes, were absorbed in a game of dominoes. He opened the newspaper he had bought earlier and began to read.

It was half past six before Ernest Boitard came into the café and went up to the bar. Even at a distance, Duval could tell how ragged his nerves were and see how difficult he was finding it to appear natural. The man drew attention with his edgy manner. Perhaps it had not been so wise to press him into service? The electrician came over carrying a glass of calvados and sat at the same table, but obliquely across from Duval. 'Do you have a light, monsieur?'

'Certainly.' Duval leaned forward and lit the cigarette, observing that the hand holding it was shaking. He turned a page of his newspaper. 'What news is there?'

'It's been very hard . . . I'm watched all the time.'

'Nonetheless, what have you seen?'

Boitard leaned closer, fiddling with the ashtray.

He spoke rapidly and so low that Duval could scarcely hear him. 'There will be fifteen pens at least – perhaps more. There are many German engineers, technicians and gangs of labourers from their Todt Organization, as well as French conscripts, like myself. Also some French volunteers, I regret to say. The concrete roofs will be flat and very thick – as much as five metres or maybe even more – the pens in a long row, like stables, and connecting by channels to the harbour. I believe there are also to be workshops and fuels stores, a dry dock, a slipway for beaching U-boats . . . all the necessary facilities and all under the same massive concrete bunker. That is my understanding.'

'What defences?'

'I don't know.' Boitard gulped at his drink. 'As I say, it's difficult. It would be very dangerous to stray far from my work.'

Duval turned another page of the newspaper. 'As time goes on, it may become easier.'

'I can tell you that there is one thing that will *not* become easier – destroying the bunkers. Once they are built it may prove impossible. The time to act is *now*.' He was resentful, as well as fearful. 'You should pass on that information to your friends in England. It's the best I can provide. Don't ask me to do more.'

He drained the rest of his drink and left. Duval stayed, reading his newspaper. After a while, someone else came to sit at his table – a small, dark man with a moustache not at all unlike the

Führer's, a near-empty glass in one hand, an unlit cigarette in the other.

'You have a light, please, monsieur?'

'Of course.'

'Thank you.' Smoke curled upwards between them. 'I have been watching you with interest.'

'Really?'

'That man who was here – I recognized him.'

'Which man?'

'The one who came to sit at your table and speak with you.'

'He came to ask for a light – as you have just done.'

'It takes only a few words to do that; he said many more. I don't know his name but I have seen him before. He is an electrician who works for the Germans at Keroman. He was conscripted – like myself.'

Duval shrugged. 'He may well be . . . it's nothing to me.'

'He was very nervous when he came in here. Very anxious. I could tell that. Then I see him talk with you, very low, and I ask myself what he is saying and why he is so nervous, and who *you* are, monsieur? What are you doing here?'

'As you can see, I am having an *apéritif*, smoking a cigarette and reading my newspaper, I hope, in peace.'

'You are not a regular and I'm not the only one in this room who has been watching you. There are several of us who meet here and talk about how we could resist the Boche. What we could do

313

against them for France. We plot and we plan and we think about little else. It helps to make things bearable.'

Duval put down his newspaper. 'Another glass, monsieur?'

'Willingly.'

He went to the bar and bought a calvados for the man and another Cinzano. He raised his glass. '*Santé*. You haven't told me your name.'

'You don't need to know it, nor do I need to know yours. Let's just say that it's Léon.'

'Very well, Léon. What do you do when you are made to work for the Germans?'

'I'm a plumber. I have my own business. Two other men are employed by me. We are all working on the U-boat bunker at Keroman – the same as your friend.'

'He's not my friend.'

'No . . . I could tell that. And he's very afraid.' The man smiled, showing tobacco-stained teeth. 'I, on the other hand, am not afraid at all.'

The next day he went on by train to Rennes. The encounter with Léon had been a piece of good fortune. Plumbers, it had been explained to him, were in an excellent position to move about and observe. Any excuse would do – mysterious blockages, the urgent need to check water flow and levels, locating leaks, fetching vital tools. A man in overalls, crawling about with a wrench in his hand and tapping pipes assiduously, went everywhere unremarked.

He watched the countryside through the train windows, thinking how much parts of Brittany resembled the south-west of England. Breakfast, he gauged, would be over at Bellevue. The rear admiral would have barricaded himself in the sitting room behind *The Times* newspaper. Mademoiselle Tindall would have gone to her room to write one of her many letters, while Mrs Lamprey would be looking for a victim to trap into witnessing her re-enact some little scene. Even the postman did not always manage to escape a soliloquy on the doorstep. He had been the victim, himself, a number of times. A snatch of Ibsen, or Chekhov, or Wilde and, once, most painful of all, the balcony scene from *Romeo and Juliet* with Mrs Lamprey perched precariously on a chair with her chiffon scarf draped round her head and speaking the lines of a fifteen-year-old girl, passionately in love – to him.

My bounty is as boundless as the sea,
My love as deep; the more I give to thee,
The more I have, for both are infinite.

He had applauded enthusiastically, of course, and helped her down from the chair. Not even Mrs Lamprey could quite spoil the beauty of the feelings expressed by the English words. His feelings for Barbara Hillyard. So deep, so true, and, to him, so miraculous.

Aunt Pauline gave him her customarily tart welcome. 'It takes another war for you to come and visit this often, Louis. I suppose I should be grateful to the Germans.'

He kissed her cheek, inhaling camphor. 'My dear aunt, I should find it hard to thank them for a single thing.'

'True enough. Would you like some tea? I always take some at this time. It's excellent for the nerves. The English have always understood that.'

'A cognac cures mine far more effectively.'

'Too much of *that* is bad for the liver, whereas tea is good for it.'

'Nevertheless, I should prefer a cognac.'

'Very well. Ring the bell for Jeanne. And put that cigarette away, Louis. You know perfectly well that I won't tolerate you smoking in here. By the way, Jeanne has some information to give you.'

The servant had, apparently, been paying regular visits to the railway station pretending to be waiting for trains, or for someone to arrive. Nobody, it seemed, took account of a little old woman clothed all in black, any more than they noticed a plumber with his tools. She had watched the German troops coming and going, seen what sort they were, how many, where they had come from and where they were going. She gave him all these details that she had kept safe in her head. And, because nobody had noticed her, she had been able to stand very close and listen to their chatter.

'You understand German, mademoiselle?'

'Oh yes, I was brought up in Alsace.'

'And what were they saying?'

'All sorts of things – the things that men talk of together. What a good time they had in Paris. How easy some of the French women were – they despise them for it, you know.'

'That seems unfair.'

She shrugged. 'Men are like that, isn't that so, monsieur? They take but they scorn.'

His aunt snorted. 'How would you know, Jeanne? Get on with it. What else did these fools talk about?'

'How good the French cooking is. And our wine.'

He said, 'Did they speak of England?'

She wriggled her bony shoulders. 'They prefer to stay in France. They say they can bomb the English without having to go where the women are as cold as the weather. And they can sink all the English ships with their undersea boats. They say that, in the end, Monsieur Churchill will have to make a deal with their Führer.'

'The sailors you noticed – can you tell me more about them?'

'They were from the undersea boats.'

'How could you tell?'

'I have learned to recognize what they wear – the special badges and clothes. Also, they are different men.'

'In what way?'

She moved her shoulders again. 'Fearless, I think. Superior to most of the rest.'

'Did they talk about their boats? Where exactly

they would be joining them? The names of their captains? Things like that.'

'No, they were more careful than the others. The train was going direct to Brest, that's all I can tell you.'

He thanked her and she left the room as silently as she had entered it. It was no wonder, he thought, that she could eavesdrop unobserved. Even so, it was not without risk.

'Tell her to be careful, Aunt Pauline. Her years will be no protection if the Germans should ever suspect her.'

'I've already told her so. At her age, she says, what does it matter? I think she's right. *You* should be careful though, Louis. You're playing with fire. And you still have a life ahead.'

'I hope so because I have found a woman to share it.'

'Welcome news. Who is she?'

'An Englishwoman.'

'That's a great surprise. I should never have imagined you with one. The English have no passion. Is she beautiful? She must be.'

'She's much more than that.'

'Well, Simone was never good for you. I hope this one will be.'

'I hope that I'm good for her.'

'You will be, Louis. I should like to meet her – one day. When this unpleasant war is over you must bring her to visit.'

As he left, he bowed and kissed her hand in homage. He knew it would please her.

Cousin André was waiting for him, by arrangement, in a café similar to the one in Lorient. The furnishings were almost exactly the same, but the *patron* at the zinc bar was thin instead of fat, and, by some miracle, could offer a reasonable cognac. He took it over to André's table. Since they were cousins with every reason to meet there was no need for the subterfuge of Lorient, and the table was out of earshot of the other customers. This time he listened, not to an account of the comings and goings of German soldiers, sailors and airmen but of the growing number of Frenchmen who wanted somehow to resist them. André could count fifty or more he knew who were willing to risk their lives, he assured Duval, his face alight with his communist zeal.

'They are ready to do anything – *anything* to make things difficult for these fascist pigs.'

'Such as?'

'Blow up bridges. Derail trains. Sabotage work in armament factories. Assassinate, if necessary.'

It was a rather different matter, Duval thought, from the stealthy gathering of information, the gradual piecing together of vital facts. He said, 'The Germans will certainly retaliate – you realize that? They'll doubtless execute innocent French civilians to discourage such things.'

'There's always a price for freedom.'

That was true enough; he could not deny it. But André's form of resistance, commendable though it might be, did not march comfortably with the activities of a secret network such as he was trying to establish. In fact, there was a real possibility that his people would sabotage not only bridges and trains and factories, but imperil the vital work of undercover agents. To become involved with his cousin and his friends would be a big mistake, he decided. Let them go their way and he would go his.

Before he left Rennes, he called on the legal firm who had dealt with the family affairs for many years. The lawyer he remembered had retired and his place had been taken by his son. First, he dictated a new will. A legacy, as before, to Simone to ensure her financial security; certain of his paintings to Gerard Klein at the gallery in Paris in recognition of his debt to him. The rest of the paintings he left to Barbara Hillyard of Kingswear, England, together with the residue of his estate. When the will had been typed, he signed it before a clerk and typist.

The lawyer offered a cigarette. 'You know England well?'

'Not well, no. Do you?'

'I studied at Cambridge for a year. It was a very happy time for me. They are in a very bad situation at the moment, of course. One must hope that, unlike us, they don't fail.'

'Yes, indeed.'

'If they go under, the war is over.'

Duval looked thoughtfully at the ceiling. 'Unfortunately, yes.'

'One wishes one could do something.'

He lowered his gaze. 'It's possible that you can.'

There was a subtle change in Paris. Duval sensed it as soon as he walked out of the railway station. Silent streets, silent people, the darkness of winter descending on the city like a widow's veil. And with the darkness, fear. It was there in the hurried steps, the averted faces, the hunched shoulders, and whenever the crunch of heavy hobnail boots signalled the passing of a German patrol. Ordinary life had ceased. Gone away. In its place was emptiness.

He made his way to the rue de Monceau. Madame Bertrand came out like a jack-in-the-box before he could reach the stairway to the apartment. She planted herself adroitly between him and the first step.

'It would not be wise for you to go up, monsieur.'

He looked down into her inscrutable old face. It was not the only time that she had given him tactful advice. 'Madame Duval is entertaining?'

She nodded. 'A German officer. SS.'

'I see. Thank you for the warning.'

'High-ranking.'

'Yes, he would be.'

'He's not the first one.' The concierge turned her head away suddenly and spat on the ground. 'And that's what I think of it.'

He said smoothly, 'Tell me, how is Monsieur Bertrand these days?'

'A little better, though he still complains.'

'Please give him my regards.'

She called after his departing back. 'It would be safer not to visit again, monsieur.'

Gerard Klein's wife, Celeste, and the five children were at the apartment and he embraced them all fondly, starting with Celeste and working his way down to the youngest child of six years old. They seemed much as ever, smiling and laughing and making jokes – the close, happy family that he had sometimes, secretly, envied. They made him sit down to eat with them – a Jewish meal of salted fish and shredded cabbage and potato dumplings which he pretended to like.

Afterwards Gerard took him off to the book-lined den that had been the scene of so many other amicable meetings. Duval opened his valise. 'I've brought you three more paintings for the gallery. That was the reason for my visit.'

'Excellent! I sold the last one at the gallery yesterday. I thought it would be the end of them, from what you said last time.'

He smiled. 'I must help to keep you in business, my dear friend. All those mouths to feed.' They sat down to drink and talk. Almost like old times, Duval thought, but not quite.

He lit their cigarettes. 'Simone has a German lover. A high-ranking SS officer.'

'Don't tell me you ran into him at the apartment?'

'Fortunately not. The concierge warned me in time.'

'Well, you can't be too surprised. Simone was always the practical type. And what better protection could she have?' Gerard brushed some ash from his waistcoat. 'Some of us could do with the same. You know, I'd been thinking of sending Celeste and the children down to the south – that is until I heard how the Vichy government is treating Jews. They frighten me, almost more than the Germans.'

'How are you treated here in Paris?'

'Like Jews are always treated, my dear Louis. There is a special police branch now for Jewish affairs. We are identified and counted like sheep; property is confiscated on flimsy excuses; if we go to the south we may not return, and naturally we are blamed for everything – but one is quite used to that. Perhaps Celeste and I should have done what you did and fled to England with the children. But it's too late now. Have you been back there since we last met?'

'Yes.'

'You're crazy, Louis – I told you that before. How is your mad scheme going?'

'It's better we don't discuss it. Let's talk of other things.' He smiled. 'For instance, tell me where in Paris one can still buy perfume.'

'Good evening, Mademoiselle Citron.' He nodded as he passed her in the hallway.

'You are quite recovered, monsieur?'

Her concern for his health was feigned, naturally. Perhaps she was hoping that if he stayed ill enough for long enough he would end up in hospital, in which case she could sublet his apartment to a German officer for double the rent. 'Yes, thank you.'

'Is that your bicycle?'

'Yes, indeed.'

'It looks different.'

'It has been undergoing repairs.'

'You wish to keep it there?'

'Unless you have strong objections.'

'It gets in the way, you see . . . when the hallway is being cleaned.'

'Very well. I'll remove it.'

He carried the bicycle up to the top floor – a considerable effort – but, on the whole, he thought it was better to keep it where it would be safe, and where it was not under her inquisitive and observant nose. At four o'clock that evening – two hours before the autumn curfew time began – he left the building again and walked out of Pont-Aven, following the road that led along the river estuary to Kerdruc. At Kerdruc he hitched a lift from a farmer driving a horse and cart piled high with muddy swedes – a bulbous orange vegetable that he had only known of as cattle food, but which the farmer was now selling for humans to eat. He left the swedes and the farmer two kilometres or so from the rendezvous at Rospico to walk the rest of the way.

By the time he reached the beach it was almost dark and he settled down for several hours of cold and discomfort, huddled in the shelter of a large rock. Cigarettes helped to pass the time and he shielded the lighted tip with his hand and buried each butt deep as it was finished. Occasional nips from a flask of brandy kept up his spirits. Every so often he checked his watch with the aid of his pocket torch. At the appointed hour he went down to the water's edge to give the arranged signal with the torch. He would see no lights from the boat, even supposing it was there. He waited on the shore, straining his ears until he heard the scrape of something broaching the shingle twenty metres or so from where he was standing. He walked in the direction of the sound. As he got closer, the familiarly insouciant voice of Lieutenant Smythson called out softly in English.

'One more for the *Skylark*, sir?'

Mrs Lamprey had cornered her in the kitchen and was recounting her memories of Ellen Terry. 'One of the greatest actresses ever, in my humble opinion. Such a beautiful voice, such command of language. I saw her with Sir Henry Irving in *Olivia* at the Lyceum once, long ago – 1885, I think it was, if I remember correctly. They were lovers offstage, of course. I heard her do the Mercy speech from *The Merchant* many times. You're familiar with the one, Mrs Hillyard – in the Trial scene?'

Before Barbara could answer, she had launched into it.

The quality of mercy is not strain'd,
It droppeth as the gentle rain from heaven
Upon the place beneath . . .

She walked about the kitchen, waving her arms – unstoppable to the end. 'She was John Gielgud's great-aunt, you know. Acting so often runs in the blood. Her sister, Marion, was also an actress but, like myself, she gave it all up to marry. And there were several other Terrys, as well . . . I remember that they all had terrible memories and were always drying up – even dear Ellen. I saw her as the Nurse when she was getting rather old and she could hardly remember a word. Romeo and Mercutio had to keep whispering every line in her ear. Fortunately, I never had any trouble myself. What is it for dinner tonight, Mrs Hillyard?'

'It's chicken.'

'*Chicken!* What a treat.'

One of the hens had grown too old to lay any more eggs and she had had to steel herself to do the deed, or rather to ask the butcher to do it. She had carried the bird down there in Fifi's carrier basket and it had squawked and flapped indignantly every step of the way. Collecting the pathetic and unrecognizable result later had been even worse and she had wept all the way back. The Rhode Island Red had been a good and faithful servant for a long time and it seemed a poor reward for it to end up in the pot and be eaten by Mrs Lamprey.

Mrs Lamprey had by no means finished her reminiscing. 'Of course, Eleonora Duse was generally considered to be the finest actress of her generation. I well remember her in *Ghosts* . . .' There was a quiet knock at the door. Mrs Lamprey halted in mid-sentence, turning. '*Monsieur Duval! Comme je suis heureuse de vous revoir.*'

'I also am happy to see you again, madame. And you, Madame Hillyard.'

Mrs Lamprey was clapping her hands. '*Quelle chance pour vous! Nous allons manger un poulet pour le dîner ce soir.*'

'And I have brought some wine that we can drink with the chicken. I have also brought a small present for you, Madame Lamprey.'

'*Pour moi?*' Mrs Lamprey opened the package at once and shrieked with delight. '*L'Heure Bleue! Quelle surprise! Merci beaucoup, monsieur.*'

There were more expressions of gratitude and pleasure, and enquiries from her about his trip to London. At last, he stemmed the flow politely.

'I have some business to discuss with Madame Hillyard. If you would excuse us.'

'Oh?' Her eyes darted to and fro. 'In that case, I'll leave you two alone.'

'Please, if you would, madame.' He held the door open.

She nudged him with her elbow. 'I know when I'm not wanted.'

He shut the door firmly after her. '*Eh bien, Madame Hillyard . . .*'

She was suddenly shy. Not sure what to say or what to do. Rooted to the spot.

'Well?'

She said softly, 'I'm so glad you're back.'

He smiled and shook his head. 'That won't do at all. Come here and show me exactly how glad you are.'

Later on, she told him about Freddie and began to weep yet more tears for her brother. He held her close.

'My poor one. Is there no hope for him?'

'They say there were no survivors. I suppose it was a U-boat.'

'It's very easy for them now that they can use the ports in France.'

She said sadly, 'Freddie was so dear to me. And all I had.'

'Not all,' he corrected her. 'Now you have me.'

He had brought her scent, too. Not Mrs Lamprey's kind but something else that he told her would suit her far better. But what risks had he taken to get it? Some black market deal, almost certainly, that could have got him into serious trouble.

At dinner that evening, he produced the bottles of wine and insisted that she join them in a glass. Mrs Lamprey, well doused in *L'Heure Bleue* and well fortified earlier with Stone's Original Green Ginger wine, had downed several in quick succession before getting unsteadily to her feet.

She brandished her glass in the general direction of his table. For once, her French had completely deserted her.

'Here's looking at you, Monsieur Duval,' she cackled. 'Mud in your eye!'

The rear admiral and Miss Tindall had also risen. Miss Tindall lifted her glass high with great dignity and a small, triumphant glance at Mrs Lamprey.

'*Vive la France!*'

Thirteen

Harry telephoned from London.

'I'd like to come down and meet this chap Duval. Go over everything. Can you set up a meeting, Alan?'

'When do you want it?'

'Friday. And let's have some time for you and I to have a bit of a chat privately together beforehand. We need to catch up.'

'I'll arrange it.'

'By the way, General de Gaulle wants to meet him too. I'm in two minds whether to let that happen. What do you think? We don't want the French pinching him from us.'

'We don't really have any right to keep him.'

'No, but we don't need to tell him about it, do we?'

Harry arrived by train two days later and Powell met him at Kingswear station. As they shook hands on the platform, the vivid image came into his mind of them both standing together on that same platform as raw young cadets years ago. Harry had clearly been thinking along similar lines. As they walked towards the car, he said, 'Haven't been down here for years, Alan. It takes me right back to the old days – makes me feel almost young again. Like we were. They were good times, weren't they?'

The men that were boys when I was a boy. 'Very good times.'

A Wren brought cups of coffee into his office and went out again. Harry stirred his sugar vigorously round and round with the spoon.

'I've got some rather splendid news, Alan. We'll be getting those radio transmitters quite soon.'

'About bloody time.'

'As you so rightly say, about bloody time. Which means that our agents will be able to stay over there for a decent period instead of popping back every so often. That's partly why I wanted to meet Duval. If we're going to go on using him, he'll need to be properly trained how to operate the damn things, as well as all the rest of it. I'd like to see for myself what he's like – before we go that far. He's something of an unknown quantity, after all. Bit of a wild card.'

'He's inexperienced at the job, but I'd say he was completely reliable.'

'He's certainly done a good job so far, I'll grant you that. That last little trip of his produced some interesting titbits. And he's recruiting a few quite useful people. Mostly small fry, of course, but they seem to have their wits about them. And it's all grist to the mill.'

331

'The information on the U-boat pens at Lorient was rather better than grist, I thought.'

'Yes, I'd like to ask him a bit more about that.'

'You read what his informant there had to say? He believes the pens should be attacked *now*, while they're still being built. That we shouldn't wait until they're finished. I think he's right. If the bunker concrete's going to be as thick as he says, bombing them later on might be completely useless. Like bouncing peas off a drum.'

'The fellow's an electrician, isn't he? With the best will in the world, he can't know much about the strength of concrete bunkers. He's not an expert and we need an expert opinion. The RAF can't just send their chaps off into the blue without a lot more facts and figures.' The coffee spoon went round and round again. 'Besides, I happen to know, Alan, that the Foreign Office are saying that on the grounds of humanity we shouldn't strike the land and people of a defeated France. We couldn't hit the Germans without hitting some French too. They're quite persuasive in their argument with the Chiefs of Staff.'

He said sharply, 'I think that's absolute nonsense. France has effectively become our enemy. Even Churchill says so. Look how their Vichy government is behaving.'

'But the Vichy lot don't represent the views of *all* the French, do they? By no means, and that's the sticky problem. Anyway, I've got another piece of news that you'll like. I've been pressing hard lately for something a bit faster than your fishing boats for you.'

'And?'

'Well, as we know, submarines are probably the best way of landing and picking up agents, but the difficulty is that they can seldom be spared unless they happen to be in the immediate area and, of course, it's damned hard to arrange for them to meet up with another boat that's under sail and dependent on the wind. High-speed motor torpedo boats have many advantages, I know you'll agree, and I have reason to believe that one may come our way very shortly, on loan from the Admiralty. One big snag, though, is we'd be stuck with using the north coast. The boats still don't have the speed or range to go further south. Not ideal, I know. Crawling with Germans and seas rough as hell, but there we go.'

They discussed the pros and cons of the high-speed boats for a while until Lieutenant Smythson arrived at the appointed hour with Louis Duval. The Frenchman came into the room and Powell introduced him and watched Harry greet him affably, pumping his hand and clapping him on the shoulder. He sensed, though, that Duval was well aware that he was under close scrutiny of some kind and was, therefore, on his guard. The Wren brought in more cups of coffee and he saw the way she blushed when Duval smiled at her and thanked her for his. He was lighting one of his Gauloises, leaning back in his chair, one leg crossed over the other, waiting quietly for whatever came next. For the first time in his life, Powell felt the miserable, gnawing pain of jealousy. Barbara was in love with this man. A Frenchman, with all the powerful attraction they apparently held for women – if Hattie was to be believed. *So different. From what? Well . . . from Englishmen.*

Harry was speaking. 'These people you've recruited, Mr Duval . . . admirable, in their limited way, of course, but you're aware, I'm sure, that we need harder facts.'

'Rome, as they say, was not built in a day, Commander Chilcot.'

'No, indeed.' Harry cleared his throat. 'Regarding the Lorient submarine bunker construction – you have another new contact working there now, I understand . . . a plumber by the assumed name of Léon?'

'That is correct.'

'What do you think he might achieve?'

A shrug that would annoy Harry. 'Who can say? He'll try his hardest, that's all.'

'Quite. You're of the opinion – it says so very specifically in your last report – that the U-boat bunkers at Lorient, and presumably elsewhere, should be attacked *now*, before they can be completed.'

'Later may be too late. It may prove quite impossible to destroy them.'

'But your theory is based on the view of an ordinary electrician. Hardly an expert opinion.

And you've never actually seen the bunkers yourself.'

'What do you expect from me, Commander? That I should go and ask one of the Todt Organization engineers? Do you think the RAF should bomb you now, or later?'

Harry smiled thinly. 'I appreciate the difficulties, Monsieur Duval. I'm sure you appreciate ours. We need a lot more technical information.'

'I'll do my best to get it for you.'

'So, you would be quite willing to return to France to continue your activities?'

'Certainly.'

'And, before you go, to undergo some rather special training here?'

'What sort of training?'

'On the assembly and operation of radio transmitters. How to send messages. How to receive them. Morse, coded messages. As well as various other things.'

'You have these radio transmitters at last?'

'We do. Or rather we will very soon.'

'And the proposal is for me to take one to France next time?'

'Assuming you complete the training course satisfactorily. It would mean a much bigger risk for you, of course. Rather tricky to explain away a transmitter to the Germans, if they happen to catch you with one. But, as you have pointed out yourself, considerably more effective than going backwards and forwards across the Channel.' Harry paused. He said casually, 'We'd rather like you to go on working for *us*, rather than for the Free French.'

'So far they haven't invited me.'

'They may. To speak frankly, before we invest considerable time and trouble in you, Mr Duval, we need to be able to count on your continued loyalty to our organization. You understand?'

'Perfectly.'

'So?'

'You can count on it, Commander. I imagine that I'll serve my country equally well, working for the British.'

'Possibly even better.' Harry stirred his coffee once again. 'By the way, General de Gaulle has asked to meet you. Lieutenant Commander Powell will arrange it for you, if you like.'

To his disappointment Mrs Lamprey opened the front door to him. 'Mrs Hillyard is out, Lieutenant Commander.' She opened the door wider, with a coy smile. 'But you can come in and wait, if you like. I don't expect she'll be long.'

He said briskly, 'Just for a few minutes.'

She took him into the sitting room and, to his irritation, showed every sign of staying. The cloying scent she wore smelled even stronger than usual and he thought from her behaviour that she was slightly tipsy.

'Monsieur Duval's not here either. He's gone to London to meet General de Gaulle.'

'Really? How interesting.' It was no surprise

since he had set up the meeting himself. The general, it seemed, was quite keen to meet Duval.

'Yes, isn't it? He's promised to tell us all about it when he gets back. We're very fond of him. All of us – *especially* Mrs Hillyard. They're having an affair, did you know?'

He said coldly, 'I hardly think that concerns either of us, Mrs Lamprey.'

'I've seen him going to her room at night . . . am I shocking you, Lieutenant Commander?'

'No.'

'It doesn't shock *me*. Not a bit. Those of us in the theatrical profession are *quite* used to that sort of thing.'

'Yes, I'm sure you are.'

She wagged a finger under his nose. 'You're in love with her yourself, aren't you?'

He stepped back one pace. 'I'd prefer not to discuss Mrs Hillyard at all, if you don't mind.'

'Ah, but I know you are. I can tell. *She* doesn't realize, though. Hasn't a clue. All she can see is *him*. Frenchmen know exactly how to treat women, that's the thing.'

'I expect they do.' It was the last thing he wanted to hear.

The finger wagged again. 'Mind you, Englishmen have their good points as well. Only they're not so obvious. I think the most attractive man I ever met was Gerald du Maurier. Did you ever see him on the stage?'

'I'm afraid not.'

'You should have seen him as Raffles. He

was simply wonderful. And, of course, he played Bulldog Drummond to perfection . . .'

For the next fifteen minutes he endured more theatrical reminiscences until, at last, he heard the front door opening. He went out into the hall, deserting Mrs Lamprey. Barbara had come in, carrying a full shopping basket.

She looked at him hopefully. 'Is there any news – about Freddie?'

He shook his head, wishing so much that there were. 'I'm afraid not. I just came by to see how you were.' Mrs Lamprey, he knew, would be listening avidly to every word.

'How kind of you, Alan. I'm quite all right, thank you. How are you?'

'Fine . . . just fine.' He stared at her, remembering exactly how it had felt to hold her close in his arms. How his uniform had been wet from her tears. How he had dried them for her with his handkerchief. 'Well, I'd better be getting along, then.'

'Thank you so much for coming.'

He went to the front door and opened it. 'Just let me know if there's anything I can ever do for you.'

It was ironical, Duval thought, that, for the first time, his story of going to London was perfectly true. The prospect of meeting the general intrigued him. He was rumoured to be aloof and arrogant; a cold man and humourless. Before the war he had had a reputation as a fine soldier and clever strategist, and when France had been attacked he had acquitted himself with courage and honour. Then he had fled to London and the Free French had made him their leader. To the Vichy government, to remain in France was proof of honour and patriotism, and de Gaulle was a traitor, sentenced to death in his absence.

He took a taxi from Paddington station to the address he had been given in Westminster. On the journey he saw the destruction everywhere by the German bombers, but he also saw a very different city from Paris. London made him think of an indomitable old lady who had been set upon by thugs but had picked herself up, dusted down her skirts and was carrying on regardless, bearing her scars and bruises with pride; Paris had been like a beautiful woman, outwardly still beautiful but mortally wounded in her heart.

St Stephen's House was a rather dingy redbrick building – a disappointing place for the headquarters of Free France. A man in some kind of blue uniform took him up to the third floor in a shaky lift to join a queue of other French civilians and servicemen. Over an hour passed before a lieutenant conducted him into a room overlooking the Thames. The general, a very tall man, rose from behind a desk and shook his hand. Duval was invited to sit, offered a cigarette; the ashtray on the desk, he noticed, was overflowing with stubs. He listened to a short, clipped speech of congratulation on his efforts in France.

'I understand that you are working with the English?'

'I am working with the English, *mon Général*, but I am fighting for France.'

The general nodded. 'We French in exile must never forget that. France has lost a battle, but she has not lost a war. We fight on. One accepts England as an ally and partner, but we must never be her servant. Nor should we ever be her bosom friend. The destinies of our two countries are not the same and never have been.' A cigarette was put out, another lit. 'I have requested the British that you report to me in person what you have seen and learned each time you return from France. Other than that, I have no objection to your continuing to work with them, if you so wish.'

He said, 'I feel a certain sense of obligation to do so. Of honour, perhaps.'

Another curt nod. 'Very well. But before you leave, I should like to present you with the emblem of the Free French – the Cross of Lorraine – to wear with pride.'

Duval rose while the general pinned a small metal brooch to his lapel. They shook hands once more and the lieutenant showed him to the door. As he went out he glanced back to see that de Gaulle had moved to the window and was standing looking out at the river. The tall, imperious figure, caught in beaky profile against the light, was unforgettable. He had the odd feeling that he was looking at France herself.

He took another taxi to the railway station, and as he gave the destination, Waterloo, to the driver, reflected wryly on the English habit of annoying the French at every opportunity. Naming the station after a French defeat was on a par with deliberately mispronouncing French words: beauchamp, belvoir, beaulieu – all anglicized beyond recognition. The train carried him out into the countryside and yet another taxi – an ancient vehicle more like a hearse – took him up a long gravel drive to one of those pleasant, ivy-covered English country houses built at the turn of the century, complete with dripping shrubbery, croquet lawn, tennis court, lake – all in the middle of nowhere.

There, in the company of others far younger than himself, he spent the next weeks learning about the workings of a radio transmitter, about sending and receiving, coding and decoding. As Commander Chilcot had promised, he also learned various other things – some of which struck him as childish games, like writing invisible messages and wearing disguises. Others, such as self-defence and how to kill a German quickly and silently with bare hands, seemed highly practical.

He also discovered how woefully unfit he was: overweight, flabby, short of breath, incapable of any prolonged or extreme physical exertion. The doctor who examined him advised him to give up smoking, which, naturally, he declined. He also politely turned down the suggestion of giving up drinking and going on a diet. All that was really required, he decided, was to carry on doing much as he had already been doing in France without it being noticed by the Germans. There was no necessity for him to be able to run five miles without collapsing. In the evenings he escaped from his prison and the terrible canteen food and walked to the nearest village, where the landlord of the Horse and Groom still had some bottles of French wine in his cellar, and the landlord's wife took pity on his offended stomach and cooked him an excellent supper.

On the phone, Harry sounded satisfied. 'He seems to have done reasonably well, Alan. Pretty hopeless on the PT front, I gather, but then he's a lot older than the rest. One wouldn't expect much there. Kept scampering off to the local pub.'

'I can't say I blame him.'

'Nor I. Those places are hell. No booze and school food. Not his sort of thing at all. He's not bad with the unarmed combat and perfectly all right so far as the R/T procedure is concerned, which is the main thing. We're not the SOE, asking him to rush around France blowing things up, thank God.'

'So, how soon do you think he can go back?'

'We'll wait till we can send him over by the MTB. There'll be two other agents with him, as well. Another week or two, I'd say. You'll have to go for a moonless night, obviously. Leave in the dark and be back in the dark. As I said, it'll have to be a landing somewhere on the northern coast, unfortunately.'

Powell said, 'We'll need a first-class navigator with pinpoint accuracy. That stretch can be treacherous – absolutely murderous in winter. I'd like to be on board for the trip, Harry. Make sure everything goes smoothly.'

'I don't think that's such a good idea, Alan. Your place is on shore, doing your job at HQ.'

He said stubbornly, 'I'd still like to go.'

'Hmm.' A long pause. 'All right, then.'

Christmas had passed quietly. The butcher had miraculously conjured up a joint of beef and Barbara had made a pudding from saved-up dried fruit and carrots and stale breadcrumbs that had worked quite well. The rear admiral had presented a bottle of wine, which Mrs Lamprey had drunk most of, and Miss Tindall had scoured the hedgerows for holly and ivy. Mrs Lamprey had contributed a bunch of mistletoe from the greengrocer's – largely, Barbara suspected, in the hope that Monsieur Duval would be back. Esme's father had sent a long letter and a present for her: a beautiful foreign doll dressed in Chinese clothes.

On Christmas Day, she took Esme to church and Miss Tindall and the rear admiral accompanied them, leaving Mrs Lamprey treating a chill with her patent remedy of hot ginger wine. Alan Powell was in the next pew and afterwards she stopped to talk to him by the lychgate. She didn't ask about Louis Duval or when he might be back. Nobody asked such questions in wartime. Instead, they talked about the church service and the cold weather and he enquired after the kittens. Then Mrs Shapleigh had come up and started to talk about the WVS canteen.

New Year's Eve came and 1941 began. The kittens grew and grew. Fifi had brought them down from the airing cupboard, carrying each one in her mouth by the scruff of its neck, and they now lived in a cardboard box in a corner of the kitchen. Before long they had started to jump out and Esme spent hours playing with them.

Late one afternoon the doorbell rang. When she opened the door Louis was standing there.

'I'm so sorry,' he said. 'I forgot to take my key away with me.'

At dinner that evening, Mrs Lamprey wanted to hear all about General de Gaulle.

'*Est-il beau?*'

'One could not say that he was handsome, but he's very remarkable. Once seen, one would not forget him.'

Her sharp eyes noticed the little brooch. '*C'est une médaille, monsieur?*'

'*Non, madame.* It's the badge of the Free French. The Cross of Lorraine.'

That night, lying beside him with his arm about her, she asked when he would have to go away again.

344

'Not for a while, I think. But next time it may be for much longer.'

She watched the glow of his cigarette. 'It's dangerous, isn't it? Very dangerous.'

'What is dangerous?'

'Whatever you do when you go away. I'm so afraid for you.'

'There is no need to be.'

There was every need, she thought.

Out of the darkness Louis said, 'When this war is over and France is free again, will you come and live with me there? In France?'

'If you want me to.'

'I want you to very much. Will you live with me, Barbara? For always?'

'Of course.'

'You understand that we could not be married? Simone, my wife, would never divorce me because of the Catholic religion.'

'I understand. And I don't care.' She curled closer to him. 'Where would we go?'

'Wherever you like.' The cigarette glowed again. 'To the south, perhaps, where the weather is good. Somewhere in Provence, maybe – St Paul or Vallauris. We could find a nice old house. One that pleases you. Make it good for us. A good home. Fifi could come too. She'd like that, so long as the Germans had gone.'

He went away less than two weeks afterwards. She was in the kitchen, talking to a woman who had come to see the kittens. The woman couldn't make up her mind whether to have a black one, or a tabby. She kept picking each one up and then putting it down again.

'Oh, dear, they're all so sweet. I just can't decide.'

He spoke to her urgently from the doorway. 'I have to leave now, madame.' It was always *madame* in front of others. 'They have sent a car for me.'

The woman was still undecided. 'Which one do you think has the best temperament, Mrs Hillyard? They say in all the books that that's the most important thing. Now, this little black one seems a bit nervous . . .'

'Would you excuse me a moment?' She went over to him. 'Can you wait?'

He shook his head. 'I'm sorry. I must go at once.' He took her hand, kissed it quickly and pressed something into her palm. 'Keep this safe for me.' She listened to the front door closing and the sound of the car driving away down the hill. He had given her the Cross of Lorraine brooch, the emblem of the Free French.

Behind her the woman said, 'Of course, I really would prefer the ginger one, you know.'

Fourteen

The motor torpedo boat slipped away from her moorings at twenty hundred hours on a cold and moonless January night. She made her way slowly and quietly downstream towards the open sea. The captain, first lieutenant and the crew of eighteen were all considerably younger than Powell himself and he felt like an old man among them. The destination was Bonaparte beach, to the west of St Malo. As Powell well knew, the north Breton coast was a notoriously unforgiving place for mariners. Even the names were sinister: the Channel of Great Fear, the Bay of the Dead, the Hell of Plogoff. The tide sweeping into the St Malo Bay could reach a height of forty feet, and when the wind blew hard the battering-ram effect of the sea was tremendous. Bonaparte beach had been selected as seeming the best out of a poor choice, but there was still plenty to worry about: currents, rocks, cliffs, German patrols, permanent and occasional sentry posts, possible new gun emplacements.

Louis Duval and the two other agents kept out

of sight below decks but Powell stayed on the bridge, revelling in the experience of being back at sea again. The pitching and rolling that began as soon as they had left the lee of the land was natural to him. His sea legs had never deserted him and the deskbound years slid away, as though they had never been.

He had taken the briefing before departure, covering the expected weather, the state of the tide, all the hazards of the low-lying rocky coastline, the need for absolute blackout and silence off the French shores. He had indicated the exact spot on the chart to which the navigator was expected, without the aid of lighthouses, lightbuoys, land-based navigation or radar, to find his way precisely. The young sub lieutenant specially assigned to this daunting task had seemed unfazed. The MTB was to anchor off the beach while a boat was lowered with two men to row the landing party ashore. The boat would then return, be hauled back on board and the MTB would return to England. It sounded straightforward enough but was very unlikely to be any such thing. An accurate landfall was crucial, for a start.

Powell went down the ladder to take a look in the cramped chart room under the ship's bridge. If the young sub lieutenant, wedged firmly against his table in order to stay on his feet, got things even slightly wrong they could spend valuable time hunting along the coast for the right beach – hampered by the fact that they would have to reduce speed and engine noise drastically, so close to France. The sub lieutenant was working away under his red-painted light bulb, the chart table spattered with the rusty salt water, the colour of weak Bovril, that kept cascading down from the bridge voice-pipe overhead.

After a time he left him to it and went back to the bridge. The MTB was wet, cold and uncomfortable and once out of port the entire ship's company, with the old-fashioned exception of himself, had put on a variety of clothing to combat the elements – seaboots, heavy jerseys, scarves, and the like. The clandestine voyage across the Channel to the enemy French coast in the darkness of night had a touch of the Scarlet Pimpernel about it.

The weather worsened. The gunboat's flared bow lifted high with each wave to slam down hard into the troughs and roll heavily to port, before the next wave lifted it up again. Speed had to be reduced to twelve knots. They pressed on until the swell was on their beam, the motion eased and they could increase to fifteen knots.

After six hours, they were ten miles off the coast of France and reduced speed to eight knots, to cut the sound and the boat's wash and the telltale phosphorescence. Through night glasses Powell could just make out the black shadow of the land, lying low and almost indistinguishable from the sea. He climbed down again to the wheelhouse. The navigator had the large-scale chart out now and was plotting with his stopwatch and checking each bearing he was given. He glanced up once briefly, smiled and nodded.

Back on the bridge, Powell watched the coast coming closer. There were no enemy lights showing. No gun flashes, or sounds from the shore. The sub lieutenant brought them in exactly off Bonaparte beach and they dropped anchor three-quarters of a mile away, using a silent coir-grass rope instead of a normal anchor chain. The surf boat, roped at each end, was rolled over the side and lowered quietly into the sea, and two seamen climbed down to take the muffled oars. Nobody spoke; it had all been rehearsed many times before. The three agents had come on deck. As Duval passed him, carrying the small suitcase that contained the radio transmitter, Powell shook his hand firmly.

He watched the surf boat through his binoculars as it headed for the beach, until it was lost to sight against the darkness of the land.

By the time they reached the shore they were well drenched by the waves breaking over the boat, and the process of disembarking from boat to beach involved another wetting. Without the need for silence, Duval would have been cursing aloud and furiously. As the surf boat left on its journey back to the MTB, the three of them – himself, another Frenchman, Pierre Galliou, and an Englishman, Charles Hunter – made their way across the beach, keeping a safe distance from the nearest German watch post up on the cliffs to the east. The hamlet of Keruzeau was less than a kilometre inland and they walked to the cottage there belonging to the sister of Galliou and her husband. Duval and the Englishman waited outside while Galliou roused his sister and brother-in-law from their beds. Presently he came back. His sister was willing to shelter them, his brother-in-law less so, but they could take refuge in the cottage attic for the rest of the night until the following day. After that they must leave. The whole area, apparently, was thick with German troops.

They stripped off their outer clothes and lay down on the bare boards, wrapped in the blankets that Galliou's sister had charitably pro-vided. The crossing, spent below decks, had been extremely unpleasant. Both Galliou and Hunter had been seasick, the Englishman violently so, and he had been on the verge of the same himself. The night air had revived him, but the drenching had produced its own discomfort. The attic was freezing, the boards hard, the blankets thin and the rafters above were, apparently, home to a large colony of bats. Sleep was impossible for him, though soon he could hear Galliou snoring. Hunter, who spoke faultless French, talked for a while before he, too, fell asleep. Duval lay cold, stiff and aching until the grey light of dawn began to filter through the shutter slats.

The sister brought up hot coffee, bread and a little cheese. She was a good woman – anxious to

351

help but more than a little afraid. Duval could see that she wanted them to be gone.

The radio transmitter, concealed in a false compartment at the bottom of his suitcase, seemed undamaged by the wetting. He replaced it carefully after he had examined it and covered the compartment lid again with the clothing, the French cigarettes and the sketch pad and chalks that he had brought with him. As arranged, they left the cottage one at a time – a gap of an hour between departures. Each was travelling in a different direction: Galliou across to the Finistère region, Hunter to Normandy, himself to Paris. It was unlikely that they would meet again.

He walked to the nearest railway station and caught the next train going in the direction of Paris. There were plenty of German troops around but none paid him, or his suitcase, much attention. There were some advantages, he thought wryly, in being his age. Vigorous young men of military years were dismissive of anyone so old. They looked through you, rather than at you. You held no interest and posed no threat – or so they thought.

In the train compartment which he shared with two Wehrmacht soldiers, he passed the journey chewing on a garlic clove given to him by Galliou's sister, and watched them edge away.

He changed onto another train going direct to the capital and slept for the rest of the journey. At Paris he booked into a small hotel in Montmartre. The Germans, he knew, would expect an artist to stay there, and as it happened it suited him. He planned to keep well away from both Simone and Gerard Klein – Simone because of her SS lover and Gerard because he had no wish to implicate him in any way. He spent a month in the city, meeting with his contacts there, as well as recruiting new ones – adding to the growing spider's web of agents. Any important information he transmitted in code to London from his hotel room. Occasionally, for verisimilitude, he made sketches of Montmartre scenes, and curious German soldiers would come and peer over his shoulder and nod and make approving noises.

He spent several agreeable evenings at *Le Petit Coin* where Michel the *patron* regaled him with Occupation anecdotes. There was, it seemed, no shortage of collaborators among the Parisian rich and famous – actors and actresses, singers, entertainers, writers, artists, film-makers and high society who had found it more convenient and to their advantage to be friendly with the Germans. Duval listened grimly to the long list and to the large number of women of Michel's acquaintance who were known to be *collabos horizontals* – to which he could have added the name of his own wife. And the city was awash with *indicateurs*, informants who eagerly denounced their fellow men, and with *corbeaux*, the crow-like writers of poison-pen letters. Jews were always the favourite target. Mademoiselle Citron was far from alone in her desire for personal revenge.

'But, thank God,' Michel assured him, 'there

are still plenty of us in Paris who aren't like this. There's not much we can do, but at least we can ignore the Germans. We don't speak to them, we don't help them, we won't tell them the way, we won't even give them a light for their cigarettes. Silence is our only weapon but it's a good one.'

On one of his visits, he saw the truth of this when two young Wehrmacht officers happened to enter the café in search of a meal and everybody immediately stopped talking and eating. In the total silence and stillness that followed, the two of them stood awkwardly by the door as the silence lengthened. No-one looked at them, no-one moved, no-one made a sound. After a while, the Germans turned and left.

Before he left Paris, he telephoned Simone. She sounded exasperated.

'Where are you *now*, Louis? You never seem to be at the studio. I can never contact you there.'

'I move around. I visited Aunt Pauline in Rennes not so long ago.'

'That old battleaxe! Whatever for?'

He said mildly, 'For old times' sake. She seemed pleased to see me.'

'Well, she always liked you. She hated me.'

He didn't bother to deny it. 'Is the bank paying the allowance on time?'

'They were five days late last month. That's why I was trying to get hold of you.'

'I'll have another word with them. How are things otherwise?'

'As you'd expect. Not easy.'

'Trouble with the Germans?'

'Not exactly. I told you, everything is in short supply.'

'But you're managing?' he said drily.

'Yes, I'm managing. I look after myself. I have to.'

'Of course you do, Simone.'

The next day he went by train to Orléans, the suitcase stowed in the luggage rack above his head. There was an inspection of tickets and papers by German railway police but all his were in perfect order. The suitcase was left unsearched.

At Orléans he stayed in another small and insignificant hotel and set about spinning the spider's web still larger. One of the contacts in Paris had given him a useful name. He met the man in a side-street café and they talked at a table in the corner. At first, the man was far from willing.

'You are asking me to work for the *English*?'

'No, for France.'

'I must make something very plain to you, monsieur. I am a royalist. I don't recognize the Republic of France. You may work for who you wish, but I shall be working for the rightful King of France who will one day be restored to his throne.'

What did the cause matter, Duval thought, so long as the aim was the same?

He spent another week in Orléans before continuing south-west to Tours where he called on his sister. It was more than six years since he had seen Albertine and he knew very well that any pleasure she might have felt at their meeting would be spoiled for her by worrying how her husband, Henri, would react. As soon as he had embraced her, he set her mind at rest.

'I'm calling by, that's all. Just to see how you are.'

He left the suitcase in the hall and she showed him formally into the pin-neat parlour where they sat on uncomfortable chairs and made polite conversation – more like strangers than brother and sister. He asked after her two children, though their names escaped him. Marcel, she told him, was now married with a baby and had followed in Henri's respectable footsteps, working at the town hall. Claudette was not yet married and had a job as a pharmacist. He remembered his nephew as a carbon copy of his father, and his niece as gawky and plain. His sister looked much older than when he had last seen her. He wondered if her dowdy, depressed look was a consequence of spending more than twenty-five years in company with the purse-lipped, pince-nez-wearing Henri, or if it was simply in her nature. They were seven years apart in age – she the younger – and so far as he could recall there had never been a single thing in common. She had no more understanding of his work or his life than he had of hers.

The talk, inevitably, turned to the Occupation, and to the Vichy government.

'Henri says that it's the duty of us all to do as

Marshal Pétain tells us – to accept the German victory and to continue to work as usual. Getting back to normal is patriotic. France should not resist. It's not in her interest.'

'I see. And what do *you* think, my dear Albertine?'

She looked at him, baffled. 'Me? I agree with Henri, of course.'

'Does Marcel also agree with his father?'

'Certainly. Claudette doesn't, though. She believes quite differently. She and her father have many arguments. It's just as well that she no longer lives here with us.'

His niece came by after work and he studied her with renewed interest. She was indeed plain, just as he remembered, but he saw now that there was a certain air about her – a fearless look. Whereas others might keep their eyes lowered to the ground to avoid encountering those of the occupiers, she, he imagined, would hold her head up to engage them directly. And she was a qualified pharmacist – clearly intelligent.

He left before his brother-in-law returned, sparing his sister the embarrassment of a confrontation. His niece left at the same time and they walked down the cobbled street together.

He said, 'It's been a long time since we last met.'

She smiled slightly. 'My father would like it to be for ever. According to him, you live a life of total debauchery and decadence.'

'If only it were so.'

'He believes you spend your time painting naked women and seducing them.'

'Alas, not *all* my time.' They passed a café and she accepted his offer of a drink. She also accepted a cigarette. Henri, he felt sure, would have approved of neither. He lit the Gauloise for her. 'Your mother tells me that you don't always agree with your father's views – for example, on Marshal Pétain's exhortations to all patriotic Frenchmen to work hard for the Germans.'

She drew on the cigarette, flapping the smoke aside irritably. 'That old man talks shit. So does my father. Plenty of people in Tours think just the opposite.'

'Really?' he said. 'How interesting. Tell me more.'

Powell caught sight of Barbara in the distance, putting up her umbrella against the rain as she emerged from the bank in Dartmouth. He crossed the road and made sure that their paths met. A pointless exercise, but he couldn't help himself. She looked up at him from under the umbrella, startled but not, he thought, too dismayed to see him, and when he suggested some tea in the Castle hotel close by she seemed perfectly willing. Considering the way the wind was blowing and the rain lashing the quayside, he thought it wasn't such a bad idea himself. Inside it was at least dry, and a good deal warmer than out. He took off his cap and shed his wet greatcoat. There was even a log fire burning and a table close beside it. He ordered tea and scones from the waitress.

She took off her gloves, looking round. 'Do you know, I've never been in here.'

'My parents used to stay when they came down to visit me at the College.'

'Then it must hold a lot of memories for you.'

'Yes, it does.' He thought fondly of his mother, elegantly dressed in the ankle-length gowns of those pre-Great War days, a spectacular hat and, always, her many-stranded choker of pearls, after the fashion of the Princess of Wales. And he thought of his father, straight-backed and handsome – the admiral who had expected an equally high rank from his son and concealed his disappointment well. He had been very lucky with his parents.

'How are the kittens?' It was a safe subject.

She smiled. 'I've found homes for all except the ginger one. He's staying until Esme can take him home with her one day.'

'I'm sure she's pleased about that.'

'Yes, she is. And she's so much easier now. I'll be very sorry to lose her when the time comes.'

He thought, watching her, what a marvellous mother she'd make and how much he'd like to be the father.

The tea and scones arrived, with jam too. She poured out his tea for him, which inevitably led to more daydreaming on his part. He knew that she must be wondering if he had heard any news of Louis Duval, though, equally, he knew that she would never ask him. Not that he could have told her much. London had received certain messages and Duval was known to be in Tours. He hoped, for his sake, that the weather was better over there.

By the time he left Tours, Duval had set up a small but dedicated resistance cell in the area with Claudette in charge. It was a nice irony, he thought, considering her father's views. She thought so too.

He went on to Nantes where an old friend of his – also an artist, had lived for years. Lucien and his wife, Denise, gave him a warm welcome, a good supper, a great deal of wine and offered a bed for the night. He had no intention of trying to recruit Lucien – he was a good man but much too fond of the bottle to be reliable. However, before the level of the nightcap brandy had sunk too low, he steered the conversation away from trivial gossip to the subject of U-boats.

Lucien raised his eyebrows. 'U-boats? What of them?'

'They say the Germans are busily building bunkers for them all along this coast.'

'We heard something of the kind, or rather Denise did. She was queuing at the butcher's and the woman in front of her was going on about it.'

'What did she say?'

Lucien shrugged. 'I didn't listen properly. You'll have to ask her in the morning. She'll be asleep by now, snoring away.'

He had Denise to himself at breakfast since Lucien was doing his share of the snoring. Yes, she told him, the woman in front of her in the butcher's queue last week had told her that her husband, a builder, had been made to work for the Germans. He was very upset about it, and so was she, but what could one do? If you refused, they shot you. He had been put to work on some concrete bunkers to house German submarines over at St Nazaire. A great big construction with room for a fleet of U-boats. How many? She hadn't asked – it was depressing to talk about such things. Night and day they were being made to work. What else had the woman said? Just that. It wasn't so much the U-boats the woman had cared about, it was the idea of her husband having to work like a dog for the filthy Boche and for a pittance. No, she had no idea of the woman's name. She had never set eyes on her before. She was just another one in a very long queue – two hours or more for a minuscule piece of tough beef.

In April Duval was back in Lorient. Ernest Boitard, his wife informed him on the telephone, had been sent elsewhere to work and she refused to say where that was. It might, or might not have been true, but the certain thing was that Boitard had reached the end of his tether and would do no more. Duval contacted Léon and arranged to meet at the same café as before. He arrived earlier than the appointed time and settled himself at the same table with a newspaper to read and a Cinzano to drink. The two old men with their blackened pipes were at their table again, apparently engrossed in their game of dominoes. Nobody seemed to take any notice of him, but he knew his presence was being observed.

Léon was ten minutes late. He went straight to the bar and brought his glass of calvados over to the table; under his arm he carried a newspaper. He was wearing an old belted raincoat and with his little moustache and slick dark hair the resemblance to Hitler was remarkable. The plumber sat down on the opposite side of the table, placing the newspaper beside him.

'You have a light, please, monsieur?'

'Certainly.' He leaned forward to oblige.

'Thank you. Well, I have something of great interest for you.'

'Is that so?'

'Something of vital importance.'

'And what is that?'

Léon lowered his voice. 'Drawings.'

'Drawings? Of what?'

'Of the Keroman U-boat pens. Specifications. Drawings for their construction. Measurements. Distances. All details.'

He didn't believe him. 'And how did you come by these drawings?'

'I stole them.'

He said coolly, 'Really? Didn't the Germans notice?'

'No. I only took them overnight. I had them

traced and took them back the next morning.' Léon swigged down some calvados. 'You see, I happened to be working near this office and I knew the man in it was important – a construction engineer, or some such, with the Toldt Organization. Big office, big desk, and so on. Then one day he was ill – so ill that he had to stop his work suddenly and go away. I watched him leave, groaning and holding his stomach, and he forgot to lock the door. So, later, I took my bag of tools and went in there and pretended to work on the heating pipes. I told you, nobody takes any notice of a plumber. If necessary I could have made the pipes leak, so I wasn't too worried.'

Duval still doubted that there was any truth in the story. 'What then?'

'From where I was pretending to work I saw the drawings lying on the desk – several of them, one on top of the other – and I could tell the sort of thing they were. I could read the words printed in big red letters on the top one: *Sonderzeichungen – Streng Geheim*. Special Blueprint – Top Secret.' Léon spread out his hands expressively – workworn, grimy hands with dirty nails. 'At first, I didn't know what to do. I went on tapping away at the pipes and thinking to myself that I must take this chance . . . somehow I must find the courage to do something. Somehow I had to.' He looked at Duval proudly. 'And in the end, I did.'

'Did what exactly?'

'I went away and fetched a length of piping. Then I took the drawings off the table – rolled them up very carefully and slid them inside the pipe. And I left the room and went back to my work nearby. When it was time to go, I walked out with them inside the pipe under my arm.'

'Surely they searched it?'

Léon shook his head. 'They were busy with somebody else much more important. A plumber is nobody, you see. And he is always carrying such things – tools, buckets, plungers, pipes. It looks natural for him.'

'And you took these drawings home?'

'No, I took them to the house of a friend. A draughtsman. He worked all night, tracing each one on thin paper. Then I rolled the drawings up again and returned them to the pipe and in the morning, when I went to work, I replaced them on the desk, exactly as they had been. The engineer was still away ill and no-one saw me. Nobody knows.'

Duval was still uncertain whether to believe him. He said slowly, 'And where are these tracings now?'

Léon indicated the newspaper lying on the table beside his glass. 'In there.'

He transmitted to London that evening from his hotel room, urgently requesting to be picked up and returned to England. Leaving the café, he had simply swopped newspapers with Léon and it wasn't until he had reached his room that he had been able to see for himself that the plumber had been speaking the truth. The tracings were there, folded over and sandwiched neatly between the pages. He had gone through them quickly, the German words leaping out at him: *sofort-program* – highest priority construction; *bunker, blockhaus, kanal, kai, trockendock, werkstatt* . . .

In the morning he caught the train to Pont-Aven. It was very cold for April and the few customers *Chez Alphonse* had kept their coats on. Alphonse was mortified.

'The boiler has broken down, monsieur, and we have no heating. There is no spare part to mend it. It's a tragedy. I can offer you some *potage paysanne* to keep you warm and there is a *filet de boeuf garni* but I have to confess that there is almost no meat in it. However, there is still some wine, I'm happy to say – specially for you, monsieur. I have still managed to save. Thank God, the summer is not far away.'

He ate with the suitcase propped against his chair leg and the newspaper beside him which, from time to time, he pretended to read. At the end of the meal, when the other customers had gone, Alphonse returned to the table with two small glasses of cognac.

'Not the best, I'm sorry to say, but it's the only kind that's left.' He sat down and raised his glass. 'Your good health, monsieur. How is it going with you? I haven't seen you for some time.'

He lifted his glass in response. 'Not so bad, thank you. But I need your help, Alphonse.'

'My help? Certainly. What can I do for you?'

'I need to hide something – just for a little while – but in a very safe place. Somewhere our friends, the Germans, would never think of looking. Is there anywhere in here?'

'How big is this thing?'

'The size of a newspaper. This one.'

Alphonse stared at it, bewildered. 'So much trouble for a newspaper . . . and a week old at least, by the look of it.'

'It's very important that it's not found, you understand?'

Alphonse shrugged. 'If you say so, monsieur. You have your good reasons, no doubt, and with the Boche one cannot be too careful. Let me think for a moment.' He frowned and then his brow cleared. 'I have just the place. The broken-down boiler. It's in the basement. The Germans are very fussy, you know. Very fastidious. They'd never dream that anyone would hide anything of importance in such a filthy, dirty place. And if they should see an old newspaper they will think it's there simply for burning, though heaven knows when the boiler will be working again.'

Mademoiselle Citron came out of her room as soon as he entered the hall, carrying his suitcase. She must spend nearly all her day at her window looking onto the street, he decided.

'You have returned, monsieur?'

'Clearly, mademoiselle.' He continued towards the stairs.

'Major Winter was enquiring after you. I told him that I had no idea where you were, but I thought you would be bound to be back soon.'

'Did you indeed?'

'Yes, it has become your habit. To come and to go.'

He turned from the stairs to see her looking up at him in her malevolent way; this time, he thought, tinged even more unpleasantly with something else. Something he could not define. 'Well, now you can inform the major of my return.'

He went on up to his studio. It was very cold, though not as cold as *Chez Alphonse*. He coaxed some lukewarm heat from the radiators. All he could do now was wait to receive the answer from London. In the evening he switched on the wireless and tuned into the BBC French language news bulletin. Among the personal messages read out afterwards was the one he was hoping to hear. *Les narcisses sont en fleur.* The MTB would leave England the following night to pick him up. First thing in the morning he would collect the newspaper from its hiding place. He would take the train across Brittany – a journey that could easily take all day with changes and delays – to St Brieuc, which would bring him within a few easy kilometres of the Bonaparte beach and the rendezvous with the boat.

He poured a cognac and lit another cigarette

and sat down to listen to some of his records: a Beethoven symphony, some Berlioz, a few soothing Liszt piano pieces. He half-expected Major Winter to knock on the door and almost welcomed the idea of a little civilized conversation to pass the time. Perhaps even another bottle of Courvoisier? But when the knock came – much later and in the middle of the night when he was in bed asleep – it wasn't the major in his smart grey Wehrmacht uniform. The visitor wore a civilian raincoat and a soft brown hat. He knew at once who he was. A member of the *Geheime Staats Polizei*: the Gestapo.

Fifteen

Harry had been very reluctant to take the risk of sending an MTB with barely enough hours of darkness available to provide effective cover.

'We don't know what Duval's on about. The message didn't give us a clue. It could be all about nothing – you know how excitable the French can be. No sense of proportion.'

'I don't believe he's like that. I think his judgement is very sound. When he says it's of vital importance, it is. A fishing boat would take far too long to fetch him back.'

In the end he'd won and there had not been so much difficulty, this time, in persuading Harry that he should go across too, and that Lieutenant Smythson could be a useful addition to the party.

'Well, it's your show, Alan. You'd better be the one to make damn certain it works.'

It was somewhat ironic, he thought, that he should be so determined to bring back a man he wished anywhere but in Dartmouth. The last information they had received from Duval had stated that he was returning to Pont-Aven to wait for the broadcast confirmation of the pickup. Providing he had been able to get from there to the rendezvous at Bonaparte beach in time and on time, everything should go according to plan. Harry was quite right, of course. The big danger lay in the shorter nights: if he wasn't there, they couldn't wait around to be spotted at dawn by the Germans. By daylight they had to be at least thirty miles away from the French coast.

There was only a moderate westerly swell and for most of the crossing they made a steady fifteen knots, creeping up to eighteen when the wind eased off and the sea became calmer. He had begun to feel that luck was with them when a faulty fuel pump caused an engine breakdown. By the time it had been repaired, much precious time had been lost. Some way off the coast the lookout reported a light flashing from the direction of St Malo which almost certainly meant enemy shipping in the area. Another hazard. They watched the light flash intermittently for a while before it stopped.

The same young sub lieutenant navigated them accurately to the spot where they had dropped anchor before. No signal could be sent to the shore, but it had been pre-arranged that Duval should flash an agreed Morse code letter with a hand-torch. Nothing could be seen: no signal of any kind from the darkness of the shore. After waiting another ten minutes, Powell decided to go ahead with the landing, in the hope that Duval would have arrived at the beach meanwhile. The surf boat was rolled silently over the side and he took Smythson along, with two of the crew at the oars. He had calculated that they would now have only fifteen minutes left to stay on the beach.

They reached the shore. There was no sign of Duval or, so far as they could tell, of any Germans. Powell walked in one direction while Smythson went off in the other. He had reached the furthest end and turned to go back when he saw a light coming onto the beach. His first thought was that it must be Duval and then he dismissed the idea: the Frenchman was certainly not that careless and his signalling would have been from a small hand-torch. This light, from a large and powerful lamp, came steadily towards his end of the beach, sweeping to and fro, and now he could hear the crunch of boots and, as they drew nearer, the sound of German voices and, still more chillingly, the savage bark of a dog.

He retreated into the shelter of some sand dunes while the night patrol went past and then back the other way, the dog straining on its lead. As soon as they saw the light the surf boat crew would have rowed away from the shore. Lieutenant Smythson, he reckoned, could look after himself. The dog, he realized, knew they were there and barked its warning several more times. All might still have been well if the German patrol had not stayed. They stopped and put down the lamp. He could hear them talking, see the flare of matches lighting cigarettes. Occasionally the dog barked knowingly again but was ignored; he heard it yelp once, presumably from a well-placed boot. The minutes ticked by and still the Germans stayed, and stayed. By the time they finally left Powell knew that it was too late for the surf boat to come back.

'Where did you get the radio transmitter?'

'A man gave me the suitcase at the railway station. I'd never seen him before. He asked me to keep it safe for him. I didn't know the transmitter was there.'

'You're lying.'

He wouldn't have believed it himself, but it was the best he could think of.

'I ask you again, where did you get it?'

'Like I said, from the man at the station—'

They hit him once more with the truncheon – across the mouth this time.

'Who are you working for?'

He spat out a tooth. 'Nobody.'

'Is it the British?'

'How could it be?'

'We know that you have left Pont-Aven several times in the past months. Where did you go?'

Thank you, Mademoiselle Citron. 'I'm an artist. It's my habit to look for new scenes to paint.'

'Have you been to England?'

'To *England*? How could I?'

'You went in a boat. You returned in a boat.

You are an agent working for the British. Who else in Pont-Aven is working for them? Give us their names.'

'I don't know what you're talking about.'

They hit him again, harder.

After the German patrol had gone, Powell went in search of Smythson. They met up in the darkness, somewhere along the beach.

'Bit of bad luck that, sir. What now?'

He had already decided the next move, which was to get to Pont-Aven and find out what had happened to Duval and why he had needed to return so urgently. Easier planned than done. Lieutenant Smythson, like the rest of the gunboat crew, was wearing civilian clothing – white fisherman's jersey, reefer jacket and old flannel trousers – and he had had the commendable foresight to carry his old French papers, whereas Powell, clinging to his traditional ways, had kept on his naval uniform and was hardly likely to walk around France unnoticed. He saw himself as Smythson must see him – a middle-aged, stuffy stick-in-the-mud, now paying the price. And he remembered, with pain, Harry's amused comment – that he'd stick out like a sore thumb in France.

The lieutenant said, 'I wonder if I might make a suggestion, sir?'

'Is it a good one?'

'I think so. We find the nearest house and get French clothes and papers for you. And money.'

'Do you imagine they're going to hand them over – just like that?'

'No, sir.' Smythson patted his pocket. 'But you see, I happen to have my service revolver.'

They made their way across the sand dunes behind the beach. With no moon and no lights to guide them progress was slow, but no night is completely dark and the better their eyes adjusted, the more they could see. About a mile inland, they came across a cottage standing on its own.

Powell said firmly, 'We have to know first if there's a man roughly my size and age. We'll wait till they're up and about.' The lieutenant, he could tell, was all for rushing in immediately. 'There's no point risking it for no gain.'

They found shelter in some kind of shed that seemed to contain a variety of tools, sacks and wooden crates and, as it gradually grew lighter, they took turns to keep watch on the house. It was Powell's turn when, at last, the door of the cottage opened and a man came out. He looked considerably older than himself, and several inches shorter, but the clothes were good – loose-fitting labourer's clothes. He motioned to the lieutenant to take a look.

'How about just asking them politely for help?'

Smythson shook his head. 'Too uncertain, sir. They might help, but they might not. More likely not. They'll be too scared, I should think.

Shall I do the talking, sir? They can be hard to understand.'

'All right. But I'll take the gun.'

They watched their quarry go towards a dilapidated chicken coop and bend down to undo some kind of hatch.

Smythson spoke low in his ear. 'He's coming this way now, sir. Probably getting food for the hens.'

They stood behind the door and the man came into the shed and, with his back turned, began to scoop out grain from a sack into a bowl. Powell stepped forward and stuck the revolver into his back. Lieutenant Smythson did the talking as though he had been holding up people all his life, and it was as well he did, since the Breton's terrified gabble was incomprehensible to Powell.

'He says his ID's in the cottage, sir. He keeps it safe in there.'

'Tell him to lead the way.'

The cottage was a dark, damp little hovel. There was a chair or two, a table with an oil lamp burning above it, a dresser against the wall, a peasant woman standing at a prehistoric range, stirring a black pot with a wooden spoon. As they came in, she turned and gave a shriek of terror and dropped the spoon.

Powell said in his polite English-accented French, 'There is nothing to be afraid of, madame, so long as you do what we tell you.'

She looked at him blankly, hand clamped over her mouth, eyes wide, and Smythson growled something else. She backed away towards a dresser and groped clumsily in a green jug on one of the shelves. Smythson stepped forward.

'Here you are, sir. This should do the trick.'

The card showed an indistinct photo of the man. *Nom: Cordet; Prénom: Jean; Né le 4.5.1894 à Trévos.* With a jolt he realized that he was almost exactly the same age as himself – same year, same month – just two days apart. *Domicile. Départment* . . . He read on rapidly down the card, translating the French. Profession: agricultural worker. Height – in metres, of course, but considerably shorter than himself. Hair: brown. Moustache: none. General shape of face: oval. Eyes: brown – something vital in common. Distinguishing particulars: none. The signature was a semi-literate scrawl, the stamp – imprinted no less than three times in different places – the proud marque of the local *mairie*. The right-hand thumb print in the corner was so smudged he doubted anyone but an expert could have deciphered it.

'Tell him to get some clothes – a jacket, trousers, and a hat, if he has one.'

The man looked mutinous but the woman spoke sharply to him and he left the room, accompanied by Smythson who had borrowed the gun. Powell was left alone with the woman who was still cowering by the dresser. He wanted to reassure her but it was safer that she remained in that state. Instead he barked out as menacingly as he could, '*Argent, madame. Tout ce que vous avez. Vite.*'

The poor wretch turned again to the green jug and pulled out a little wad of franc notes and then, delving deeper, some coins. She put them on the table and stammered something at him. It was probably all their savings, he thought, and swore to himself that after the war, he would see that the exact sum was returned to them.

Smythson came back with the man carrying a bundle of clothes. 'His Sunday best, sir. He doesn't have much of a wardrobe.'

'I've got all the money they seem to have.' He looked again at the woman. 'Tell her they'll get it back one day.'

Smythson said something in kinder tones. 'I'm afraid she doesn't believe us, sir. She thinks you're German, by the way. Something to do with your accent and the uniform. They have been known to muddle us up. I didn't enlighten her.'

They left the cottage and headed for a nearby copse where Powell changed into the farm-worker's Sunday best – black jacket, trousers, shirt, waistcoat. They smelled of damp and sweat and mothballs, with a greenish tinge to the shiny black and, by the age and style of them, were probably handed down from a previous gener-ation. They were also far too small, the trousers ending above the ankles, the jacket sleeves half-way up his arms. He couldn't get the man's shoes on at all but fortunately his own, normally highly polished ones were dull and dirty from seawater and sand. Smythson produced a beret apologetically from his pocket.

'This was the only hat he had, sir.'

He would have drawn the line at wearing it, except for the fact that it covered his very English haircut. The lieutenant, he could see, was biting his lower lip.

'Excuse me, sir. That's not quite how they wear it. Shall I show you?'

They buried his Royal Navy uniform and, with it, the gun. It had served its purpose and if they were searched for any reason, it could only get them into trouble. As they covered the burial spot with leaves, he said, 'The gun *was* loaded, wasn't it, Lieutenant?'

'Actually, no, sir.' Smythson smiled brightly. 'But of course, they didn't know that, did they?'

'I will ask you again, who gave you the radio transmitter?'

'I told you – a stranger at the railway station. He asked me to look after his suitcase.'

'We do not believe you. The transmitter was made by the British. You are working for them, as an agent.'

'How could I be? I'm a painter. I know nothing about such things.'

'Where do you go when you leave Pont-Aven?'

'To Paris, to sell my work and to visit my wife.'

'Where else?'

'I look for places to paint. I go everywhere. It's my habit.'

'What are the names of other people in France who are working with you?'

The questions went on and on. In between there was the pain. Terrible pain. But they would never learn the names. Jean-Claude, Marthe, Jacques, Paul, Léon, Jeanne, André and all the others . . . they would never learn them from him.

The train compartment was full. Powell sat in a corner seat with Lieutenant Smythson opposite. A large country woman next to him, her elbow in his side, was taking up far more than her fair share of space. She had a wicker basket on her broad lap, covered with a cloth, and from time to time she lifted the cloth to take out something to eat – a hunk of bread, a piece of strong-smelling cheese, a wrinkled sausage which she bit into with a guillotine chop of her front teeth, before returning it beneath its covering. Her jaws worked away, masticating in a slow sideways movement like a cow. He closed his eyes. He was hungry enough to envy the woman her snacks and wished he and Smythson had had the sense to steal some food as well from the cottage.

His plan seemed the only sensible one, in the circumstances. Go to Pont-Aven. Find out what had happened to Duval and why he had wanted to be picked up. He knew the names of the people in Duval's network – their real names as well as those used for cover. One of them would surely have news of him. What then? Get back to England somehow. If he could find Duval and the radio transmitter he could send a message to London to arrange for a pickup. And if not?

Head for the Pyrenees and Spain and go back that way. Get back he must. There was a job to do. Harry, with good reason, would be furious that he'd got himself into this situation. He was angry with himself. He should never have gone ashore, never have left the gunboat without a clear signal from Duval on the beach. Presently, lulled by the rocking of the train, he fell asleep.

He was woken by a German railway policeman in a grey and black uniform, demanding to see all papers. The Frenchwoman beside him heaved her bulk around to extract hers from a pocket, jabbing him hard in the ribs. The German passed from one passenger to the next, examining each document carefully. There was some irregularity with the woman's identity card: all was not exactly in order and the official was not pleased. He pointed to the card, haranguing her in bad French. The woman shrugged and answered in the Breton patois. It was clear that neither understood each other and, in the end, the German gave up and thrust the card back at her. When Powell offered his for inspection, the man barely glanced at it, or at Smythson's either; he was still muttering angrily to himself, throwing the woman threatening glances over his shoulder. She took no notice; she was attacking the sausage again, taking another gigantic bite and chewing away placidly.

'Are you Mrs Hillyard?'
'Yes, that's right.'

'Well, I'm Esme's mum. And I've come to get her.'

Her hair was dyed blonde with a row of snail-shaped curls carefully arranged across her forehead beneath the brim of a red felt hat. The smart costume was red, too, and so were her high-heeled, peep-toe shoes, and her Rexine handbag.

Barbara said, 'Please come in.' She showed the woman into the sitting room and shut the door against Mrs Lamprey's cocked ear. Esme's mother looked round first at the room, and then at her.

'It's not like I thought it'd be. Didn't know she was in such a posh place. Where is she, any-way?'

'She's upstairs in her room, reading.'

'You can tell her to come down, then, and be quick about it. I've got someone waiting in a car outside.'

'Someone?'

'My fiancé. He's a Canadian. We're going to be married, soon as I've got the divorce from Esme's dad. Steve's arranging for us to go to Canada – to get away from the war. So, I've come to fetch her.'

'Would you sit down for a moment?'

'What for? We haven't got time. Steve's got to get back.'

'There are some things we ought to discuss.'

'What things? Oh, you mean money? I thought they paid you for looking after her.'

'No, I didn't mean money,' she said coldly. 'I meant Esme.'

'What about her? She's not ill, is she? Is something wrong with her?'

'No, she's very well, as a matter of fact. She's settled down here now but it took her quite a time. It will be a bit of an uprooting for her . . . to be taken away so suddenly, and so far.'

'Oh, she'll love Canada. She's lucky. Steve's going to fix it all for us.'

'Yes, I'm sure he is. Does her father know?'

'Vic? God knows where *he* is. I can't very well get hold of him at sea, can I?'

She said stubbornly, 'But I think he has a legal right to know what's happening to his daughter – about her being taken out of the country.'

'He won't care . . . he's always away. Off on some bloody ship.'

'Not always. He came here to see Esme when he was last on leave. And he writes to her regularly. I think he'll care quite a lot.'

Her eyes narrowed under the hat brim. 'Vic's got no say. I've always looked after Esme. It was me got her sent away, safe from the bombing and everything. And, if you don't mind, it's nothing to do with *you*, neither. So p'raps you'll kindly go and tell her to come downstairs right now. This minute.'

She went upstairs to find Esme who was lying on her bed, reading a book. Tom, the ginger kitten, was curled up beside her. It was a picture of peaceful contentment.

'Your mother's here, Esme. She's come to see you.'

The child sat up with a start. '*Mum*! Come *here*?'

'That's right. She's waiting for you in the sitting room.'

Esme ran down the stairs and Barbara followed more slowly to give them time alone together. Well, that's that, she thought. I can't do much about it and maybe it *is* the best thing for her in the end. Canada will be safe, well away from the war, and a wonderful opportunity for a better life than she's likely to have in England. She went into the sitting room expecting to find Esme all smiles, in her mother's arms; instead, she was standing at a distance, head bent, digging at the carpet with the toe of her shoe. Her mother gave a shrug.

'She's grown, I'll say that, Mrs Hillyard. Still got that sulky way with her, though, hasn't she? She gets that from her dad, not me. Gets her looks from that side of the family, too – more's the pity. I've just told her what I said to you – about going to Canada. You'd think she'd be thrilled about it, wouldn't you? Lots of kids'd give their eye teeth to go. And just look at her.'

'I expect she needs a little time to get used to the idea.'

'Well, we haven't got any. Steve's waiting, like I said, and he's not a patient man. Soon as her bag's packed, we'll be off.'

Esme lifted her head. 'Can I bring Tom?'

'Tom? Who's he?'

'My kitten.'

'A *kitten*? Don't be stupid. You can't take a kitten to Canada. They won't let you.'

Esme's chin went up. 'Then I'm not coming.'

Her mother folded her arms. 'You can't take the kitten, and that's that. I dare say we might let you get one over there. I can't promise. I'll have to ask Steve about it.'

'I don't want another one. I want Tom.'

'Well, you can't have him. Go and get your things together. We're leaving.'

Esme didn't move. She was staring at the carpet again, working the toe of her sandal deep into the pile.

'I'm not coming without Tom. I don't want to go to Canada, anyway.'

'You're an ungrateful little so-and-so, aren't you? You can't stay here. Mrs Hillyard doesn't want you round her neck for ever.'

Barbara said firmly, 'Esme's very welcome to stay as long as she likes.'

Esme gave her a grateful look. 'Anyway, Dad says he'll come and get me, soon as the war's over.'

'Does he, indeed? How's he think he's going to look after you, I'd like to know?'

'He says we'll manage somehow.'

'Well, I'm not having that. You're *my* daughter and you'll come with me.' Esme's mother grabbed hold of the child's arm. 'You go upstairs right now and get your things.'

Esme jerked herself free and backed away towards the door. 'I'm not coming with you, Mum. I won't. I'm staying here with Mrs Hillyard till Dad fetches me. We'll manage without you – just like he said.' She ran out of the room. They could hear her pounding up the stairs.

Her mother drew a long, indignant breath. 'Well . . . of all the cheek! It's Vic's fault. He's been setting her against me, that's what. Saying all kinds of lies, I've no doubt.' A car horn hooted outside – harsh and impatient. She snatched up the smart red handbag. 'I've got to go. If that's the way they both want it, it's fine by me. Esme always was a bloody pain. She won't be much loss, I have to say. You can tell her father from me – *if* he ever comes back – that, as far as I'm concerned, he's welcome to her.'

The front door slammed and there was the sound of a car driving away fast.

Barbara went upstairs to Esme's bedroom and opened the door quietly. She was sitting on her bed, holding Tom in her arms, her face buried in his ginger fur.

'Your mother's gone, Esme. Are you all right?'

A muffled answer. 'Yes.'

'Are you sure . . . about not going with her? *Quite* sure?'

'Yes.' She looked up, her face very white. 'You don't mind if I stay, do you? Till Dad comes for me?'

She went and sat on the bed beside her and put her arm round the child and the kitten. 'Of course I don't mind. You can stay here for as long as you like. You and Tom.'

She held them both against her as Esme started to cry.

'Is there any news of Monsieur Duval, Mrs Hillyard? He's been away much longer than usual.'

'I'm afraid not, Mrs Lamprey.'

'Oh. I just thought he might have been keeping in touch with you.'

'No, he hasn't.' She removed Mrs Lamprey's plate and the vegetable dish. 'Will you have some pudding?'

'What is it today?'

'Sultana roll. And custard.'

'Just a teeny helping. I really mustn't overdo it.'

She had learned long ago, in Mrs Lamprey's case, to ignore such pleas. She moved on to the rear admiral's table and he looked up at her as she took his plate away. There was sympathy in his eyes, and understanding. 'Will you have the sultana roll, Rear Admiral?'

'Certainly, my dear. It's one of my favourites.'

Miss Tindall smiled cheerfully at her. 'They said on the wireless that it's going to rain later. I expect you could do with it for the garden.'

'Yes, it has been rather dry lately. Pudding for you, Miss Tindall?'

'Please. Not too much though, if you don't mind.'

Sixteen

There were stops and starts on the journey to Pont-Aven, changes of train, delays and another inspection of papers – this time by a French gendarme who was, ironically, far more thorough than the German railway official. The man took so much time over the stolen identity card that Powell feared the worst. If he had to answer any questions, he knew, the game would be up. His accent might pass muster with a German who spoke bad French, but never with a Frenchman.

Smythson took him down to the port and he could see at once why, as an artist, Duval would have found the place so appealing. Buildings, boats, shapes, shadows, colours, water, light . . . all spoke of what he had seen of Duval's work. The primitive-seeming execution – the dabs and daubs and distortions like that of a child, and yet not childish at all – had surely found its inspiration here.

Smythson pointed out the shuttered windows of Duval's studio on the top floor of a house close to the quayside. As he did so, a German officer emerged from the building and walked away down the street. A major, Powell noted. An older man with the stiffly erect carriage of a past age. Major Winter, perhaps? The cultured one who had so admired Duval's paintings and had supplied the *Ausweis* and the gasoline coupons and the Courvoisier cognac. For a moment, he debated the possibility of simply going to the door and asking for Duval, and then dismissed it. The landlady, Mademoiselle Citron, was not to be trusted – Duval had stated this clearly in his report. The next question was whether they dared to approach any of the contacts, or whether they, and Duval, had all been compromised.

They walked on beside the river Aven in the direction of the town centre. Smythson paused at a café in the rue du port. 'We could get something to eat in here, sir. And see if we can find out anything at the same time.'

'Did Duval come here?'

'I'm afraid I don't know, sir. But it's near his studio so there's a good chance they might know him.'

The café was called *Chez Alphonse*. The whitewashed walls had faded prints of modern French paintings and there was a very French aroma of garlic and wine and tobacco. It was also rather cold. They sat at a corner table, away from the other customers who were intent on their food, conveying it to their mouths, tearing at bread, drinking wine.

The *patron*, presumably Alphonse himself, was

a small, dark man with a white apron lashed to his hips. He moved fast and furiously among the tables and with the resigned look on his face of one who invariably expected the worst. When he came to their table, a napkin hooked over one arm, Powell let Smythson do the talking. There was a choice between fish soup or pig's liver. Alphonse, personally – if asked – would recommend the soup. It was not the same as in the old days when one knew exactly where the pig had come from, whereas he could vouch for the fish having been caught by the Pont-Aven fleet only that morning. And he could offer some passable bread. Naturally, they would understand the impossibility of giving his customers anything like they were accustomed to. The shelves were bare, the cellar almost empty . . . but, it so happened, he had a few bottles of *ordinaire* that one could drink without feeling disgraced.

He went away, returning shortly with a carafe of wine. While it was being poured Smythson enquired casually after Louis Duval. The *patron* paused, holding the carafe aloft.

'Monsieur Duval? You know him?'

'Yes, indeed. An old friend of ours. We hope to see him while we're in Pont-Aven.'

'Alas, you will be disappointed. He has been arrested. The Gestapo. They came to his studio and took him away. A very sad affair.'

'But what for?'

Alphonse shrugged his shoulders. 'Who knows? They don't need to give reasons. They arrive at the door, they make an arrest, and that's that. In my opinion, it was Mademoiselle Citron who was responsible – the *logeuse*, you know. She had a grudge against him. A woman scorned – you understand? They are the worst of all – the most dangerous.'

'Do you know where he has been taken?'

'No. As I say, they take somebody and nobody knows why or where or what will happen to them. It's horrible. But what can we do?' He poured more wine. 'He was one of my best customers, too.'

He went off to another table. Smythson said, 'Not very good news, sir.'

'Very bad. There's nothing we can do for him, but we need to find out why he wanted to be picked up.'

'Maybe he knew the Gestapo were onto him?'

'Or he might have had some important information. Something he wanted to bring back himself.'

'We could see if one of his contacts knows anything?'

Powell frowned. 'It's risky – for them, as well as us – but we'll have to try. You'd better do it, I think. I suggest you start with the bicycle-repair man – Jean-Claude Vauclin. Make the excuse that you're looking for a bike to buy and take it from there.'

'What about you, sir? Will you be all right?'

He said coolly, 'I'm not entirely incapable of looking after myself.'

'Of course not, sir.'

'I'll make myself as inconspicuous as possible. Buy a newspaper, sit in a bar and drink. Smoke Gauloises. We'll rendezvous back here.'

'Right, sir.'

The wine was certainly no disgrace and the fish soup excellent. They ate quickly, paid and got up to go. If anyone had been watching them, Powell thought, their suspicions might have been aroused at the speed with which they had finished their meal compared with true Frenchmen. Alphonse, running after them, enquired anxiously whether it had all been to their satisfaction. As they went out of the door, two Wehrmacht sergeants came into the café, one of them pushing Powell roughly aside. The *patron*, he noticed, gave them his full attention, escorting them with a flourish to a good table. Who could blame him? The man had a living to make.

Lieutenant Smythson went off in search of Jean-Claude Vauclin and Powell walked around the town, pausing to buy some French cigarettes and a newspaper. He sat on a convenient bench and looked at the paper with some interest. It was little more than a propaganda tool for the Third Reich. All their recent triumphs were trumpeted across its pages – the siege of Tobruk, the fall of Belgrade, the British retreat in Greece. It made depressing reading. He folded it under his arm and walked on, finding himself outside the *hôtel de ville*. The conversation he had had with Duval on his return from his first mission came back to him. The mayor, Maurice Masseron, Duval had told him, had been extraordinarily helpful. He was not one of the network but, evidently, Duval had trusted him enough to confide in him completely.

On an impulse which he knew was probably foolhardy, he walked into the building and, summoning up his most convincing French accent, asked to see the mayor. His business was very urgent, he told the hard-faced woman at the reception, and private. What was his name? He gave the first French name that came into his head – Renault. The mayor was an old friend of his from past years. A *very* old friend. She stared at him, he thought, with deep scepticism and went away. For all he knew, she could be phoning the French police or even the Gestapo, but he waited, looking as unconcerned as he could. After some time she returned. The mayor would see him – only God knew why was implicit in her tone and expression.

He was shown up an impressive flight of marble stairs and into the mayoral office, the woman holding the door open for him. The man who rose from behind the desk was broad-built with a mass of thick, greying hair. He held out his hand.

'What a pleasure to see you again after all these years, my old friend. Come and sit down.'

Powell was gestured to the chair in front of the desk and heard the office door click shut behind him. The mayor went on, speaking in loud tones.

'How have you been? You must tell me all your news.' He held a finger to his lips, went over to the door, opened it and shut it again before returning to his desk. 'We can talk now. That woman is admirable in many respects but she sees her role as my guard dog and she has a naturally suspicious mind. She tells me that you have a strange foreign accent, which intrigued me. I couldn't recall any very old friend of mine with any such thing and, naturally, the moment I saw you I also realized that we had never met in our lives. Also, I realized – which fortunately she did not – that you are almost certainly English, in spite of the clothes and that newspaper that you are carrying.'

'Is it that obvious?'

'To me, yes. To others, perhaps not so much. I have come across a number of Englishmen over the years. They have a particular look. A certain style. There is something about them that sets them apart. But what in the name of heaven are you doing in Pont-Aven?'

He said, 'I'm here to find out what has happened to Louis Duval.'

'Ah . . . that explains it, in part, at least. I am aware that Louis has been active in certain directions, shall we say.'

'Do you have any news of him?'

'Nothing good, I regret to tell you. The Gestapo arrested him two days ago.'

'I've already learned that. Do you know on what grounds?'

'My dear friend, this is not as in your free country. Our Nazi masters make their own laws. They can arrest whom they please and keep them incarcerated for as long as they like. They don't need to give public reasons. They may have had reason to suspect Louis, or somebody may have denounced him with a trumped-up story.'

'His landlady, for example?'

'You've heard about her? Yes, it's very possible. Women are often at the root of any trouble, in my experience. I warned him to be careful of her. You should stay well away from her at all costs. They are probably watching the place. Cigarette?'

He accepted the Gauloise and the light, with thanks. The French tobacco made him cough. 'Do you know where they've taken him?'

'No idea. And it would be difficult – perhaps even suspicious – to try to find out. I regret to say that there is nothing that can be done to help him. We can only hope for the best. It's very sad.'

Powell said, 'He had a radio transmitter and he sent a message, asking to be returned to England urgently. Do you have any idea why? Did he talk to you about it?'

'No. I haven't seen or spoken to him for a long while. I didn't even know that he was back in Pont-Aven – not until I heard about the arrest. Bad news travels fast in a small town like this. But if the Gestapo found the radio, then he's in real trouble.' Masseron pulled open the bottom drawer of his desk. 'A little cognac, monsieur? I think we could both do with one.'

He took the glass of brandy that was passed across. 'I see you have one of his paintings.'

'Good, isn't it? I bought it from him years ago – before he got expensive. Those standing stones are near here. If you were a tourist I should advise you to go and see them, and a good deal else of interest. This is a delightful area. As it is, I can only advise you to leave as soon as possible. Do you have some kind of plan for returning to England – if I may ask such an indiscreet question?'

'We'll probably go south to the Unoccupied Zone and try to cross to Spain.'

'*We?*'

'There's another Englishman with me. A naval lieutenant.'

'My God! Two of you at large in my town.'

Powell smiled. 'He's actually half-French and looks rather more convincing than me.'

'Just as well. No offence to you, of course. But you will need papers, my friend.'

'We have them – identity papers, at least.'

'That's something. But if you wish to travel into the Unoccupied Zone you will need more than that. A special *Ausweis*, for example. The Boche adore papers and they insist on them.'

'I was hoping that you might be able to help us in that respect.'

'It's dangerous for me.'

'I realize that.'

The mayor studied his brandy glass thoughtfully for a moment. 'You can, perhaps, do me a favour in return.'

'What favour?'

'I have a son – an only son – sixteen years old. Luc is a fine boy but also a foolish one. Like most young men of his age, he has a hot head and no sense of self-preservation. His principal recreation is to bait the Germans in every way he can. It's only a matter of time before he is arrested. Sent to a labour camp, or forced to join their army, or something equally undesirable. In return for my helping you, I should like you to take him with you. Take him to England for the duration of the war. He'll be safe over there.'

'You've a great deal of faith in us – considering how things stand with the war at the moment.'

'We French must have faith in something, my friend. It keeps us going. So, will you take him?'

'If you accept the risk to him – yes.'

'It's smaller than if he stays here. And he could make himself useful to you. He could pass as your son. We can arrange papers for that. Invent some good story.'

Smythson could pass as another son, Powell thought wryly. A family group, no less, with him as *paterfamilias*. He glanced at his watch. 'I've arranged to meet the lieutenant soon.'

'Where?'

'A café in the rue de port: *Chez Alphonse*.'

'Louis went there all the time. Alphonse might have some news. He hears all the talk.'

Powell shook his head. 'We've already asked him. He knows nothing.'

'So, what will you do after that?'

'Find somewhere to stay the night.'

'You can stay with us, my friend. We have a large house with an attic and you'll both be safe enough up there. My wife, Anne-Marie, will make a big moan about it, but she'll cook you a superb meal, I guarantee you.' The mayor smiled. 'And we must do something about those clothes that you are wearing. They don't fit you at all.'

The café was empty except for its proprietor. Powell could see him through the glass door, laying tables and flicking and flapping about him with a napkin. He opened the door and went in. Alphonse came forward, lifting his hands.

'Ah, monsieur . . . I regret that I am not yet prepared. If you would care to return in another half-hour . . .'

'Just a glass of wine – if possible.'

'A glass of wine is *always* possible, monsieur. Please be seated – anywhere that you choose.'

He chose the same corner table, well away from the windows, and sat down, the newspaper beside him. After a moment the proprietor returned with a small carafe of red wine. 'The same as you had before, monsieur. It's the best I can do. And there is more, if you wish.'

'Thank you.' He lit a cigarette. 'My friend is meeting me here in a while.'

'Well, you are welcome to drink until he arrives.' Alphonse picked up a glass, breathed on it and polished it with the napkin. 'You said that you were old friends of Monsieur Duval?'

'That's right. He comes here regularly?'

'He used to – before this terrible war started. Since then he has not been here so much. He went south, you know – to Toulouse, I believe. And then he came back. Then off he went again, somewhere else. Of course, artists are not like others. We ordinary people must stay put, but they have restless souls. They must always look for things to paint, to be inspired. It's a tragedy that he has been arrested – all because of a spiteful woman.' Alphonse flapped his napkin in the direction of the prints on the walls. 'Monsieur Duval's work is just as good as those, in my opinion. He is already well-known in France and one fine day, without doubt, he will be world-famous.'

'When was he last in here?'

'Only the other day. In fact, it was the very day that he was arrested. He had been away, I think – I don't know exactly where – and he came in here for some lunch. I remember that he had the soup and then the *filet de boeuf*, though, as I was obliged to confess, there was scarcely a morsel of meat in the dish. One has to call it something and it keeps the spirits up if people can pretend a little. The soup was nothing to boast about either, but at least it was warming. It was a cold day, you know – and, as you may have noticed, there is no heating in here. The boiler has broken and who knows when it can be mended. There are no spare parts, you understand. But then everything is scarce in France, isn't that so? It affects us all. It's a disaster.'

'What did he talk about?'

Alphonse shrugged. 'He did not come here to talk, monsieur. He came to eat, though, naturally, we had a little conversation. Monsieur Duval is always most agreeable – as you will know yourself, of course, being a friend of his.' He put his head on one side, consideringly. 'Forgive me for being personal, monsieur, but clearly you are not French. One can tell that from your accent, though I can't place it exactly.'

'My mother was English,' Powell said, with perfect accuracy. 'I picked it up from her.'

'That explains it. Does she live in England?'

'She died some years ago.'

'My condolences, monsieur. One has only one mother. More wine?'

When the glass had been refilled, Powell said, 'Monsieur Duval had something of great interest to tell me but I don't know exactly what it was. It's rather a mystery. That's why I wondered if he had said anything about it to you.'

Alphonse shook his head. 'Not a word. And I regret that he made no mention of you, monsieur. None at all.'

'Never mind.'

'Unless, of course, it was to do with the news-paper.'

'Newspaper?'

'Yes, it was very strange. He had a newspaper with him – already several days old. He wanted to hide it somewhere very safe. I have no idea why. People are always hiding things these days, isn't that so? Anything that is precious to them, they hide from the Boche – money, jewels, valuable ornaments, paintings, wine . . . they make sure it can't be taken away from them. The Boche take everything, don't they? The swine.'

'Do you know where he hid it?'

'I hid it for him, monsieur. In the broken-down boiler in the cellar. It's a very safe place. The Germans would never search there – it's too dirty. Besides, who would imagine an old newspaper to be of any interest? I wondered myself if Monsieur Duval had had some kind of brainstorm. Painters are often disposed to such things, I believe. Like Van Gogh, for instance. They say he went completely mad.'

Powell said casually, 'Is this newspaper still there?'

'Certainly. I have left it there, as he wished. God willing, he will be able to return to collect it.'

'Could you show me? Perhaps it has something to do with what he wanted to tell me. Some article of particular interest to me, perhaps.'

'If you wish.'

He picked up his own newspaper and followed the proprietor through to the back of the café and the kitchen beyond, where an immensely fat woman, busy filleting fish, ignored them completely. Alphonse waved the napkin again. 'My wife. She does the cooking. I do all the rest.' A door led to stone steps going down into the cellar – a dark dungeon of a place, lit by one low-wattage electric bulb hanging on a cord from the centre of the ceiling. Alphonse indicated the near-empty wine racks. 'Naturally, the best is elsewhere. I also hide what I can. The boiler is over here.' He swung open the mouth of the iron monster crouched in the corner and groped around inside. 'And here is the newspaper that Monsieur Duval left. But I doubt that it can be of any interest to you – or anybody else.'

'May I look? Just in case.'

'Certainly. But if you'll forgive me, monsieur, I must get on with my work. Customers will be arriving soon for the evening and things are not ready.'

The newspaper was rolled up into a cylinder and covered with ash. Powell brushed it clean and unrolled it carefully. The light was poor but he could feel and see that other sheets had been laid between its newsprint pages – very thin sheets that had been folded to the same size. He rolled up his own newspaper in the same way and buried it in the ashes before closing the boiler door. Duval's paper he tucked under his arm.

Upstairs, Smythson was waiting at the corner table, drinking the remains of the wine. Alphonse was spitting on a knife before polishing it energetically.

'Another carafe, monsieur? Now that your friend has also arrived.'

He ignored Smythson's hopeful expression. 'Unfortunately, we have to leave.'

'Was it of any interest – the newspaper?'

'None at all that I could see. I replaced it.'

Alphonse shook his head. 'Poor Monsieur Duval. It's like I thought, he must have taken leave of his senses.'

The German officer was smiling. He looked freshly shaved, his uniform well pressed, the buttons brightly polished, and the scent of some kind of expensive cologne hung about him. French cologne, Duval thought. Bought, no doubt, in Paris. The officer was holding out a silver box, the lid open.

'Cigarette, Monsieur Duval?'

Why not? He took one, though to hold it between his damaged lips was painfully difficult. Not French cigarettes though, an American brand: Chesterfields. Simone would have been pleased. The officer leaned across the desk offering a flame from a gold lighter. The flame met the end of the cigarette, stayed there a moment, as he inhaled. He let the smoke trickle out of the side of his mouth. The officer was lighting one for himself, sitting back in his chair and blowing the smoke up over his head.

'So . . . things have been a little unpleasant for you, I understand.'

An understatement, if ever there was one. Duval shrugged. Even that small movement made him wince. Speech itself was an effort.

The officer looked sympathetic. 'I'm sorry. Some of our people have rather crude methods. Personally, I'm against all that. I have nothing to do with the *Geheime Staats Polizei,* but you can understand why they were so suspicious – a radio transmitter concealed in a suitcase, and given to you by some stranger. On the face of it, it seems an unlikely story, but then the most unlikely are sometimes perfectly true.' His French was stilted but faultless. A model of grammatical correctness. Another neat exhalation of smoke ceilingwards. 'There is no reason to suspect you . . . an artist of renown who can surely have no interest in the dirty and dangerous business of espionage. And yet, some small explanation seems to be required. You do see that? I'd like to help get you out of here, so that you can get back to your painting as soon as possible. Tell me, by the way, what do you think of the work of our German artists today?'

His answer was mumbled, but clear enough. 'Mostly crap.'

The officer chuckled. 'I agree with you. Our Führer has very sentimental tastes and we have to pretend to appreciate them. You and I know better, of course. They interrogated your wife, Simone, in Paris by the way. It seems she knows nothing.'

'We haven't lived together for years.'

'So she says. She has other interests. Other loyalties, it seems. She did mention that at the start of the war you had been thinking of going to England – before we arrived in France – but that you changed your mind. Is that correct?'

He nodded slowly. Thank God he had never told her anything else.

There was a short silence. 'For myself, I have always admired the English. It's a great pity to be at war with them. You know England?'

He drew carefully on the cigarette without answering.

'Of course you do. You lived there for a while. In St Ives, isn't that so? I have never been there but I hear that it's delightful. Something of an artists' colony, like Pont-Aven, which is even more charming. To tell the truth I prefer France to England, though I'm not so sure about the French. Perhaps the French should go and live in England and the English come to live in France and then this country would be perfect.' Another chuckle. 'I'm joking, of course. Where were we? Oh yes, trying to find some way to get you out of here. We must give them something to satisfy them, you see. Nothing very much. A name or two. Let's start with people in Pont-Aven whom you know are engaged in a little amateur spying . . . you understand what I mean? Watching us, Germans, and passing on what they see and hear to somebody else, who passes it on to somebody else . . . that's the sort of thing, isn't it? Gossip, really. And mostly harmless, of course. There would be no question of severe punishment. Who do you know who is like that?'

'Nobody.'

The officer sighed. He flicked at some invisible speck on his sleeve. 'Monsieur Duval, I'm trying to help you, please believe me. A name or two, that's all, and you can be released. Go back to your studio, pick up your brushes and continue with your life.'

Another silence, but longer. Since it hurt to speak, why bother when there was nothing to say?

After a while, the German continued pleasantly, 'I assume you know what the alternative will be? Unless you give them this information, you will be shot. So, I do advise you to be sensible. Let's start again, shall we?'

Madame Masseron – small and thin with black frizzy hair – was not pleased to see them. A stream of protest directed at high speed to her husband made that clear. As she left the room, the door shut behind her with such force that the walls shook. The mayor, however, seemed quite unmoved. He clapped Powell on the back.

'Take no notice. She'll be all right. Let's have a drink while she gets on with the cooking. I'd have got rid of her long ago, but she's a marvel in the kitchen. No good anywhere else, but there we are. We can't have everything, can we?'

He poured wine for them – far superior to the *ordinaire Chez Alphonse* – and a toast was drunk, first to France and then to England. Powell put down his glass.

'Monsieur Masseron, it's very urgent that we get back to England as soon as possible.'

'Of course . . . I understand.'

'I said before that we had thought of going south and over the border to Spain, but I realize now that it would take far too long. We must find a quicker way.'

'All very well, my friend. But how do you suggest? By plane would be the fastest but that's impossible.'

'By boat. From here. Could you arrange it? A fishing boat that we could take to England.'

'My God! I can't work miracles. The fishing boats belong to people; they make their living from them. And then there would be all the papers and permits necessary. The Germans are very strict now. They make searches all the time.'

Powell said carefully, 'About your son . . . We'd take him with us, of course. Look after him in England, until the end of the war. Just as you wished. As a matter of fact, my sister has a son very near his age. I'm sure she'd help.'

There was a pause. 'It would take time to arrange.'

'How long?'

'Several days. A week perhaps. Even if I can find a boat, there would be no fuel. It's too scarce. You would have to sail. And how could you do that? Impossible.'

Smythson was grinning all over his face. 'We're in the Royal Navy, sir. We know how to sail.'

There was a single bed in the attic – a narrow, iron affair obviously intended for a maidservant. Madame Masseron had grudgingly provided some threadbare blankets and two thin pillows which she threw at Smythson who caught them deftly. Earlier, however, she had provided a memorable supper of onion soup, crabs stuffed with herbs, Normandy cheese, apple crêpes. Masseron had produced several bottles of cold white wine, followed by one of Armagnac. The mayoral household was clearly not suffering too badly from the shortages.

Powell had hauled Smythson, who was in a state of collapse, up the stairs and onto the iron bed and made himself as comfortable as possible on the floor with one of the pillows and a blanket. Duval's newspaper, in its rolled-up state, was tucked under his arm like a child's favourite bedtime toy. A look at one of the tracings concealed between the pages had instantly told him why the Frenchman had been so keen to return to England. He had shown Smythson but decided not to take Masseron into his confidence. The less he knew, the better. And it still remained to be seen whether he would be able to arrange a boat. The papers, it seemed, were not a problem, but a boat was another matter. It would have to be a boat large enough and seaworthy enough to make the journey safely.

It was all very well for them to choose to risk their lives if they wanted to, the mayor had told them over the cognac, but he had to consider the life of his only son. The voyage would be very dangerous – not only because of the Germans with their patrols and inspections, their planes, their E-boats, not to mention their U-boats – but also because the coast of Brittany was treacherous even for the most experienced local sailors. The seas rounding the Pointe du Raz were a veritable cauldron, did they realize that? With an engine it was bad enough, but under sail they would be at the mercy of wind and tide.

Powell had reassured him. He was familiar with the coastline and well aware of the dangers. So was the lieutenant. They would keep well away from the Pointe du Raz, steering a westerly course that would take them clear of it and of the Ile de Sein and the islands off Brest. In which case, Masseron had pointed out, they would be outside the fishing limit and a target for any Germans who spotted them. Either way, it would be very dangerous. The more the mayor thought of it, the less he liked the whole idea. Far better if they reverted to their original plan to get out through Spain.

And then the boy, Luc, had come back, breezing cheerily into the room. He was tall for his age, with his father's thick curly hair and his big build. It was long after curfew time and Masseron had been angry. Where had he been? What had he been up to this time? The boy had shrugged. He and some friends had met and hung around. Doing what? Nothing much. Just a trick or two to annoy the Boche. A little sugar in a fuel tank; a truck tyre let down; a few rude words written on a poster. The mayor had turned to Powell despairingly.

'You see how it is? One day the Germans will lose their patience. Or he'll do something really stupid.'

He had said gravely, 'Then the sooner we leave, the better.'

Luc, it turned out, was all in favour. The little tricks played on the Boche were not enough to satisfy him. What he really wanted to do was join the Free French navy and fight them properly, like a man. He was already an excellent sailor, he told Powell proudly. He had sailed his own dinghy since he was seven and been out many times with the fishing boats. He would be happy to crew for monsieur on the voyage to England.

And so the matter was settled. The necessary papers and permits would be obtained as fast as possible. And, somehow, a boat would be found.

He lay on a truckle bed in the corner of the cell, smoking his last cigarette. At least, he assumed that it would be his last since he had none left and at daylight he was to be taken out into the prison yard and that would be the end of it. So he had been informed. He was not afraid, but he had regrets – the chief one being that now he would never know the great happiness of a life with Barbara. After all, it was not to be. She would find someone else in time, of course – or someone else would find her. That was only natural, and he wished it for her. But he was deeply sad at his own loss.

Another regret was that he had not been able

to get the tracings back to England. He had been careless again, just as he'd been with the restaurant bill. He had ignored the threat of Mademoiselle Citron. He should have shut his eyes and slept with her, and he might not be where he was now. And he should have hidden the suitcase and transmitter in the boiler and not taken them up to the studio – except that to have done so could have endangered Alphonse. The old newspaper would never be noticed. The tracings would stay in their hiding place until the boiler was mended and they were burned. Nobody but he knew they were there. He had failed.

Even so, he had achieved something for France. His little network was still in place, still unknown to the Gestapo but known to the people in England. It could be used and it could spread across northern France. And other similar networks would be set up – he had no doubt about that. Thousands of pairs of eyes watching the Germans. French resistance would surely grow and grow as time went by. Every town and village would have its eyes, observing and informing. The Boche would not have it all their own way.

The cigarette was almost finished. Another one would have been good. A drink, too. A glass of fine cognac. Two glasses, even. If the good Major Winter could have visited, he would have certainly brought him some. In England, in similar circumstances, he would probably have been offered a cup of tea. He smiled at the thought. And later, they would have asked him so politely if he'd *mind* stepping outside to the prison yard. The cigarette was burning his fingers now and he took another final, long, slow drag, letting the tobacco smoke reach deep into his lungs before he leaned over and stubbed it out on the stone floor.

They had taken away his watch and so he was not sure of the time, but there was a faint and perceptible change of light at the cell window above him and he knew that dawn could not be far away. He lay, watching the light increasing little by little. A while longer, and he heard heavy footsteps approaching and the harsh scrape of the door bolts being drawn back.

The *Isabelle* was a yawl, not a fishing boat. She had been built in the Thirties for pleasure sailing until her owner, an industrialist who had named her after his wife, had grown bored with both the boat and the wife. The French Navy had bought her and used her for a while as a training ship for coastal pilots. Later, she had been sold again and used for tunny fishing – being built on similar lines to the local tunny boats. The spacious mess deck had been converted, ignominiously, into a fish hold. She had an auxiliary motor but it was unreliable and not very powerful, and, in any case, there was no fuel available. Masseron related all this to Powell, well pleased with his find. The tunny boats were allowed outside the limit to work in the Bay of Biscay, which provided the excuse they needed. It was early in the season but not unreasonably so. At the moment the *Isabelle* was lying at anchor some way downstream – another convenience. Her present owner had, apparently, had the misfortune to fall foul of the port authorities over certain irregularities and his permit had been cancelled. Wouldn't he object to his boat being appropriated? Object? Nobody would ask him. He wouldn't know about it until it was too late.

The papers were ready and they discussed the plan in detail. They would leave the house in time to walk down the river to the yawl and set sail by six o'clock. In that way they would have the tide in their favour and be able to join up with the other fishing boats in order to arrive in their company at Port-Manech, the German inspection point at the river mouth.

'They usually board every other boat,' Masseron told them. 'Your papers are all in order and so there should be nothing to worry about, though, of course, one never knows with the Boche. Sometimes they just like to throw their weight around.'

Powell reckoned that the crossing would take roughly three days – if they managed a steady five knots or so and kept out of trouble. He was well aware of the dangers so feared by the mayor. He was also aware of a sense of elation such as he had not felt for years.

Madame Masseron, who had thawed slightly over the days of waiting, produced bread, cheese, cold meat and the mayor added several bottles of wine. Powell and Smythson turned away tactfully as they said goodbye to their son.

Masseron gripped his hand. 'You'll look after him for us?'

'You have my word on it.'

'Thank you, my friend. We'll meet again after the war.'

His elation increased at the sight of the *Isabelle*. She still had the graceful lines from her pleasure-sailing days and had kept her two masts – the tall main and much smaller mizzen abaft the stern. And her sails, like those of the other Breton tunny boats, were made up of different colours. She was a boat to lift the heart of any sailor.

They tacked downstream, joining a dozen or so fishing boats from Pont-Aven and other small ports, all heading towards the checkpoint at Port-Manech where they formed a line, moving up one by one for inspection. If they search us, there is nothing to find, Powell thought. An old French newspaper, days out of date and stuffed casually in a locker together with Madame Masseron's provisions, would surely be of no interest whatever. Even so, he held his breath as the *Isabelle* came alongside the jetty. There must have been fifteen or more German officials there, and a party of them went aboard the boat ahead, clumping noisily round the deck, making a thorough search. When it came to their turn, Smythson, at the wheel as pre-arranged, was the one to show their papers. He even made a joke as he did so and the German even laughed before he waved them on. The boy, Luc, with all the cheek of youth, actually waved back.

He took over the helm from Smythson once they had left the port behind and set the yawl on a north-westerly course. The wind was Force 4 – ideal for getting a move on – and the bows cut cleanly through the water, the multicoloured sails overhead a glorious sight. When he had the chance, he asked Smythson what he had said to the German.

Smythson grinned. 'I told him we were English spies disguised as French fishermen. He thought it was a hell of a good joke.'

The *Isabelle* sailed on steadily, bearing away from France on her course for England. Powell flung back his head and laughed.

Seventeen

'Just a very small portion, Mrs Hillyard, if you don't mind. I do have to be careful.'

Barbara served her the usual amount of lemon curd tart and passed on to the rear admiral and Miss Tindall, who murmured their appreciation and thanks.

Mrs Lamprey lifted her spoon and fork. 'Still no news of Monsieur Duval, Mrs Hillyard?'

'No, I'm afraid there isn't.'

'You'd think he would have been in touch. He's usually so considerate. Quite strange.'

'I expect he's been very busy in London.'

'I suppose so. There seem to be an awful lot of French over here now. There was a group of them on the ferry yesterday – French sailors in those funny pompom hats they wear. I had a word with one of them but I don't think he understood what I was saying. I don't know why because I spoke very clearly. Monsieur Duval never has the slightest difficulty.'

'Perhaps he came from a country region of France and was used to a different way of speaking,' Miss Tindall suggested tactfully.

'Yes, that must have been the reason. It's amazing how badly people speak – simply swallow their words. That's where speech training is such a help. Actors are taught to project their voices so that they can be heard in the last row of the gallery – without shouting, of course. It's quite an art, you know. I particularly remember how beautifully Sybil Thorndike always enunciated her words.'

Barbara escaped to the kitchen. She had finished washing up the first-course dishes when the doorbell rang. She took off her apron and went to answer it.

'Mrs Hillyard? I'm Lieutenant Reeves. We've never actually met – only spoken on the telephone.'

He looked very much like he had always sounded: spruce, brisk, keen-eyed, and with a handshake that made her wince. 'I'm afraid all my rooms are taken, Lieutenant – if that's what you've come about.'

'Actually, I came to let you know that Monsieur Duval won't be needing his any more.'

She went quite still. 'What do you mean?'

'He won't be returning here.' He smiled at her. 'It was jolly good of you to take him on at such short notice. Much appreciated. I came to get his things, as a matter of fact. Take them off your hands so you can let the room – if you'd be good enough to show me where it is. It shouldn't take a tick.'

'Has something happened to him?'

'Just a change of plan. You know how it is when there's a war on.'

'Lieutenant Reeves, as it happens, I know exactly how it is when there's a war on. I lost my only brother recently. So, would you please tell me what has happened to Monsieur Duval?'

He had stopped smiling. 'I'm sorry, but I'm afraid I can't give you any details, Mrs Hillyard.'

'You see, I know the kind of activity he was involved in. I found out quite by accident. He never told me and we never talked about it, but I discussed the matter with Lieutenant Commander Powell. Perhaps you're aware of that?'

'Really?' He wasn't, she could see.

'It's very important to me. Very important. You understand? Is Louis Duval dead?'

He was silent. After a moment, he said quietly, 'Perhaps you could show me the room now, Mrs Hillyard. I'll do the rest.'

She led the way up the stairs and along the corridor. He was quick and thorough, taking the battered suitcase from the top of the wardrobe and laying it on the bed, undoing the two leather straps, snapping open the metal clasps, opening drawers one after the other, reaching into the wardrobe. She realized that it was something he had done before: clearing personal effects, or whatever they called it. This was what someone else would have done with Freddie's things. Gone to his lodgings and gathered it all up to go in the suitcase that had been sent to her. She had gone through it numbly: the clothes, the books, the photos in their frames . . . all that was left of him.

She watched the lieutenant deal with a jacket expertly – sleeves aligned precisely side by side, then the whole flipped over in half so that it fitted neatly into the case – the familiar loose black linen jacket, rather creased as always and faintly exuding the aroma of French cigarettes and France. When he had finished with the drawers and the wardrobe, the lieutenant inspected the canvases propped against the wall, the tin of oil paints, the jar of brushes and the sketchbook lying on top of the chest of drawers. He glanced rapidly at each page of the book, flicking them over in succession. 'Perhaps you'd like to keep these? Shall I leave them?'

'Yes, please.'

He snapped the suitcase clasps shut – click, click – buckled the leather straps and hauled if off the bed. She could remember Louis holding it when he had first arrived, looking like a tramp. The lieutenant nodded to her. 'Thank you, Mrs Hillyard. I'll find my own way out.'

When he had gone, she picked up the sketchbook and turned the pages, looking through the sketches that Louis had made – the house, the garden, the hillside, the estuary, the harbour, the boats, Fifi curled up asleep, Esme holding Tom kitten on her lap, and herself sitting on the wall. He had written her name beneath it and underlined it. She could hear his voice saying it the French way: *Bar-bar-a*.

She covered her face with her hands.

'Commander Chilcot will see you immediately, Lieutenant Commander.'

A different woman admitted him to the house in London, but she was cut from the same cloth. No smile, no expression in either face or speech. Harry, however, had plenty of expression in both.

'What the bloody hell have you been up to, Alan? What sort of damn-fool game have you and Smythson been playing, getting yourselves marooned over there?'

'It was no game, Harry.'

'I should bloody well think it wasn't. You're damn lucky to have got back at all – God knows how. I want to hear the full story.'

He told him most of it. Harry listened, shaking his head periodically. 'Madness, Alan! Sheer lunacy! Lord knows how the Germans didn't spot you. Smythson might have got away with it but you certainly wouldn't. You said yourself that the mayor knew at once that you were English. You took the most frightful risk going to Pont-Aven and hanging about like that.'

'I thought it was important to find out what had happened to Duval.'

'I could have told you. He was executed not long after he was arrested. Shot. The Free French passed on information that one of their people brought back.'

He said heavily, 'I'm very sorry to hear that. Very sorry indeed.' He would always regret the failure to rescue Duval. He may have felt jealous of him but that had never, for one moment, lessened his respect for the man.

'So was I. Damn bad show. When they found that transmitter, of course, he didn't have much of a chance. He was never what you might call a professional at the game.'

'He established a very useful network over there.'

'Indeed he did. Nothing of major importance, of course, but we can take advantage of it. Maybe expand some of our operations along those lines – in conjunction with the trained agents we send over. Apparently, he didn't spill any beans – so his contacts are still secure. No doubt the Gestapo tried plenty of persuasion. By the way, I got hold of Lieutenant Reeves down your way and told him to get all Duval's things cleared out of the place where he was staying. Just in case there was anything we wouldn't want anyone else to get hold of. It can all go to the wife in Paris after the war.' Harry had simmered down now and smiled wryly. 'You know, Alan, to tell the truth, I rather envy you that bit of excitement. Being over there – right in the thick of the enemy. Cloak-and-dagger stuff. Something to tell your grandchildren one day – if you ever have any. Cigarette?' Harry leaned forward with his case. 'We never did discover why Duval wanted to get back here so urgently.'

Powell lit his cigarette. 'Actually, I did manage to find out.'

'You did? Well why the hell didn't you say so?'

'I didn't finish telling the whole story.' Powell produced the rolled-up French newspaper and laid it on the desk. 'It was because of this.'

'Lieutenant Reeves? It's Lieutenant Commander Powell speaking.'

'Yes, sir?'

'I gather you've been round to collect Louis Duval's things?'

'That's right, sir.'

'I take it you saw Mrs Hillyard?'

'Yes, sir.'

'What exactly did you tell her – about Duval?'

'I told her that he wouldn't be returning, that's all.'

'Was she very upset?'

'Well, she tried not to show it but I could see that she was. Very upset indeed.' The lieutenant cleared his throat. 'I'm afraid I hadn't quite realized the situation there.'

'Do you think she understood . . . why he wouldn't be coming back?'

'Oh, yes, sir. I couldn't tell her in so many words, of course, but she understood all right. She said she knew about what he was doing. She'd found out by accident and she'd talked it over with you.'

'Yes, she did. It won't have gone any further, I'm quite sure of that.'

The lieutenant cleared his throat again. 'I left all his paintings with her, sir. And a sketchbook. It seemed the right thing to do.'

'Yes it was. Exactly the right thing.'

'Henrietta? It's Alan. I'm in London for a couple of days . . .'

'That's wonderful! Come round for dinner this evening.'

He watched a young couple walking arm in arm along the Embankment – the man in army uniform, the girl in WAAF blue. 'Who else will be there?'

'Just William and Julian. He doesn't go back to school until the end of the week. He'll love to see you.'

The florist had no roses of any colour, so he bought white narcissi mixed with blue iris which pleased her very much.

'They smell gorgeous, Alan, thank you. I'll put them straight in water. Go on into the drawing room. William's late, as usual, but Julian's in there, up to no good, I expect.'

As he opened the door, his nephew whipped a cigarette behind his back.

He said loudly, above the head-splitting noise of some jazz record playing on the gramophone, 'Hallo, Julian. How are you?'

His nephew grinned. He brought the cigarette out of hiding and took a nonchalant drag. 'I thought you were Ma. You won't split on me, will you?'

'Good heavens, no. I'll join you.' He lit a cigarette. 'Do you think we could have the volume down a bit?'

'If you like. Fantastic isn't it? Benny Goodman, you know. He's terrific.'

'Yes, he's very good.' He watched the boy. Not so much a boy any longer. The man was emerging fast. At seventeen he was only an inch or two shorter than himself, the shoulders broadening, the voice deepening, the features changing. Only a year away from call-up papers. He thought, I hope to Christ the war's over before that can happen. 'How are things, then?'

'Pretty bloody.' His nephew pulled a face. 'They're making me go back this term. I wanted to join up but they won't let me.'

'You're too young.'

'Only just. I could easily lie about my age. Lots of people do.'

'And lots of people get found out and sent home. I shouldn't advise it.'

'The thing is if I don't get a move on, the whole show will be over and I'll have missed it all. I want to join the RAF, you see. Train to become a fighter pilot. And that takes time.'

'Finish your schooling first.'

'You're sounding just like the parents.'

'They do know what they're talking about.'

Another airy drag on the cigarette like a veteran smoker, the smoke puffed casually into the air, then the giveaway, involuntary cough. 'Yes, but they don't really understand. Everything's different now. It's fighting the Jerries that's the important thing, don't you agree? I can always go to university later on. You fought in the last war, didn't you? So you know exactly what I mean.'

'Yes,' he said. 'I know what you mean.'

'I bet you wouldn't have missed it for anything. It must be pretty grim to have to take a back seat now. Really boring for you.'

He smiled. 'I should get rid of that cigarette before your mother comes in.'

Henrietta appeared with the flowers more or less arranged in a vase and he poured drinks for them – gin and tonic for her, pink gin for himself, lemonade for his nephew, despite the protests. After a while, his brother-in-law returned from the hospital. The talk, naturally enough, centred on the war and its progress – or rather the lack of it.

William said grimly, 'They're booting us out of Greece and it'll be Crete next. I'll lay any bets on that. After that it'll be North Africa. Everything's going their way and we can't seem to do a damn thing about it.'

Henrietta was knitting some curious khaki garment. 'You mustn't be a pessimist, William.'

'I'm not. I'm a realist.'

'Well, at least they're not bombing London quite so much.'

'They've got other fish to fry, that's why. What do you make of it all, Alan?'

'It certainly doesn't look too good at the moment, but I think things will turn around eventually. It's taken time to recover from

Dunkirk and to regroup, and the Luftwaffe have kept us pretty busy.'

His nephew seized his chance. 'The RAF keep on advertising for men to join up, Dad. Posters everywhere.'

'You're still a schoolboy, Julian, and you're staying on for at least another year. That's final. No more discussion on the subject. How are you getting on down in Devon, Alan?'

'Fine.'

'Interesting work?'

'Routine desk stuff, mainly.'

'All part of the war effort, though.'

'I hope so,' he said.

After dinner – a brave attempt by Henrietta at something she called Smothered Sausage, found in a wartime recipe book, followed by Orange Mould from the same source – Julian went off to his room and William was summoned by phone to return urgently to the hospital. Powell sat down with his sister and talked for a while over cigarettes and the Benedictine that she had unearthed from the back of a cupboard.

'Bless the monks . . . my favourite. Bless you, too, Alan.'

He raised his glass. 'And you, Hattie. May I ask you a favour?'

'Ask away. If it's something I can do, consider it done.'

'There's a young French boy who's arrived recently in Dartmouth – a year younger than Julian.'

'Don't tell me *he* wants to join up too.'

He smiled. 'As a matter of fact, he does – but the Free French navy, not the Royal Air Force. Of course, he's too young – like Julian. He's on his own – the parents are still in France.'

'How on earth did that happen?'

'Bit of a long story. I promised that I'd keep an eye on him, you see. I've managed to get the Naval College to take him. It's an ideal solution, really. He'll be looked after during term time, doing exactly the sort of thing he wants, but there's the problem of the holidays. Where he goes then. They'd keep him there if necessary, of course, but I wondered if you'd have him to stay? I think he and Julian would get on rather well, and it would be some sort of family life for him.'

'Of course I will. Poor boy. We'd be glad to have him.'

'Thank you, Hattie. It's very good of you.'

'How's his English?'

'Non-existent, but it's bound to improve fast.'

'Actually, Julian's not bad at French. Rather surprising really. I used to speak it pretty well in the old days, when I was at the Paris finishing school. You remember my telling you about my Frenchman – the one I fell desperately in love with? His English wasn't up to much and that did wonders for my French.'

'Do you still think about him? After all these years?'

'Yes, I do. I'll never forget him. But he belongs to the past. I take him out and think about him and then he goes back in his box again – if you see what I mean. Women are like that, you know. They keep their memories safe, like old love letters tied up with ribbon in the attic. Once in a while, they'll bring them out and go through them and remember. The rest of the time, they stay hidden away – out of sight and out of mind. I think every woman should have at least one unforgettable love affair in her life – preferably with a Frenchman. By the way, is that girl you met still in love with *hers*?'

'As a matter of fact, he's not around any more.'

'Ah. That makes a difference. It gives you a chance.'

'I'm afraid there's not much hope.'

'Be patient, Alan, that's my advice. Give her time. She'll notice you one day.'

Eighteen

The roses were in midsummer bloom, the long bed making a swathe of colour across the garden – yellow, white, apricot, pink, crimson. She'd been weeding and now she sat on the seat to rest and admire the roses, and the Scots pines on the hillside below, and the green-blue glitter of the sea through their branches. This was where she had sat with him and where she came when she wanted to remember him.

'Yoo-hoo, Mrs Hillyard! Are you there?' Mrs Lamprey appeared at the top of the terrace steps, one hand extended, her scarf trailing from the other. Pause for applause before she descended with the swaying, loose-kneed gait of a Busby Berkeley chorus girl – halting halfway down. 'Lieutenant Commander Powell is here for you. He's waiting in the hall.'

'Thank you, Mrs Lamprey.'

'Such an *attractive* man. A trifle stiff and starchy on the surface, but he's not really at all like that, is he? Not underneath. Still waters run deep. You can tell that from his eyes – they have hidden depths.' Another sashaying step down-wards. 'It's a long time since we've seen him. I wonder what he's come about.'

'I've no idea, Mrs Lamprey.'

'Perhaps he knows some naval gentleman who wants a room. You're full up, though, since that Belgian person arrived.'

That Belgian person – always referred to dis-paragingly in those terms – had been a great disappointment to Mrs Lamprey. She had expected to be able to continue improving her French, but the elderly and reclusive refugee from Antwerp had turned out to be Flemish-speaking.

Mrs Lamprey pursued her back to the house, her eager scramble up the steep steps in contrast to her floating descent. 'Of course, the lieutenant commander has always been a *great* admirer of yours, Mrs Hillyard. But I expect you realize that. He's always carried a torch for you.'

Alan Powell was standing in the hall, ex-amining Louis's painting of the house which she had had framed and hung on the wall. He was in his Royal Navy uniform. Tall, upright, correct and not carrying any torches – only his cap in his hand. He had called by, he said politely, just to see how things were. They would not discuss the painting, she knew; nor would they discuss the painter. After the war she would perhaps find out everything that had happened, when careless talk no longer cost lives.

Mrs Lamprey was hovering close by, panting audibly from the climb and curiosity.

'Would you come into the kitchen, Alan?' she said. 'I ought to get on with supper.'

Fifi was asleep in her basket but Tom stretched and strolled over. Alan picked him up and stroked him. The ginger cat started purring. 'This must be Esme's. How is she?'

'Fine. She's doing much better at school. And her father came to see her again on his last leave.'

'What about her mother?'

'Gone to Canada. She wanted Esme to go with her but she refused. It meant leaving Tom.'

'Tom?' He had lifted his head so that she could see straight into his eyes. Mrs Lamprey had been right about them having hidden depths. They were smoke-grey and very hard to read.

'You're holding him.'

'Well, I don't blame her. He's a very fine animal.'

She sliced up the onions and put them in the pan on the stove. 'Would you mind very much giving these a stir now and again, while I get on with the rest?'

'If you trust me not to make a hash of it.'

She laughed. 'Actually, that's just what it's supposed to be – a hash. Corned beef hash.'

The tins of American corned beef were a novelty at the grocer's, and she'd soon discovered how useful they could be for eking out the rations. She fetched one from the larder, opened it and began cutting up the processed meat. The potatoes were already cooked, so the rest was easy – once the onions were done.

Alan was still holding Tom, cradled in the crook of his left arm, while he stirred the onions. She watched him covertly. Mrs Lamprey was right, too, about him not being nearly so stiff and starchy as he seemed – she had known that anyway – but wrong about the torch-carrying. Quite wrong.

Then, just as she was thinking this, he turned his head and looked at her. And smiled.

THE END